Rebel Hearts

Also by Tanya Byrne

Heart-Shaped Bruise
Follow Me Down
For Holly
Afterlove
In the Shallows

Rebel Hearts

TANYA BYRNE

HODDER

HODDER CHILDREN'S BOOKS

First published in Great Britain in 2025 by Hodder & Stoughton Limited

1 3 5 7 9 10 8 6 4 2

A CIP catalogue record for this book
is available from the British Library.

ISBN 978 1 444 97222 1

Printed and bound in Great Britain by Clays Ltd, Elcograf S.p.A.

The paper and board used in this book
are made from wood from responsible sources.

MIX
Paper | Supporting
responsible forestry
FSC® C104740

Hodder Children's Books
An imprint of
Hachette Children's Group
Part of Hodder & Stoughton Limited
Carmelite House
50 Victoria Embankment
London EC4Y 0DZ

The authorised representative in the EEA is Hachette Ireland,
8 Castlecourt Centre, Dublin 15, D15 XTP3, Ireland (email: info@hbgi.ie)

An Hachette UK Company
www.hachette.co.uk

www.hachettechildrens.co.uk

For the young activists demanding change and to all those who came before them who passed the megaphone and told them to keep resisting.

Stand before the people you fear and speak your mind – even if your voice shakes.

– Maggie Kuhn

What's your earliest memory? It's something lovely, isn't it? Like the first time you tasted chocolate ice cream. Or the first time you saw the sea. Or waking up on Christmas morning to find the rollerblades you'd asked Santa for under the tree. Or maybe it's your uncle showing up on your birthday with a wriggling, pink-bellied puppy that you loved so much, you understood why your mother kissed you on the cheek for no reason sometimes.

Or perhaps it's something sharper, like that time you got lost in the supermarket. Or the first time you fell off your bicycle and there was no one there to stop it happening.

My earliest memory isn't as traumatic, but it has still imprinted on me in an enduring, indelible way. It was the summer of 2014. I was seven and my mother had taken me to a Greenpeace protest. It wasn't my first protest (technically, that was a Climate Rush rally when she was eight months pregnant with me) but it was the first one that I remember, probably because it was also the first time I was on the six-thirty news.

There we were, me and forty-nine other kids, outside Shell's headquarters in London, building Arctic animals out of massive LEGO pieces to protest their long-running partnership with Shell. Well, that's what Greenpeace was doing. I was building LEGO. But then I turned away from adjusting the eyes on the snowy owl to show my mother and saw that we were surrounded by people. Some looked slightly bewildered as they passed on their way to grab a sandwich for lunch, but most cheered us on and stopped to sign the petition. And of course there was that crew from Channel 4 News, who asked me why we were there and I pointed up at the people peering down at us from inside the Shell building and said, 'They're listening.'

'Can you feel it, querida?' my mother asked, squeezing my hand as she led me over to join the other kids behind the large *SAVE THE ARCTIC* letters that we'd made out of white LEGO. And I did. It was several years before I was able to articulate exactly what it was, but it's the same thing I feel every time I go to a protest. That moment when the number of faces I recognise in the crowd are outnumbered by the ones I don't as people stop whatever they're doing long enough to pay attention.

Some laugh. Some sneer. Some stay and ask questions. It's the people my age that tend to be the most curious, though. But then, if I saw a load of teenagers shouting and waving signs, I'd ask myself why. I see them watching us sometimes, trying not to stare while they're with their family, or frowning down at us from the top deck of the bus. Later, when they're bored, I hope they google us to see what we were protesting and find one of our videos. And while I'm sure most of them will probably roll their eyes then go back to their For You page, I've been doing this long enough now to know that not all of them will.

Some will watch another video.

Then another.

And another.

And another.

2

And that's how you start a revolution: one bored teenager at a time.

It can only happen in that moment. I still it feel nine years later. The moment when a crowd becomes a congregation, when milling becomes marching and chatter becomes chanting and suddenly everyone is calling for the same thing. Our energy – and purpose – fusing, flaring, spreading until you can feel it sparking off the hair on the back your neck because this is it.

It's about to happen.

We're about to change the world.

1

Riley calls it the *TICK TICK* before the *BOOM*, but for me, it feels more like a wave that's building and all I can do is stand there and wait for it to hit me. Today, I feel it as soon as Riley and I get off the bus, this buzz in the distance punctuated by the steady beat of Sasha's drum that we walk in time with.

As we approach The Dorchester, I see the Out of Time crew. They're outnumbered by a wall of police officers on the other side of the road guarding the entrance to the hotel, which is overkill for thirty teenagers sitting cross-legged on the pavement holding a sign. I mean, most of them have such chronic anxiety that they're unlikely to make direct eye contact with you, let alone storm a hotel, but whatever.

Roll out the tanks, I guess.

Tab is on Live as she paces back and forth with a megaphone leading a call of, 'Earth before . . .' that everyone responds to with, 'Profit!' They chant it over and over, each pause filled by Sasha's drum as people stop to take photos. As soon as they do, Tab approaches to tell them why we're there and while most recoil (rightly so given they've just been charged at by someone with a megaphone), some lean in and listen.

When everyone sees Riley and me, they cheer and Sasha bangs her drum with renewed purpose. With that, the call and response gets louder, which is enough to make the row of police officers look across the road at us. As soon as they see me, it prompts a domino line of turned heads as they step forward just enough to let me know they're there, but not enough to discourage me from doing something that will give them an excuse to close the distance between us. But I just smile sweetly, making sure to wave at them as Tab laughs, then lowers the megaphone.

'Here she is, guys,' she announces on Live, 'our fearless leader!'

Tab knows I hate it when she calls me that, but before I can object, she slings her arm around my waist and pulls me into her so my face appears on the screen as well. Given that we haven't spoken for the last two weeks, I can't help but tense at the unexpected contact, her cheek warm against mine. My head swims as I'm forced to remember the smell of her, that lavender and geranium shampoo I've used so many times and the perfume I bought her for her birthday.

With that, any self-control I thought I had immediately abandons me as she smiles. I was worried that it would be weird seeing her again, but Tab's so normal – so brazenly, painfully normal – that when I see my smile slip on the screen, I catch myself and beam brightly before she – or anyone else – notices.

'Hey, guys!' I salute everyone on Live with two fingers. 'Who's ready to raise hell?'

Tab squeezes her eyes shut, throws her head back and screams, 'Yes!'

It's echoed by the Out of Time crew sitting at our feet as Riley jumps in behind Tab and me and sticks his tongue out, then points at the screen and says, 'Let's fucking go!'

There's a flurry of cheers as I crouch down on the pavement. Riley and Tab do the same – him to my left, her to my right – her phone on me now as I check in with the others.

'Have they gone in?'

Tab nods. 'Twenty minutes ago.'

I'm pissed I missed it but at least the others were here.

'Have the police said anything?'

All at once, their gaze flicks over my shoulder to the wall of officers on the other side of the road.

When they look back at me, everyone shakes their heads.

'So they haven't put up any notices or given anyone a leaflet or anything?' I ask.

Tab shakes her head this time. 'No, nothing.'

'Good.' I nod. 'OK, let's go.' I clap my hands and they cheer again. 'You know the drill, guys, stay on the pavement. Make sure everyone can get past. If they can't or if we go into the road, they'll bust us for Obstruction of the Highway. Remember, keep it peaceful. We can't do *anything* that can be construed as' – I count off each one on my fingers – 'disorder, damage, disruption, impact or intimidation.'

'What about Sash's drum?' someone asks.

'I doubt anyone paying a grand a night to stay here is going to be thrilled, but for the police to intervene it has to be *significant and prolonged*.' I use air quotes. 'We'll only be here for a couple more hours, so they'll leave us alone if we stay across the road, say our bit and go. Which is fine. We're not here to confront anyone, are we?'

Everyone nods.

'We're just making Jeremy Casey aware that we know that he's in there' – I thumb over my shoulder – 'schmoozing BP execs and helping them make even more money, and that's not OK. It's not OK that our Secretary of State for Environment, Food and Rural Affairs is sucking up to a company directly responsible for the climate crisis while we're out here without coats because it's the warmest February on record.'

Everyone claps and Tab turns her phone to say, 'Fuck yeah!'

'So when Casey and those execs walk out later, let's make sure they know that we're not going to let them get away with it.'

'Earth before . . .' Tab shouts.

Everyone responds with, 'Profit!'

When Sasha starts banging her drum again, Tab gestures at Riley and me to get up, then gives someone her phone and tells them to keep going.

As soon as they start chanting, she tugs us away. 'Ren, don't look now but the BBC are here.'

She grins, but I frown. 'Why? We're protesting a lunch.'

Tab and Riley raise their eyebrows at each other as I glance across the road.

'I don't like this, guys. Maybe we should call it a day.'

'You're kidding?' Tab says, appalled. 'We *want* the BBC here.'

'But there's nothing to film. We're not climbing a crane, or anything.'

'They don't know that.' She holds the megaphone out to me. 'So now's the time to say something, Ren. Before they realise that this isn't worth their time and leave.'

I look around to discover that as well as the BBC News crew, there are half a dozen photographers in the crowd gathering in Hyde Park behind us. When I spot a cluster of people in Out of

Time hoodies, I wave them over then stop to take photos before Riley helps them over the low fence so they can join us. But as the crowd gets bigger, it's clear that most of them have no idea who we are. I guess they heard us chanting and are now looking between us and the police across the road, phones poised for whatever is about to happen, which is exactly what we want. For people to stop. To ask questions. To google Out of Time and tag us on their social media.

So I don't know why I suddenly feel so uneasy.

'Come on, Ren,' Tab says, pupils swelling. 'Give them something worth filming.'

When the corners of her mouth twitch, my heart beats wildly as I take the megaphone from her and climb up on to the fence. It's more of a railing so it takes me a second to get my balance. Tab and Riley reach up to steady me, but before I can raise the megaphone, I'm aware of a commotion behind me and look over my shoulder as the crowd parts and a police officer strides towards me.

'Renata Barbosa!' he bellows. 'Get down from there!'

'Sergeant Sykes.' I turn to face him with a grin. 'Long time no see.'

When he stops in front of me with a stern frown, Riley initiates a chorus of pantomime boos.

'Leave her alone!' Tab yells. 'She's not doing anything wrong!'

Sergeant Sykes ignores her. 'Come on, Renata. Get down. You're blocking the pavement.'

'I'm not on the pavement.'

He tips his chin up at the Out of Time crew who are now on their feet, facing him. 'They are.'

'They're not blocking it. If anyone wants to get past there's plenty of room. Right, guys?'

They back me up with a cheer, but Sergeant Sykes shakes his head. 'Come on, Renata. Get down.'

When he raises his arm, I think he's going to grab me and almost lose my footing. Luckily Tab and Riley reach up to steady me as I say, 'It's still legal to peacefully protest in the UK, last time I checked.'

Another officer I don't recognise appears then. 'Come on, kids. That's enough now. Break it up.'

My gaze narrows at *kids* and when the booing from the Out of Time crew burns out, I make sure I look him in the eye when I say, 'There's nothing to break up. We're just standing here.'

That prompts a cheer as Tab and Riley jump up on to the railing to stand either side of me, Tab's phone pointed at the officers as she leads everyone in another call and response.

The officer chuckles sourly, then turns to Sergeant Sykes. 'You were right about her, Dan.'

He raises his eyebrows. 'You know her mum's Lady Fernanda Barbosa, right?'

Professor Dame Fernanda Barbosa, I'm about to correct, but the officer chuckles again and looks up at me with a smirk.

'I don't care who your mum is; this is over.'

'Back off!' Riley roars. 'We're allowed to protest!'

Tab has her phone in the officer's face now. 'Careful, Ren has four million followers and they're watching.'

But the officer just laughs as the chants turn to shouts and we're swallowed by a sea of neon yellow. In the scrum that follows, my foot slips from the railing, but when I reach for Tab and Riley, they're not there.

2

Sitting in a cell at Kensington Police Station waiting for my mother to arrive certainly wasn't on my bingo card for today. I figured I'd go to The Dorchester, raise hell, give Jeremy Casey and the assholes from BP the finger, then go to the pub with Tab and Riley, like we do after every protest.

Still, it's not the first time that the police have made me sit in a cell 'until I've calmed down' – or until they need the cell, whichever comes first – but it is the first time that they've told me they can't question me without an adult present and I'm not going to lie, I'm nervous. Questioning me implies that there's something to question me about, and if there's something to question me about, that means there's something to charge me with.

If Riley was here, he'd tell me not to worry, but my mother isn't going to be as blasé. It's bad enough when the police let me go with a slap on the wrist, so I dread to think how she's going to react when she finds out that they might charge me. It's enough to have me considering the logistics of Shawshanking my way out of here using the leaflet the custody sergeant just gave me informing me of my rights.

DC Abbell seems as anxious as I am about her arrival because he keeps opening the hatch every few minutes to check I'm still here, until, finally, the door swings opens and I sit up.

'Your mother is on her way,' he says, his face a shade of pink I immediately recognise.

I try not to smirk. 'How do you know Mum, DC Abbell?'

'I used to work at Number 10.' He nods solemnly. 'She's a remarkable woman.'

'And by remarkable you mean . . .'

He hesitates, his gaze darting around the cell, before settling back on me as he dips his head and lowers his voice. 'Terrifying. I've done two tours of Afghanistan and if I did another, she's who I'd want by my side.'

Try being her daughter, I think as he hurries out and when he does, I'm almost certain that I see the custody sergeant behind the desk opposite my cell hastily tidying papers as it swings shut.

As soon as I hear it lock again, I ask Our Lady of Aparecida to watch over me because this isn't going to end well for me. My mother is formidable enough when she's on *Question Time*, deftly dismantling anyone naïve enough to disagree with her. But that's Professor Dame Fernanda Barbosa DBE, CBE and about twenty-seven other letters I've stopped trying to memorise because every time I do, she earns another three. She can bring anyone to their knees with a cutting quip and an equally cutting smile, but when it's just us and there's no audience watching, her carefully curated Oxbridge accent vanishes and she's like every other Brazilian mother.

So, when the door opens again, I brace myself.

But it isn't her.

It's the last person I expect to see at Kensington Police Station on a Friday night.

'Pearl Newman,' I say with a slow smile as they lead her in.

She stops and stares at me, her eyes almost neon green in the severe fluorescent light. 'Renata Barbosa.'

'You know each other?' DC Abbell seems relieved. 'Good. You won't mind sharing, then.' When I continue to smile and Pearl continues to look horrified, he adds, 'It's busier than usual tonight thanks to you lot, so trust me, when the pubs close and it really kicks off, you'd rather be together.'

Pearl's eyes widen.

But I wave my hand at him. 'Don't worry, DC Abbell. We'll be fine.'

When he leaves, locking the door behind him, I slide along the bench so Pearl can sit, the mattress squeaking comically as I do. 'Mattress' is generous. It isn't much thicker than a yoga mat and made of crayon-blue-coloured rubber, so I don't blame Pearl for looking down at it, then up at me, then crossing her arms.

'I never thought I'd see you here, Miss Newman,' I say, my smile sharpening to a smirk. 'What happened? Forget to return a library book?'

'Wait.' She blinks at me. 'Are you actually acknowledging my existence, Renata? I'm honoured. But then' – she stops to look around the tight cell – 'you can't run away this time, can you?'

For the record, I've never *run away* from Pearl.

But I have avoided her.

And that hasn't been easy. We've been in each other's orbits for years. We go to the same protests and we've been invited to the same conferences, so it's taken some effort to ensure that we've never been introduced. That probably sounds harsh because she seems sweet enough – the sort of friend that your mother checks will be there before she agrees to let you go anywhere – but I've seen enough of the insipid, inspiring posts on her Instagram, GreenGirlPearl, to know that we won't get along.

Still, I get why people want us to be friends.

But let me get one thing straight: I'm an activist.

Pearl is an influencer.

There's a difference.

That's definitely harsh, but it's hard not to be when I'm out here, being detained every week for holding companies like BP accountable, while Pearl is sitting behind a computer, posting cute, colourful infographics.

Still, maybe she isn't as sweet as she looks because when I smirk at her again, she doesn't flinch, and I'm almost impressed. I've always thought Pearl was kind of, well, *blah*, so she should be in tears by now.

Even in the brutal light of the cell, I can see that she's as pretty as her photos. She's not my type, but she has this whole Elle Fanning thing going on that people swoon over. All blonde hair and big eyes and pink cheeks. Perfect Pearl with her perfectly pressed shirt and her perfectly straight hair that's parted perfectly in the centre.

Even her white VEJA Campos are pristine.

Meanwhile, here I am, a smear of black. Between the hoodie I borrowed from Riley and my favourite pair of jeans that are being held together by gaffer tape and prayer, I look every bit the cliché. Even if wearing black is less about showing how misunderstood I am and more an effort to avoid being picked out of a crowd.

When I don't respond, she continues, 'I guess that's one of the benefits of sharing with a regular, you get the best cell.'

'Nah. My favourite is the last one on the left,' I tell her. 'More light.'

Her smile is swift – deniable – but I see it.

When her eyes linger on my face, I know she sees my mother. Technically, half my DNA belongs to my father, but you wouldn't know it to look at me. He left before I was born and it's as though he didn't leave a trace in me, either, because I am all my mother. Same dark hair and eyes. Same deep, copper skin. Same constellation of freckles across the bridge of our noses. We even have the same mole below our bottom lip, hers on the left and mine on the right, as though we're looking at one another in a mirror.

If I didn't know better, I'd say that when my father left, my mother smirked at him in that way she does – in that way I do as well, I'm told – and said, 'Well, if you don't want her, she's going to be all mine.'

'You should sit down,' I suggest, patting the mattress. 'It's going to be a long night.'

'You'd know. How many times have you been detained now, Renata?'

'Only my mother calls me Renata. My mates call me Ren.'

She doesn't miss a beat. 'Like I said, how many times has it been now, *Renata*?'

ZING, I think, swallowing a chuckle as I imagine a scoreboard somewhere registering the point.

When I close one eye and begin counting, she holds her hand up. 'If you have to think about it, it's too many,' she tells me as she considers where to sit, her options limited to the toilet in the corner and the floor.

She seems to be contemplating the floor when we hear a voice on the other side of the cell door wailing.

When she looks over her shoulder then paces towards me, I expect her to sit as far away as possible, wedge herself in the corner against the white tiled wall, but instead she drops next to me on the bench with a sigh.

'Did they tell you what's going to happen next?' I ask as she stares at the door.

'Yeah,' she mutters, uncrossing her arms to show me the leaflet they've given her as well.

'Is someone on their way for you?'

'They called my mum.'

'Did you accept the caution?'

Pearl looks alarmed. 'You mean that thing they say when they arrest you?'

'No, when the police brought you in, did they offer to let you go with a caution?'

'Yeah, but someone in the police van warned me they were going to do that, so I didn't.'

I feel a pinch of pride as I realise that was probably Riley.

That's how we met, actually, in the back of a police van after a Just Stop Oil protest.

'They make it sound like it's nothing,' I tell her, 'but it's an admission of guilt and stays on your record.'

Pearl nods, then crosses her arms again. 'I didn't say anything.'

'Keep it that way until your mum gets here. Even then, don't say anything without a solicitor.'

She nods again, but I feel bad because I've obviously scared the shit out of her.

'Listen. Don't worry. They're running out of cells, so they'll want us out of here as soon as possible.'

She nods, then resumes glaring at the door, her long blonde hair falling between us like a curtain.

'I knew I shouldn't have gone to your ridiculous protest,' she mutters, her back straightening as the wailing outside becomes more urgent.

'Why did you? You've never been to an Out of Time protest before.'

She flicks her hair with a theatrical sigh. 'It's an inset day. I didn't have anything better to do.'

'And there isn't a sale on at Next?'

The scoreboard registers a point for me this time as she glances down at what she's wearing, then scowls.

'Actually, I was taking photos for a piece I'm writing for *The Good Trade*.'

'Yeah? I didn't see you.'

'You were too busy getting us all arrested.' She turns to glare at me, but when I snigger as I play with the strings on Riley's hoodie, she huffs. 'It's not funny, Renata. They're going to charge us.'

'No, they're not. They'll just send us home with a slapped wrist. Trust me.'

'Trust you?'

'Not my first rodeo, remember?'

I give her the double finger guns, but the seemingly permanent groove between her eyebrows deepens.

She uncrosses her arms to gesture at the door. 'They *just* told me that they're going to charge us.'

'With what?' I snort.

'When the police found out about the protest, they put a Section 14 order in place.'

I snigger again, tickled at the thought of the police scrambling to justify why they arrested a load of teenagers for standing in the street. I hope BBC News got a shot of them hauling off fourteen-year-old Sasha.

That'll look great on the six o'clock news, won't it?

'There was no Section 14.' I wave my hand at her. 'They're just trying to scare you.'

'Why would they want to scare me?'

'So you accept a caution. If we do, they can tell themselves that this wasn't a complete waste of time.'

'How can you be so sure?'

'Because when they impose a Section 14 order, they have to communicate it and they didn't. I checked.'

'Well, they did. They've called the duty solicitor for me.'

'They didn't say any of that to me,' I tell her when she tosses the leaflet on the mattress between us.

'Because they know your mum's going to arrive lawyered up.'

'They're full of shit.' I sniff. 'Section 14 notices aren't for thirty teenagers protesting a lunch.'

'Forgive me for believing a police officer over someone wearing jeans held together with gaffer tape.'

'Do you know how many protests I've organised, Pearl? I've memorised the Public Order Act.' I tap my finger against my temple. 'This is what they do. They find a flimsy reason to haul us into custody so they can keep us here until it's calmed down, then give us a telling-off and send us home. It's a way of shutting down the protest.'

'You'd know,' she says, but there's no sting to it this time as she crosses her arms again.

'We didn't do anything wrong. We shouldn't have been arrested. We're allowed to protest the fact that our politicians are cosying up to an industry directly responsible for the climate crisis.'

Pearl stares at me. 'You don't know, do you?'

'Know what?'

But instead of answering, she asks, 'Who organised today's protest?'

'Tab and Riley. Why?'

Pearl exhales through her nose and shakes her head. 'Be careful, Renata?'

'Of what?'

'Out of Time is so big now that you're going to lose control of it eventually.'

My throat tightens like a fist and in that moment, I realise why I've never liked Pearl.

People think they know why: Pearl's jealous of me because I'm the face of environmental activism. And I'm jealous of her because she's coming for my crown. She hates me because I'm cooler than she is. And I hate her because she's prettier than I am. Plus, we're both queer, so we're secretly in love with each other.

'See' – I lean back against the tiled wall – 'this is why I can't with you, Pearl.'

She turns to me, her pink cheeks pinker. 'What's that supposed to mean?'

'I get enough of this at home. I don't need it from you as well.'

19

Pearl seems delighted, her eyelashes fluttering as she says, 'Well, if you're comparing me to your mother, then that's a huge compliment. She's *brilliant*.'

'Yeah,' I tell her, fighting the urge to roll my eyes. 'She's also insufferable.'

Pearl gasps, one hand flying to her chest as though I've just called Zendaya ugly, or something.

'Neither of us would be here without your mother, Renata.'

'Be sure to remind her of that when she gets here, will you?' I ask, tipping my chin up at the cell door.

'Your mother—' Pearl starts to say, but I cut her off.

'Don't,' I warn because I can't hear it again.

I can't hear how brilliant my mother is while I sit in a police cell waiting for her to bail me out.

So, instead I say, 'Yeah, Out of Time is growing quickly, but that's because nonviolent civil disobedience *works*, Pearl. I know you don't agree—'

'It's not that I don't agree,' she interrupts, her brow puckering again. 'It's that I'm not convinced those tactics work. I'm concerned they do more harm than good.'

'There it is,' I mutter with a bitter chuckle as I turn away from her and lean back against the wall again.

My mother's favourite refrain.

Be careful, Renata.

You're damaging the cause, Renata.

'There *what* is?' When I don't respond, Pearl snorts and says, 'And this is why I can't with you, Renata.'

I make myself look at her and as soon as I do, she tilts her head at me.

'You do know it's possible to have two different approaches to the same problem, right?'

I sit up so suddenly, the mattress shifts beneath us. 'You literally *just said* nonviolent civil disobedience does more harm than good. Like, *four seconds* ago. You can't have forgotten already.'

'No, I said that *I'm* concerned that those tactics do more harm than good. I.' She points at herself. 'Me.'

'What's the difference?'

'The difference is that what works for me and what works for you are not necessarily the same thing, but that doesn't make one inherently better than the other, does it?'

'No, the implication that one does more harm than good makes one inherently better than the other.'

Pearl rolls her eyes and that's it, I see red.

'Listen, Pearl. I don't give a fuck. Every year there are more wildfires. Storms. Floods. Ocean temperatures are at an all-time high. The Great Barrier Reef is literally *cooking*. 2023 is set to be the hottest year on record and there's *no way* the government's reaching net zero by 2050. I'm done playing nice.'

'Is that what you think I'm doing?' She stares at me. 'Playing nice.'

I hold my hands up. 'GreenGirlPearl is great at what it does. Impeccable vibes.'

'Impeccable vibes?' she repeats, an eyebrow raised.

'Truly. But you can take your little photos –'

'I'm a *Teen Vogue* Digital Storytelling Fellow but go on.'

That's actually kind of impressive, but I'm on a roll and can't stop.

'And you can do your little thrifted clothing hauls –'

21

'Say little one more time,' she warns.

'But let's face it, it's not enough. The war isn't going to be won with empathy, Pearl.'

'How is it going to be won, Renata.'

'By getting in people's faces. Making them listen. Making them do something about it.'

'I know what you think and—'

'Why do you care what I think?' she cuts in. 'I thought you didn't give a fuck?'

'I don't,' I tell her, but it doesn't sound as convincing as I hoped. When she smiles in a way that lets me know that she notices, I sit up. 'What?' I push. 'Just say it.'

She thinks about it for a moment then says, 'I don't trust them, OK?'

'Who?'

'Tab and Riley. Actually, Riley's harmless. He just does as he's told. Tab's the one you need to watch.'

'Why?' I ask, even though I know she's wrong.

'She loves the chaos. The drama and the police and being on the news. But to keep that up, Out of Time will eventually have to cross the line from nonviolent civil disobedience into full on anarchy.'

I laugh, but she keeps going. 'Tab and Riley need you for now, because you're the face of Out of Time.' Her right eyebrow quirks up for second. 'But you won't be able to control them much longer.'

I laugh again, but it sounds hollow. She tucks her hair behind her ears as she says, 'Just make sure that those two aren't using you because of who your mum is.'

That is enough to make me glare at her again. 'Why would you think that?'

'Because until the whole *impeccable vibes* thing, I refused to believe that you were that much of an asshole to purposely embarrass your mum.' She smiles sweetly. 'But maybe you are.'

'Calm down, Pearl. The protest had nothing to do with my mother.'

'I knew it,' she mutters. 'You don't know.'

'Know *what*?'

'That your mum was at that lunch at The Dorchester today.'

I stare at her for a second, then shake my head. 'No, she wasn't.'

'*Yes*, she was.'

'She's my mother. Don't you think I'd know something like that?'

'She was talking about it on the *Today* programme *this morning*, Renata. She's facilitating a deal between BP and the Crown Estate to create Scotland's largest offshore wind hub in the Port of Leith,' she says, the silence that follows a sharp, sheer drop that turns my stomach inside out as I ask myself how I didn't know that.

But I was so worried about seeing Tab again that whatever my mother is up to wasn't even on my radar.

'Tab and Riley organised the protest today not you, right?' Pearl reminds me, tugging me back.

I don't hesitate. 'They didn't know. They would have told me.'

I know things are weird with Tab, but Riley one hundred per cent would have told me.

Pearl's still staring with that smug look on her face, though.

'They wouldn't do that to me,' I say and I mean it.

23

Feel it, somewhere deep in my bones.

'You might think you know me because you've seen me on TikTok, or whatever, but you don't,' I tell her, trying to keep my voice even. 'You have no idea what Tab and Riley are to me. They're my family. They'd *never* use me to get back at Mum and I think it's fucking shitty that this is literally the first time we've ever spoken and you're trying to make me doubt the two people who mean the most to me.'

Pearl stares at me, her cheeks flushed, but before she can say anything else, I turn my face away.

3

My mother's timing is nothing if not impeccable.

I'm still stinging from what Pearl said, so I don't notice the door swing open. I just feel a rush of cold air fill the stuffy cell and the relief that follows, which is immediately extinguished when DC Abbell strides in, his face pinker than before and his back straighter as he announces my mother's arrival.

Pearl leaps to her feet with such urgency, the leaflet flutters to the floor like a broken bird. She smooths her shirt with her hands, then does the same with her hair. Usually, I'd laugh and tell her that it's OK. *It's just Mum.* But after what she just said, she's been promoted to the top of my shit list. *I hope she makes her cry*, I think as my mother marches in, ushering in a cloud of jasmine and sanctimony as 'The Imperial March' plays in my head.

Much like Pearl, she seems absurdly out of place, like a video I saw once of a peacock swishing around a supermarket. And much like Pearl, she's immaculate. A straight black line in a knee-length shift dress, a long wool coat and a pair of heels so sharp, I don't know how they aren't puncturing the grubby grey lino.

When she stops in the middle of the cell and exhales wearily, she looks like an exclamation mark, arms at her sides as she

25

peers down at me on the bench, her dark eyes darker and her signature red lips pursed as she turns towards DC Abbell and says, 'May I have a moment with my daughter, please?'

He seems relieved to be dismissed, hurrying out as she turns back to me and slowly raises her eyebrows.

Which is my cue to stand.

'Renata,' she says tightly when I pull myself to my feet to face her. 'Are you OK?'

I nod once and tuck my hands into the front pocket of Riley's hoodie.

'Mum, listen . . .' I start to say, but she shakes her head and raises a finger.

Which is my cue to shut up.

Her eyes flick up to the camera in the corner of the cell, then back to me. 'Wait for Giles.'

Giles is her solicitor, a friend from Cambridge with skin like wet pastry and an accent so plummy it sounds as though it's a struggle to get each word out. Still, he'll make sure that I don't get carted off to Bronzefield.

I nod again and when I look at her from under my eyelashes, her face softens and she smiles.

It takes me a second to realise that it isn't directed at me, though.

'Pearl Newman?' my mother says.

'Professor Dame Barbosa,' she says stiffly, then bends slightly at the knees.

'Did you just curtsy?' I ask, appalled, as my mother frowns earnestly at her.

'What are you doing here, darling?'

You have to know my mother like I do to know that was for my benefit.

First to remind me that I haven't given her a reason to call me darling for a very long time.

And second to remind me that it's a shock to find Pearl in a police cell.

Me? Not so much.

'I was taking photos of the protest,' Pearl says sheepishly.

'Do you need a solicitor? If so, you can use mine. He's excellent.'

'That's very kind, but it's OK. The duty solicitor is on their way.'

'Don't use the duty solicitor,' I mutter. As soon as I do, Pearl and my mother turn to look at me as though they've forgotten I'm there, which makes the tips of my ears burn as I shrug and say, 'Duty solicitors are shit.'

The corners of my mother's mouth lift for just a second, but then she catches herself and raises her voice slightly as she looks up at the camera again. 'Duty solicitors are heroes, but Renata's right; you need someone who specialises in this sort of thing. Use Giles. He's an expert, thanks to my daughter.'

Nice.

'What about Tab and Riley?' I ask with a frown.

'Oh, those two hoodlums will be fine.' My mother waves her hand at me. 'They've been arrested so many times that I'm sure they can represent themselves at this point.'

'It's OK.' Pearl shakes her head. 'The duty solicitor will be fine.'

My mother must realise why she's hesitating because she says, 'Don't worry, it's on me. You deserve it after being stuck in a cell with this one.'

'It's been fun, actually.' I smirk. 'We've been bonding, haven't we? She just called me an asshole.'

Pearl gasps, her whole face aflame.

But my mother just laughs. 'How long have you been in here with my darling daughter?'

'About half an hour.'

'That seems about right.' She laughs again – bright and easy – then turns to me. 'Pearl and I met at the *Teen Vogue* summit last year. She was on the panel that you and I were supposed to do,' she explains as I wait for her to make a dig about me refusing to travel to Los Angeles. 'Pearl was brilliant,' she says with the sort of enthusiasm usually reserved for selling a used car. 'So insightful.'

I brace myself and count back from three because I know what's coming.

Sure enough, my mother sighs theatrically and says, 'I've never understood why you can't be friends with Pearl instead of those Out of Time anarchists, Renata.'

There it is.

Mercifully, the cell door opens and DC Abbell reappears to tell us that Giles has arrived.

'Thank you. We'll be right there,' my mother says, but I'm already striding towards the door, my hands fisting in the front pocket of Riley's hoodie.

4

Pearl was right; the police did impose a Section 14 order outside The Dorchester.

'This is such bullshit,' I say, shivering with rage as my mother and I walk out the back door of the police station into the car park. 'But if Giles isn't worried, neither am I. If they had anything on me, they would have charged me, not released me under investigation.'

When she doesn't say anything, just adjusts one of her gold earrings, I should let it go, but I can't.

'This just proves that what Out of Time is doing is working, Mum. They're doing everything they can to stop us speaking out, but we have to, otherwise nothing will change.'

She tosses her head back and laughs, her dark eyes shining as she looks at me as if to say, *Do not cite the deep magic to me, witch. I was there when it was written.* I'm tempted to remind her that the police did the same thing to her when she protested animal testing as a teenager, but before I can, two officers approach. I tense, but my mother just smiles, as they nod at us on their way into the station.

As soon as they do, her smile recedes, and I know that she has no intention of discussing it.

Not now.

Not here.

When she begins tapping on her phone, I give up and take mine out of the back pocket of my jeans. It's my burner because I don't bring my personal one to protests. Only Tab and Riley have the number so when I take it off airplane mode, I see that I have a string of messages from Riley checking on me, but nothing from Tab. That stings but then I realise that she's probably still being interviewed.

I check Instagram, but again, there's nothing from Tab. Just a flurry of notifications from people pleading for an update. I should go on Live to let them know that I'm OK, but before I can, Riley sends a screenshot to our group chat of the BBC News homepage. I click on it to find a photo of me being led away by the police with the headline, *RENATA BARBOSA PROTESTS MOTHER'S BP DEAL*.

To my surprise, Tab responds a few seconds later with, *Yes, Ren!*

So, she's out then, I realise and it needles at me that she hasn't checked in with me. But then she replies with a string of laughing emojis and I feel a full-on scratch as I ask myself what's so funny.

'Renata, come on,' my mother snaps, tugging me back as a Range Rover pulls up in front of us.

'What is *that*? Where's Maurice?'

'It's his wedding anniversary so I gave him the night off,' she tells me as a driver in a neat black suit hops out and greets us with a practised smile, then opens the passenger door for my mother.

'I can't get in *that*,' I tell her as she walks towards him. 'I was just arrested at a climate change protest.'

She stops and turns on her heel. 'Renata, I am capable of a great many things but finding a horse-drawn carriage at half eleven on a Friday night is beyond even my capabilities.'

'Mum, please,' I plead as I stare at the hulking black Range Rover.

'Renata,' she says through her teeth, 'there are photographers outside and—'

'Exactly! And if they get a shot of me in this *beast* it will undermine everything I'm saying!'

'Fine,' she says as she climbs into the backseat. 'Ask Tab to pick you up on her bike, then.'

A photo of me leaving on the handlebars of Tab's lime-green Wayfarer would be amusing, but as soon as I think it, I hear Pearl saying, *Tab would love being in the papers, wouldn't she?*

I pick at the thought like a scab as I watch the driver stride around the back of the car to open the other passenger door for me as the window on my mother's side slides down and she arches an eyebrow at me.

'Renata, get in,' she says crisply.

As much as I don't want to be seen in a chauffeur-driven Range Rover, I conclude that it's wise not to piss her off any more than I already have.

I join her in the backseat, then tug up my hood and duck down as the gates to the car park slide open. There are only two photographers, but when the backseat stutters with light, it feels like a lot more. They rush at the car, my heart hiccupping every time their lenses knock against the windows, but I don't look up as the driver finally passes them and speeds off.

We don't get far before we have to stop again and I panic as we join a procession of cars waiting to turn on to Kensington High Street, sure that the photographers are going to take advantage of the fact that we can't go anywhere to get their shot. I brave a peek over my shoulder to check, but as I do, something knocks against the window on my side, and I duck down again. But it's just the wing mirror of a scooter as a Deliveroo driver threads between the Range Rover and the row of parked cars.

When it darts away, I risk another peek from under the hood as we finally pull off. I've grown up travelling with my mother, bouncing from hotel rooms and short-term rentals around the world as she moves from one project to the next, so London is hardly home. But it's the first city I remember living in, and even though I've lived in dozens of others since then, it will always be my favourite.

After being locked in a cell for most of the day, Friday night in London is overwhelming as cars honk and people cling to one another with such abandon I don't know if they're shrieking with horror or delight. It's almost midnight, so it's dark. Except it isn't at all; the street a riot of light. Most of the storefronts are lit up, even though they've long been closed, and the neon signs of the ones still open glow red and green and hot, hot pink, promising everything from vapes to burgers while the streetlamps pick out groups of friends as they gather in rowdy clumps along the high street to decide whether the night is ending or getting started.

That should be me, I think as we pass them.

Out with my friends on a Friday night.

Tab and Riley are probably at the pub, regaling everyone with tales of the protest. Or at Riley's, eating pizza in his cluttered living room that always smells of weed and the incense he lights to disguise it from his landlord.

And here I am, clutching my phone in one hand and my tote bag in the other, which contains most of my worldly possessions that don't add up to much. Just a toothbrush, deodorant, a change of clothes, Riley's lucky lighter, which I've ended up with somehow, lip balm, a twenty-pound note and some loose change, and the book I was hoping to finish, which was astonishingly naïve given how the day turned out.

I brave a glance at my mother to find her frowning at her phone, the rectangle of bright light making her eyebrows look even sharper and her lips even redder as she mutters something, then looks up. I tense, waiting for her to turn to me, but she presses her phone to her ear and begins talking to her publicist.

She then proceeds to talk to everyone but me. Her publicist, Max. Someone from British Airways about a flight to Austin tomorrow. Tia Aline, who obviously has some sort of Google alert set up for me. Max again.

They start going through her schedule for Austin but she has to put him on hold to answer another call, and as soon as she does, I hear her tone harden. She tells whoever it is that she's already issued a statement and ends the call with a sharp sigh. When she goes back to Max to ask how *The Sun* got her personal number, I realise that she's probably been fielding calls like that since the protest and feel a swift stab of guilt, the tips of my ears burning as she tells Max that she'll have to change her number again.

When she hangs up, she pinches the bridge of her nose. In

the silence that follows I hear a voice in my head, the one that so often leads me astray, telling me, *Do it now, Renata. Tell her you're sorry.*

But I can't.

I know my mother well enough to leave her alone.

She'll let me know when she's ready to talk and she won't say a word before then.

And even if she was ready, she wouldn't want to do it here, in front of a driver we don't know.

But the guilt is gnawing at me. I can't just sit here with it between us on the backseat because I can feel it growing, spreading, filling the car and pushing us further apart.

'Mum, about today. I didn't know that you were at The Dorchester. I thought—'

She holds up a hand to stop me. 'Not now, Renata.'

It's enough to make the words shrivel up on my tongue because that's it.

She doesn't want to talk, so we won't talk.

So, I leave her to make her calls while I check my phone again, figuring that I'd better reply to Tab and Riley before my battery dies. As I'm about to, Tab's name flashes up on my screen and my heart hiccups. But when I open the message, she's not asking how I am – or how my interview went – she's sent a link to the *Guardian* to the group chat with a crown emoji. I click on the link to find myself looking impossibly cool as I smile at Sergeant Sykes beneath the headline, *FERNANDA BARBOSA'S DAUGHTER LEADS OUT OF TIME PROTEST.*

The article is surprisingly measured given the *Guardian* is assuming that my appearance at the protest was a fuck you to my mother. But before I can read it, I notice that we've stopped and when I look up, I turn to her with a fierce frown.

'You have *got* to be kidding me,' I hiss as someone steps forward to open my door.

'Welcome back to The Dorchester, Miss Barbosa,' the doorman says with a bright smile.

He waits for me to get out, but when my mother nods at him, he nods back and closes the door again.

The driver takes the hint as well, stepping out of the car.

'Mum, is this a joke?' I ask.

She looks genuinely confused. 'What do you mean, Renata?'

'Are you bringing me back here to punish me, or something?'

'Of course not.' She laughs lightly as she slips her phone into her bag. 'I'm supposed to be in the ballroom right now. I've been nominated for an *Architectural Review* Future Projects award for the hospital we designed in Copenhagen.' She sweeps on a fresh layer of red lipstick, then snaps the compact shut and tosses it back into her bag. 'So given that I have a breakfast meeting here in the morning, it made sense to stay overnight.'

I feel another stab of guilt, but my discomfort is soon swallowed by irritation as I look back at the hotel and say, 'Mum, you could have literally stayed anywhere else but here.'

'What's wrong with The Dorchester?'

'Exactly the same thing that's wrong with this car and *that bag*.'

When I gesture at it, I feel something in my head begin to fray as she blinks at me a few times.

She looks down at the bag, her forehead creased, then back up at me.

'Nossa,' she mutters and I know that look.

35

It's her *Stop being so dramatic, Renata* look.

'This is hardly fast fashion,' she scoffs, stroking the black quilted leather. 'It belonged to your grandmother. Tia Aline didn't speak to me for a month when Vó gave it to me.'

'It's not about the bag,' I say through my teeth.

I tell myself to calm down because there's still time to turn the car around before I say something that will send her into a blur of curls and jasmine-scented rage that concludes with her threatening to put me on the first flight to São Paulo to live with my grandparents.

So, I take a deep breath and exhale slowly through my nose. 'I just thought things would be different.'

'How so?'

'I don't know,' I tell her, playing with the straps of my tote bag. 'I thought that now you're teaching at UCL you'd rent an apartment for us, or something. But you're never here. Every other day you're on a plane somewhere. You're away so much I pretty much live with Riley. We're talking about getting a two-bedroom.'

It's not easy to catch my mother off guard, but I clearly have, the flutter of alarm that disturbs her brow confirming what I've always suspected.

She hasn't noticed that we haven't spent a night under the same roof since the new year.

I'm not surprised, but it's still a blow.

She recovers quickly, though.

'You're not moving in with Riley, Renata. You're sixteen years old. You're not old enough to move out.'

'Move out of *where*? We don't have a house.'

I laugh and it sounds so harsh – so bitter – that I realise that we're hurtling down that road again.

I can see the edge of the cliff approaching.

So I try a different tack. 'Listen, Mum. I get it, OK? You travel so much that it's not right to leave a house sitting empty when someone else could be using it. When I was a kid, I didn't even realise it was weird that we didn't have one because home was always your home in São Paulo. Where you grew up. Wherever we were in the world, we'd always end up back there. But that's your home, not mine.'

'It is your home, Renata.'

'I know,' I say, waiting for the air to warm again. But she just fusses over her earring, then her hair, then her earring again, so I try to find the right words, desperate to steer the car away from the cliff and towards some common ground. 'You know how your room in São Paulo is exactly the same as the day you moved out? The CND poster still over your bed and the wardrobe full of stuff you haven't worn since you were eighteen.'

She chuckles gently. 'Mamãe will never throw out that sticky bottle of White Musk.'

'Exactly. She still washes your sheets every week so they're fresh in case you come home.' I press my hand to my chest. 'I've never had that, Mum. I've never slept in the same bed for more than a few months. I've been living out of a suitcase my whole life.' I shrug and start fiddling with the straps on my tote bag again, wrapping one of them around my finger. 'I watch people on TikTok, getting ready in their rooms, and they have fairy lights over the bed and a noticeboard covered in photos and I wish I had that. Somewhere of my own. Somewhere to go back to that smells like the first bottle of perfume I bought for myself.'

I wait for her chin to shiver as she nods.

Or to reach over to quiet my bouncing knee with her hand.

But she just gives me that look again.

'Renata, por favor.'

'What?' I ask with a wounded frown.

'No, you've never had your own room,' she says and I recognise that tone. It's the one I've heard her use on *Question Time* so often. The one she uses when she wants someone to think that she agrees with their point, right before she eviscerates them. 'But you've seen the world, Renata.' Do you know how many people your age would trade a single bed in a box room to spend Christmas at an elephant sanctuary in Rambukkana or to watch the turtles hatch on the Galápagos Islands?'

'I know,' I tell her as my cheeks burn. I look down at the piece of gaffer tape on the knee of my jeans. It's started to curl up in one corner again, so I smooth it down with a defeated sigh. Not just because she's right but because there's no way of saying that Riley's tiny flat over a kebab shop in Earl's Court still feels like the closest thing I've ever had to a home without sounding unforgivably ungrateful.

Still, she must know that because she says, 'But you'd rather sleep on Riley's sofa than be with me.'

'Mum, stop it. You know I'd rather be with you, but I can't.'

'Why not?' she says and it's all I can do not to scream because I'm not buying the wounded mother act.

'You know why. We've discussed it *so many* times. You know I can't be out here, advocating for climate justice, then jump on a plane with you every other day. It goes against everything Out of Time is doing.'

She bristles. 'Out of Time is virtual. Everything you do is on Instagram or TikTok—'

'Not *everything*,' I correct before she can finish.

'Most of it is,' she says, even though I was literally just arrested at a protest.

'As long as you have your phone, you can keep up with Out of Time, but I *have* to travel. The work I'm doing is important.'

And mine isn't? I want to say, but I don't.

Her legacy is undeniable.

Unavoidable.

Wind farms and hospitals and elephant sanctuaries that will be there until the sun burns out.

Whereas all I do is post TikToks, apparently.

'Renata,' she says with a sigh. 'I remember what it's like to be sixteen and desperate to change the world.'

'Do you?' I ask, because I'm not so sure.

'In September, it will be *thirty-one years* since I started that first petition to ban animal testing and sometimes I ask myself if anything's changed, but it has. Yes, it's slow, but it's happening. Be patient, Renata.'

But all I hear is, *Be careful, Renata.*

You're damaging the cause, Renata.

'In an ideal world, I'd only accept projects based here, but it isn't an ideal world. It's on fire.'

I know that.

I grew up hearing that every single day.

I used to have nightmares about the oceans rising up and swallowing us all.

When I was nine, I wrote a story about a magical tree that we could climb and it would save us all. Thinking about it now, it was just a rip-off of *The Giving Tree*, but whatever my inspiration, despite the dire, sleep-stealing predictions I grew up hearing at my mother's dinner parties, I really did believe there was an answer.

We just had to find it.

'I'm doing everything I can,' she says.

'So am I,' I tell her.

'I know you're trying, Renata.'

'*Trying*? I have *four million* followers. Most of them are my age and about to inherit a world that, as you just pointed out, is on fire. So, yeah, most of what we do is virtual, but that's the point. We want people to know that even if they can't come to a protest there are still plenty of things they can do. Over one hundred thousand people signed our petition on private jets so now Caroline Lucas is leading a debate in parliament next month.'

She snorts, but I persist. 'Besides, not *everything* is virtual. I've organised concerts and been invited to speak everywhere from the United Nations to Glastonbury and I've done it all without getting on a plane.'

But she doesn't budge. 'Yes, but what I'm doing and what you're trying to do are completely different.'

I point at her. 'And there it is again. *Trying*.'

'I didn't say that one was better than the other,' she's quick to clarify.

'No, just that you're succeeding and I'm not.'

'When did I say that you're not succeeding, Renata?' she asks with a frown. 'You know how proud of you I am. You're *thriving*, despite everyone telling me that you should be in boarding school, not travelling with me. But we proved them wrong, didn't we?' She raises her chin with a smug smile. 'You speak five languages and earned all nines in your GCSEs and you got to see the world while you were doing it.'

But that isn't what I'm talking about and she knows it.

'Really? Because that's not what you said in *Observer Magazine* three months ago.'

'Meu Deus!' She throws her hands up. 'I don't know how many more times I can tell you: I was misquoted.'

'Misquoted?'

Come on.

My mother, who has rendered politicians speechless with a single sentence, was misquoted?

'Sure.' I pull a face. 'You weren't trying to distance yourself from me *at all*.'

'Renata,' she says sternly, 'I had *no idea* that they had asked you to write that essay about Out of Time. And I certainly had no idea that they were going to tack it on to the end of my interview.'

'What did you think the interview was for, then?'

'I told you: I thought it was a profile because I'd won the Royal Gold Medal.'

'So how did Out of Time even come up, then?'

'They asked me in passing what I thought about Extinction Rebellion. Not you. I never even mentioned Out of Time. I just made an off-the-cuff remark about how nonviolent civil disobedience is counterproductive—'

'Oh, I know that, Mum,' I sneer, cutting her off.

'It was after the interview. We were done. I thought it was off the record. How was I supposed to know they were going to put it on the cover to make it seem like we're at odds?'

'We are at odds, Mum!'

She seems stunned.

So stunned that she actually says it out loud this time. 'Don't be so dramatic, Renata!'

'Mum, *please*. You hate Out of Time. You think we're making things worse!'

'I don't *hate* Out of Time,' she corrects.

But she doesn't disagree.

'What was it you said?' I remind her. '*The war will not be won by climbing cranes and spray-painting windows.* How will it be won, then? By doing business with BP? BP, Mum! You think you can win the war by playing the game with people like *them*?'

She nods. 'That's exactly how it will be won, Renata. By playing the game, then changing the rules.'

'*How?* I know you talk the talk on *Question Time* and you're an advisor to all of these people, but when was the last time you actually used these relationships to push for changes in legislation? I know our private jet debate is probably going to be laughed out of parliament, but at least I'm trying to do something. Yet *I'm* the one damaging the cause! The world is burning and you're being ferried around in a Range Rover, going to lunch with the people responsible for setting it on fire in the first place!'

42

I hear that voice in my head again, pleading with me to turn the car around.

But I can't. Just remembering how excited I was to read my essay in *Observer Magazine*, how Tab and I got up early and ran to the newsagent that first Sunday morning in January to buy it only to discover my mother's face on the cover with the words *MOTHER KNOWS BEST: FERNANDA BARBOSA'S ADVICE TO HER WAYWARD DAUGHTER* makes me slam my foot on the gas and point the car towards the cliff, not away from it.

'So, is this is your solution, huh? How you're *changing the rules*?' I emphasise the words with my fingers. 'Boozy lunches with BP and helping the king make even more money with his offshore wind farms?'

She studies me for a moment and I wonder if she's thinking the same thing I am.

That for the first time she doesn't see herself reflected back.

'Is that all you think I do, Renata?'

I hear her voice catch and I feel wretched because no, I don't think that.

I don't think that at all.

I just want her to acknowledge what I'm doing as well.

And I don't know how this happened.

When it became about who's trying harder to save the world.

But before I can remind her that we're on the same team, she's gone.

5

'Are we weird?' I ask Riley when he finds me sitting on our favourite bench.

He doesn't hesitate. 'Yes.'

'No, I mean, is it weird that we always meet at this particular bench?'

'Why is that weird?' he asks with a frown.

I gesture at the headstones, and he looks slightly startled, as though he hadn't seen them before.

'I mean, yeah.' He shrugs. 'I guess it is kind of weird to hang out in a graveyard.'

'That seems to be the consensus,' I tell him with a sigh as he flops down next to me. 'I just went on Live and when everyone saw where I was sitting, someone called me Wednesday Addams.'

When I turn to scowl at him, he peers at me, then says, 'You do look like Jenna Ortega, actually.'

I wish.

Still, where else are two misfits with nothing to do on a Saturday afternoon supposed to meet?

Plus, we're lazy. Brompton Cemetery is exactly equidistant between his flat and Jimmy's, which is the only place near here that offers vegans something other than falafel and hummus. That's reason enough to favour it even if despite it being worryingly warm yesterday, the temperature has since dipped dramatically enough to remind us that it's still only the first weekend in February. But I don't care. The sun's out, even if I can't feel it, so after being stuck in a police cell most of yesterday, I can endure a cold nose if it means I can see the sky.

'Hey, Scully.' Riley salutes his cat, who's black, of course, because what would this scene be without a black cat? She's sitting by my elbow, surveying the headstones to make sure everyone is staying put.

'She was here when I arrived,' I tell him as I give her cheek a swift tickle.

'She hangs out here all the time. She likes the peace and quiet.'

'Same, Scully,' I lean in and whisper as she watches a squirrel scuttle up a tree trunk.

'Sorry I didn't wait up for you last night,' Riley says, his head dipped as he dumps his tote bag on to the bench between us then starts rooting through it. 'I tried, but I was beat.' He stops to yawn then blinks a few times and says, 'I tried listening to a Radio 4 podcast about Defra's latest Environmental Improvement Plan in an effort to keep myself awake, but it ended up having the opposite effect.'

'You don't say?'

'Anyway' – he produces a small cardboard box and holds it up to me – 'I repent with moujadara.'

'You're a good man, Sōta Riley,' I tell him as I take it from him. Then I remember something and reach into the pocket of my coat. 'Let me give you this before I forget.'

'My lucky lighter!' He beams when I hold it up. 'I thought I lost this!'

He kisses it and when he starts looking through his bag again, I feel my phone buzz in my hand. My heart hitches, but it's only Tia Aline and my shoulders sag because I haven't heard from Tab since she sent that link to the group chat last night so you can add that to the lengthy list of reasons why I barely slept.

I reply to Tia Aline, then check when Tab was last on WhatsApp while Riley pulls stuff out of his bag.

'Someone tried to steal my order in Jimmy's. Can you believe it?' he huffs as my heart hitches again when I see that Tab is online. 'The guy clearly said Riley. Riley doesn't sound anything like Kelly, does it?'

'Uh-huh,' I say, but I'm not listening because all I can think about is whether he's heard from Tab.

I shouldn't ask because given that she can't even wait in line for coffee without calling me because she's bored, he'll know something's up and that's *exactly* what Tab doesn't want, isn't it?

For things to be weird between the three of us.

But I have to know.

'Hey, Riles,' I say, feigning nonchalance as he pulls out a wooden fork. 'You heard from Tab today?'

I make sure to add a little shrug, but there's no need because Riley isn't even looking up.

He just hands me the fork and says, 'Yeah, she called me, like, fifteen minutes ago.'

'She did?' I say as I tell myself that it's fine that he's heard from her and I haven't.

It's fine.

I'm fine.

Everything is fine.

It's not like I want to throw up on my shoes, or anything.

'Yeah.' He pulls out another box and points it at me. 'She called to tell me that she saw Suella Braverman at Waterloo' – he tears into it and reaches for his Quorn burger – 'she shouted, *Fuck the Tories* at her.'

He creases up and I join in, but it's not as enthusiastic because usually, I would have been Tab's first call. Then I realise that if she's at Waterloo, she must be getting the train home for the weekend. It's the first time I haven't gone with her since she started at Imperial and it finally hits me: it's over.

'You OK, Ren?' I hear Riley ask and look up to find him offering me a chip.

'Yeah, I'm fine,' I tell him, even though each heartbeat feels like a punch.

February 4th, my brain pulls from nowhere.

I look down at my phone to check then sigh tenderly.

Her mother's birthday.

I rest the cardboard box on my knees for a moment, terrified that I'm going to drop it and send rice everywhere as I think about the book I bought from Brick Lane Bookshop last month that's still sitting on the sideboard in Riley's living room. Rebecca Boyle's *Our Moon* because, like me and Tab, her mum loves the moon. She's always dragging us outside to look at it. But how am I going to give the book to her now?

Oh God, *why* did I say that to Tab?

Are you ashamed of me, or something?

Every time I think about it, it makes me feel so sick I can't breathe.

I should have just left it alone because everything was fine.

We were fine.

Except I want more than fine.

I jump then as Riley waves his hand in front of my face.

'Ren, your phone's ringing.'

My heart hitches again, hoping to see Tab's name, but it's a number I don't recognise.

'It's probably another journalist,' I grumble, and let it go to voicemail.

A few seconds later, I get a text.

'What?' Riley asks around a mouthful of burger when I let out a pained groan. 'Is it the *Daily Mail*?'

'Worse,' I groan again, then read aloud. *Just calling so you have new number. Please memorise it. F.B.*'

'Who's F.B.?'

'Fernanda Barbosa,' I tell him, then feel a flutter of panic at missing her call, which passes as soon as I realise that she knows I never answer calls from numbers I don't know so she had no intention of speaking to me.

'Your mum signs off texts with her initials?'

'Only when she's mad at me.'

Riley's so used to us that he isn't fazed by that in the slightest. He just plucks a pickle from his burger and pops it into his mouth as I think about how unhinged it is that I can read my mother's mood by how she signs off her text messages. They're like the symbols on a weather forecast. If she ends with *M xx* we're good – nothing but sunshine – but if she omits the *xx*, something's brewing and I need to proceed with caution. However, if she signs off *F.B.*, batten down the hatches because she's furious.

'I saw your Live about what happened at the police station before I fell asleep last night so I figured your mum would be pissed. Was it bad?' Riley asks with a snort. 'What did she say?'

'She didn't say a word, actually.'

'Is that better or worse than the *Observer Magazine* incident?'

'Definitely better,' I tell him with an uneasy chuckle.

But just as things are beginning to thaw between us, I had to turn the hourglass over again, didn't I?

'How did it end this time?' he asks around a mouthful of burger.

'Like always. With her telling me that she's doing the real work while I'm fucking around on TikTok. Except this time, I told her that if she's doing deals with BP, then she's lost sight of the cause.'

His eyes widen.

'I'm surprised she gave me her new number at all,' I say, exhaling sharply through my nose.

'And that's the first time you've heard from her since?'

I nod.

'Have you tried calling to apologise?'

'How do you apologise for shitting over everything someone has accomplished?'

He tilts his head from side to side. 'True.'

'Besides, I know Mum. Even if I tried to apologise, she wouldn't listen.'

'Just give her a minute,' Riley tells me as he bites into a chip.

'You know what she's like. Every time you have a big blow-out, she ignores you for three to five working days then calls like nothing happened.'

I let out another pained groan.

'So stop beating yourself up and eat your lunch before it goes cold,' he tells me, nodding at the cardboard box still sitting on my knees. 'I nearly fought someone called Kelly for that.'

I chuckle, but as soon as I lift the lid, the smell of spices and crispy fried onions hits me and I'm blindsided by the memory of the three of us at Glastonbury last year. I close my eyes as I try to catch my breath, but that just makes it worse, everything a dizzying kaleidoscope of sound and colour as it comes at me, all at once. How suddenly the day dimmed and there was that seamless shift from glittery cheeks and sunburnt shoulders to weed and white teeth. Riley dancing with someone in pink fairy wings. Tab and I sneaking kisses when he wasn't looking. Those pints of warm pear cider that made Tab's mouth taste of autumn while we queued up at the Goan Fish Curries stall in West Holts as we waited for Little Simz to come on.

With that, I don't just remember the smell of the curry, I remember it all. How even though it was our second night there, Tab still smelled the same, of lavender and geranium shampoo and the perfume I bought her for her birthday. But there was something else. I still don't know what it is, whether it was the sunshine or being outside or the suncream I kept rubbing into her shoulders. Perhaps it was a combination of all three, but it was something I hadn't smelled until then. Something I'll never smell again if I don't fix this.

And I remember laughing. The three of us laughing and

50

dancing until we couldn't catch our breath and had to push our way through the crowd back out into the open. As soon as we did, we lifted our faces up to the big, black sky, gulping for air, Tab's hand in mine as we staggered away, looking for somewhere to sit. I'll never forget it, the three of us on that hill, looking down at the Pyramid Stage and the constellation of lights below.

'So you get it, right?' Riley says.

He's obviously been talking for a while because it's like turning on the radio and catching the end of a song. I try to look like I've been paying attention, even though I'm still on that hill with the world at my feet.

Riley knows me, though. He's caught me drifting off enough times while he's telling me about a paper he's reading on advancing snowmelt to know when he's lost me.

So he raises his eyebrows and says, 'You get why Tab and I had to get out of there.'

'Out of where? The police station?'

'No, the protest, Ren.'

'Huh?'

When I still don't catch on, he adds, 'Tab and I managed to get away as it was kicking off.'

'Wait.' I sit back and hold my hand up. 'You guys weren't detained yesterday?'

He shakes his head and all I hear is Pearl saying, *Well, that's convenient.*

I shake my head. 'I just figured the police put you in another van.'

I must look as dismayed as I feel because he puts his burger

51

down and says, 'We had to get out of there. Imperial are threatening to stop my bursary after Out of Time protested the debate they hosted with Bjorn Lomborg last month, so they'd kick me out for sure if I got arrested. Then what? I'm not like you and Tab,' he reminds me with a fierce frown. 'Do you know how many of my friends got into uni? Shit, do you know how many of them even finished school? Plus, Tab's parents will kill her if she gets kicked out of Imperial. Her mum's an alumnus. Do you know how embarrassing it would be if her daughter's expelled?'

But it's fine to embarrass my mother, right? the voice says then.

Except it isn't Pearl's this time, it's my own.

The trouble is, I wear my heart on my face so as soon I think it, his flushes.

'We agreed, Ren, right from our first protest. We agreed that if it all comes on top and Tab and I can get away, we should because *you're* the face of Out of Time. It's your name that gets us coverage. So there's no need for us to risk getting kicked out of uni when no one gives a shit if we're at the protest or not.'

'I know,' I tell him, and I feel wretched because he looks so disappointed.

As though I've betrayed him, or something.

Two days ago, I wouldn't have thought twice about it.

'Fucking Pearl,' I mutter.

'Huh?' he grunts as he picks up his burger again.

'Nothing.'

Luckily, he continues as though I didn't say anything, his tone lighter. 'Besides, you said it yourself: you've got nothing to lose, not like us. Your mum has the connections to get you out of anything, doesn't she?'

I didn't say that.

Tab did.

She's the one who's always saying that I have nothing to lose when I have plenty to lose, don't I?

Fucking Pearl.

'What?' Riley asks as I start stabbing at my rice with my fork.

'Nothing,' I mutter. 'Just something Pearl said yesterday that's been bugging me.'

I force a forkful of rice into my mouth before I can say anything else.

'Pearl as in GreenGirlPearl?' Riley asks with a frown.

I nod.

'When were you talking to her?'

'We ended up in the same cell yesterday.'

'Ah.' He nods, then chuckles. 'So that explains why you followed her back last night.'

I shoot a look at him. 'How do you know that?'

'Ren, come on. You know what your stans are like. As soon as you liked Pearl's photo, they went nuts. Between the ones who think you hate each other and the ones who ship you, it was carnage. It took them all of three seconds to check and see that you'd finally followed her back.'

'Are you serious?' I don't know why I ask because I've spent enough time on the internet to not be surprised by anything any more, but I'm still stunned. 'Pearl took the photo the *Guardian* used so I figured it was only polite to like it and follow her back. This is what I get for being nice.'

'Just admit it, Ren,' Riley tells me, pretending to swoon. 'You love her.'

'God, Riles. Be serious,' I sneer, reaching over to steal one of his chips.

I can't look at him, though, because I'm not thinking about Pearl, I'm thinking about Tab.

After scrolling through GreenGirlPearl's Instagram for a few minutes on the night bus last night, my mind drifted to Tab and I finally surrendered to the temptation to check her timeline. I haven't looked at it since she suggested that we *cool things down for a bit*, terrified that I'd be confronted by her, happy and unburdened. But I let go of a breath when I saw that she'd uploaded a photo of me from the BP protest, winking at the camera as Sergeant Sykes and his chuckling friend led me away.

With that, I tumbled down the rabbit hole of us. Starting with our last photo together, at that protest in Oxford two weeks ago, a few hours before I tried to kiss her on the train back to London and something became untethered when she moved her face away.

Being forced to remember it was like running through a burning house. Actually, it felt like I was the one who was on fire as I looked at the photo, Tab's head back, megaphone raised while I sprayed *EARTH BEFORE PROFIT* on the window of Barclays bank. But once the sear of shame passed, I realised she was right. Once everyone found out, they'd be talking about us, not what we were doing with Out of Time.

I don't want that, either, but I don't understand how everyone doesn't already know.

Can't they see it?

I could, as I spent the rest of the bus ride scrolling through Tab's Instagram.

It's right there.

Everything.

Every protest.

Every night out.

All of it her and me.

Me and her.

My sixteenth birthday, her kissing my cheek. New Year's Eve on the beach in Poole, fireworks blooming over our heads. Her pinning an Out of Time badge to the Christmas tree outside Shell's headquarters while I point and cackle. The two of us sitting, side by side, on the edge of the stage in an empty Brixton Academy while we wait for sound check to start for the Radio 1 Out of Time gig last November.

Then everything else – her first day at Imperial, that week in Cornwall with Riley learning to surf, Glastonbury, her eighteenth birthday – all of it, right there. A mosaic of everything Tab and I have done all the way back to the moment we met outside Downing Street just over a year ago. I missed my stop reading the caption she'd written under that first photo of us, her in a homemade Out of Time hoodie, me trying not to stare at her. *Got the 05.40 train from Poole this morning just to meet @ rebel_ren and she's everything I knew she would be.*

'Hey.' Riley nudges me. 'Now you and Pearl are besties, word is out that you're going soft because another sustainability influencer keeps DMing me, trying to get in touch with you. Melody something . . .'

It takes me a beat too long to get what he's saying, but when I do, I stare at him. 'Melody Munroe?'

'Yes!' He reaches for a paper napkin and wipes his mouth. 'Who is she?'

'No idea, but she's been blowing up my DMs as well,' I tell him, which isn't *strictly* true.

I do know who she is, actually, but he'd tease me mercilessly if he knew why.

I first heard the name Melody Munroe a month ago when I was lurking on SimplySabrina's Instagram. Sabrina was the original sustainability influencer and I developed a debilitating – and some might say misdirected – crush on her when I was thirteen, despite the fact that she's hopelessly heterosexual and eleven years older than me.

She was my first – albeit unrequited – love so I still have a soft spot for her and continue to follow her even though most of her content revolves around her upcoming wedding. But then last month, in a break from her posts about vintage wedding dresses and how to source flowers that are 'grown not flown', Sabrina tagged Melody Munroe in a photo saying that she was gonna save the world, and curiosity got the better of me.

'I googled her on the night bus home,' I lie.

Riley smirks again. 'How bored were you on that night bus?'

'She's one of those old school YouTubers. She had a channel in the early noughties called MelodyLoves.'

'Is she American?' he asks as he finishes his burger and sits back against the bench.

'Nah. She used to live in Brighton, I think. She was part of that first wave of YouTubers who used to do make-up tutorials and vlogs mucking around with their mates, and stuff.'

'So she's one of the OGs.'

'She was an influencer before anyone thought to give it a name. She was one of the first to start her own skincare line. She was about to sell it to Estée Lauder, but then the night cream started burning people's faces.'

He crosses his arms and stretches out his legs. 'Nice.'

'She disappeared after that, but then she launched a podcast last year.'

'Have you listened to it?'

'I might have if she didn't insist on referring to herself as a sustainability influencer.'

'She's one of *those*,' he sneers, reminding me why I can never tell him about my crush on SimplySabrina.

I get it, though. It's a title that's always made me feel slightly nauseous. Not only because adding 'sustainability' doesn't make you different from any other influencer – your sole purpose remains to flog products, even if they're vegan – but because if the war isn't going to be won by climbing cranes and spray-painting windows, then it certainly won't be won by making your own facial oil.

'That explains why you've been ignoring her.' Riley chuckles. Then he scratches his beard and asks, 'I don't get it, though. Why is she so keen to interview you?'

'I don't know,' I say as I tease Scully with my fork. 'She has a new book out, or something.'

'There it is.'

'What?' I ask when he points at me.

'She's using you to flog her book.'

I roll my eyes and resume teasing Scully. 'So young, yet so cynical.'

'Just because I'm paranoid, doesn't mean I'm wrong.' I roll my eyes, but he wags his finger at me. 'There's a reason she's being so persistent. I'm sure the fact that you have *four million* followers has nothing to do with it. Ten quid says that she wants to do the interview at Waterstones.'

The Feminist Bookshop in Brighton, actually.

But I don't tell him that.

Luckily, I'm saved as my phone rings again.

It's another number I don't recognise, so I ignore it as he says, 'You know I'm right, Ren.'

'Probably, but who cares? I'm not doing the interview,' I tell him as my phone buzzes this time.

I assume it's a voicemail, but when I glance down, I see that it's a text.

It's me. Call me back. – F.B.

'Renata,' she answers sharply. I shouldn't have put her on speaker, not with Riley sitting next to me, but given that he's constantly warning me that mobile phones fry your brain, it's become a habit at this point.

It's so quiet in the cemetery that my mother's voice rings out, sending the birds fleeing from the tree we're sitting under as Riley sits up straight and starts furiously smoothing his long hair with his hands.

She can't see you, I mouth as Scully jumps down from the arm of the bench and runs off.

But before I can take her off speaker, she says, 'Melody Munroe.'

Then I'm so freaked out that I forget to, as I look around the graveyard.

'She emailed Max,' she says, reading my mind. 'She's been trying to reach you.'

'Yeah,' I finally say, 'she wants to interview me.'

'She's quite persistent.' My mother sighs and I'm not sure if she's appalled or impressed.

'Sorry, I'll message her now,' I promise, annoyed that this influencer is bothering my mother.

Calm down, Melody, I think.

It's only been a week since she first DMed me.

'Are you going to do the interview, Renata?'

'Of course not. Giles told me to keep my head down while I'm under investigation, didn't he?'

'Well,' my mother says in a way that makes me tense as I wait for her to complain about being pulled into this. But instead she says, 'I'd never heard of her, but she's *very* keen to speak to you. I just sent Teresa to Waterstones to pick up her new book, *Sustainable Sustainability*.' I can hear pages turning through the phone as she flicks through it. 'It's quite interesting, actually.'

'It is?' I say, slightly stunned to hear my mother say that about a book with a hot-pink cover.

'It's a Ladybird Learners *My First ABC of Sustainability*, but that seems right given the target audience.'

'OK,' I say, looking at Riley, who seems as confused as I am.

But then she finally lands the plane. 'I think you should do the interview.'

I'm so surprised that I burst out laughing. 'What?'

'I've discussed it with Max, and we think it would be good for you.'

'*How?*'

'It wouldn't hurt to be associated with someone like Melody Munroe right now. She's harmless. Young. Fun. Approachable. Max just spoke to her, and she pitched an event at a bookshop in Brighton.'

'Yeah, I know.'

'She wants to do a panel on the future of activism with you and Pearl.'

I almost laugh again as I realise that this is my mother's solution to what happened yesterday.

The Renata Barbosa Rebrand.

Sure enough, she says, 'We need to do something to soften your image, Renata.'

When I look at Riley, his eyes widen as he leans back against the bench.

'Giles agrees,' my mother says, letting me know that it's been decided. 'People need to see you as something other than the girl who is always on the news for being arrested.'

'I'm not *always* being arrested,' I insist.

'Twelve times in two years, Renata.'

'That's hardly *always*, Mum,' I start to say, then stop, because what's the point?

Resistance is futile.

My mother must sense I've surrendered because she softens. 'It will be an easy interview. This Melody is hardly Emily Maitlis, is she? Just let people see the real you. Not the one on the news.'

Is there another one? I think as she hangs up.

6

Melody is everything I thought – and feared – she would be.

A squealing ball of energy that charges at me as soon as I step into the bookshop.

'Thank you so much for doing this, Renata!' She puts the mug she's holding down on the counter, then grins and pulls me into a hug so tight it knocks the air clean out of me. When she eventually lets go and takes a step back, she keeps her hands on my shoulders, her grin a little more conspiratorial. 'This is going to be amazing!'

'Amazing,' I repeat as I try to smile back.

I'm guessing it's more of a grimace, though, because the truth is: I'm not a hugger.

Tab?

Always.

My mother?

Rarely.

Someone I haven't even been introduced to yet?

Absolutely not.

I want to run away and find Tab and Riley in the pub on the corner and forget I ever agreed to this.

Not that I can with Melody clutching my shoulders. 'It's Ren, right? You prefer Ren?'

When I nod, she takes that as her cue to start talking. Not

to me, *at* me. I don't even know what she's saying, just that she's so close that I can smell the coffee on her breath and her sweet, sweet perfume as she talks and talks and talks. I can't even see her face. She's just this *blur* of white teeth and dark eyes and pink lips and the way it makes my head spin is not unlike that moment right before you throw up.

If Pearl is annoying, then Melody is on a whole other level. She has the energy of a children's television presenter, this pantomime sunshine happy that's slightly unsettling, if for no other reason than I'm terrified that she's about to grab a guitar and burst into song. When she stays still long enough for me to take her in, I discover that she looks like one as well, in pink DMs and a pair of colourful Lucy & Yak dungarees. Or she does until I note that they're made of a print of Andy Warhol-esque breasts. So maybe she looks less like a children's television presenter and more like she should be in a comedy club somewhere, cracking jokes about smear tests.

'Is your mum with you, Ren?' she asks, hands still clasping my shoulders, and I try not to laugh as I picture my mother being confronted by Melody, bounding towards her in her boob dungarees.

It almost makes this whole ordeal worth it.

'She's on her way,' I assure her.

'Oh, that's amazing!'

Amazing, I almost parrot, but I tell myself to control my face as someone appears next to us.

'Hey, welcome to The Feminist Bookshop,' they say with a small wave. 'I'm Ruth.'

Melody finally lets go of me to sling her arm around them. 'Ren, this is Ruth. She owns this place.'

'It's lovely,' I tell her.

'Isn't it dreamy, Ren?' Melody interrupts, grabbing her mug from the counter and pointing it at me. I hope it's decaf otherwise it's going to be a long night. 'I used to come here all the time when I lived in Brighton.'

'Where are you now?' I ask, more out of politeness than any real curiosity. But as soon as I do, I curse myself because Melody's clearly an oversharer.

When she takes a swig of coffee, I say a little prayer that she's just going to say something like, *I'm living in London*, or whatever, and leave it at that. But of course she rolls her eyes as she says, 'I moved out to the sticks a few years ago but, God, I miss it. I love Brighton. I was born here. I used to live in a house in Montpelier Villas, didn't I, Ruth?'

She nods and says, 'Yes, she lived in a gorgeous house around the corner.'

'Gorgeous,' Melody says with a theatrical sigh, then shakes her head. 'But when everything went tits up with my skincare line, I lost everything. So did my parents. They went bankrupt paying my legal fees and ended up getting divorced. So, my mum, my baby brother, Oren, and I had to move in with my nan in Newport, which, after living in a million-pound house and driving a Range Rover, was a shocker, let me tell you. But as humbling as it was, as ports in a storm go, being somewhere I could go to the corner shop without someone asking for a photo was a pretty good one. So, I made the most of my newfound anonymity and got a job at the hospital, transcribing medical notes. If you ever need to know how to treat a pituitary adenoma, I'm your girl.'

She thumbs at herself and the way she does it – her pink lips parting with an exaggerated wink – tells me that she's told this story before. She doesn't stop for breath and keeps going as though she's on *BBC Breakfast*. 'By 2019, the storm had passed, and things were calmer. Then I was just Melody again. Melody who got the 29 to work every morning and went to Sainsbury's on Friday nights and ironed her work shirts on Sundays, but when I realised it was my new normal, I lost it.' Her eyes widen. 'It had been three years and the thought of sitting at a desk all day with a pair of headphones, listening to a voice drone on about gonadotropin deficiency for the next thirty, made me want to jump off the Transporter Bridge. I couldn't do it. I needed to do something. So, I decided to start a podcast because my brother's sixteen and a *huge* fan of yours, Ren. He's always berating me about fast fashion and not recycling and shopping at Sainsbury's when I should be supporting local farmers at Newport Market, and it made me realise how different teenagers are now. They really care about this stuff, don't they?'

She finally stops talking, no doubt waiting for me to nod, but I just stare at her because *my God*, if I'd know that asking where she was living now would prompt all of this, I wouldn't have done it.

Melody blushes and presses her hand to her forehead. 'I'm talking too much, aren't I? Sorry! I do that.' She winces and looks at Ruth, who's still standing next to me. 'I do that, don't I, Ruth?'

She smiles sweetly. 'That's why we love doing events with you, Melody. You're always so engaging.'

That's one way of putting it, I suppose.

Melody shimmies with excitement and when she squeezes my arm, it feels like being cornered in a pub bathroom by a

64

drunk girl telling you that she loves you as she says, 'I'm sorry. It's just that I'm so excited to meet you, Ren! You and Oren are the reason I started my sustainability journey.'

I'm glad Tab and Riley aren't here because they'd howl at *sustainability journey* as Melody continues gushing. 'All of this is kind of my fault, isn't it? I'm the Amazon generation, right? We ushered that in. Amazon. ASOS. Deliveroo. All of it. We had to have everything right away.' She clicks her fingers. 'There was no next-day delivery before us, and I actively encouraged it with my clothing hauls and discount codes and sponsored posts. So I guess I wanted to try and undo some of the damage I did, which is why I started my podcast. To make people my age think about what they're consuming in the way my brother made me think twice before doing another Boohoo order after three glasses of Pinot Grigio on a Saturday night. That's why I called it *You Don't Need Another Tote Bag*. But the response was so underwhelming that I thought no one was listening. By the sixth episode, I was ready to give up because it was *so much* work, but then my arch nemesis, Zoella, got in touch.'

She smirks, clearly waiting for a reaction, and when she doesn't get one, she says, 'You're sixteen. Of course you haven't heard of her.' She rolls her eyes. 'Zoella was my Pearl. We were rivals. We hated each other.'

'I don't hate Pearl,' I tell her with a frown.

But Melody carries on as though I haven't said anything. 'It turned out that when Zoella and I actually spoke, we didn't hate each other at all. She's a sweet baby angel. So let that be a lesson to you, Ren.'

She wags her finger at me and I try not to stare because what is she on about?

I only asked her where she was living. How did we get here?

'I regret the time I wasted competing with her,' Melody says with a wistful sigh. 'We could have been working together, not against each other.'

Here it comes, I think, bracing myself for whatever nugget of wisdom she's about to impart.

Girl power. Rah. Rah. Rah.

But instead she resumes talking about herself, which is no less predictable. 'Zoella offered to come on my podcast and it blew up!' She beams. 'She persuaded me to get back on to social media and rebuild my following and here I am!' She almost spills her coffee as she waves her hand. 'The shiny new Melody Munroe!'

Did she actually answer my question?

'Then, the podcast got even bigger during the pandemic,' Melody ploughs on, 'and I finally had enough money to move out of my nan's spare room. The plan was to come back to Brighton, but my sister told me about a farm that was for sale in her village. After living with Nan for so long, I kind of liked the idea of being near family again, so I bought it! It's in Chanctonbury, which is about forty-five minutes away. I know nothing about farms, so it's been a steep learning curve, but it's the best decision I ever made. Especially as my mum and brother came with me so, without meaning to, it's unintentionally turned into an intentional community. There's currently about ten of us in the village. I think you know one of our crew, actually. Celeste Calder.'

That gets my attention. 'Aunt Celeste?'

She blinks back. 'Wait. Is she your aunt as well?'

'No, I've just always called her that. She went to Cambridge with Mum. I've known her forever.'

'No way! What are the chances! She married my uncle Dan when I was four. She's always lived in Chanctonbury so we used to spend the summer at their house and I loved it. My sister and I would charge around on the South Downs, then camp overnight with them on Chanctonbury Ring, hoping to spot aliens.' She chuckles to herself, then shakes her head. 'It's no surprise that we all ended back there. It was always our happy place.'

'Sounds blissful,' I tell her.

'It still is,' she says, but before she can go on, she's interrupted by her phone ringing.

When she apologises, then puts her mug down on the counter, I let go of a breath, grateful for the reprieve. I watch her pulling stuff out of her bag as she tries to find her phone. First, a pink metal water bottle with cherries all over it, then a green-and-white striped notebook, then a pair of yellow mohair mittens, before she finally holds her phone up to us with a triumphant cheer. She has an orange Miffy phone case and when I see it, I tell myself to stop being an asshole because Melody is basically a six-year-old in boob dungarees.

When I glance at Ruth, she looks as wrung out as I feel, watching Melody skip around the shop while she chats to whoever called her. I try not to laugh as I say, 'This place really is beautiful.'

The white wooden front door and bay windows look original, so I suspect it was a house at one point and we're standing in what was once the living room, the walls now lined from floor to ceiling with rows and rows of books. Everything from Susan

Sontag to Clarice Lispector. I can't wait for my mother to see it because I know she'll swoon. I spot a collection of Penguin Little Black Classics and feel the same burn of longing that I get every time I see something in a shop then realise that I have nowhere to put it. A book is one thing because once I'm done, I can leave it on a train for someone else to find or donate it to a charity shop, but I've long given up collecting things for the bedroom I'll never have. I did for a while, but then I got tired of unpacking then repacking everything every time we moved somewhere else.

'That's a great book,' Ruth says, nodding at the copy of *Braiding Sweetgrass* that I'm smiling at.

Except I'm not smiling because of this book; I'm smiling as I realise that in a couple of years, I'll be at university and I'll be able to keep my books in a room of my own instead of having to give them away.

'I've been meaning to read this,' I tell her as I slip it off the shelf.

'I love that book!' Melody interrupts to tell me.

When she resumes yapping on the phone, I turn back to Ruth. 'Thanks for having me, by the way.'

I was going to say that anyway, so there was no need for my mother to warn me to be nice. *I'm always nice*, I told her when she called as Riley and I were getting on the train to Brighton, but she still insisted on reminding me to be polite. Say please and thank you. Remember everyone's name. Offer to help. Don't be difficult.

Don't embarrass me, basically.

'Of course, Ren,' Ruth says. 'Thanks for coming. We're all very excited.'

68

'Are we doing the panel here? Do you need help setting up the chairs?'

Melody almost chokes on her coffee as she tosses her phone back into her bag.

'Ren, you're so funny!' she shrieks. 'Of course we're not doing it here!'

'I would have *loved* to.' Ruth smiles and there's something so refreshingly normal about her that she makes Melody look even more like a cartoon caricature. 'But the shop's too small. So we're doing it at St Mary Magdalen' a few doors down. Even so' – she shrugs, her smile a little looser – 'when people heard you were coming, the tickets sold out in half an hour and almost three hundred people signed up to watch online.'

'Oh wow,' I say, my cheeks warming.

I wish that my mother was here to hear that.

Not bad for a girl who's only known for being arrested.

'That's why I wanted us to meet here first,' Melody explains, 'so we can go through the questions and get to know each other a bit so we don't go into the interview cold. Gotta give them a good show!' She winks at me then thumbs over her shoulder. 'Why don't we head downstairs. We don't have long.'

'Sure.' I nod, as she grabs her coat.

'Let me wrap that for you,' Ruth says, reaching for the copy of *Braiding Sweetgrass* that I'm still holding.

'I'll see you downstairs,' I tell Melody, then follow Ruth to the till.

I take my phone from the pocket of my coat, but she shakes her head and slips the book into a tote bag. 'I've sold *a lot* of books because of you, so this one is on me.'

'Buying that so you can hide a nail file in it?' Pearl asks, suddenly behind me.

I'd forgotten that Melody was interviewing her as well and roll my eyes before I turn to face her.

'Miss Newman,' I say with a slow smile. 'How lovely to see you again.'

'Ditto.' Her smile is a little sharper. 'But it will be nice to have the opportunity to escape this time.'

'Aw, shucks. What am I going to do with this nail file, then?'

'Don't worry. I'm sure you'll have cause to use it soon.'

'Or we could lock ourselves in the bathroom, you know, for old times' sake.'

I wink at her, but she ignores me as she looks me up and down.

'You look decidedly less anarchic tonight, Renata.'

'And you look less like you're about to throw up.'

'I guess you just have that effect on women.'

'So, that's a no to the bathroom thing, then?'

'Oh, Renata. Irrelevant as always.'

'I think you mean *irreverent*.'

She tilts her head at me. 'Do I?'

I try not to laugh as Ruth waves from behind the till. 'Hi, Pearl.'

'Hey, Ruth.' She waves back with a sweet smile. 'Sorry I'm late. I got stuck at work. This drunk guy came into the café and wouldn't leave. We had to call the police. The joys of working in North Laine.'

'We don't have that problem in Hove. It's more middle-class rage if we don't have the new Zadie Smith.' She chuckles, then

70

says, 'Can I get you guys something to drink? We have tea, coffee, hot chocolate?'

'Do you have any herbal tea?' Pearl asks.

'Of course! Anything for you, Ren?'

I think about Melody waiting downstairs for us and say, 'Coffee, please. Black.'

I guess Pearl notes my tone, because when Ruth goes to make the drinks, she sniggers.

'First time meeting Melody, huh?'

'Oh yeah,' I say, suddenly exhausted as I realise that the night hasn't even started.

'How much do you hate her?'

'I want to extract her essence, lock it in a jar and throw it into a volcano.'

She nods, then says, 'She's my godmother, by the way.'

Of course she is.

'I mean, she's not that—' I start to say, but Pearl holds her hand up.

'It's OK. I know Melody's a lot, but she has a good heart.'

When she unwinds her scarf, her hair fizzles with static and I feel an unsettling urge to reach over and smooth it down with my hands. But she's already doing it, the warm light of the shop making it look gold this evening as opposed to white, like it was in the cell. Other than that, she looks the same, her eyeliner perfect and her cheeks pink. Except the tip of her nose is as well, obviously from the cold as she tugs her grey wool gloves off and adds, 'Melody and Mum went to school together.'

School?

Before I can do the maths in my head, Pearl says, 'Mum was sixteen when she got pregnant with me.'

'Oh,' I say a little too cheerfully, but I hope she realises that's out of surprise rather than horror.

Pearl doesn't seem bothered.

'Yeah, it was all very Lorelai Gilmore but without the coffee and rich parents to bail her out.'

I'm not sure what to say, surprised – and disoriented – by how open she's being.

But then I hear Tab's voice in my head, saying, *She's trying to have a conversation, weirdo. You know? She says something. Then you say something. It's how you connect with people.*

Luckily, before I say something excruciating like, *It must be cool to have a young mum*, Melody saves me, calling out my name from downstairs.

She leaps on Pearl as soon as we find her.

When they step apart, Pearl gives her a look not unlike the one I must have given her when I first saw her as she asks, 'Aunty Mel, are there breasts on your dungarees?'

'Oh my God! You're obsessed!' Melody cackles, swatting at her.

Pearl blushes furiously, then composes herself and says, 'Those are definitely breasts, Aunty Mel.'

'They're *bears*.'

'Bears?'

'Yes! The person in the shop told me that these are part of Lucy & Yak's Bearing All range.'

'Bearing or *Baring*?' Pearl checks.

Melody looks down at the dungarees and gasps. 'They're breasts!'

72

When she looks over at me, I nod. 'Definitely breasts.'

She looks between us and gasps again. 'How did I not notice that they're breasts?'

'It's like a Rorschach test,' Pearl tells her with a shrug. 'You heard Bearing All and saw bears.'

'I can't go on stage like this! I'll be arrested!'

'Don't worry.' I wave my hand at her. 'It's Brighton. No one will even notice.'

'And if you are arrested' – Pearl thumbs at me – 'Renata has a nail file in her book.'

Half an hour later, me, Pearl, Melody and her boob dungarees head to St Mary Magdalen. Because it's so close to the bookshop, we leave it until the event is pretty much ready to start, which gives Melody plenty of time to have a panic attack about bursting into flames as soon as she walks into a church covered in breasts.

To my surprise, I find the whole thing oddly endearing. Melody – or MelodyLoves, I should say – used to be so perfect. Perfect hair. Perfect smile. Perfect teeth. Perfect make-up that you can achieve as long as you watch her tutorials and buy all the products she recommends. She even used to pull the perfect faces in her YouTube thumbnails that were just the right side of kooky before they tipped into ugly.

Because, yeah, MelodyLoves was perfect, but she was *so normal*.

She was your best friend!

I guess for a lot of thirteen-year-olds, she probably was.

I feel kind of sorry for them, thinking that she actually cared about their periods and pimples because, as she told them, she understood. She had bad skin days as well. So here's a discount code for antibacterial cleanser.

But that was MelodyLoves. Now she's Melody Munroe, podcast host and 'recovering consumerist' who definitely isn't perfect. Case in point: she's currently wearing boob dungarees that she's just spilt coffee down and mismatched socks. There's something so delightfully chaotic about her, it's disarming. So when Ruth came down to tell us that it was time to go and Melody said again that she was sure that she was going to burst into flames when she walked into a church covered in breasts, I reminded her that Pearl and I probably would as well.

Unless the Catholics have changed their mind about the whole gay thing since I last checked.

Luckily, we're fine, but we do walk in at the same time as someone who's running late.

They stop and stare when they see us.

'Oh my God! Ren! I love you! Can I please have a photo?'

They thrust their phone at Melody without even looking at her and I'm mortified given that she's no doubt used to being in the photo rather than taking it. But Melody is charmed, chatting to them while they tell us about how they started Earth Day at their school and have asked for a membership to the Marine Conservation Society for their birthday because they want to study marine biology at university, like I do.

Melody nudges me as we walk towards the stage. 'Guess you don't need a hype man now, huh?'

I laugh, scanning the crowd as I feel my chest warm at the thought of my mother walking into the church to be greeted by all of these young people in Out of Time hoodies and finally seeing that climbing cranes and spray-painting windows is doing more than getting me arrested.

But I can't see her.

Tab and Riley are in the front row, though.

Riley mouths *Good luck*, and I wave as Ruth walks out to introduce us.

'Look how many people are here,' Melody whispers, shivering with excitement.

'I know,' I mutter, looking back out at the crowd.

'Don't forget to turn your phones off,' Melody tells Pearl and me, then chuckles to herself. 'My nan called me once while I was doing an interview on Capital to say that she could hear me on the radio.'

I nod, but when I take mine out of the back pocket of my jeans I have a new text.

Sorry. Meeting ran late so not going to make it. Call me when you're done. M xx

'You OK?' Pearl asks.

'Fine,' I manage to say even though it feels like my throat is closing up.

'What's wrong, Ren?' Melody leans in. 'I know you've been getting a lot of shit online since you got arrested, but don't worry, if anyone starts anything, I've got your back.'

She balls her hands into fists and even though I don't feel like it, I can't help but snigger.

It's the least menacing thing I've ever seen.

'I got you,' she tells me with a wink, then scampers away when Ruth calls her on stage.

But Pearl's frowning. 'It's not that, is it?'

I clear my throat and shrug. 'Mum's not coming.'

Pearl casts a glance out at the audience, then turns back to me. 'I'm sorry, Renata.'

But I just shrug again.

'Hello, Brighton!' Melody roars into the mic as I try not to wince.

Then I try not to laugh as I glance down at Tab and Riley to find them looking utterly horrified.

The audience are equally bemused as I watch them turn to one another, then clap politely. If they're anything like the teenagers who usually turn up at Out of Time protests, then most of them rarely leave the house so it must be quite a shock to be suddenly stuck in a room – a church, no less – with Melody.

'I'm Melody Munroe, but as most of you aren't old enough to be served in a pub, you have no idea who I am, do you?' That raises a gentle titter as she holds her hand up. 'Don't worry, I'm not here to read you a CBeebies Bedtime Story.' The titter is a little less restrained this time. 'All you need to know is that I started a YouTube channel in 2006, back when most of you were in nappies. I was one of the first influencers, even though we didn't know what influencing was. I was just doing favourites videos and getting paid to recommend foundation I'd never use, blissfully unaware that I was creating a culture that you guys would grow up to despise.'

There's a low hiss, but Melody laps it up. 'I made a lot of money flogging shit to kids who couldn't afford it. I mean, why was I doing luxury skincare hauls when most of my subscribers were thirteen? Spoiler alert' – she cups her hand to her mouth and stage whispers – 'because why pay for La Mer when I can get it for free? I even started my own skincare line. Not bad for a girl who went to Varndean, right?'

That prompts the first cheer and as I watch the audience giggle and nudge one another, I sit back in the armchair and smile to myself as Melody says, 'I was a millionaire at twenty-five. But then my manufacturer had the bright idea to change the formulation, so we'd make even more money and it literally *burned* people's faces.'

She waits for a gasp and is rewarded. 'I was done. Or cancelled, as I believe the kids say now. I was sued and I lost it all. The Mini Cooper. The Range Rover. The house in Montpelier Villas. I even lost all the friends I used to vlog with every day because they were scared that they'd get cancelled as well.

'Nice, right?' she says when there's a pantomime boo. 'I was twenty-seven and I had less money than when I was sixteen and I worked in TopShop. I couldn't even move in with my parents, back into the bedroom I started my YouTube channel in, because they had to sell their house to bail me out. They ended up getting divorced over it. Because of me.' She presses her hand to her chest. 'I was making a hundred grand a month and I didn't save a penny of it. I spent it all on clothes and holidays to Ibiza so I could show off on Instagram. And for what? I had nothing. I was qualified for *nothing*. I didn't go to uni because why would I when I was making so much money on YouTube?' She held her finger up. 'So let that be a lesson to you. Stay in school, kids.'

There's a flurry of nods from the handful of adults in the audience. 'The plan was to keep my head down until the dust

77

settled, but while I was gone, a dozen more influencers had taken my place and the thought of getting back on the merry-go-round, of hustling all the time, of not doing anything unless it generated content. Cursing myself every time I watched a sunset because I should have taken a photo of it. Not experiencing *anything* because I was never in the moment, I was just thinking about how I could exploit it. Make money off it. Not spending time with anyone who didn't want to vlog or didn't have a big account I could collaborate with. Changing the way I smiled because I didn't like how I looked in photos. Always sucking my stomach in and sticking my arse out and blocking people when they tagged me in a photo I hadn't pre-approved.'

She shakes her head. 'It was *exhausting*. I didn't want to do it again, but I didn't know what else I could do. I had no experience. No qualifications. I even applied for a job at ASDA in the marina, but I never heard back. But every time I went in there, someone would recognise me and ask for a photo. It was *surreal*. Imagine signing autographs in a supermarket you can't even get a job in? But do you know what saved me?'

When she leans forward, everyone in the audience does as well. 'These two. When I was their age, I was pouring products down the sink so I could do empties videos and pulling April Fool's pranks with my baby brother, pretending he was my secret love child with Joe Jonas. I know!' She nods, her eyes wide, when the mention of Joe Jonas's name prompts a mixture of amusement and disgust. 'But look at these two!'

She gestures at us. 'Look what they're doing at sixteen. They're literally changing the world. Full disclosure, Pearl is my goddaughter, so I'm understandably and unrepentantly biased, but I didn't see much of her when she was little, which is my fault,' she admits, looking at her with a sad frown. 'Like I said, when my YouTube channel blew up, I stopped hanging out with anyone who didn't want to vlog or didn't have a big account I could collaborate with, so I lost touch with Pearl's mum. Which is the polite way of putting it. The impolite, and probably more accurate, version is that I disappeared so far up my own arse that I couldn't see out of it any more.'

Melody waits for the audience to stop laughing, then asks, 'But guess who was there for me when everything fell apart? Pearl's mum. So I got to watch Pearl blossom into this brave, brilliant, breathtaking human being, which I take no credit for whatsoever, but I'm so proud.' The corners of her mouth lift to a smile. 'She's a *Teen Vogue* Digital Storytelling Fellow, she writes for *The Good Trade*, *Wonderland* and *Vanity Fair* and her Instagram, GreenGirlPearl, has over a hundred and fifteen thousand followers.

'Then there's this one.' She thumbs at me and there's a huge cheer that makes my cheeks burn as I look down to see Riley clapping wildly as Tab sticks her fingers in her mouth and whistles. 'Ren Barbosa, who needs no introduction, I'm sure, given how many of you are wearing Out of Time hoodies.'

That prompts another cheer as people throw their arms in the air or point at their friends. 'Two years ago a photo of Ren at an Extinction Rebellion protest went viral. She now has *four million* followers and has gone toe-to-toe with everyone from Piers Morgan and Trump to big brands cashing in on the green pound. What is it she says? *Forget eco-friendly, it's time to start eco-shagging.*'

My mother loved that one, I think as Tab whistles again. 'Ren is a rock star. She's an Ocean Ambassador for Greenpeace and the Marine Conservation Society. She spoke at the 2021 United Nations Climate Change Conference and last week, *Time* included her in their Top 100 Most Influential People of 2023, and I love her.'

I turn to blink at her, but Melody isn't looking at me as she leans towards the audience as though she's telling them a secret. 'Ren is fucking *fearless*. While everyone's talking and making pledges, Ren is actually out there, doing the work, making a difference. I mean, look how many people are here tonight because of her. She's everything I wish I was when I was sixteen. Shit, she's everything I wish I was *now*.

'Do you know why these two are so special?' she asks, and the audience is suddenly so quiet that I hear a car beeping outside. 'Because they remind me that everything I need to change the world is right here.'

She points at her chest and in the silence that follows, I watch each of the faces looking up at us still, as their eyes widen and their lips part. 'Because they, the government, big corporations, the experts who tell you not to listen to Ren because she's too young and she doesn't know what she's talking about because she's been radicalised by her mother, want you to believe that they've got it handled. That there's nothing to worry about. Keep using your paper straws and your tote bags and everything will be fine. But we know it's not, right?'

Everyone nods.

'Right?'

'Yes!' the audience barks back.

80

'We read the news, don't we? We see the ice caps melting and the Great Barrier Reef cooking and we know they're wrong. We're in trouble and no one is coming to save us.' Melody points wildly. 'So that's why they don't want you to listen to Ren and that's exactly why you have to. Because she's right. Everything she says is true and they hate that she's brave enough to stand up and tell them we're not putting up with it any more.'

Melody is looking at the audience, but I'm staring at her as I feel my throat closing up again, for a very different reason. I'm so used to defending myself – explaining myself, excusing myself – that I just want to put my head in my hands and weep because no one has *ever* said that about me before.

I just wish my mother was here as Melody says, 'We have the power to make a difference. We are brave enough and resourceful enough and clever enough to change the world. It's already inside us. Oh! Oh! Oh!' She waves her hands and grins. 'I just realised what's happening! You know that bit in films when the main character finds out that they have a superpower?'

The audience nods.

'Well, this is that moment for you. For all of us. If we put our superpowers together, we're unstoppable. And yeah, I know that people like me are to blame for the position we're in and I have to spend the rest of my life repenting for that, but who says that we can't change things? That we can't fix it? Or at least not make it worse? Why are we waiting for them? We don't need them. We can do it ourselves. There are more of us than there are of them. Ren's right. We need to be a problem to those in power because we're out of time. We tried reasoning with them, but they're not listening. So we have to *make* them listen. And the only way to do that is to break shit!'

'Yeah!' I hear someone in the audience yell as Melody points to the door of the church.

'So, go out there and raise hell!'

There's a *roar* as everyone in the audience leaps to their feet.

Even I'm overwhelmed, tears in my eyes as I join in the applause.

I can't remember the last time I felt so fired up, my heart thundering and my hands shaking.

'That was amazing,' I tell Melody later, as we're walking off stage.

And I mean it this time.

She looks sad, though. 'Your mum didn't come, huh?'

'It's fine.' I shrug. 'Her meeting overran. It happens all the time.'

Melody considers that for a moment, then nods and says, 'Ren, your mother is brilliant, but her work will always come first.' She reaches for my hands and squeezes them. 'Now it's time for you to put yours first.'

7

Melody puts on her best RuPaul voice and leans closer to the mic. 'OK. Come on. It's just us girls.'

'Just us girls and everyone listening to your podcast,' I point out, reaching for my coffee.

'Minor detail.' She waves her hand. 'So, tell us. What happened when you two were in that police cell?'

Pearl groans. 'Is this still a thing? It's been three months, Aunty Mel.'

'What?' She feigns confusion, but her eyes are alight with mischief. 'The people want to know.'

'Do they?' Pearl pulls a face. 'Or are you just bored because you're trying to give up caffeine?'

'Seriously, though.' She reaches for the stack of paper next to her on the desk. 'Do you know how many emails I received after I said that you guys were going to be on the show?' She holds it up, pretending to struggle. 'But then, I shouldn't be surprised. You just hit five million followers on Instagram, right, Ren?'

'I did?'

'I love that you don't know that! But take it from an old lady who remembers the internet when it was all fields, it takes *years* to earn that many followers, yet you can lose them like that.' She clicks her fingers. 'So if I can offer a word of advice to the new generation of influencers, I would urge you guys not to attach your worth to that number because, at the end of the day, it means nothing.'

I try not to bristle at being lumped in with the *new generation of influencers*.

But Pearl turns to Melody, her nose in the air. 'Renata doesn't think she's an influencer.'

She raises an eyebrow. 'Really? Why not?'

Pearl raises her shoulder, then lets it drop again. 'Because she's a snob.'

I shouldn't take the bait, but I can't help myself.

'Haven't you removed *sustainability influencer* from your profile, Pearl?'

But she doesn't flinch, her green eyes shining as she says, 'I didn't realise you were paying such close attention, Renata. But come on, if you're not an influencer, what are you, then?'

I shrug. 'An environmental activist who has a lot of followers.'

'Followers whom you have no influence over, right?'

'I'm not selling them anything.'

'What about Out of Time merch?'

She thinks she's got me, so I almost feel bad for her when I say, 'We don't sell merch, Pearl.'

'I think you need to check the Out of Time website, Renata.'

But before I reach for my phone to prove her wrong, Melody makes her hands into a T.

'Time out, guys. That's an interesting distinction. Is selling some Out of Time T-shirts the same as what I used to do on

MelodyLoves? I'm sure most brands would kill for Ren to endorse their products, but I'm guessing most of them don't bother asking. It's not like you're going to do a Dove campaign are you, Ren? I mean, you're heading to a meeting at Greenpeace straight after this.'

Before I can respond, Pearl says, 'There's a statement on the Out of Time website telling brands not to send Renata anything and if they do, it'll be donated to Refuge.'

I'm impressed, but still counter with, 'Man, you've really been studying our website, haven't you?'

'Almost as much as you've been studying my Instagram.'

'Zing! Point to Pearl!' Melody holds up a finger, delighted. 'But I have to let my listeners know that, since our event back in Feb' – she stops to put on a cheesy voice – 'to promote my new book, *Sustainable Sustainability*, which is out now in all good bookshops, and probably a few bad ones' – she stage winks at us across the desk then continues in her normal voice – 'we've been hanging out, haven't we, Ren?'

'Yeah, we have.'

I'm as surprised as anyone, but after Melody's speech at our event at the church went viral, I received an email from an editor at the *Guardian* asking if I'd consider co-writing an article with Melody countering online misinformation about climate change.

That's how it started, I guess. With a coffee at the Tate Modern on a damp afternoon to discuss it. I told her that I only had an hour because I had to be somewhere else, as though it was a first date and I needed an exit strategy. But we ended up spending the rest of the day together, wandering from room to room, gazing at the artwork, the article forgotten as I told her about everything going on in my life.

I say *everything*, but let's be real, we only talked about one thing. Tab.

Thinking about it now, I'm astonished at how quickly Melody and I bonded given that she's twice my age, but then Tia Aline always says I'm an old soul. Or perhaps Melody is a young soul. Whichever it is, after all of this weirdness with Tab, being with Melody was so easy.

Like talking to a wise older sister.

Melody pulls a face at Pearl. 'I'm cool now I'm hanging out with Ren.'

But she just laughs. 'You'll never be cool, Aunty Mel. You literally have yogurt on your shirt.'

I hide my snigger behind my coffee mug when she looks down to check, then say, 'It's been fun, Melody.'

'It has!' she says. 'Everywhere we go, someone wants a photo or to tell you about a petition they've started. Last week we went to an event and people came up to us all night. It was like being with Beyoncé!'

'Sure.' I snort. 'If Beyoncé gets the bus and sleeps on her friend's sofa.'

'I'm serious, Ren. You're the Beyoncé of climate justice. And they're all teenagers. Every single one. Yeah, we've had a few miserable middle-aged assholes tell us that you're ruining your mother's legacy—'

'What?' Pearl gasps, looking between us.

I'm so used to it now that I just laugh it off. 'Mum's legacy is fine. Nothing I do will ever change that.'

'Exactly!' Melody points at me. 'But you're activating a new generation, Ren.'

My cheeks warm. 'We're trying to.'

'You are!' she insists. 'Out of Time reaches the demographic that every group is *dying* to attract. You're getting teenagers to actually care about the planet they're going to inherit in a way that no one else has.'

'I have a question,' Pearl pipes up then and I turn to find her looking at me with a wolfish smile. 'Out of Time has changed the game in digital activism. So why bother with the protests?'

That catches me off guard.

I thought this interview would be like the night at the church – light and fun and peppered with playful banter – so I didn't expect to be questioned about the direction Out of Time is going in.

So I just smile back. 'Is it our protests you object to or the way we protest?'

She sidesteps my misdirection. 'Methods aside, why not keep it virtual?'

'That's a good point,' Melody says, tipping her chin up at Pearl. 'Does Out of Time need to protest when groups like Extinction Rebellion, Just Stop Oil and Fossil Free London are doing it anyway?'

'For me, personally,' I say, ignoring the pinch of irritation that prompts, 'protesting is how I show up. I've been going to them since I was a kid. They're central to my activism and always will be.'

'I get that' – Melody nods – 'but Pearl's not saying that you *can't* protest. She's saying your time would be better spent focusing on the online stuff instead of organising elaborate stunts.'

'Exactly.' She nods. 'Most of them have been done already anyway. So what's the point?'

That makes my jaw tighten because every time Tab suggests another protest, I think the same thing.

But I keep smiling as Melody asks, 'Isn't that what Out of Time used to do? Didn't you start out attending protests rather than organising them? That's how you met Tab and Riley, right?'

'Yeah,' I say as I wind the wire from my headphones around my index finger. 'I met Riles at a Just Stop Oil protest a couple of years ago and Tab at a Fossil Free London one just over a year ago.'

'So why'd you stop doing that?'

'We haven't. We promote and attend *everyone's* protests.'

'So, why bother organising your own, then?'

'Because the more noise we make the better.'

Then Melody says it.

The one thing that is guaranteed to make me want to Meryl Streep scream every time I hear it.

'Yeah, but doesn't it piss you off to be called Junior Extinction Rebellion?'

That makes my scalp burn, but I shrug as I say, 'Of course not. We love Extinction Rebellion. We're not trying to compete with them; we're trying to support them. It's about amplifying everyone's voices to make them louder and keep the conversation going.'

She shrugs back. 'I know, but perhaps your time is better

spent doing digital activism because that's what makes Out of Time so special. No one does it like you guys do.'

'Why can't we do both? Digital activism is for nothing if it stays online.'

'True,' Melody concedes, nodding to herself. 'Like the girl who came up to you as we were walking into our event in Feb. She told us she'd organised her school's first Earth Day and wants to study marine biology, like you do, so I guess that's what it's about, right? Getting these teenagers to raise hell in real life as well.'

Pearl chuckles. 'Yet Renata doesn't think she's an influencer.'

'That's my point,' Melody says, slightly breathless. 'What makes an influencer? Is it being able to sell people the latest primer or getting them to change the world? Are they the same thing?'

Pearl nods. 'I think so, which is why I don't deny that I'm an influencer.'

I register the dig, then smile and ask, 'So why did you take it out of your profile, then?'

When she hesitates, her cheeks a little pinker, Melody leans forward.

'Zing! Point to Ren!' She holds up a finger again and wriggles in her chair. 'This is what I wanted.'

Pearl frowns at her. 'What? Me and Renata fighting?'

'No.' She waggles her eyebrows. 'Flirting!'

I have to put my mug down as I fight the urge to scream-laugh into the mic.

Pearl looks appalled. 'Jesus, Aunty Mel. Why don't you have a latte and maybe you'll calm down.'

'OK, Kim Richards,' Melody and I say at the same time, then point at each other across the desk.

'Ren Barbosa is a *Real Housewives of Beverly Hills* fan!' Melody shrieks.

'It was the pandemic,' I say, pressing my hands to my face. 'I'd completed Netflix.'

When she stops laughing, Melody rolls her chair back towards the desk and says, 'Seriously, though. I am intrigued about what you guys talked about in that police cell.' She waggles her eyebrows again. 'Please tell me it was more than your shared passion for climate justice. Oh, by the way' – she stops and holds her hand up – 'for anyone listening who doesn't know what climate justice is, basically, in the same way that feminism is intersectional, the climate crisis is as well. It's a social and political issue because it doesn't affect everyone in the same way. Some countries and companies are more responsible for the damage that's been done than others, yet the rest of the world is suffering. Like with fast fashion, when people buy a dress from SHEIN, or wherever, and it falls apart the first time they wash it, what they don't realise is that it will probably end up in Ghana.'

'Exactly,' Pearl says.

'Even if we take it to a charity shop or put it in a clothing bin, right?'

'Yeah, because many of them can't cope with the number of donations they're receiving. As a result, the Korle Lagoon in Accra has become one of the most polluted water bodies on earth, which is disrupting the natural ecology. Google "clothing waste in Old Fadama". The photos are devastating.'

'It's the same with plastic waste, right, Ren?' Melody says. 'Recycling, like clothing bins, is another placebo devised to make us feel like we're doing something to help the environment. We dutifully separate our recycling every week, blissfully unaware that it's going to be shipped somewhere like Malaysia, which is causing widespread environmental contamination.'

'Yeah.' I nod. 'But that's decreased significantly since China banned exports in 2017. Now we're sending it to places like Turkey and the Netherlands instead. My concern is what happens to the plastic waste that remains here in the UK, though. The majority of it is incinerated, which releases all kinds of shit into the air. Of course they do this in areas already struggling. When they tried to open an incinerator in Cambridgeshire, for example, the council rejected it because it wasn't in keeping with the listed and historic buildings in the area. Yet they were happy to open one in Edmonton where sixty-five per cent of residents are people of colour.'

'Fuckers,' Melody mutters, then shakes her head. 'Listening to you two, it's clear that you're painfully aware of what we're up against, but you have wildly different approaches. Pearl, you're all about reasoning with people. Meeting them where they are. Whereas, Ren, you have a more radical approach, right?'

Pearl thumbs at me. 'This is what we talked about in the police cell, actually.'

I thumb back at her. 'She called me an asshole.'

'Pearl! I'm shocked.' Melody gasps theatrically. 'I don't think I've ever heard you swear.'

'What can I say?' I smile sweetly. 'I bring it out in people.'

I turn to wink at Pearl and she blushes.

Even her ears are red as she says, 'It was a long day, Aunty Mel, and she was being—'

'An asshole?'

Melody points at me over the desk and cackles, then claps her hands and says, 'OK. I was going to do this later, but we may as well do it now. So . . .' She pauses for dramatic effect. 'Let's play Activist Death Match!'

She dips her head to tap on the screen of her phone and when a braying crowd starts cheering, I snort.

'On one side' – Melody raises her arm to Pearl, putting on a wrestling commentator voice – 'we have Team Empathy. And on the other' – she raises her arm to me now – 'we have Team Anarchy. Let's get ready to rumble!'

Melody drums her hands on the desk as the crowd sound gets louder, then taps on her phone again. When the intro of 'Eye of the Tiger' kicks in, Pearl groans and crosses her arms, but I'm sniggering so much that I have to put my mug of coffee down as Melody pumps her shoulders up and down, then punches the air.

'OK, ladies. We're going to have a fair fight. Let's keep it clean. No hair pulling or eye gouging. Just a good old-fashioned verbal throwdown. Pearl, why don't you take to the ring first for Team Empathy.'

She looks slightly stunned, her eyes wide as Melody turns the music off to play the sound of a bell.

'OK,' Pearl says warily, uncrossing her arms and sitting forward. 'I believe the key to urging the government and society into action is finding common ground because people are more likely to be receptive. Blocking roads so they can't get to work is going to have the opposite effect.'

I snort. 'Sure, the ocean is about to rise up and swallow us all, but we can't be late for work, can we?'

'That isn't apathy, that's capitalism,' Pearl counters. 'We need people to listen. If they do they'll understand that it's not too late and there are still things that can be done to mitigate the climate crisis.'

'I mean, that's lovely,' I say, 'but it's bullshit.'

Pearl tilts her head. 'And *that's* why I called her an asshole.'

Melody just laughs. 'Playing devil's advocate for a moment, I just got done reading Dave Eggers' *The Every*, which is incredible, by the way, but kind of disheartening because there were times that I found myself asking if we're even capable of empathy any more. I mean, your generation have learned to condense the most devastating statistics about the state of the planet into three-minute videos, thanks to TikTok. And even when you do, most of your followers just respond with a broken heart or crying emoji. Or they say something eye-wateringly offensive, which means that you guys are always in fight mode, so is empathy even possible at this point?'

Before I can respond, Pearl waves her hand and says, 'Oh please. That's just another way of shutting us down. We're just braindead teenagers who are on our phones all the time.' She gestures at me. 'Why do you think Renata has *five million* teenagers following her? It's because they care about what's happening to the planet and she's the only one telling them that they're right to be worried.'

'So why doesn't empathy work, then?' Melody asks me.

'Because we've tried it,' I tell her with a shrug. 'I know a lot has been said – and will continue to be said – about my relationship with my mother but you need to know two things. First' – I hold up a finger – 'I love her fiercely. I give her hell, which is well documented, but if anyone said a word about her, I'd rip their heart out.

'And second' – I hold up another finger – 'don't forget that she raised me. I am who I am *because* of my mother. I grew up listening to her and her friends talking about global warming and melting ice caps and carbon emissions. I know better than anyone the work she's been doing since she was my age. I've sat at dining tables and watched her on *Question Time* while she tries to reason with people. Educate them. Change things from within. I mean, she's on half a dozen steering groups and government committees and has won awards for the work she's doing with things like mycelium, algae-grown limestone and pollution-absorbing bricks. I'm so, *so* proud of her, but why do you think I chose Out of Time? Because we're running out of time.'

'So, what's the solution, then?' Melody asks with a frown.

'We need to start breaking shit.'

'This is where Renata and I part ways,' Pearl says. 'She's *trying* to piss people off.'

'Are you?' Melody asks me.

'Absolutely.'

Her eyes light up. 'So you're an anarchist?'

'Of course I am. Pearl's right: people's reluctance to acknowledge the issue isn't apathy, it's capitalism. There are only a handful of people who actually have the power and resources to change things, but all they care about is money. So, if their staff are late for work because Out of Time are blocking a bridge, that costs *them* money. If their private jet can't take off because I'm on the runway, that costs *them* money. If they have to shut down a building site because I'm climbing a crane with an Out of Time banner, that costs *them* money. We have to hit them where it hurts: their pockets. That's the only way we'll get their attention.'

'But they're too pissed off to listen, Renata,' Pearl insists. 'That's the point.'

'Yeah, but the next time Mick from Grays is on the news, complaining about being late for work, at least it's followed up with a shot of us in our Out of Time T-shirts.'

'Yeah, but everyone hates you guys.'

'I don't give a fuck.'

'Wouldn't you rather reason with them?'

I shouldn't laugh, but I have to. 'Do you know when Mum organised her first protest? 1992. *1992.* Thirty-one years later and where are we? They've banned shopping bags. Big whoop. And they only embraced that because it means they can charge an obscene amount for "bags for life" that are, guess what? Made of plastic. Then you have the people on TikTok who are queuing up outside Target so they can buy another Stanley cup to make sure they have one in every colour, when the whole point of Stanley cups is to reduce plastic.'

Pearl shrugs. 'I don't agree with it, but I'm not going to judge them for it, either.'

'I'm not judging them. I'm saying that most people are so far down the rabbit hole of consumerism that they can't hear us. All they have the energy for is going to work and taking care of their families, so saving the planet feels like this Herculean thing beyond their control. Especially when they hear people saying that using tote bags and paper straws is never going to counteract the damage big corporations are doing. Which' – I stop to raise my finger – 'not only gets them off the hook, but means they don't have to make the connection that these big corporations are producing the shit that they keep buying to distract themselves from how miserable they are.

'So,' I conclude, 'if Out of Time blocking a bridge knocks some people off course for long enough to think about something other than getting to work on time and they go home and google us, it's worth it.'

Pearl throws her hands up. 'But that will only work for so long. The government is passing all of these laws to discourage protests because of groups like Out of Time. Look at the Section 14 they imposed on your protest at The Dorchester. Three months later and we're both still under investigation.'

'If I'd written a letter to my MP, would we have gotten any coverage?'

Pearl exhales sharply through her nose and crosses her arms.

'And they haven't charged us, have they?' I remind her when she turns her cheek away.

'They still might,' she mutters.

'It's been *three months*. If they were going to charge us, they would have by now.'

Pearl stares at me. 'Some of us don't have mums who can bail us out, Renata.'

Melody raises her hand, but the words are already rushing out of me like a car jumping a red light.

'You're using my mum's solicitor, Pearl, so we're in *exactly* the same position, actually.'

I shouldn't have thrown that at her.

Especially on a podcast.

The wounded look she gives me confirms it.

'We're not in *exactly* the same position *actually*. You've got nothing to lose, do you, Renata?'

'Why did you even come to the protest, then, Pearl?' I ask.

'I told you: to take photos.'

'Photos that ended up in the *Guardian* and on the BBC News and Sky News websites.'

She shakes her head. 'Not worth it.'

'Absolutely worth it,' I tell her. 'That's why we protest. Civil disobedience works. Look at Rosa Parks.' I count each one off on my fingers. 'The suffragettes. The miners' strike. Reclaim the Streets. Shit, look at everyone who refused to pay their poll tax in the eighties. I'm sick of being told that we can't do something. That things are so far gone that we just have to sit here and wait for the sun to burn out. Fuck that. I'm going out fighting.'

'What a note to end on,' Melody says and when I look over the desk at her, she's beaming.

She records her outro and when she's done, Pearl rolls her eyes and waves a tissue at me.

'That was fun,' I tell her with a wink as she tosses it back on the desk.

'It always is for you, Renata,' she says under her breath.

But before I can ask her what she means, Melody tugs off her headphones and shrieks, 'That was amazing, guys!'

She jumps on me, sending my chair rolling into Pearl.

'What time is it?' I ask when she finally lets go. 'I'm not going to miss my train, am I?'

I can hear my phone ringing in my coat pocket and curse myself as I try to find it because I was supposed to put it on DND while we were recording. I'm sure I did. Actually, I *know* I did, because Melody made a point of reminding us. Then my heart stutters as I realise that there's only one person who can override my DND.

Luckily, I remember not to put it on speaker because when I answer, my mother is *livid*.

'Renata, where are you?' she hisses.

'Brighton,' I say warily, unsure what I've done now.

She is quiet for a beat, then asks, 'Why are you in Brighton?'

'Recording Melody's podcast with Pearl.'

I thought she'd be thrilled, but now she sounds confused. 'Wait. So, you're not at Greenpeace?'

'Not yet. The ambassador's meeting got pushed to three o'clock. Why?'

She curses under her breath.

'Renata,' she says tightly, 'I suggest you check in with Tab and Riley then call me back.'

8

I don't think I've ever been so angry in my life.

Even my mother, who has perfected the art of making me go from mildly irritated to wanting to burn everything to the ground in less than three seconds, has never made me feel like this. As I'm walking towards the pub, I understand what it feels like to be raging. Like, actually, physically *raging*. Hands shaking. Teeth grinding. Jaw clicking. Each breath quick and sharp and not enough as I make my way down Earl's Court Road.

I can see the pub at the top of the road, but it feels very far away, my eyes swimming in and out of focus every time I think about what happened yesterday. It feels like when I used to wear my mother's reading glasses as a kid. Distorted. Disorienting. Everything too bright and too close, all at once. The scalding streetlights. The violent stutter of traffic. Stop. Start. Stop. Start. Stop. Start. Cars barking. Buses panting. Weary commuters pinballing their way around piles of bin bags and the people pleading for a pound outside Earl's Court station.

It's as though everyone needs to be somewhere that isn't here.

Everyone except me because this is exactly where I need to be.

I just need to get to the pub, but I'm shaking with this feeling of utter, world-shifting helplessness. As though one more step and my legs will give way and I'll be on my knees on the pavement. Me and the cigarette butts and trodden-in chewing gum. Yet I've never felt stronger, my hands balled into fists and my back straight and sure. I feel like I could tip over a bus if one got in my way. Punch clean through the windshield.

It's a strange thing to feel both of these extremes at once.

To feel both broken and unbreakable.

So when I get to the pub, I pace back and forth a few times outside the door in an effort to calm myself down because if I don't, there will be no coming back from this. I'm not even sure if there is, but if there's still a chance, I can't burn that bridge before we've had a chance to cross it.

I glance through the pub window to see Tab and Riley waiting for me in our booth in the corner, just talking. Talking and laughing. They look so normal, as though this is any other Thursday night and I'm meeting them for tofu pad Thai, that I feel the shift of something in my stomach.

Why are they laughing?

This isn't funny.

This isn't fucking funny.

With that, I'm pushing through the door and when Riley sees me, he immediately slides out of the worn velvet booth, then dips his head, hiding behind his long hair as he walks past me.

'Where are you going?' I call after him, but he doesn't look back as he slopes off to the bar.

Then it's just Tab and me.

Given it's the first time we've been alone in months – well, as alone as we can be in a packed pub – I wait for a feeling that doesn't come. For that familiar weakness to return to my knees or for my hummingbird heart to betray me as I look at her, sitting there in a green T-shirt that I don't recognise.

She's dyed her hair lilac since I last saw her and changed out the silver barbell in her septum for a hoop with a green stone. An emerald. Her birthstone. *It's her nineteenth next week*, I remember. We talked about spending the weekend in Brighton. We were going to have a fancy dinner at terre à terre and go on the zip line and get matching helix piercings but when she turns her cheek to glance out of the window as an ambulance screams past, my heart hiccups as I see that she has a gold stud I've never seen before at the top of her ear.

I want to ask her why she got her helix pierced without me, but I know why. We're not going to Brighton next week, are we? Or to Glastonbury. Or to see BLACKPINK at Hyde Park in July. The summer is suddenly empty, my heart throbbing now as I realise there will be no falling asleep under trees in Kensington Gardens, like last year, or sharing a blanket while we sit side by side on the stretch of beach outside her parents' house, looking up at the moon. We won't suck on Fruit Pastilles lollies until our tongues turn purple or chase one another around the fountain outside the Southbank Centre or get covered in chocolate at Carnival.

We're not doing any of it.

The summer is over, before it even began.

With that, the rage that just propelled me down Earl's Court Road burns away and I feel myself shiver as I watch Tab turn away from the window and wait for her to take advantage of the few seconds we're alone before Riley returns from the bar to acknowledge me. Or at least show some discomfort that she can't. To shift awkwardly and reach for one of the beer mats. Start tapping it on the edge of the table while she waits for Riley to rescue her.

But she just sips her pint and looks at me as though I've come to check if there are any empty glasses.

When I lean in to ask her why she's being like this, I smell it. Something strange. New. A slight smokiness filling the space between us. It takes a moment to recognise that it's Riley's incense. She must have been at the flat before they came to the pub. So what? That's no reason to make my heart quiver like this.

But then I realise why.

I can smell it because she's not wearing the perfume I bought her for her birthday.

Until now, everything I've felt for Tab has been so sure. So loud. All of it in capital letters. And what I'm feeling in this moment is no less sure because I know now that we're done.

'You got nothing to say to me, Tab?' I ask at last.

She doesn't flinch. 'I'm waiting for Riles.'

'Not about yesterday,' I tell her, and I see something flicker across her brow, just for a second, before it stills again as I'm rewarded with the awkward shift in the booth I've been waiting for.

She still doesn't say anything, though, and I realise that Melody's right: sometimes the things that people don't say, tell us much more than the things they do. So, Tab leaving me to dangle for four months rather than just saying it's over, tells me everything that I need to know.

Riley returns then, putting an orange juice down on the table.

There it is, I note as I watch him slide into the booth next to Tab.

He's picked his side.

I shrug off my denim jacket and join them, the table between us, as I wait for them to speak first.

To explain.

Apologise.

Plead for forgiveness.

But Tab just looks at me while Riley looks down at his pint and I feel a fresh surge of fury.

'Guys, what the fuck?'

Nothing.

Not even from Riley.

But then, I'm almost certain, he's been instructed to let Tab do the talking.

'Why the fuck would you go after Greenpeace?' I ask when they just look at me.

'Don't be so dramatic, Ren,' Tab says at last.

I've never been punched in the throat, but I'm pretty sure this is what it feels like.

I don't know how I don't hurl my orange juice at her because I don't even recognise her.

This girl who murmurs my name in her sleep and makes me dance to Robyn when I'm in a bad mood.

Who are you? I want to yell across the table, but I make myself suck in a breath.

'So *Out of Time*,' I make sure to use air quotes, 'didn't occupy Greenpeace's offices yesterday?'

But Tab just shrugs. 'We did.'

My temple throbs to the beat of the song playing because that *we* doesn't include me. And the way Tab is looking at me – while Riley won't – lets me know that it never will again. It's a moment or two before I can focus on anything other than what I've just lost so I don't notice that the song playing is 'VOID' by Melanie Martinez. When I do, I want to weep as I remember that Tab and I have tickets to see her in November. We were going to dye our hair green and I don't know how this happened.

How we got here.

But as much as I want to ask her how, instead I ask, 'Why, Tab? Why would you go after Greenpeace? It makes no sense. We should be focusing on the people doing the damage, not the ones trying to fix it. Besides, Extinction Rebellion occupied Greenpeace years ago and they got a ton of shit for it, so what was the point? If we're trying to shake off the Junior Extinction Rebellion thing then constantly recycling their ideas isn't going to help, is it?'

'XR don't care.' Tab waves her hand at me. 'We're all fighting the same war.'

'Maybe so,' I concede, but something kicks at me as I remember what Melody said yesterday, 'but I care. I care that we've stopped doing the digital stuff that made Out of Time so special in favour of focusing on protests that Extinction Rebellion, Just Stop Oil and Fossil Free London are doing anyway. That's what we used to do, remember?' I say to Riley and he nods. 'We need to get back to supporting these groups instead of doing what they've already done. It's embarrassing.'

'I love Greenpeace.' Tab presses her hand to her chest with a pained look that's so theatrical I feel the anger bubble up again because here it is. The speech she's been rehearsing. 'I grew up supporting them.'

'So why did you target them, then?'

'Because we're running out of time and Greenpeace isn't doing enough. We need to send a message that mass civil disobedience is the only way to avert the impending climate crisis.'

'That's not how Out of Time works,' I remind her as I tell myself to stay calm because Melody said that will throw her. She called me before I left Riley's and when she heard how angry I was, she warned me that Tab is expecting me to come flying into the pub, ready to fight. So if I do the opposite, it will catch her off guard and she might actually be honest with me.

Plus, staying calm means that I'll be able to say everything that I want to say rather than unravelling into surliness and swearing, like I usually do, so I try to keep my voice steady as I say, 'We decide everything together, Tab. I have no issue with Greenpeace and, until yesterday, I didn't think you did, either. But if you do, you should have come to me, and we would have put it to everyone. That's how it works. How it's always worked.'

When she sniffs, then reaches for her glass, I feel something in me spike, but I wait for the sting to pass before I say, 'And that's how it will continue to work. We can't allow one person to dictate the message Out of Time sends. It defeats the purpose of the group. Of the people, by the people, for the people, remember?'

'Is that so?' She looks me in the eye at last. 'Why does everything we do go through you, then?'

It doesn't and she knows that.

So I ignore her and get straight to what's really bothering her. 'Tab, I know it sucks that I'm the one everyone talks about, but the truth is, if my last name wasn't Barbosa, no one would give a shit about me, either.'

It's not a dig, but she takes it as one. 'I'm not the only one who has an issue with Greenpeace.'

I don't believe her.

If that's the case, then why were she and Riley the only ones there?

And why have Out of Timers been blowing up my phone, furious about the whole thing?

But I humour her and say, 'It should have been brought up in the monthly meeting, then.'

Melody's advice to keep calm is working because I see Tab's jaw click as she takes another sip of cider.

So I keep going. 'Tab, you know that a lot of what Out of Time does has been influenced by the groups that went before us, like ACT UP. We've always followed their philosophy of not demanding full agreement from the group for our campaigns because if we wait for everyone's consensus, we're never going to get it and we'll just end up doing nothing. So even if not everyone agreed with your plan to occupy Greenpeace, we wouldn't have stopped you, *but* anyone who wanted to take part would have been able to.'

I arch an eyebrow at her. 'Same with the Out of Time merch. We should have discussed it, agreed on the designs, colours, all of it. It wasn't up to you to just start selling it.'

'Relax,' she sneers. 'I'm not trying to steal from you. All the money is going into the Out of Time PayPal.'

When Riley sneaks a look at her, it's clear he also assumed that people have been making their own Out of Time merch, not getting it from our website. After all, the three of us have always said – from the first time we sat in this booth, in this pub – that we'd never profit from Out of Time.

Tab's glaring at me, though, as she says, 'You wanna talk about taking advantage of people, Ren? You've been crashing with Riley for five months and you haven't given him a penny.'

That hurts more than anything she's said so far as I turn to stare at Riley.

He looks as appalled as me, though. 'Yes, she has! *I* never asked, but Ren still insists on paying half the rent and bills, even though she's only sleeping on the sofa. So I don't know where you got that from, Tab.'

She ignores him and when she reaches for her phone, he finally tags in.

'Listen. Fuck all of that, Tab. Let's stay on topic.' He looks at me, his brow creasing. 'Ren, I'm sorry about yesterday. We didn't tell you because we know how much Greenpeace means to you.'

When Tab chuckles to herself while she types something on her phone, I want to snatch it out of her hand. Tell her that speaking on the Greenpeace stage at Glastonbury last year was one of the greatest moments of my life. Remind her that Ben from Greenpeace – who also happens to be my godfather – called this morning and asked me how I could do that to them, then requested that I step down as an Ocean Ambassador.

But she knew that.

They both did and they did it anyway.

Tab doesn't look up from her phone, though.

At least Riley has the decency to look miserable as he reaches for his pint. 'Don't look at me like that, Ren. We didn't tell you so you'd have plausible deniability when it all came on top.'

I tilt my head and peer at him across the table. 'Really? So is that why you timed it when I was supposed to be at Greenpeace for a meeting so it looked like I was signing off on it?'

When he shoots a look at Tab, that confirms that this is *all her*.

With that, I'm done talking to him and turn to her.

'Just like you knew that Mum was at The Dorchester in February, right, Tab?'

There's a beat of silence as the song playing ends. Then it's so quiet in the pub that I can hear my phone ringing in my jacket pocket. I'm about to reach for it to turn it off when Tab shrugs.

'We needed coverage.'

'Coverage?' I ask, appalled. 'Is that all you care about?'

'I care about saving the planet, Ren. If you and your mum are collateral damage, so be it.'

She shrugs again and it's so pathologically unrepentant, as though she's an anime villain who's about to toss her head back and laugh, that Riley looks ready to dive under the table.

He probably should because all I can think is, *Pearl was right. She was fucking right.*

It should be like a knife in the heart, but I feel something turn instead.

Lock, actually.

'So that's twice that you've deliberately targeted Mum?' I check.

She pretends to look confused. 'Twice?'

'The Dorchester and yesterday,' I tell her, but she knows that.

Riley obviously doesn't, because he frowns. 'Yesterday?'

I don't look at him, only at her. 'Mum's on the board of Greenpeace.'

Then he turns to look at her as well. 'I didn't know that.'

'Me neither,' Tab lies and this is excruciating enough, but she could at least be fucking honest.

'Yes, you did.' When she ignores me, I feel something in my chest give way. 'OK. We're done.'

Tab's pupils swell. 'No, you are, Ren. You're out!'

I blink at her a few times, then bark out a laugh. 'Wait. Are you trying to fire me?'

'You can't fire her,' Riley says, stunned. 'Ren *is* Out of Time. There's no Out of Time without her. She started it.'

Tab glares at him, clearly furious that he isn't backing her up as she points at me.

'Didn't she just try and fire me, Riles?'

But before I can ask her who's being dramatic now, he says, 'Look, I don't know what's going on with you two' – he looks between us – 'but things have been weird for months.'

She ignores that and says, 'We've discussed it. Ren doesn't give a shit about Out of Time any more.'

I note how he blushes at *discussed it* and realise what Tab is trying to do.

This is a fucking coup.

It isn't working, though, because whatever they discussed, it clearly wasn't getting rid of me.

'What are you doing?' he says, which makes her throw her hands up and sit back. 'Just let Ren explain.'

'Explain *what*?' I ask.

Tab leans forward again, her arms crossed. 'How you're neglecting Out of Time for Melody Munroe.'

I can't help but laugh again.

Louder this time.

'Melody?'

'Yeah.' She nods. 'It's weird, Ren.'

'What's weird?'

'Hanging around with a forty-year-old.'

'She's not forty, Tab. She's thirty-three.'

'It's still weird. She's, like, twice your age.'

She waits for me to bite back and I'm glad I listened to Melody because the calmer I am, the more agitated Tab becomes. She's usually so chill, so it's strangely satisfying to see her like this, her back straight and the skin between her eyebrows pinched, as she looks me in the eye and finally tells me the truth.

'I've seen you all over her Stories, Ren. You went to the David Bowie exhibition, when you knew I wanted to see that. And you went to see that Celine Lowenthal Riot Grrl play at the Southwark Playhouse.'

So, this isn't about Melody.

She's pissed that I'm doing stuff without her.

When Tab sits back again and looks out of the window with a huff, the relief of realising that she does still care about me – even if it's not in the way I want her to – makes me

110

soften. But before I can admit that I'd rather have done that stuff with her but she wanted to 'cool it', Riley presses his palm to the table.

'Listen, Ren. We're just concerned about how close you and Melody have become. It's only been, what, three months, and you guys are hanging out pretty much every day.' He winces. 'It is kind of weird. What do a sixteen-year-old and a thirty-three-year-old even have in common?'

'You mean, apart from trying to save the planet?'

Tab snorts. 'Please. Melody's just using you for clout.'

I don't dignify that with a response because now she's just being spiteful.

When I look back at Riley, he rolls his eyes at her, so I exhale sharply and say, 'Riles, it's more of an older sister thing. You know I don't have any siblings.'

'But you're always with her, Ren. You never come to protests any more.'

'Yes, I do! I went to the Stop Rosebank protest *last week*.'

'With Melody,' Tab pipes up.

'So what? You know my mum's lawyer wants me to keep my head down while I'm under investigation.'

'The planet's on fire,' Tab snaps. 'Who gives a shit if you get arrested again?'

I do, because I want to go to university, I almost say, but stop myself because she's right.

The planet is on fire so who gives a shit about going to university?

Riley says something under his breath that is enough to make Tab huff and cross her arms.

111

When she does, he turns back to me. 'Ren, you have to admit that your methods have changed.'

'They had to. If I can't go to protests, I had to find another way to get our message out.'

After that article Melody and I co-wrote for the *Guardian*, we were asked to write another for the *Telegraph* about protecting green spaces, which led to being asked to speak at the United Nations on World Wildlife Day. I guess someone at Penguin saw our speech, because we were then asked to contribute to an anthology that's being curated by Sir David Attenborough, and it all kind of snowballed from there.

So Riley's right, something has changed.

My work has become more reasoned.

Respectable, I'm sure he and Tab think.

But as I'm asking myself why that's a bad thing, Tab says, 'It's the Renata Barbosa Rebrand.'

That one lands because she's right.

This is exactly what my mother wanted, isn't it?

For me to be on the news for the sort of activism that gets the 'right' attention.

The back of my neck burns as I reach for my orange juice and take a gulp.

'OK,' Riley tries again, holding his hands up. 'Can we please just stay on topic?'

'Fine,' I say tightly. 'What's the topic? To force me out?'

'No! We just think that you should separate Out of Time from your friendship with Melody.'

'Why?'

He fidgets in his seat, his cheeks flushing as he tucks his hair behind his ears. 'Well—'

But before he can say it, Tab does.

'Because we don't want to be associated with someone who flogs hair vitamin gummies.'

Melody hasn't done that for years and Tab knows that.

'So Melody's not cool enough to be associated with Out of Time, is that what you're saying?'

'Well, yeah,' Riley admits with a shrug.

At least he's honest about it, but Tab hisses at me, 'Ren, we're anarchists.'

'Your parents are millionaires,' I remind her. 'You live in Sandbanks, for fuck's sake.'

She looks like she's about to fly across the table at me. 'All of *this*' – she waves her hands wildly – 'this whole rebrand with your lovely articles in the Torygraph and your lovely speeches at World Wildlife Day and your sponcon posts with Melody, skipping around, eating ice cream—'

'When have I ever done a sponsored post?' I snort as I hear my phone ringing again.

Even Riley's frowning at her, his lips parted, as he looks at her as if to say, *Are you OK?*

But she ignores us both. 'None of it is in keeping with Out of Time's ethos.'

I stare at her for a moment, then burst out laughing.

'*Out of Time's ethos?* Since when do we have an ethos? Tab, you sound unhinged.'

'Do I, Ren?' She leans forward and yells in a way that does nothing to convince me otherwise.

'You do a bit,' Riley mutters, frowning at her, then turning back to me. 'Listen, Ren. We don't want you to lose focus. All this shit you're doing with Melody is fine, but we're not here to make nice with the *Telegraph* and the United Nations; we're here to make them listen. Don't let Melody distract you.'

'How am I distracted from Out of Time? If anything, I'm more resolved than ever.'

'You are?' he asks with a frown.

'Yes!'

'Good.' He nods, then reaches for his pint and raises it to me. 'Let's keep raising hell, then.'

Tab and I hesitate, then do the same, clinking our glasses together, if not as enthusiastically.

But I'm not toasting us.

I'm toasting Tab because I have to give it to her.

I strode in half an hour ago, ready to crucify her and Riley, but Tab did *exactly* what Melody said she was going to. Tab was the one who fucked up. She not only undermined me yesterday, but she pissed off one of our closest allies, not to mention most of our supporters. Yet, she still managed to turn the whole thing on me so I'm the one sitting here, reassuring them of my commitment to a group that I started.

It's brilliant, when you think about it.

I might be able to appreciate it if she hadn't just broken my fucking heart.

'Shall we get some food?' Riley asks as though nothing's happened.

And I don't know how, because it's over.

Not just me and Tab but the three of us.

We'll never be the headstrong, heart-eyed rebels plotting to save the world over tofu pad Thai again.

'I'm good,' I mutter, reaching for my jacket. 'See you back at the flat, Riles.'

Don't cry, I tell myself as I walk out of the pub.

Not yet.

When I step out on to Earl's Court Road, I hear my phone ringing in my jacket pocket again and for one wild moment, I think it's Tab, calling to apologise and plead with me to come back. To tell me that she didn't mean it, that she was just being a stroppy cow because she's hungry. And the thought makes my eyes blur with fresh tears so I can't see the screen as I answer, then hold my breath and wait for her to say it.

But it's not Tab.

It takes me a second to recognise the voice, and when I do, I stop so suddenly that someone almost walks into the back of me. I turn and hold my hand up to apologise as he swears at me and keeps going.

I don't like talking on the phone in the street – especially on Earl's Court Road where any one of these people on BMXs can whip it out of my hand as they pass – but I suspect this can't wait until I get back to Riley's.

'Renata,' Giles says tightly. 'I'm calling you before I speak to your mother.'

Oh shit.

This can't be good.

'Renata, the police are charging you.'

'What?' I gasp. 'I had nothing to do with what happened at Greenpeace yesterday!'

'No. Not that. The Dorchester.'

'What?'

'You've been instructed to attend Westminster Magistrates' Court on June 26th.'

9

I'm charged with *failing to comply with a condition imposed under section 14 of the Public Order Act.*

I'm stunned.

My mother is furious.

Not her usual furious, but a new, even more terrifying kind that makes me long for the halcyon days of her signing off texts with *F.B.* She's calm. Quiet. So quiet that we only communicate through Giles. The silence is excruciating. It's the longest we've gone without speaking, then, on day twenty-one, she instructs Giles to tell me to join her for breakfast the next morning at The Mandrake.

We usually meet on the terrace, so when she summons me to her suite instead, I panic because it's the middle of June and my mother never passes on an opportunity to sit in the sunshine. That means she doesn't want to be overheard – or any witnesses – so I make the sign of the cross before I knock on her door.

When she answers, she looks as immaculate as always as she greets me with a nod, then turns and leads me out on to the balcony where the table is set up with breakfast that we're probably not going to eat.

I watch warily as she pours a coffee, then hands it to me.

'Everything's going to be OK, Renata.'

I stare at her for a moment, unsure what to do.

My mother isn't the *Everything's going to be OK, Renata* type.

She's more the *How are you going to fix this, Renata?* type.

So I hold my breath as I wait for the other half of that sentence.

Something that involves a punishment far worse than whatever is coming my way in court.

But she just reaches for a copy of *The Times* and hands it to me. I look up at her, then down to find it open on the Letters to the Editor. The top one reads *THE TEENAGERS JEOPARDISING THEIR FUTURE TO ENSURE OURS* and it's followed by a scathing letter saying that the Section 14 restrictions imposed on me, Pearl and the rest of the Out of Time crew at The Dorchester were unlawful.

It's signed *Melody Munroe*.

'A handwritten thank-you note from Professor Dame Fernanda Barbosa, you should be honoured,' I tell Melody ten days later as we wait in the corridor at Westminster Magistrates' Court.

She pretends to swoon and while I make a show of rolling my eyes, I'm grateful for the distraction from asking myself what's about to befall me as I wait for my mother to arrive. I thought she'd be with Giles, so when Melody and I arrived to find him alone, I had to accept the very real, very likely possibility that she isn't going to show for fear of what being seen in court with her wayward daughter will do to her already tarnished reputation. But as Melody pointed out when we were greeted by the handful of photographers waiting outside, my mother's failure to stand by me would be more juicy than whatever the verdict is so Melody's sure she'll come.

'You OK?' Melody asks as the corridor swells with a storm of grey and pinstripe. In contrast, she's wearing an ankle-length *Atonement*-green cotton dress and a pair of gold wedges.

Looking at her makes me think about that video.

The one of the peacock swishing around that supermarket.

Which makes me think about my mother again.

'Don't be nervous,' Melody tells me. 'You didn't do anything wrong, Ren.'

I mutter something, distracted by the fact that there's still no sign of my mother.

Or Tab and Riley, which isn't entirely unexpected.

Melody must know what I'm thinking, because she asks, 'Where's Thelma and Louise?'

That makes me chuckle at least. 'Tab's not going to show up, is she?'

'When was the last time you guys spoke?'

'Not since what happened at the pub last month.'

I shrug it off, but I had hoped Tab would have put our shit aside and joined the Out of Time crew making a racket outside. But according to her Instagram, she's on her way back from Glastonbury, which isn't entirely unexpected, either, but still hurts enough to make me feel lightheaded.

'What about Riley?' Melody asks.

'He has a meeting with his head of department this morning. Imperial have already suspended him over getting arrested at the Greenpeace protest so it's not looking good for him.'

'I feel bad,' Melody says, exhaling heavily, 'but Riley shouldn't have let Tab talk him into that ridiculous Occupy Greenpeace stunt. He knew Imperial were going to be pissed. Isn't that why he and Tab ran off and left you at The Dorchester? Because they didn't want to get kicked out of uni.'

'They didn't run off and leave me,' I tell her, even though that's essentially what happened.

I wait for Melody to disagree but she lets it go and asks, 'Is Riley going back to Manchester?'

'No, Tab's convinced him to stay in London for now.'

'So, are you gonna rent a two-bed place together?'

'We can't. I can't sign a tenancy contract.'

'Not even if your mum acts as guarantor?'

'She's already told me that I can't live with Riley so I'm not even gonna ask.'

'I'd sign it for you, but my credit rating's still shot to shit after my skin line imploded.'

'That's so sweet, but it'll be OK.'

'So, what's the plan?'

'According to Riles, he and Tab are taking a year out to focus on their activism.'

I wait for it and sure enough, Melody's gaze narrows. 'What does *that* mean?'

'I have no idea. But he's super excited about how to grow Out of Time.'

Her eyes almost disappear. 'What are he and Tab going to superglue themselves to now?'

'Nothing, hopefully.' I snigger. 'All I know is that he and Tab are looking for a new place.'

She frowns. 'What about you?'

'I guess I'm back to travelling with Mum wherever she goes.'

She looks about as happy with that as I am.

But Melody pushes her shoulders back and smiles brightly. 'At least you'll be at my farm for the summer.'

As soon as she says it, I look around because this would be the moment my mother chose to arrive.

I lower my voice. 'Can we keep that on the downlow until I've spoken to Mum? With everything going on, I haven't had a chance. But then, in about an hour, I may not need to tell her because she'll know exactly where I'll be living for the next three years thanks to His Majesty's Prison and Probation Service.'

'Don't worry about that.' Melody waves her hand. 'But you do need to worry about Tab and this year she's taking off to *focus on her activism*, especially after what she tried to pull last month.'

'I'm not worried about Tab,' I snort. 'The Out of Time crew let her have it for the Greenpeace thing. She knows they want her gone, so if she comes for me again, she'd better succeed this time.'

Melody smirks. 'You come at the king, you'd best not miss.'

'*King Lear*?'

'*The Wire*.'

I laugh, but Melody's right.

I know what Tab's like when she gets something in her head.

For whatever reason, she's decided that I'm steering the ship in the wrong direction and wants to take the wheel. And as long as I keep trying to steer Out of Time away from the sort of thing that happened at Greenpeace and back towards digital activism, she's going to keep making a grab for it until she gets her way.

So I know Tab isn't avoiding me because she's embarrassed.

She's regrouping.

Rallying the troops.

Starting with Riley.

But I can't think about that right now.

As if on cue, I hear someone say, 'Don't worry, Ren. We've got this.'

I look up to see that it's Sasha and salute her with two fingers as she passes with her parents.

The doors to the courtroom swing open and I hear a voice call out the next case.

There's a flutter in the corridor and my heart leaps in my chest as someone appears next to me.

But it isn't my mother.

It's Pearl.

'Sorry!' she says, turning to mouth the same at Giles. He nods at her but keeps talking to whoever he's on the phone to as she turns back to us, pink-faced and out of breath. 'I had to get the bus. The Circle line's down.'

When Pearl fusses over her shirt, I'm grateful for a new distraction.

She looks like a blonde Audrey Hepburn.

All big-eyed and fresh-faced in a white shirt and black capri pants.

Meanwhile, there I am, all in black, sweating in a pair of tights that are a size too small and already have a ladder in them, my top lip wet and my toes numb from the heels my mother insisted I wear.

'She's sixteen, perv,' I sneer at the middle-aged guy in a suit who leers at her as he passes.

He puts his head down and keeps walking, but Pearl doesn't even notice.

'What was that?' she murmurs, looking around as she smooths her hair with her hands.

'Nothing. You look nice, Miss Newman. Are you in court, or something?'

'Not now, Renata,' she says through her teeth. But it isn't with her usual playful ease as she asks where the toilet is, then darts off.

As soon as she does, Melody squeezes my arm. 'Go easy on her, Ren. She's terrified.'

'I'm not exactly doing cartwheels myself.'

'I know, but' – she stops to lower her voice – 'Pearl has a lot to lose today.'

I resist the urge to make a smart remark as I realise that, like Riley, Pearl's probably poised to be kicked out of college as well, and while I don't have to worry about that, I think I'd rather deal with that than my mother.

I must summon her because there's another flutter in the corridor. Actually, it's more like the parting of the Red Sea as everyone sweeps aside to create a path. Then there she is, heels snapping as she strides towards us in sunglasses and a black trouser suit, her lips redder than I've ever seen them.

She stops in front of me and checks what I'm wearing, the corners of her mouth lifting for a second as she sees that I've put on everything that she had sent to Riley's yesterday.

Satisfied, she leans in to kiss me delicately on each cheek. 'Renata.'

'Mum,' I murmur, when she steps back. 'Thanks for coming.'

'Of course,' she says, as though there was never any question that she would.

I turn to Melody to introduce her, but before I can, she steps forward. 'Hi, Fernanda.'

I wince at *Fernanda*, an indiscretion that is rewarded with a slow turn of my mother's head and a slower glance up and down that tells Melody in no uncertain terms that she isn't to refer to her as that again.

At least Melody doesn't try to hug her.

'Mum, this is Melody,' I say quickly, and it feels like snatching a toddler from the path of a speeding car.

'Ah, yes.' Her smile sweetens. 'Thank you again for writing that letter to *The Times*.'

When my mother extends a hand, Melody shakes it carefully.

'Of course. Hopefully it helps with Ren and Pearl's case today. But even if it doesn't, at least it's opened up a conversation about the tactics being used to discourage protesting.'

My mother nods, but I'm sure she regrets bringing it up because she won't – or can't, in fairness – be drawn into this conversation. Perhaps in private with me, but she'd never risk it with someone she's only just been introduced to and certainly not here, in the corridor, where anyone could hear.

'I heard you on the *Today* programme last week, Melody,' she says instead, changing the subject. 'You made an interesting point about the role of social media in climate change misinformation.'

I smile as I watch her take off her sunglasses, touched that she's making an effort.

Melody beams, then gestures at me. 'Thank goodness for Ren

and Out of Time for countering that misinformation otherwise we'd have no idea what state the planet is in.'

'Well.' My mother's smile splinters to a smirk as she slips her sunglasses into their velvet case then snaps it shut. 'I can certainly see why my daughter is so taken with you, Melody.'

'The feeling's mutual. You must be very proud of Ren. She's going to change the world, you know?'

The shift is so slight that you have to know my mother well enough to spot it.

A sudden sharpness at the corners of her eyes – just for a second – before she recovers.

'Of course I'm proud of my daughter, Melody.'

But it sounds more like a warning than a confirmation.

Mercifully, Giles interrupts. 'Fernanda, you're here.'

'Shall we go in?' she says as soon as he does.

'I think they let us know when they want us to go in, Mum,' I tell her.

But as I say it, the doors swing open again and someone steps out to announce our case.

If I didn't know any better, I'd say that they've been waiting for my mother to arrive.

'Can we go in now, Renata?' she asks as I fight the urge to stuff my entire fist in my mouth.

I start walking towards the doors, but my mother reaches out to stop me.

She leans in and lowers her voice. 'Remember what I told you?'

'Yes, Mum,' I mutter. 'Let Giles do the talking. Only speak when I'm spoken to. Be polite.'

Don't embarrass me.

'Good. Now come along.'

As we're about to go in, Giles whispers something to her and she stops and turns towards him.

Pearl reappears then, still pink-faced and breathless. 'I didn't miss anything, did I?'

I thumb at the open doors. 'Don't worry. They only just called our case.'

Pearl nods and when she gulps – actually cartoon gulps – I remember what Melody told me earlier.

'It's gonna be OK,' I tell her. 'The Section 14 was unlawful. We didn't do anything wrong.'

'You've been saying that for the last five months, Renata. Yet here we are,' she huffs.

Melody comes to stand between us and slips her arms around our shoulders.

'Listen, girls,' she says. 'Whatever happens, just know that you did nothing wrong, OK?'

10

The judge dismisses the charges.

But as sure as I was, the relief still brings tears to my eyes.

It's so overwhelming that I don't realise Melody is hugging me until she peppers my cheeks with kisses.

'I'm so proud of you, Ren!' she tells me, holding my face in her hands. 'You were right!'

When she lets go and steps back, someone else hugs me. Leaps on me, actually, and it isn't until I get a mouthful of blonde hair that I realise it's Pearl.

What's weirder, though, is that it's actually kind of comforting, her arms tight around me and her forehead warm against my neck. She gets it, I realise, as I feel her heart hammering in time with mine. So maybe it's not that weird because she's the only person in the courtroom who knows exactly how I'm feeling. It's a strange thing to have in common – escaping three years in prison – but I suppose that warrants a hug.

If I'm weak with relief, then she's shuddering with it and it's a minute or two until she's steady enough to let go. When she does, I pretend not to see as she turns her cheek to swat away a tear with the tips of her fingers. I make a show of looking for Melody, spotting her walking out of

127

the courtroom with someone who has their phone pointed at her while Melody talks furiously, hands waving.

'Sorry,' Pearl says with a sniff, then clears her throat.

'S'alright,' I tell her with a shrug.

'Renata, come along,' my mother says, suddenly at my side.

And that's it.

No hug.

No *well done*.

No indication whatsoever that she's as relieved as I am that it's over.

But she manages a smile for Pearl as she asks how she's getting home.

'I'll go back to Brighton with Melody,' Pearl says as she looks around the courtroom.

'I just saw her leaving with Oliver Sutton from the *Guardian*,' my mother says, nodding at the doors.

'I guess I'll see you, then,' Pearl says with a small shrug.

I nod and as soon as she walks away, my mother's face hardens. 'Come on. We're going to be late.'

'Late for what?'

She doesn't tell me, though, just turns on her heel and marches out of the courtroom.

'Hey, guys,' Melody says when we get back into the corridor, then slings her arm around Pearl's shoulders. 'Let's celebrate! I've booked us a table at The Landmark across the road.'

I see a tremor in my mother's eyebrow at *celebrate*, before she smiles smoothly.

'That's very thoughtful, Melody, but Renata and I have a meeting at the U.S. Embassy.'

'The U.S. Embassy?' Melody and I say unison.

My mother isn't used to explaining herself and the look she gives us tells us that she isn't going to.

She simply says, 'It was a pleasure meeting you, Melody. Have a safe journey home.'

'Is that it?' I ask as soon as Maurice pulls away and we can no longer hear the photographers shouting our names.

'Is *what* it, Renata?' my mother says as she takes her bag off the backseat and puts it in her lap.

'You're not even going to acknowledge what just happened?'

'Well,' she scoffs, 'if you're expecting a celebratory lunch, you're certainly not getting one.'

'I wasn't expecting that, trust me, but did you hear what the judge said?'

'I did,' she murmurs as she takes her phone out and peers at the screen.

'I was right,' I say, because she's not going to, is she? 'The Section 14 restrictions were unlawful.'

I hope that prompts something.

A nod.

A raised eyebrow.

Anything.

Anything to acknowledge that the last five months have been worth it.

But there's nothing.

I persevere, hoping the sixteen-year-old Fernanda who used to break into labs and throw red paint on people is still in there somewhere and she's proud of me, even if forty-seven-year-old Fernanda isn't.

'Mum, this is *huge*. Judge Barton all but said the police abused their powers to stop the protest. Do you know what that means? It's a win, not only for Out of Time, but for our right to protest. Melody says—'

'Renata, por favor.' My mother raises her hand, killing the thought before I can finish. 'Para com isso!'

'Stop what, Mum?' I ask as she slips her phone back into her bag.

'Stop trying to retcon this into some sort of moral victory.'

'But it is.'

'Don't be ridiculous,' she hisses. 'I'm sure that's *exactly* what Melody was doing when she left with Oliver Sutton, spinning this into a feelgood story about a gang of plucky teenagers who stood up to the man and won. But we both know that you weren't making a stand about our corroding civil liberties at The Dorchester. You didn't even know what the protest was for, did you? You just showed up out of mindless loyalty to Tab.'

'That doesn't mean that this case didn't bring attention to the tactics being used to stop people from speaking out.'

'Fine.' She takes off her sunglasses to glare at me. 'You're Rosa Parks. Is that what you want me to say?'

'No, I want you to acknowledge that this wasn't my fault.'

'Well, I'm not going to.'

'But the judge said—'

'I don't care what the judge said, Renata. You attended a protest you knew nothing about, which isn't only naïve, but could have put you in danger. I know there's a rush to climbing cranes—'

'But the war will not be won by climbing cranes and spray-painting windows, right?'

'No! You're my sixteen-year-old daughter and every time my phone rings . . .'

When she trails off and turns to look out of the window, I feel wretched as it dawns on me that maybe she doesn't hate Out of Time because we're damaging the cause.

She's just scared that the next call won't be from the police.

But before I can acknowledge that, Maurice clears his throat, and I realise that we've stopped.

'Thank you, Maurice,' my mother says, her tone cooling again as she says, 'Let's go, Renata.'

'Where are we?' I ask, peering out of the window.

'I told you. The U.S. Embassy.'

'Wait. What?' I turn back to find her taking out her compact and lipstick. 'You were serious about that?'

'Why on earth would I lie?'

'I thought you were making an excuse to get out of lunch with Melody.'

I can see that she's trying not to smirk as she sweeps on another layer of red.

'Melody Munroe is not someone I would ever feel the need to make excuses to.'

Nice.

'Why are we here, then?' I ask as she snaps the compact shut.

'To pick up our visas.'

'For what?'

'Renata,' she says with that *I am not explaining myself* look she just gave Melody and me.

But it doesn't work this time. 'Mum, how do I know this isn't a home for wayward daughters?'

'Don't tempt me,' she warns.

'Mum,' I push.

'Fine.' She huffs, then lifts her chin. 'We're spending the summer in Austin. We leave on Wednesday.'

She's hit me with so many things at once that my head spins like one of those colourful, flashing wheels on a game show before it finally settles on, 'Wednesday? But today's Monday, Mum.'

'That's why we can't miss this appointment. Now, hurry up. Let's go.'

'Maurice, no!' I hold my finger up to him as he goes to get out to open her door. When he freezes, I turn back to my mother. 'What do you mean we're spending the summer in Austin, Mum? What's going on?'

'We don't have time for this, Renata. I'll tell you when we get inside.'

I don't budge, though. 'Why are you shipping me off to Austin?'

'Don't be so dramatic, Renata. This trip has always been on the cards, but now I know that you're not spending the next three years at HMP Bronzefield, we can go. But we need to be there by July 6th.'

'Why?'

'You know the company I met with in the spring that's developing that 3D printer?'

132

'Yeah,' I say, crossing my arms more tightly when I realise where this is going.

'We're collaborating on a project to build a public library in Austin.' Her eyes light up and I hear her breath hitch as she says, 'It's going to be the first of its kind to be built using 3D-printed construction.'

'How long will it take?'

'Technically, it only takes about three hundred hours to print, but from start to finish, we think about three months.'

'*Three months?*'

I don't know why I'm so surprised.

In fact, that's pretty quick for one of my mother's projects.

So it's not surprise, I realise.

It's panic, hot and quick, suddenly fizzing through me, my dress sticking to my back as she checks her watch and says, 'Now come along. You know I don't like to be late.'

When she reaches for her bag, Maurice turns to get out of the car again and it all happens so quickly that I don't know what to do. So in my rush to stop them, I hold my hands up. 'No!'

I don't mean to shout, but it's enough to make them both freeze.

'No?' my mother repeats, clearly stunned as I tell myself to put my hands down.

It's not a word she hears often, even from me.

Perhaps when I was a fractious toddler, but even as a fractious teenager, I wouldn't dare.

'What do you mean, no?' she asks when I stare back at her.

'Mum, I can't go with you to Austin,' I tell her, my voice quick with panic.

I probably should have tried to soften the blow, but I only have a few seconds before the shock passes and she reaches for the car door again because I know what she's doing. What she always does when it's time to move on somewhere else. Rushing me. Blindsiding me. Not saying a word until we have to leave, then it's already happening. We have to go right now. On to another trailblazing project that she *has* to do because it's going to change the world, and I can't object because who stops their mother from building a children's hospital?

Or a library, in this case.

'Why not?' she asks as I continue to stare at her, my heart hammering. But she doesn't wait for me to catch my breath as she throws her hands up and says, 'Renata, por favor. It's OK to fly sometimes. But I can ask Teresa to look into any cargo ships that are heading to Texas in the next few days.'

'It's not that,' I say.

Again, she doesn't wait for me to tell her why. 'Já deu, Renata. You've punished me enough for that *Observer Magazine* interview.' She holds her finger up when I try to tell her that it's nothing to do with that either. 'It's been six months. Tia Aline told me to give you some time otherwise I'd lose you altogether and I did, but that's enough now. You're not spending the summer on Riley's sofa and you're certainly not moving in with him. And while I'd rather not physically drag you somewhere you don't want to go, I will if I have to, because until you turn eighteen you are my responsibility and you will do as I say. Você tá entendendo?'

'Mum—' I try, but she shakes her head.

'No, Renata. Enough. Besides, isn't Riley going home for the summer? Tab will be as well, I assume. Is that it? Has Tab asked you and Riley to spend the summer with her family at their house in Lucca again?'

'Not this year,' I manage to say around the knot of pain suddenly lodged in my throat.

I shouldn't lie, but this is difficult enough without having to explain the demise of our friendship as well.

'Well, whatever the three of you had planned for the summer, it's not happening.'

When I look up, she looks down and I feel awful because I know what she's thinking.

'Mum, this is nothing to do with you.'

'Why won't you come to Austin, then?' she asks, but doesn't look at me.

'Because I was hoping to do something else this summer,' I confess with a shrug.

'What?'

'Melody's invited me to spend the summer at her farm.'

I brace myself, sure that she's going to throw her hands up and yell, *Não vou deixar, Renata!*

But her response is uncharacteristically muted as she simply says, 'Melody.'

I hold my breath while she considers that then says, 'I should have known this had something to do with her. That certainly explains why the pair of you were so alarmed when I said that we were coming here.'

I wait, sure that I'm going to get another lecture about how we're spending too much time together.

That it's weird.

Unhealthy.

But she says, 'Well, now I've met her, I can see why you're so fond of Melody. She reminds me of Aline.'

That's never occurred to me, but Melody is *exactly* like my aunt.

Bright.

Loud.

Mutinous.

They have that same energy – that same purity – that makes you feel like you can do and be anything.

'I can't picture Melody living on a farm, though,' my mother says with a smirk.

'Me neither, to be honest.' I chuckle.

'Where is it?'

'Chanctonbury.'

She goes quiet and I know I should leave it because if I push her, she'll go the other way. But when I glance out at the embassy gleaming in the sunshine, panic pinches at me because we don't have the three to five working days that she usually needs to process something like this.

We have two.

So I say a prayer to Nossa Senhora Aparecida and say, 'Melody lives with Aunt Celeste.'

That makes her turn to look at me. 'Celeste? My Celeste?'

'Yeah, except she really is Melody's aunt.'

'She is?'

'By marriage. Uncle Dan is Melody's mother's brother.'

She stares at me for a second or two.

'Wait. Is Melody *Mel*?' She doesn't wait for me to answer,

just shakes her head and says, 'Celeste has been telling me about an intentional community she's creating with someone called Mel and her family.'

'Yes!' I point at her, delighted. 'That's the one. There's, like, ten of them.'

'Celeste has been trying to get me to visit for months. Apparently, they've been doing wonderful things with Sussex Wildlife Trust's Nature Recovery Network.'

I feel a rush of hope. 'I know you've never been there, but if Aunt Celeste—'

She arches an eyebrow. 'Hold on, Renata. Why has Melody invited you to spend the summer there?' she asks, with a suspicious frown. 'Does she want you to join this community, or something?'

'No, nothing like that.'

'Why, then?' she pushes, as I try to find the best way of putting it.

'You know Melody's book, *Sustainable Sustainability*?'

She nods.

'Well, we're going to co-write the follow-up.'

'Is that what the meeting the two of you had yesterday was about?'

Shit.

I forgot I told her that.

'It was just a coffee with Melody's editor,' I tell her with a shrug.

The crease between her eyebrows deepens. 'And what did you discuss?'

'Her editor wants us to write something about how social

media is the best and the worst thing to happen to the environment. The first half will be Melody talking about how, as one of the first influencers, she used social media to get her generation hooked on mass consumption, and in the second half I'll talk about how I'm using social media to mobilise my generation to undo the damage.'

My mother thinks about that for a moment, then says, 'That could be interesting, actually.'

I'm so stunned she's even considering it that I just murmur, 'I think so.'

'So, what's the plan? You spend the summer at Melody's farm working on it?'

I nod.

'Why can't you do it on Zoom?'

'Writing an article on Zoom is one thing, but a whole book that we haven't even outlined yet is going to be a nightmare. Especially with the time difference between here and Austin. What is it, like, five hours?'

'Six. When is the first draft is due?'

'The end of September.'

'When I'm due back from Austin,' she snorts. 'How convenient.'

'Mum, I found out about Austin four minutes ago.'

She snorts again, but she uncrosses her arms. 'What about school? You still have almost a month of term left.'

'I do everything online so I can do my tutorials anywhere, can't I? Just like if I was in Austin.'

'And writing this book won't interfere with them?'

'It won't, I promise. Melody's brother, Oren, is sixteen as well and he's homeschooled. By Aunt Celeste, in fact. I mean, who better to teach me biology than someone with a PhD in plant sciences?'

'Well,' she says with a huff. 'I suppose it's better that you're with Celeste, doing something productive, rather than being by yourself all day while I'm on site. Some structure will do you some good, actually,' she says with another huff, but then she turns to me with a fierce frown. 'But you're not putting your name to a book until I've read it. In fact, you're not writing a word until Giles has read the contract. You didn't sign anything, did you?'

'Of course not,' I tell her.

'Good.' When she nods, I try not to smile, but she catches me and arches an eyebrow. 'That isn't a yes, by the way, Renata. I'm not agreeing to anything until I've spoken to Celeste, OK?'

'But it's not a no, right?'

The corners of her mouth twitch. 'It's a *We'll see*.'

11

I walk out of Chanctonbury station to find Melody waiting by a battered green Land Rover Defender. As soon as she sees me, she cheers and charges over, almost knocking me down.

'You're here!' she says, kissing my cheek while I laugh and try to hug her with one arm.

'I'm here,' I say when she lets go, heaving the strap of my holdall back on to my shoulder.

'Oh my God, Ren. Look at you.' She steps back and I can tell she wants to laugh. 'It's, like, a hundred degrees and you're still wearing black. How are you not dying right now?'

I am. It's unbearably hot today and while I'm relieved not to be stuck on a train carriage any more, the heat is showing no sign of simmering even though it's almost six o'clock. Still, I refuse to give her the satisfaction of being right. If for no other reason than that she always teases me for wearing black, regardless of the weather.

When she reaches down to tug at the piece of tape that's curling away from the knee of my jeans, I protest. 'Hey! That's my emotional support gaffer tape. Leave it alone or these jeans will literally fall apart.'

When I swat her hand away, she cackles. 'I respect your commitment to being a goth.'

'I'm not a goth,' I correct. 'I just like black. It's chic.'

'Real chic,' she snorts, trying to rip the gaffer tape off again.

But if I look like my usual teenage cliché self, then Melody looks completely different. In fact, she looks positively demure compared to the swirling tempest of pattern and colour that I'm usually assaulted with.

No boob dungarees.

No hot-pink lipstick.

No gold wedges.

Farm Melody is channelling noughties Kate Moss at Glastonbury in navy Hunters, a pair of frayed denim shorts and a Stevie Nicks T-shirt that I suspect was once black and is now a patchy grey. I'm relieved to see that she's wearing bright green Wayfarers, though, so the Melody I recognise is in there somewhere.

I guess I've never seen what Melody looks like when she's at home. Not about to go on stage with Pearl and me or standing by our side in court. There's no one to perform for here, I suppose. To impress.

Even so, it's strange seeing her like this. She's usually so put together. Granted, she's not as polished as my mother, but I've learned that Melody is no less precise. Everything she chooses is carefully curated, down to her nail polish, even if she tends to favour Miami pink over the fierce red my mother always wears.

But today, Melody's nails are bare and there's a black crescent of dirt under each of them. Even her hair looks different. It's only been two days since I last saw her at Westminster Magistrates' Court, but the sunlight we're drenched in exposes rivulets of bronze that I don't normally see and it isn't teased

141

to achieve that just-rolled-out-of-bed look she likes so much. Today it looks like she really did just roll out of bed. Actually, it looks like she's just finished a hard day, working the land, her knees bruised with mud and her Hunters filthy. They're almost as filthy as the Defender she's standing next to, which looks like it's been driven into war more than once.

'Where's your stuff?' Melody asks, looking down at my feet.

'Here,' I tell her, patting the black canvas holdall hanging from my shoulder.

'*That's* it?' she asks, horrified. 'I take more stuff to the gym.'

'I travel so much that I've learned to keep it light.'

'*That's* all you've brought for three months?'

I nod.

'Christ,' she says, taking it from me. 'Oren is going to love you. Whenever we're in a shop he's like' – she pulls a face and puts on an annoying voice – '*Do you really need that, sis?*' She scowls and opens the back of the Defender. 'No, I don't need another scented candle, but they bring me joy. Why can't he just let me live?'

'Mum has a thing for scented candles as well,' I tell Melody as she mutters to herself.

As with her nail polish and lipstick, she only likes one kind, though.

Diptyque Figuier.

It's the one constant in the hotel rooms and short-term rentals that we bounce between so, in a weird way, whenever I smell it somewhere else, it always reminds me of home.

'Well, I needn't have bothered cleaning this out,' Melody says, sliding my holdall into the trunk.

'Most of it is coffee, in fairness.'

'You brought your own coffee?' she gasps, slamming the door shut. 'I know you're Brazilian, but you can trust me when it comes to coffee, Ren. At any given time, I'm at least twelve per cent caffeine.'

'I thought you'd given up?'

'Please,' she scoffs, jumping into the driver's seat. 'That lasted for, like, four hours.'

'But you only drink herbal tea when you're with me.'

'I have cut down,' she concedes when I climb into the passenger seat beside her, 'but I'll never be able to give up completely because if I don't have a coffee in the morning, my brain refuses to function.'

'I feel that,' I tell her, dumping my tote bag into my lap and tugging on my seatbelt.

'What are you reading?' she asks.

I look down to see that my book is poking out of my bag and take it out to show her.

She peers at it with a frown. '*Learning to Breathe Underwater: How to Survive the Climate Emergency.*'

She looks appalled, but I smile sweetly. 'Just some light reading for the train.'

Given my mother's penchant for commenting on what I read – like last year, when she caught me buying *The Uninhabitable Earth* in a bookshop in Edinburgh and thoroughly embarrassed me by insisting that I buy *Twilight* instead – I wait for Melody to say something. But she just slips her sunglasses back on and claps.

'You ready for your one perfect summer?'

'Don't,' I warn, rolling my eyes.

143

But she cackles again because she knows that's the only reason my mother agreed to let me stay on the farm. 'Your mum said that we can spend the summer working on our book as long as you promise to, what?'

'No petitions,' I say with a surly sigh because she knows full well what the terms are. 'No protests. No arguing with strangers online. Just ice cream and lime-green nail polish and falling asleep in the sunshine.'

'And maybe a summer romance.' She winks lasciviously.

'Not much chance of that around here,' I tell her, tipping my chin up at the deserted street.

As if on cue, a tractor rolls by and I smirk at her as if to say, *See?*

'Have a little faith, Ren,' she says, then winks again as she starts the engine.

It lurches to life with less of a roar and more with the cough of a forty-a-day smoker. But after some sweet talking – and a few pumps on the gas – she coaxes a more promising response. Then we're off.

'Look at this, Ren!' she says when we pull away. 'Chanctonbury put her best dress on for you!'

She certainly has. The sun is loud and bright, amplifying everything so the village looks like a page from one of those Shirley Hughes books that my mother used to read me as a child. The blue, blue sky. The green, green hills. The scruffy black-and-white dog waiting outside the butcher's. It's perfect. Everything you'd expect from an English village, including the Union Jack bunting that's still there from King Charles's coronation last month.

Not like the London I fled an hour and a half ago. Me sweating and saying, *Excuse me*, every other step as I navigated the cluttered concourse at Victoria station, my holdall bouncing against my hip as I tried not to spill my coffee, the abiding soundtrack of buses belching and cars honking scoring my efforts to catch the 16.35.

No, here it's quiet. Still. Birds sing and butterflies bob as the Defender chugs through the village.

'I'd give you a tour, but this is pretty much it,' Melody says, gesturing at the neat row of brick buildings that we're rolling past. 'It's just like being back on Earl's Court Road, right?'

I shouldn't laugh, but I doubt I'll be able to get an onion bhaji pitta at 2 a.m. here.

I'm guessing the shops were houses at one point. They're small. Sweet. Each with the same lichen-mottled roof and crooked leaded windows with a stone surround framing the door and bay windows either side. Yet, each one looks distinct. Some painted white with black windows, others with striped awnings and baskets bubbling with hot-pink geraniums hanging outside, each one with a different-coloured door.

'There's not much,' Melody says with a shrug, 'but we have all the essentials. A butcher. A baker. A candlestick maker.' She laughs. 'OK. Maybe not a candlestick maker, but this' – she points at a shop with blue windows – 'is the village store. It's a mish-mash of everything. A newsagent. A post office. An off-licence. There's a cash point in there as well, but it never works. So, if you need cash, you're better off heading into Steyning, which is about twenty minutes from here. Don't get your hopes up, though. There's no Starbucks on every corner, but it has *way* more than we do here. A bank. A hairdresser. A curry house. All that good stuff.'

As we approach a sage-green shop with matching windows, someone with long grey hair strolls out.

'Hey!' Melody grins when they wave at her.

She doesn't look, just stops the car, and I gasp, checking over my shoulder, but there's no one behind us.

'I thought I heard you coming, Mel,' they say, stopping at her open window.

'Ren, this is Martha,' Melody says. 'She's part of the farm fam. She owns this café.'

Martha's face lights up as she dips her head inside the Defender and reaches her hand out to me. 'Ren! I'm so thrilled that you're spending the summer with our community! How was your journey down from London?'

'Great, thanks,' I tell her as I shake her hand.

'Look what she was reading on the train,' Melody says, grabbing the book from my lap.

'Oh, I've read that! It's brilliant.'

'Of course you have,' Melody mutters as she hands it back to me.

'I'm so looking forward to spending time with you, Ren,' Martha tells me with a warm smile. 'I met your mother at a Woodland Trust event about ten years ago. Such a remarkable woman. I love that she's still fighting the good fight and has passed the baton on to you. My youngest granddaughter is off to Exeter in October to study marine science because of you. You give me hope that the tide is turning.'

'Oh wow,' I say, my cheeks warming.

Melody lets go of the wheel to ball her hand into a fist. 'Of course it is!'

Martha chuckles, then steps back. 'See you at the house, OK? I just need to close up.'

'Do you want us to wait?' Melody asks, but Martha shakes her head.

'Oh no. It's fine. I'll walk. It's a beautiful day.'

'If you're sure. I'll see you back at the farm, then.'

Melody doesn't look in the mirrors when she pulls out either, but again, there isn't anyone behind us.

Aside from that tractor, I haven't seen anyone else on the road since I arrived.

'Everyone always calls her Mother Martha, but I didn't want to confuse you,' Melody says as we continue on along the high street. 'I don't know why, we just do.'

'You'd be surprised how many mothers I've met at protests over the years.'

'I bet.' She chuckles. 'You're gonna love her, though. She's Canadian and was one of the first members of Greenpeace. I know there's that old joke about if you sit next to anyone in a bar in Vancouver, they'll claim to have founded Greenpeace, but Mother Martha really did. She was a stringer at the *Winnipeg Tribune* in the 60s with Bob Hunter and was one of the original members of the Don't Make a Wave Committee.'

'Shut up!' I turn and stare at her. 'She knew Bob Hunter?'

Melody nods as we stop to let someone with a red tartan shopping trolley cross the road. 'She knew all of them. Jim Bohlen. Bill Darnell. Dorothy and Irving Stowe. She even has the first Greenpeace button that Jim Bohlen's son, Paul, made. I'm sure she'll show you. Her photos from that time are amazing.'

'I'm sorry' – I hold my hands up – 'but that is cool *as fuck*.'

Tab will die when she hears this, I think, but the thrill sharpens to something that makes me suck in a breath as I remember that we haven't spoken since the night I walked out of the pub.

'This is the Chanctonbury Arms,' Melody says when we reach the end of the high street. She sticks her arm out to point at a large black-and-white building that is the only deviation from the cute row of houses. 'They do a mean Sunday roast. There's no vegan option, of course, but they'll do all the trimmings.'

'That's good to know,' I tell her. 'I couldn't find a menu.'

'Wait.' Melody shoots a look at me. 'You googled it?'

'I googled the village.'

'Why?' She flashes me a mischievous smirk. 'Don't you trust me?'

'Of course I do, but I've travelled to some pretty remote places with Mum, so I wanted to make sure that when you described Chanctonbury as a "rural idyll", that meant running water and electricity.'

'Come on. It can't be that different from your mum's village.' She throws her head back and laughs. But when I don't join in, she turns to look at me again, this time with a frown. 'What?'

'Mum's from Jardim Europa, which is one of the most affluent neighbourhoods in São Paulo.'

'Shit.' Melody's shoulders jump up as she winces. 'Sorry.'

I wave my hand at her. 'Don't worry, you're not the only one who thinks that. But my grandfather worked for the government and my grandmother owned a chain of pre-schools that she franchised all over Brazil.'

'Wow. So they're, like . . .'

'Loaded?' I say when she trails off. And I don't know why she's so reluctant to say it, but I guess she's being careful not to make another assumption. 'I mean, yeah. She grew up in a fifteen-thousand-square-foot house with a pool, tennis courts and a full-time staff. She even had a bodyguard who went everywhere with her. So this whole thing about her surviving the favela to become a world-renowned architect is nonsense.'

'Sorry, Ren,' Melody says again. 'I hope I didn't offend you.'

'Of course not.' I nudge her with my elbow. 'And I'm sorry for being defensive. It just bugs the hell out of me that everyone thinks Brazil is this lawless hellhole with drug lords roaming the streets and chickens running around. Which' – I arch an eyebrow – 'is kind of true in some areas, but the rest of it is lovely. I mean, I've been more scared walking back to Riley's from Brompton Cemetery when Chelsea are playing at home.'

She giggles, then stops when someone calls her name.

'Hey, Art!' she calls back, sticking her arm out of the window to wave as we pass. 'Give Sue my love.'

'So is this one of those villages where everybody knows your name and no one locks their door?' I ask as we approach a tall black wrought-iron sign with a painted coat of arms and *CHANCTONBURY* in white letters.

'Pretty much,' she says. 'After three years in Newport, where my nan referred to her neighbour as *that cow next door*, moving somewhere that strangers say hello to you in the street took some getting used to.'

'It must be nice, though,' I say, thinking about all of the hotels I've stayed in and their seamless rotation of staff with their practised nods and smiles who never looked me in the eye.

'Of course – I love it here,' she says as my gaze drifts out of the open window to find another row of houses with neat lawns and a low stone wall separating them from the road. They're more uniform than the ones on the high street but just as sweet, with white windows and white front doors and neatly trimmed hedges with clouds of lilac hydrangeas and lavender speared with hollyhocks that blush pink in the sunshine.

Once we pass them, the houses become much bigger and farther apart until there's nothing but green.

Green.

Green.

Green.

Great clouds of trees and fields that roll on and on.

The sky so wide that it feels like I can see every corner of it as the road gets narrower.

So narrow that I don't know what we're going to do if we encounter another car, let alone another tractor.

But there aren't any.

Just us on the hairline of a road that parts the fields.

'It's good and bad,' Melody admits as she tilts her head from side to side. 'I've always harboured a fantasy of riding around a village like this on a bicycle with a dog in the basket, solving crimes.' She takes her hand off the steering wheel to hold a finger up. 'Which could still happen, by the way. But it's also bad,' she says with a small sigh, gripping the wheel again, 'because you can't turn your pillow over without someone knowing. And let's just say that not everyone in the village is as open-minded about what we're trying to create at the farm as we are. At best, they think we're harmless hippies who are all shagging each other—'

'At best?' I interrupt with a snort.

'Well, the alternative is that I'm heading up some sort of doomsday cult, so when the rapture comes, someone will have to sneak in and take me out like Scarface before I make everyone drink the Kool-Aid.'

I shouldn't laugh, but I full-on howl at that.

So hard that my book slides off my lap and into the footwell.

'Everyone loves Aunt Celeste and Mother Martha, though,' Melody says as I reach down to pick it up. 'So while I'm sure there's much debate about what we're up to, everyone leaves us to it. Plus, my sister and her family have been living here for eight years now so they know we're not freaks. They just don't understand, you know? And whenever I try to explain it to anyone, it sounds unhinged. But I really believe that these sorts of communities, where we look out for each other and are as self-sufficient as possible, are the only way that we're going to survive the climate crisis. The funny thing is, it's the older people who get it because that's what Chanctonbury used to be like before, you know, capitalism. Now everyone works a sixty-hour week and is more likely to know the name of their DPD delivery driver than their neighbour.'

'I'm sorry,' I say, holding my hands up as I laugh again. 'You know I agree with you, Melody, but I can't get the image of you as Tony Montana out of my head.'

'Careful,' she warns. 'Or you could be starting your one perfect summer with a horse's head in your bed.'

'That's *The Godfather*.'

'Oh yeah. Anyway' – she shakes her head – 'I do need to warn you about something.'

When she cringes, I immediately stop laughing.

'I was right, wasn't I?' I groan. 'There's no running water, is there?'

Or electricity.

What if the farm's falling apart and there's no roof?

What if we have to camp?

Sharing a tent with Tab and Riley at Glastonbury is one thing, but camping for *three months*?

Absolutely not.

But Melody's older-sister intuition kicks in again because she immediately reassures me, 'There's running water, I promise. And Wi-Fi. You even have your own room. But . . .'

'What?' I say warily as she turns to look at me.

'Pearl's there.'

I blink at her. 'Pearl?'

Melody nods and looks back out at the road.

'For how long? The whole summer?'

I try to disguise the disappointment in my voice because despite rolling my eyes when my mother insisted that I needed to have one perfect summer, while I'm not one for ice cream, lime-green nail polish and falling asleep in the sunshine, I did agree that I needed a break. Or at least an escape from listening to Riley complain about how he and Tab will never find a flat that they can afford.

But now I have to spend the summer with Pearl?

I thought the book was our thing.

Just Melody and me.

But she reads my mind again. 'Don't worry. Pearl's not working on the book.'

'So why is she at the farm, then?'

She shifts slightly in her seat as she says, 'All you need to know is that she's living with us now.'

'Living as in *living*. Like, all the time?'

She nods.

'Just her?'

She nods again.

'How come?'

'I'll leave it to Pearl to tell you.'

'Why? What's going on? Has she had a fight with her parents?'

'No, nothing like that.'

But the way Melody shrugs confirms that it's definitely something to do with her parents.

'Did they kick her out, or something?'

'Ren, stop,' she whines. 'I promised I wouldn't say anything and you know what a big mouth I have.'

'Fine,' I say, because it's none of my business, is it?

I mean, I wouldn't like it if Pearl was asking questions about my relationship with my mother, would I?

If she wants me to know, then she'll tell me herself.

'Well, I hope she's OK,' I murmur, turning my cheek to look back out at the expanse of green.

'She will be,' Melody says when I stick my arm out of the window, letting the sunlight warm the bones in my fingers as I remember what she said in the corridor of Westminster Magistrates' Court.

When she told me to go easy on Pearl.

That she had a lot to lose.

I thought she was going to get kicked out of college but is this what she lost?

Her parents?

That would explain why they didn't show up in court.

I feel a rush of affection for my mother then because whatever I've done – and however vehemently she disagrees with it – she *always* shows up. It's easy to forget that not everyone does. Most of Out of Time's followers don't get involved in person because they can't, because their parents are terrified something will happen to them. And while Pearl didn't fall off a crane, getting arrested or kicked out of college is no less life-altering.

'Stop it,' she says, reaching over to flick me.

'Ouch,' I hiss, rubbing my arm.

'Pearl will tell you when she's ready. Just give her a minute.'

12

I'm still thinking about Pearl, so I don't realise that the Defender has slowed down until we're turning left.

Again, Melody doesn't look, just swings between two trees that look exactly like the other trees and pulls on to an even narrower road. I say road, but it's just two grooves in the ground, separating the fields, so I have to reach for the door handle as the Defender wades through the sea of grass suddenly surrounding us.

The way it shudders as something I can't see – and hope isn't essential – rattles every time we hit a bump, reminds me of being on that boat in Svalbard when I was ten, my mother beside me, pointing out polar bears while we carved through the sea ice. Except here, everything is green, not white. And instead of polar bears, birds soar skyward – godlike – while the grass swishes, applauding our arrival as a house finally comes into view.

'Welcome home, Ren,' Melody says, turning to me with a proud smile.

The roof seems to be intact, I'm relieved to note. And while it isn't as quaint as the houses we just passed in the village, it makes sense because this is a farmhouse. It's solid. Practical. Built to withstand muddy boots and dogged winter winds that have nowhere else to go but right at it.

If this was a zombie apocalypse film, it's the sort of house the main characters would hope to stumble upon because there'd be enough canned food to see them through and a couple of shotguns. I know that doesn't sound like a compliment, but when I look up at the house, something in me settles.

All I've known for the last several years are cities that flash blue at night as babies are born and people don't come home and others don't wake up. The circle of life completing its turn before the sun rises and a cavalry of carts roll out to sweep away the empty beer bottles and pizza boxes so everyone can go to work and the tourists can pose for photos in front of statues of people who would no longer recognise the city that's so proud of them.

I guess I'm used to it now. To being surrounded by people. There's always someone walking too slowly in front of me. Or pushing on the Tube before me to get the last seat. Or asking for spare change at the cash point. I thought I liked it. Not being alone. I like overhearing conversations on the bus or in the elevator of whatever hotel I'm in. Knowing things I have no right to know about people I'll never see again. And I like that it doesn't matter what I'm wearing or if I trip on a paving slab, because no one sees me. And even if they do, in a few minutes I'll be gone, and they'll have forgotten me by the time I turn the next corner.

That's kind of liberating but it's also exhausting because I'm always on edge. Always making sure that my phone is in my pocket and that I have one hand on my bag and that there isn't a car coming so I can cross the road to avoid the guy smoking outside the betting shop who always whistles at me and calls me Nenita.

But one thing I'm not used to is being in the same place long enough to grow weary of it. So as much as I complain about having to flit from city to city, hotel room to hotel room, with my mother, after six months in London with its relentless traffic and bullet-grey sky, every day the same, nothing but noise and teeth, my feet – and heart – are getting restless. And nothing could be more different from Riley's stuffy flat above a kebab shop than a farmhouse in the middle of nowhere with nothing but green for miles.

But when Melody told me about it, I'd pictured a spread from *Architectural Digest*, her floating around barefoot in a colourful kaftan, picking wildflowers while tiny birds flutter around her. But I see no trace of her, which is strange given she's been here for three years. I thought she would have painted the front door Miami pink and put bay trees either side of it, but there's nothing. Just a worn wooden bench under one of the windows and a carpet of biscuit-coloured gravel that splashes beneath the soles of my trainers as I climb out of the Defender.

'Is that an attic?' I ask Melody when she jumps out.

'Yeah, but don't worry. I haven't banished you up there!'

She cackles, but it's drowned out by barking and I look over as two Golden Retrievers fly around the side of the house and charge at me in much the same way she just did outside the station.

I'm equally amused – and unbalanced – by the greeting, reaching down to pet them as they circle me.

'Where were you two?' Melody asks, then walks to the back of the Defender. 'Were you sleeping in the barn again? You're farm dogs, you know? You're supposed to be working.'

'You're too pretty to work,' I tell them, rubbing their heads.

'Ren could be here to murder us all,' Melody calls out as she opens the trunk. 'And yet here you two are, running past me to get fuss from a complete stranger. I'm your mother. You should be protecting me!'

They throw their heads back and howl, as though defending themselves.

'Yeah, yeah,' she tells them as she slams the trunk shut.

But they continue barking as they circle her this time, one of them going between her legs.

'Buffy! Willow!' Melody wails as she almost trips.

'Buffy and Willow?' I tilt my head at her. 'And *I'm* the goth?'

'I didn't name them.' She scowls, trying not to drop my holdall as one of them tugs at the strap. 'Oren did. I wanted to name them Rachel and Monica, but I was outvoted because it wasn't fair to leave out Phoebe.'

'Well, she is the best one.'

She stops in front of me, still scowling. 'You and Oren are going to gang up on me, aren't you?'

When she rolls her eyes, it occurs to me that if I like Melody so much because she reminds me of Tia Aline, maybe she likes me so much because I remind her of her younger brother.

'Come on, you two,' she says to the dogs, who are now sitting at her feet and looking up at her, their blonde tails splashing in the gravel as they pant happily, 'shall we show Ren her new digs?'

They respond with a howl, then run up to the front door and wait for Melody to push it open. As soon as she does, they barge in first, heralding our arrival with a series of increasingly excitable barks. I can hear them being greeted with cheers somewhere in the house as I follow Melody in time to see Buffy and Willow run into what I'm assuming is the kitchen, if the heady waft of garlic is anything to go by. It smells so good that

158

I swoon, and when I do, I realise that all I've eaten today is the falafel wrap I had with Riley in the cemetery at lunchtime.

'Just to warn you,' Melody says with a theatrical sigh, holding her hand up, 'it's chaos in there.'

I hear overlapping voices and the swift *taptaptap* of a knife on a chopping board. When I hear Simon & Garfunkel's 'Kathy's Song' playing, the strum of the guitar plucks at something in my chest as I remember those weekends at Tab's house, all of us crowded around the kitchen island, making lunch while her father sang along to it, and I suddenly miss her so much it's as though someone has kicked the back of my legs.

'Let's go upstairs first,' Melody suggests as I try to swallow back the pearl of pain suddenly lodged in my throat. 'You can dump your stuff and freshen up before everyone jumps on you.'

She heads up the stairs and I follow while Melody points at doors.

'That's my room at the end. And that's Oren's. The door opposite that is our bathroom.'

I smile and nod, following her finger as it darts back and forth, but I'm not listening, too furious with myself for letting Tab back in when I haven't thought about her for weeks. But then I have, haven't I? I'm always thinking about her. Even when I skip a song so I don't have to think about her, I'm thinking about her. Or when Riley's not in the room and his phone buzzes and I have to resist the urge to check if it's her. Or when I have to resist the same urge when my phone buzzes because I know it won't be.

I was supposed to leave all of that in London, not bring it with me. That's one of the reasons I'm here – perhaps the only reason – because I can't bear the thought of spending the summer without Tab while Riley dutifully divides his time between us, like a kid trying not to choose between his divorcing parents.

Just the thought of sitting by myself in the flat eating brigadeiro, or wasting an afternoon at the cinema because he's with her, makes me ache in a way that has me leaning against the wall as I remember him in the living room last night, sorting through his books. 'Have you read this?' he kept asking as he agonised over which ones he should keep and which he should take to the charity shop.

Every day, the cluttered living room got a little less cluttered. I kept reaching for things that weren't there any more as gaps appeared on the shelves like bullet-holes. That's it, isn't it? By the time I get back to London – if I go back to London – Riley will have moved in with Tab and it won't be the same, will it?

At some point, he'll grow weary of splitting his time between us. Then I'll lose them both and Riley will become another of my friends, like all the others I've met while flitting from city to city, hotel to hotel, that I'll promise to keep in touch with and come back and visit but never do. Then we'll only communicate by trading memes because that's how it goes.

That's my life.

Five million followers and a friend in every port, but I've never been so lonely.

'Hey,' Pearl says, suddenly stepping out of the door in front of me, because of course – of fucking course – this is the moment she chooses to remind me that I'm stuck with her for the summer.

And of course she asks the one question that gets me right in the gut.

She feigns confusion as she looks around the hallway. 'Where are your sidekicks?'

She says it with a smile that I want to bite off her face, but then I remember what Melody just told me.

So I make myself take a steadying breath and say, 'Tab and Riley are in London.'

'What are they supergluing themselves to this time?'

I have a comeback ready in the chamber, but Melody's eyes widen as if to say, *Please*.

'Oh, Miss Newman,' I say instead. 'I can't wait to spend the summer with you.'

She huffs and glares at Melody. 'You told her I was here. That's no fun.'

'Listen, I didn't think that putting you in rooms across the hall from each other was going to be an issue, but if it is, I can ask Oren to switch.'

'We'll be fine,' Pearl says.

As I say, 'We'll be fine.'

When her gaze flicks to me and I counter with an arched eyebrow, Melody doesn't look convinced. 'If it's going to be a problem, it's best to let me know now before everyone gets settled.'

But I shake my head and say, 'I'm cool, Melody. I can sleep anywhere.'

When I flash Pearl a sweet smile, she flashes me one right back. 'I'm sure you can, Renata. Besides, sharing a bathroom with only one person will be a luxury for you after all of those communal showers in prison.'

That's it, I think, but Melody takes me by the shoulders and turns me around.

'OK, then,' she says, pushing me through the open bedroom door. 'See you downstairs for dinner.'

Melody closes the door and presses her back to it.

'Wow,' she says, blinking a few times.

'*I'm* the asshole?' I hold my arm out. 'I've only been here ten minutes and she's already starting on me.'

I don't get it.

The last time I saw her, she hugged me and now she's back to making prison jokes?

'First of all' – Melody steps away from the door to give me a thumbs up – 'proud of you, babe.'

But the look I give her lets her know that isn't going to cut it.

She winces and says, 'Listen, Ren. I know I asked you to go easy on Pearl and, well' – she stops to close her eyes and shake her head – 'she's certainly testing you. But don't let that performance fool you.' When she opens her eyes again, she thumbs over her shoulder. 'Pearl's really fragile right now. She could do with a friend.'

Me too, I want to say.

So I could do without Pearl's digs.

Melody takes another step towards me. 'Once we find our rhythm, it'll be fine.'

But when she flashes me a hopeful smile, I'm not sure who she's trying to convince.

Me or herself.

13

In an effort to calm down, I check my phone and cackle when I see a comment on my last video saying that if I care so much about the environment then I should be walking, not getting the train.

That's nothing new. If you point out that the planet is burning, you can't go anywhere, apparently. Or eat anything. Or wear anything. Do anything at all, in fact, because everything I post – however innocuous – is enough to prompt someone to question my commitment to the cause. Even having a phone to post from means I'm part of the problem, so I've waived my right to complain about the whole the planet-is-burning thing.

I should ignore it.

I promised my mother that I wouldn't argue with strangers on the internet while I'm here, but sorry, freethinker_76. If I have to go easy on Pearl, then you're going to get it instead.

It's as though my mother knows because as soon as I've fired off a scathing reply, she calls me.

'Oi, Mãe,' I answer breezily so she doesn't get suspicious and ask me what I'm doing.

But she sighs happily when she hears my voice, which is equally suspicious.

'Olá, minha querida filha. Tudo bem?'

Minha querida filha?

Either this is a trap or my mother has been partaking of the champagne in the first-class lounge at Heathrow because I haven't been her dear daughter for quite some time.

'Are you at the farm?' she asks as I hear a voice announcing the final call for the 19.20 to Tokyo.

'Yeah, I just got here.'

'What's it like?'

'It reminds me of that village,' I realise, clicking my fingers. 'The one with all the trains.'

'Paranapiacaba?'

'Yes!'

'Very green, then?'

'And *very* English. Like something from a postcard. Vó would love it.'

'What's the house like?'

'I just got here so I haven't had a chance to check it out yet.'

I hear her sip something before she asks, 'Do you have your own room?'

'Of course,' I say, then roll my eyes because I know where this is going.

Sure enough, she gasps theatrically and says, 'Wow. A whole room to yourself, Renata? Do you even remember what it's like to sleep somewhere with a bed and a door?'

The farm must be working its magic on me already, because instead of barking back, I chuckle.

'It's nice,' I tell her as I finally look around.

'How pink is it?'

I chuckle again because it's almost minimalist by Melody's

standards. There isn't so much as a lick of pink anywhere. No leopard skin, either. No Monstera colonising one corner of the room. No framed prints on the walls demanding *GOOD VIBES ONLY*. No wallpaper with massive peonies.

'You'd like it,' I tell my mother, because she would. It's natural. The stone around the window is exposed, along with the floorboards and beams, and the rest painted sage green, which makes the green outside look even more vivid. Nothing matches, which my mother would approve of. The cotton sheets are white and the bedframe is black and the wooden tables either side are slightly darker than the floorboards and beams, while the chest of drawers and wardrobe are stained a washed-out denim blue.

But even though it looks nothing like Melody, that in itself is hopelessly *her* because it's unexpected. The ikat wool blanket at the end of the bed looks like it's just been thrown there and the pillows are different colours and sizes, but they're not an afterthought. The room is as put together as Melody is. Every detail considered, from the spray of eucalyptus in the terracotta vase on the windowsill, to the *EAT. SLEEP. REVOLT. REPEAT.* mug sitting on one of the bedside tables. There are no cottagey florals or vases of pink roses. Instead, the blanket is a mix of orange, dark blue and white that picks out the orange, dark blue and white in the pillows and the worn rugs on the floor, which in turn picks out the various shades of wood and the denim-blue furniture.

It's the perfect balance of colourful, without being migraine-inducing, and stylish, without being sterile. And when I toe off my trainers, I feel able to do that here. Not like

165

at my grandparents' house, which is stunning (and has been in *Architectural Digest*, actually), but it's not the sort of house where you can leave your trainers by the bed. It's the sort of house where you dress for dinner and have caipirinhas on the terrace at five o'clock.

I can't even go into the kitchen to make myself a coffee without someone rushing over to do it for me.

But as nice as the room is – and as inviting as the bed looks – I can't help but miss the chaos of Riley's flat with the circuit board that trips out if you dare to use the microwave and kettle at the same time and the shower that is either tepid or skin-meltingly hot. Mind you, I won't miss trying to sleep on his narrow, lumpy sofa while a couple argue outside the kebab shop at four-thirty in the morning.

'Oh, that's me,' my mother says. 'I have to go, my flight is boarding. Remember, Renata—'

'I know,' I interrupt with a sigh. 'Be polite. Say please and thank you. Offer to help. Don't be difficult.'

Don't embarrass me.

'No,' she says. 'Well, *yes*, but one perfect summer, remember?'

'One perfect summer,' I repeat as I hear her finish whatever she's drinking.

'Tchau, um beijo. Vá com Deus. Eu te amo muito, minha querida filha.'

'Eu te amo demais também, mãe. Call me when you land.'

'Espera, Renata.'

'Vou sentir sua falta, mãe,' I tell her, and I can't remember the last time I told her that I'll miss her.

'Já vou sentir sua falta,' she says back.

As soon as she blows me a couple of kisses and ends the call, there's a knock on the door.

'Come in,' I say as I brace myself for Pearl to sweep in, ready for round two.

But it's Melody who sticks her head around the door with a smile. 'Dinner's ready.'

'Oh great.' I smile back, gesturing at her to come in as I look around for my holdall.

It's still on the floor where she left it and when I walk towards it, she frowns.

'Do you need to borrow some slippers, Ren?'

'I'm good,' I tell her, trying not to laugh as I picture what she'd produce if I did.

Something with hot-pink satin and feathers, I'm sure.

'I brought some,' I say, unzipping my holdall and pulling out my black Havaianas.

She pulls a face when she sees them. 'Was it too much to hope that they'd be pink?'

'My pyjamas are pink, actually.'

'Really?'

She sounds so surprised that I almost feel guilty when I look at her as if to say, *Come on*.

'I will lure you over to the pink side one day, Renata Barbosa. Mark my words,' she warns, but when I go to follow her out, she nods at my phone, which is still in my hand. 'Would you mind leaving that here?'

'Sure,' I say, putting it on top of the chest of drawers.

'It's just that we have a screen-time thing here.'

'Oh, OK. No problem,' I say and I shouldn't be so surprised

because I've been to a few retreats with my mother that had strict no-phones rules.

A three-day retreat is one thing, though, but I need my phone. It's the Out of Time July monthly meeting on Saturday and we're discussing how we're going to protest COP28 without travelling to Dubai. Plus, I've been asked to take over Friends of the Earth's TikTok next month. Then it's Climate Week NYC at the end of September. Plus, as thrilled as I'm sure my mother will be that I won't be on my phone all the time, how am I going to keep in touch with her? I can't not talk to her for three months. What if something happens?

I must look ready to grab my phone and run back to the station, because Melody laughs.

'Breathe, Ren.' She holds her hands up to me. 'You can still use your phone.'

When I take a breath, she laughs again.

'We just prefer to use our phones for an hour in the morning and an hour in the evening, but if you have something going on with Out of Time, we can work it out.' She waits for me to look at her again, then says, 'It's so we're more present, you know? What's the point of creating this community if we're going to sit in the same room, scrolling through our phones and not talking to each other? That's not living together, that's just sharing a house. I want us to actually be together. Enjoy each other's company.'

As she says it, I see my screen light up and when I look away to see who it is, I prove her point.

'Sorry,' I mutter, when the screen lights up again, then reach for it and put it in the top drawer.

Melody smiles. 'Give it a few days and you won't miss it, I promise.'

'Yeah, but what about Tab?'

I'm sure Riley has told her that I'm not around for the summer, so I dread to think what she has planned.

Melody just snorts. 'Don't worry about her. Everyone's still pissed at her for the Greenpeace thing. But even if she succeeds at usurping you, you don't want to be part of a group that forgets about you, and everything you've done, just because you take a few months off.'

A few months off?

I press my palm to my forehead, my head suddenly spinning because is that what I'm doing?

All of this happened so quickly that I didn't think it through.

Two days ago, I was in the back of a car outside the U.S. Embassy, telling my mother about the farm, and now I'm here, taking three months off, apparently.

I haven't even thought about how I'm going to explain my absence.

Melody reaches up to tug my hand away from my forehead. 'Ren, *you* are Out of Time. It doesn't matter if you take three months or three years off; Out of Time doesn't exist without you. So you don't need to tell anyone anything about where you are this summer.'

She lifts her right shoulder then lets it drop again. 'But if you want, you can start teasing that you're working on something. Then, as soon as we sign the contracts, Penguin will announce the book and everyone will know that's why you're here. Plus, Aunt Celeste is doing all this stuff with the Sussex Wildlife

Trust's Nature Recovery Network, isn't she? I'm sure they'd *love* it if you put your name to it. Why don't you tell everyone that you're doing that as well?'

That makes me feel slightly steadier.

'Besides,' she adds with another snort. 'I know that two hours with your phone doesn't sound like much, but you'd be surprised how much you can get done when you're not doom scrolling and arguing with trolls.'

She's right, I realise as I think about the time – and energy – I just wasted on freethinker_76.

Melody reaches for my hands and squeezes them. 'You need this, Ren. You've been in fight mode since you started Out of Time. If you burn out, you'll be of no use to anyone, and we need you to win this war. So, it's OK to take a break. What is it your mum told you when she agreed to let you spend the summer here?'

'Rest. Reset. Regroup.'

'Exactly.' She kisses me quickly on the cheek. 'Now come on. You must be starving.'

Melody walks out into the hall, then I stick my head out, checking for Pearl. There's no sign of her, so I follow to discover that it's equally understated out here. The floorboards are hidden by a long, worn runner and the walls painted a muted stone colour and lined with framed photos of what I'm assuming is Melody's family, but we pass them too quickly for me to do much more than glance at them.

At the top of the stairs, there's a grandfather clock stuck at ten to four and more photos follow us down the stairs, but, again,

Melody skips down them so quickly that all I see is another series of faces.

I manage to pick out the odd one, though. Melody at her First Holy Communion, looking angelic with her palms pressed together. Melody at someone's wedding in a surprisingly tasteful dark pink bridesmaid's dress. Melody on her grandmother's birthday, the pair of them beaming with a cake that says, *HAPPY BIRTHDAY NAN*.

Melody's life. Each of these bright moments dotted among photos of holidays and birthdays and sunny afternoons sitting on picnic blankets. I can't help but think of my grandparents' house again and the photos of my mother and Tia Aline that sit on shelves and end tables in every room. There are several of me as well, but most are from when I was a baby. Any taken since then are in my mother's phone and I suppose they'll stay there because in the absence of a house of our own, there are no walls or end tables to put them on.

The thought makes my chest feel tight as we reach the bottom of the stairs. I notice that there's another door to the left – directly across the hall from the kitchen – but it's closed. Melody doesn't say what's in there, though, as she passes the front door, which is open so I can see the dogs sleeping outside, flopped on the grass.

I glance up and see the word *HIRAETH* painted over the front door in dark green sloping letters. I ask Melody what it means, but she doesn't hear because she's already marching into the din of the kitchen.

When I join her, I'm greeted by a cheer.

Buffy and Willow charge in, barking, as Melody gestures at

me and says, 'Ren, this is the fam.' She throws her arms out. 'Fam, this is the infamous Ren that I keep talking about.'

'Hey, Ren!' they all say at once.

They seem thrilled to see me as they wave and raise whatever they're drinking with another cheer.

I spot Mother Martha, but as I wave back, I hear a voice I know so well say, 'You're here!'

I smile and turn around to see Aunt Celeste walking towards me with her arms open.

She pulls me into a hug.

When she steps back and puts her hands on my shoulders, her cheeks are pink.

'Where's Uncle Dan?' I ask, looking around.

'He's on a dig in Greece.'

'Why aren't you with him?'

'And miss spending the summer with you?' She presses another kiss to my forehead. 'Never!'

'You didn't have to stay for me!'

'Of course I did! It's been forever, Ren.'

'It hasn't been that long, Aunt Celeste,' I tell her as she takes my face in her hands.

'It's been six months,' she reminds me.

'Sorry I haven't been in touch,' I say sheepishly.

But she just laughs. 'I get it, darling. You're busy saving the world.'

I can't help but smile because she looks exactly the same. Where I'm creased and sweating, she's effortlessly elegant, in her gold wire-frame aviator glasses and a grey denim jumpsuit I'd look like a toddler in. But at almost six feet tall, she looks like she should be sitting outside a café in Berlin, nursing a doppio, her black hair smoothed into a low ponytail and parted in the middle to accentuate the streak of grey that frames her face.

'Ren, you've grown!' she says, pinching my chin between her forefinger and thumb.

I haven't, but that's what aunts say, isn't it?

'How was your journey?' she asks, adjusting my silver Saint Christopher medal so it sits on my throat.

It's the only piece of jewellery that I'm wearing and when she presses her finger to it, I wonder what she's thinking given she's always layered in gold necklaces and bracelets and that pearl choker with the C that I thought was for Celeste, but now I actually look at it, I see that it's a gold crescent moon, which is equally apt.

'It was fine,' I tell her with a shrug.

'Come on, Ren,' Melody says, slipping her arm around my shoulders and tugging me away. 'Let me introduce you to the rest of the fam.'

The kitchen is a blur of activity while Nick Drake's 'Pink Moon' – my mother's favourite song – plays. They're all doing something – chopping and slicing and taking glasses out of one of the cabinets and there's a flow to it.

A rhythm.

'This is my older sister, Jacinta,' Melody says, holding her arm out to her.

She smiles at me, then glares at Melody. 'Was the *older* really necessary, Mel?'

But she just cackles. 'This is her husband, Hunter.' She points while I try to remember their names. 'This is their daughter, Iris, and her husband, Marcus. And you know Mother.'

'Hello again.' I nod as she reciprocates with another warm smile.

'Mum is usually with us as well,' Melody says. 'You're in her room, actually.'

'You didn't give me her room, did you?' I ask, mortified. 'You know I don't mind sleeping on the sofa.'

'Don't worry. Mum hasn't lived here for *months*.'

Jacinta waves her hand at me. 'Mum didn't come back from Newport with us after Christmas because, bless Nan, I love the bones of her, but she's being a bloody nightmare. She's ninety next month and fighting the good fight about going into a home. So Mum's living with her until she sees sense.'

'And this' – Melody grins when someone comes into the kitchen behind us – 'is my baby brother.'

As soon as I see him, I try not to laugh.

He must know what I'm thinking because he rolls his eyes. 'AKA her secret love child with Joe Jonas.'

I can see why Melody tried to pass Oren off as his love child because they have the same dark eyes and hair but Oren's definitely more indie rock than *Camp Rock* with his Radiohead T-shirt and long hair that's the right side of unkempt in a way that would make most girls go feral. Plus, he's taller than Joe Jonas. Like, ridiculously tall. Has to duck to get through doorways kind of tall. So tall that I don't see Pearl until she steps out from behind him and as jump scares go, it's got to be up there with that girl crawling out of the television in *The Ring*.

'And you know Pearl, of course,' Melody says slightly manically, as she takes me by the shoulders and turns me to

174

face the living room. 'So, this is where we hang out most of the time.'

I recognise it from Instagram, but it doesn't look as big in real life. It's one open space with the kitchen and island at one end and a long wooden dining table running alongside the windows. Opposite that are two dark grey linen sofas and a brown leather armchair in a horseshoe around the fireplace.

It's not as tidy as on Instagram, either. There's a stack of vinyl next to the record player on the sideboard and the pillows on the sofas are messed up. It looks lived in. Comfortable. There's a cardigan hanging on the back of a dining chair and a half-drunk mug of tea on the coffee table. And like my room, it's warm. Natural. Mismatched furniture on layered rugs with lamps dotted around and piles of books everywhere.

'Let's eat!' Jacinta announces, heaving the pot from the stove.

I follow the others to find that the table's already been set. I hang back until Melody sits at the head and pats the spot to her left, next to Aunt Celeste and opposite Oren. Pearl sits next to him and I brace myself for another dig, but she doesn't even look at me as everyone passes their bowls up the table to Jacinta, who is decanting steaming ladles of green soup. Not that it's soup weather, but I'm so hungry I'll eat anything.

'Pea and potato.' Oren grins. 'Courtesy of Aunt Celeste's vegetable garden.'

She pats my hand. 'I'll show it to you tomorrow, darling.'

'And Mother Martha made the bread this morning,' he says, passing me a wooden chopping board.

'Renata's vegan,' Pearl mutters when he offers me the butter dish.

'Am I the only one?' I ask with a frown.

'Aunt Celeste and Mother Martha are as well,' Melody says. 'The rest of us are only vegan when we're not at the farm because here we can consume eggs from our own hens and dairy products from local farms where we know about the welfare of the animals.'

She stops to pile some salad on to her plate, then hands me the bowl. 'We try to be as low impact as we can. Nothing we eat has travelled more than thirty miles, which is easy because there are so many farms nearby. Not using a car is harder, though. Especially as Jacinta and Iris need to drive for work. Jacinta's a vet.'

'And Iris is a midwife,' Jacinta says with a proud smile, 'which'll come in handy in a couple of months.'

When she winks at her daughter, Iris rubs her belly.

It takes me a second, but then I gasp and say, 'Congratulations!'

I hope Iris doesn't think that I'm a self-absorbed asshole who didn't even notice. But she was standing behind the island earlier so I couldn't see that she was pregnant.

'Only two months to go.' Marcus beams, reaching for her hand. 'We're very excited.'

Something brushes against my leg then and I shoot a look across the table at Oren and Pearl to find them absorbed in conversation, his hands – and hair – everywhere as she laughs. It happens again, but as I'm about to push my chair back, a blonde furry head appears from under the table.

'Hello,' I say, looking down as one of the dogs rests her chin in my lap.

'Buffy!' Melody hisses.

I laugh as she ducks under the table again and sits on my feet.

'How can you tell them apart?' I ask. 'They look exactly the same.'

She gestures at her neck. 'Buffy has the black collar and Willow has the purple one. You'll be able to tell them apart soon enough, though. Willow is marginally better behaved than Buffy.'

She tips her chin up and I turn to see that Willow is sitting next to me, her tail slapping the floorboards.

'They know that we're not allowed to feed them from the table,' Aunt Celeste says, reaching for her wine glass. 'But they're obviously hoping that you haven't been told that rule yet.'

'Stop tag teaming her, you two,' Melody warns. 'It's not going to work.'

It might.

I can't take Willow looking at me with her big eyes and sweet, hopeful face.

Melody must know that I'm about to give in because she says, 'Just be strong, Ren.'

'You'll need to be strong around here,' Hunter tells me as he smears butter on to a hunk of bread. 'Not just with these two monsters, but there's plenty of work to be done around the farm. Right, Mel?'

'Hunter, stop!' she says, then laughs as she waves her spoon at him, spilling soup down the front of her Stevie Nicks T-shirt. 'You make it sound like I invited Ren here to be a farm hand!'

'I'm looking forward to working on the farm, actually,' I say as I try to avoid eye contact with Willow.

I wait for Pearl to pipe up. Ask me the last time I made my own bed. But Oren leans in to whisper something that makes her laugh so hard that she throws her head back and all I see is the pale length of her throat.

Actually, it's not as pale as I remember. Much like Melody, Pearl looks different at the farm. She's still perfect, of course, in a pink-and-white gingham sundress that my grandmother would love to see me in, but her white Campos are scuffed and her hair isn't straightened to its usual flawless gloss. Instead it looks like she slept on it while it was wet, so it's a mess of uneven waves that spill over her shoulders. Plus, her chest is pink with fresh sunburn and freckles have bubbled up across the bridge of her nose and cheeks.

Or maybe they've always been there. I don't know. I've never seen her without make-up on. New or not, though, she looks nothing like the pale, shaking Pearl I saw at Westminster Magistrates' Court who hugged me so tightly that she left creases in my dress. She looks the complete opposite. Content. Healthy. Her cheeks flushed and her eyes bright as Oren steals a piece of bread from her plate and she tries to snatch it back with another startling surge of laughter that makes everyone at the table stop eating and smile at them.

After dinner, I join Iris and Marcus at the sink to help with the washing-up, but Iris shoos me away.

'You're so sweet, but don't worry. We take it in turns to wash up. Check the rota.' She points over at the fridge. 'You'll see when you're on.'

'I don't mind,' I try to tell her, but she shakes her head.

'Trust me, there's so many of us that you'll be sick of washing up soon enough!'

When she turns back to the sink, I suddenly have no idea what to do and I hate this bit. It's the feeling I get every time my mother and I arrive in a new city. An awkward sort of dread as I realise that I have to start all over again. Find another coffee spot where they don't mind if I sit there for a couple of hours, reading a book. And somewhere that does decent vegan food, so I don't have to subsist on crisps and hummus. Maybe even make a few friends, if I'm lucky, who'll open a door I didn't know was there so I can explore the city anew. Before I leave again, and they become just another name that pops up on my phone when they see me on the news or another of my videos blows up on TikTok.

I check to see where everyone is and find Pearl and Oren by the record player, deciding what to put on next. I don't have the energy for her right now, but I should make an effort. With Oren, at least, because I'm curious to know if we're as similar as Melody says we are. I was hoping to talk to him over dinner, but I didn't get a chance when Melody told us that she's giving a talk at the University of Sussex in August and asked us what she should focus on. So I should talk to him now because he kind of reminds me of Riley. They both have that sleepy-eyed stoner thing going on where they don't say much, but when they do, it's enough to let you know that they've heard every word you said. But when Pearl giggles and nudges Oren with her hip, I don't want to intrude.

I look back at the others to find Jacinta on her knees at the coffee table, laying out a Scrabble board, as Aunt Celeste calls out to me to grab a bottle of wine from the fridge and join them.

I don't have a clue when it comes to wine. Luckily, there's only one bottle, but when I close the door, I see the rota and I'm confronted by an exhausting list of chores that is divided between everyone. We're paired up. I'm with Mother Martha, then it's by couple. Iris and Marcus. Jacinta and Hunter. Aunt Celeste and Uncle Dan. And Pearl and Oren.

'What you looking at, bug?' Aunt Celeste asks, suddenly at my side.

That makes me laugh because I haven't been called that for years.

'Sorry,' I say, handing her the bottle of wine. 'I was just looking at the rota.'

'Ah, yes. I promised your mother that I'd take a photo of you cleaning out the chicken coop.'

I laugh again, but she frowns. 'You OK?'

'I'm good.'

'You were quiet during dinner.'

'I'm just tired, I guess.'

That isn't strictly a lie because I'm suddenly heavy with something that feels a lot like exhaustion. But I don't know how to articulate what it is exactly beyond saying, *I hate this bit*.

Besides, I need to be careful because if Aunt Celeste thinks something is wrong, then it'll get back to my mother and if she finds out that this summer is anything other than perfect, I'll be on the first flight to Austin.

So, I flash Aunt Celeste a smile I hope is convincing.

'Did you know that you and Oren are doing the same A levels?' She slips her arm around my shoulders. 'So, from tomorrow morning, it'll be you, me and him.'

'Yeah?' I say, surprised by the pinch of excitement that prompts. But then it's usually just me, my laptop and the army of online tutors that my mother hired. I figured it would be the same at the farm, so it will be nice to have someone to discuss the structure of the endoplasmic reticulum with.

Aunt Celeste nods. 'You guys have lessons with me. But Pearl's doing humanities, so she has hers with Melody because I have no humanity, as you know.'

'Stop.' I nudge her with my elbow. 'You're literally the kindest person I've ever met, Aunt Celeste.'

'That's sweet, darling, but while I can talk about homeostasis all day, don't ask me to explain Impressionism. I had no idea that Monet and Manet weren't the same person. I thought it was a typo.'

I laugh for real this time and the tickle of it in my chest makes me feel better.

'Sorry,' I hear Oren say, and we turn to find him and Pearl standing behind us. 'I didn't mean to eavesdrop, guys, but did I just hear that we're doing the same A levels, Ren?'

'Yes!' Aunt Celeste says, pulling me closer. 'Biology, chemistry and geography.'

'No way!'

He looks so thrilled that I try not to stare as he grins and sweeps his hair out of his face with his hand.

I guess I've been hanging out with Tab and Riley too long because I can't remember the last time I was around someone this unafraid to show that they're genuinely excited about something and it's sweet.

Disarming.

'Ren wants to be a marine biologist as well,' Aunt Celeste tells him with a proud smile.

'I know!' he says and he sounds out of breath, his whole face pink. 'Sorry to sound like a total fanboy, but you're the reason I want to be a marine biologist, Ren. You talk about it all the time and it sounds so cool.'

I'm aware of Pearl watching us, no doubt waiting for me to say something that she can pounce on. When I risk a glance at her, I expect her to look bored, but she seems thoroughly charmed by the whole exchange, her green eyes shining as Oren fists his hand in his hair and grins.

'I'm taking a gap year to volunteer on the *Rainbow Warrior*.'

'Shut up!' It's my turn to sound out of breath. 'I'd love to do that! How did you get on? It's so hard.'

'My uncle's really into deep-sea fishing so I grew up on boats. I'm only going to be a deckhand, but still.'

'I'm so jealous!'

But before I can ask him when he finds out where he's going, Melody interrupts.

'Can I steal Ren?' she says, reaching for my hand. 'I want to show her something.'

'Sure.' Oren takes a step back, then grins at me again. 'Can we talk more later, Ren?'

'Of course,' I tell him as Melody tugs me away.

As she's leading me out of the kitchen, I hear Pearl say, 'See, Oren? Told you she wasn't scary.'

I wait for her to follow it up with something less flattering, but when she doesn't, I catch myself smiling.

The dogs follow us, then head outside and turn left. When Melody and I do the same, she hooks her arm through mine as we follow Buffy and Willow around the side of the house.

'I'll let you into a little secret: walking the dogs is the easiest job on the rota,' Melody says with a mischievous smirk as we leave them under an elderly elm tree, 'because all you have to do is open the door for them in the morning and then make sure they've gone out again before you lock up at night.'

Not that they're doing much walking, I think as I turn back to see them still sitting there.

'You OK, Ren? You were quiet during dinner,' Melody says.

How quiet was I?

Concerned that she'll think I don't want to be here, I make myself smile and say, 'I'm good. I was just distracted, thinking about our book. Did you get the rough outline I emailed you yesterday? I—'

She waves her hand at me before I can finish. 'Oh, don't worry about the book right now. I'm more concerned that you're regretting your decision to come here.'

'Of course I'm not,' I tell her, making sure I look her in the eye this time.

'Then what is it?'

'It's nothing. I'm just tired,' I lie again. 'I've been travelling all day.'

'*All day?*' The gravel hisses beneath Melody's feet as she stops walking. 'Ren, please. It's an hour and twenty-eight minutes to

183

Chanctonbury from Victoria. It takes longer to walk to the gate at Gatwick.'

'I just hate this bit, you know?' I surrender with a tender sigh. 'When I get somewhere new and it's weird and awkward and I don't have a routine yet. I wouldn't know because I've never been, but I guess it's kind of like the first day of school when you don't know anyone and you're scared that you won't make any friends.'

As soon as I say *friends*, she nods.

And I realise why I feel so unsettled.

'I guess seeing Pearl and Oren tonight triggered some shit about Tab and Riley. Things are already fucked up between us, but when I go back to London, they'll be living together and it'll be even worse, won't it?'

I feel my heart sinking, melting like a sugar cube in a cup of coffee, because that's what it's going to be like when I'm around Tab and Riley from now on, isn't it?

The whispering.

The sniggering.

The private jokes.

Me watching on.

I glance back over at Buffy and Willow, who are still looking up into the tree. 'It's hard making friends when I'm always on the go. Actually, it's hard *keeping* friends,' I correct. 'I meet people all the time, but then, I go and they stay and we keep in touch, but it's not the same. I have five million followers but no one to go to the cinema with on a Wednesday afternoon.'

Melody nods again.

'I guess I thought it was different with Tab and Riley,' I say with another shrug. 'I thought we were working on something together, you know? Building something. But now it's all gone to shit.'

'Come on.' Melody holds my arm tighter and leads me away. 'I want to show you something.'

As soon as we pass the side of the house, the sky opens up and there it is.

The view I've seen on her Instagram so many times.

'God, it's beautiful,' I say, sucking in a breath as I look out at the uninterrupted stretch of green.

And I swear it even tastes green.

Like wet grass and thick moss and apple skin.

Not like London, which is even more unbearable in the summer, the heat amplifying the sour smell of piss and weed and overflowing bins, so I have to hold my breath otherwise I'll heave.

But I can breathe deep because there's no smell of rot here, the air thick with pollen and promise.

This is what I came for, I think as I try to breathe it in.

Even though the heat has simmered slightly as the sun prepares for its descent, the sky is still brilliantly blue, and when I look at it, I know why I'm so weary of London. It's not just all of this shit with Tab and Riley, it's London itself. The relentless noise and traffic and soot. The layer of filth that dulls everything it touches to the point that I can feel it inside me. Not just when I blow my nose, but actually *inside* me. I don't even notice people sleeping in the street any more and someone throwing themselves in front of a train at Gatwick has me groaning on the platform with everyone else.

But that's what happens when you can't see the sky.

185

When there's no light.

It can't get in.

'Hiraeth,' Melody says with sigh.

'Hiraeth,' I repeat.

'It means a homesickness for a home to which you cannot return. A home which maybe never was.'

As soon as she says it, something opens up inside me.

Somewhere deep.

Around a corner I've never dared turn.

'It's Welsh. Nan has a framed needlepoint of it over her fireplace, but it wasn't until I came here and stood at this spot,' Melody says, pointing at her feet, 'that it made sense. That itch I'd spent years trying to appease with the big house and the white Range Rover and the holidays to Ibiza. I thought that when my channel hit a million followers, it would go away. But it didn't. And it didn't when I hit five. Or ten. It was always there. Always making me want more. More. More. But then everything went to shit, and I had nothing.'

She chuckles sourly. 'I only went back to Newport because I had no choice. But as your mother always says, rest. Reset. Regroup. Where better to do that than the place I was born?' She tilts her head from side to side. 'But that thing in me still didn't settle. All I could think was, *This isn't it*. So, when I finally had the money together to buy somewhere, I just wanted to go home, but I didn't know where home was, you know?'

She knows I know.

But that's why she's telling me this, isn't she?

'That's why I came back here.' She stops to take a deep breath, then exhales slowly through her nose. 'Because wherever we were, we always came back here. This has always been my happy place, you know?'

I nod like I do, but I don't.

I've never had that.

But then the ground suddenly doesn't feel as steady beneath my feet as I realise that I do.

It's Riley's, isn't it?

Shit.

Maybe I'm not weary of London. Maybe I'm scared. Scared because I can feel myself taking root. I've got used to having coffee with Riley in the cemetery every morning and standing in his tiny kitchen every evening, peeling onions and chopping peppers while he skins up and tells me about whatever lecture he had that day. And I love it. This little life that I've made for myself where the guy in the corner shop knows my name and gets the roasted pistachios that I like and I know what time the last Tube is. I shouldn't have done that because when Riley moves in with Tab and I'm back to travelling with my mother, I'll be homesick.

Homesick for a home that wasn't even mine to begin with.

'Listen,' Melody says. 'It took me thirty years to find somewhere that I felt safe. So it's OK if you haven't found it yet, Ren.'

When I don't say anything – can't say anything – she looks back out at the horizon.

She's quiet for a few minutes, before she says, 'It's quite a life that your mother has chosen for herself.'

I hadn't thought about that before, but Melody's right. My

mother chose this life, didn't she? Over sipping caipirinhas at five o'clock on a nice terrace with a nice husband and a couple of nice children who sit nicely and don't interrupt conversations to correct her guests that the capital of Turkey is Ankara, not İstanbul, like I used to.

She *wants* to flit from city to city, hotel to hotel, doesn't she? To not be in one place for more than a few months before she's on to the next place. The next project. I'm just along for the ride and I can either fit into that life or not. Like now. I didn't want to go with her to Austin, but she still went. So, here I am, in someone else's happy place while she's in Austin, building another library, because she was always going to go, wasn't she?

With or without me.

'It's a remarkable life, but yours is going to be even more remarkable, Ren, because do you see those trees?' Melody raises her arm to the uneven line of darker green separating the field from the blue of the sky. 'They've been here for hundreds of years and thanks to people like you, they'll still be here, long after we've all gone. So don't worry about Tab and Riley. People come and go. Like my YouTube friends. We were inseparable for almost ten years, but when I lost everything, I lost them as well. I was bitter about that for a long time, but now I look back on it, I'm grateful to them. They helped me build my channel. We travelled the world. Celebrated birthdays and new houses and engagements. And yeah, I wish they weren't only there for the highs, but when they left, Pearl and her mum came back into my life, and I got to spend that time with her before . . .'

She trails off, then shakes her head. 'Whenever I resent my YouTube friends for abandoning me when I needed them most and I check their Instagrams to see that they're still grinding, still churning out content now that the engagements have turned into weddings and babies and bigger houses, I come out here and look at those trees and remind myself that I'm just passing through.

'We all are, Ren. One day, we'll be food for the wildflowers, but not today. How lucky are we that we get to see this? Your mother isn't the only one trying to fix the problem. You are as well. So am I, even if I have to resist the urge to flog SHEIN's new sustainable collection. There's certainly more money in it.'

She snorts. 'But I can't. I have to keep going. Keep trying. Keep pushing for change. Trust that it will happen. That I'm making a difference, in whatever small way. Because between now and whenever I become food for the wildflowers, I need to be able to say that I did everything I could. So, every time I'm offered a load of money to do a brand deal and I think about how many metres of fencing that would pay for or how I could use it to replace the boiler, I come out here and look at these trees and I remember why I'm doing it at all.'

I nod again and when she nods back, we stand there, looking out at the trees, the sky a blue that makes me ache – that makes me feel very small – as everything shifts from green to gold and the sun begins to dip. Then it's even more beautiful, the light piercing the branches of the trees so they're haloed in yellow, like a lighthouse on the horizon, and the thought that one day, all of this could be gone brings tears to my eyes.

'It's important to have someone to go to when we need to remember why we're doing this,' Melody says, her arm still hooked through mine. 'For me, it's here. For your mum, I'm

189

guessing there's somewhere in São Paulo. A place that she loved so much that she didn't want it to change, but she knew that she had to leave to make sure it didn't. I don't know if you have a place, Ren,' she says as the sun sets light to the sky, 'but if you need to borrow mine until you find it, I'm happy to share it with you.'

14

I don't even remember falling asleep, just opening my eyes and seeing gold.

I'm so used to waking up in the sweaty darkness of Riley's living room that all I can think is that I'm either dreaming or dying because I can't remember the last time I woke up to daylight. Even when I fall asleep with the curtains open in London, it's not like this. The light has to force its way between buildings or is reflected off car roofs, so when it eventually arrives, it's dull from being filtered through metal and concrete.

But this light is loud.

Pure.

The deepest, most perfect yellow that warms my face until I feel my bones shift beneath my skin like ice cubes settling in a glass. It takes a moment for my eyes adjust and when they do, I see the terracotta vase with its spray of eucalyptus and the sash window framing four squares of orange. Then I remember where I am, the sunlight bright and unafraid, drenching me as I sit up.

I kick off the sheet and walk over to it, leaning closer to the glass to watch the broken yolk of the sun, spilling, spreading, settling, until it's everywhere. I need to be out there, arms wide and head tipped back, gulping it down until I can feel it everywhere, right down to my marrow. So, I reach for the jeans and T-shirt I wore yesterday and tug them back on. I slip on my Havaianas and grab my phone from the bedside table, but as I head out of my room, I collide with Pearl as she's coming out of the bathroom.

'Sorry!' we both say at once and jump back.

But as we do, I whack my elbow on the wall.

'Sorry!' she gasps, covering her mouth with her hand as I yelp.

The shock of it knocks the air clean out of me. The air and the romantic notion of starting my first day on the farm by dancing in the sunlight. Instead it's starting with blinding pain while I try not to curse at Pearl. Which is probably a more appropriate way to mark my first full day here.

'It's OK,' I tell her when I catch my breath.

I managed to successfully avoid her last night, making sure that I waited a beat when I heard her bedroom door close before I dared open mine. But three months is a long time to be sharing a bathroom, so until we establish some sort of routine, I doubt this will be our last awkward collision.

At least neither of us is naked, I think as she takes her hands away from her mouth to apologise again.

'It's not your fault,' I tell her when the pain dulls to a hum. 'I didn't think anyone would be up this early.'

'I should have been looking where I was going.'

'Wait. How have you showered already?' I ask, blinking at her when I notice the hot-pink towel wrapped around her head. 'It's, like, five in the morning.'

'We all get up early. That's why there are no curtains in the house. Melody says it's better for us to wake up naturally.'

It probably is.

I'm usually woken up by police sirens or when Scully uses my face as a launchpad to leap off the sofa.

'It's so we can regulate our circadian rhythms, or something,' Pearl says, and while she doesn't roll her eyes, there's an edge to her voice that lets me know that she doesn't agree with Melody. 'She says that exposure to sunlight as soon as you wake up increases cortisol, which makes you more alert.'

Pearl doesn't seem more alert as she stops to yawn.

When it passes, she steps out of the doorway and as soon as she does, the smell hits me and I sigh.

'What?' Pearl asks with a frown.

'Sorry.' I shake my head, then I tip my chin up at the open door. 'It just smells so good in there. I forgot what it's like not to have to share a bathroom with a nineteen-year-old boy.'

It doesn't just smell good.

It smells of something that makes my heart shiver.

But that's not it.

It takes me a moment to realise what it is and when I do, I chuckle again.

I press my hands to my cheeks as they flush at the memory. 'It smells like PMB.'

'PMB?'

'Para Mi Bebé. It's a baby cologne.'

She looks confused. 'Baby cologne? As in cologne for babies? Or a cologne that smells like babies?'

'Cologne for babies.' I hold my hand up because I know what she's thinking. 'They're super popular in Brazil. My grandmother used to douse Mum in one called Mamãe e Bebê.'

She still looks confused, but when I smile wistfully she nods.

'It reminds you of someone,' she says, the corners of her mouth twitching.

Usually, I'd roll my eyes because why would I share that with Pearl, of all people?

But I can't stop smiling and I don't know if it's the farm working its magic on me again, or if it's smelling PMB after all this time, but I give in to the swoony flutter I feel as I recall those three months my mother and I spent in Oaxaca while she was working on a wind farm last spring. I'd discovered the bottle of PMB in a tiny pharmacy near Templo de Santo Domingo de Guzmán and became besotted with it.

I wore it every day until the bottle ran out. When it did, I was devastated because Tab *loved* it. The first thing she did when I returned to London was grab my arm and pull me to her. But as I remember the way I shivered when she leaned in, the tip of her nose grazing my neck and her eyelids fluttering dreamily as she told me how good I smelled, I can only shrug and say, 'You know what first crushes are like.'

The way Pearl laughs lets me know that she does.

'OK. I have a confession,' she says, then winces. 'My first crush was called Wren.'

'Is that why you call me Renata?' I gasp. 'I thought it was because you know it pisses me off.'

'That too.' She smirks then says, 'She worked in a café and the first time I saw her, I was besotted. I knew I liked girls, but she confirmed it because she was *so* my type. Dark hair. Nose ring. Tattoos.'

'Really?' I say, slightly surprised. 'Pearl likes the bad girls, huh?'

'I don't know about bad, but she was moody as hell.' She rolls her eyes, then adjusts the towel on her head. 'I could never get more than a few words out of her, but I tried. I talked and talked and talked—'

'That doesn't sound annoying at all,' I interrupt, eyes wide.

She ignores me and says, 'But she would just shrug and give me one-word answers. It was *infuriating*. I refused to give up, though. I found out that she only worked on Saturdays, so I dragged my mates in there every week for, like, a month, and *nothing*. She just took my order, then gave it to me.'

'You mean, like she was paid to?' I pretend to be appalled. 'What a bitch.'

Pearl glares at me. 'How was she supposed to fall in love with me if she didn't talk to me?'

'How could she not when you're harassing her while she's at work?'

'Anyway, one Saturday, I saw the café was hiring and I figured that she'd *have* to talk to me if I worked there. So, I applied because I was convinced that if she just gave me a chance, we'd fall in love.'

'And did she?'

Pearl gives me a look as if to say, *What do you think?*

I snort. 'Don't tell me, she had a boyfriend.'

They always have a boyfriend.

'She went travelling. It turns out I was her replacement.'

I shouldn't laugh, but I can't help it as Pearl huffs. 'And I couldn't quit because I didn't want to leave them in the lurch. So, I ended up working there for a year. I only left because I moved here.'

195

'Oh good, you're up!' Melody says, suddenly at my side. 'What are you two talking about?'

She turns her head between us with a suspicious frown. When she sweeps her hair up into a ponytail, I see that she looks as laid back as she did yesterday, in the same denim shorts, but she's in a Blondie T-shirt today.

'The things we'll do for love,' I tell her with an exaggerated sigh.

'OK,' she says, still frowning. 'Well, sorry if I'm interrupting, but as it's your first morning here, Ren, I thought you might like to join me to call back our magic. You're welcome to come with, Pearl.'

'Sure,' she says, unwinding the towel from around her head and shaking her hair.

As soon as she does, I'm struck by another pretty pink wave of PMB and it's enough to knock my eyes out of focus for a moment as she leaves the towel on the side table in the hall by the bathroom.

She waits for Melody to turn and head for the stairs, then whispers, 'Don't let Aunty Mel see that.'

It takes me a second to realise that she means my phone, which is still in my hand. 'Oh shit. Thanks.'

I hide it under Pearl's towel.

'What does she mean by *call back our magic*?' I lean in and whisper.

'Just go with it and try not to laugh,' Pearl warns.

I follow her down the stairs to find the front door already open, letting in a warm rectangle of light that's so bright I have to squint as we head outside. As soon as I step out into the sunshine, Buffy and Willow appear, blonde tails swishing as if to say, *Where we going, Ren?*

Over to the grass, it seems, the gravel crunching loudly, disturbing the early morning stillness as Melody walks towards the field that rolls down to the road. She stops in the middle and waits for us, hands on her hips.

'I always do my morning affirmations here, Ren,' she says when Pearl and I join her. 'It's the point where the ley lines connect so the energy is more focused.'

She kicks off her lilac Birkenstocks and when Pearl does the same with her pink flip-flops, I slip out of my Havaianas the soles of my feet shivering as I press them to the cool grass. As soon as we do, Buffy and Willow immediately collapse on to their sides beside us in the sunshine and Melody smiles down at them.

'See?' she says. 'They know.'

I smile back, but I'm not sure that has anything to do with ley lines connecting.

'You ready?' she asks with an eager smile, holding her hands out to us.

Probably not, I think, shooting a look at Pearl as she presses her lips together, clearly trying not to laugh.

'OK,' Melody says, letting out a long sigh. But when Pearl and I each take one of her hands, she tips her chin up at us. 'You two need to hold hands as well. We need to create a circle, so our energies flow.'

Then it's my turn to press my lips together because I already know that I'm going to hate this.

Don't get me wrong. I've done plenty of energy circles at

festivals and on the retreats that my mother has been taking me to since I was a kid, but the way that the usually clumsy – and slightly manic – Melody is suddenly super serene and talking in a slow, smooth voice is more disconcerting than calming.

But then Pearl reaches for my hand and when our palms touch, the shock of it makes me tug away.

'Sorry,' I mutter, shaking it off before I offer her my hand again. 'Electric shock.'

'I didn't feel anything,' she mutters back, but her cheeks are flushed.

'OK,' Melody says in that silly serene voice as she threads her fingers through mine. 'I want you to take this moment to close your eyes and just be here with me.'

I try to ignore her voice and focus on the words instead, otherwise I'm going to lose it.

So I close my eyes and inhale deeply as I think about where we are. About the stretch of unbroken blue sky over our heads and the blanket of grass beneath our feet as Melody says, 'I want you to feel your whole body. From the breeze in your hair to the sun on the back of your neck. Let the light spill down your spine and seep into each of the bones in your legs. Let it warm your feet first, then your soles as you press them into the earth, so you're connected. Rooted.'

I do as she says and it works, my toes curling in the grass.

The absurdity of Melody's performance forgotten as I let it in.

The sun bright.

Cleansing.

Burning the night away.

And everything else with it as I tell myself that this is exactly where I want to be.

Where I've chosen to be for the first time.

'Take a deep breath in through your nose,' Melody says. 'Hold it. And exhale fully through your mouth.'

I do.

It's so quiet, I can hear the breeze stirring the grass and I can taste green again.

'Now, we're going to take another deep breath in,' Melody says. 'Hold it. That's it. And now I want you to exhale fully, letting go of anything that is no longer serving you as you do.'

My first thought is Tab.

Sitting in the booth in the pub with that helix piercing she got without me.

My chest – and heart – shudder as I picture turning away from her and walking out of the pub.

And it feels good.

I feel lighter.

Lighter and stronger, all at once.

'We're going to do this one last time,' Melody says gently. 'Hold the breath. And exhale completely.'

When I do – imagining walking away from Tab in the pub as I exhale – she says, 'Now, allow your breathing to return to a rhythm that feels natural. Take this moment to just be with whatever thoughts, feelings and sensations arise and accept them without judgement as you repeat after me: I call my power back to me.'

'I call my power back to me,' I repeat with a nod.

'I call my energy back to me.'

'I call my energy back to me.'

'I call my magic back to me.'

'I call my magic back to me.'

'I am cleansed and disconnected from anything that may drain me.'

'I am cleansed and disconnected from anything that may drain me,' I repeat, then suck in a sharp breath as I remember walking out of Riley's flat yesterday afternoon with my holdall.

How I couldn't look back because I knew that I'd never be there again.

'I am shielded from any energy that does not serve me,' Melody says gently.

'I am shielded from any energy that does not serve me.'

'I am safe.'

'I am safe,' I repeat as Melody squeezes my hand.

'I am protected.'

'I am protected,' I repeat as I squeeze it back.

'I am whole.'

'I am whole.'

'And so it is.'

'And so it is,' I say with one final nod.

'Thank you, girls,' Melody says, raising each of our hands to her mouth and kissing them.

'Thanks,' Pearl and I say at once.

Melody squeezes my hand again. 'You know you're safe here, right, Ren?'

I squeeze it back. 'Of course.'

'I just want to make sure you know that because you've been getting a lot of shit online recently.'

'That's nothing new.'

'Yeah, but it's really ramped up since your case was dismissed. You've been getting death threats.'

'That's nothing new, either,' I tell her with a snort, slightly startled by the handbrake turn given that we've just let go of negative energy. 'I've been getting them since I started Out of Time. It comes with the territory.'

'I get stuff like that as well,' Pearl says with a shrug. 'It just means you're doing something right.'

I turn to chuckle and nod at her. 'Right?'

But when I turn back to Melody, she's frowning. 'It's still scary, though.'

'I know, but like you said, I'm safe here. Especially with these two.'

When I nod down at the dogs, who are still dozing in the sunshine, Pearl cackles.

Melody doesn't, though. 'Why do you think I implemented the screen time rule? I'm going to make social media work for me this time. I'm not going to let it ruin my mental health, or my career, again. Or yours.' She frowns fiercely. 'It's not good for your nervous system to be on edge all the time, Ren. Yeah, I've met some of my dearest friends online. But I dread to think how much of myself I've lost arguing with strangers over the years. At some point you have to stop defending yourself to people who are committed to misunderstanding you.'

'Hey!' I grin at Melody. 'I love her! Do you follow her on TikTok as well?'

The crease between Melody's eyebrows deepens. 'Who?'

'Franchesca Ramsey.'

'Franchesca Ramsey?'

'She said that. *Resist the urge to explain yourself to someone who's committed to misunderstanding you.*'

'Oh yes. Yes. I love her. Anyway, as I was saying, taking a break from social media will be good for you. Just be in the moment with us. You'll be surprised by how much better you'll feel. Like now,' she says with a satisfied sigh as she lets go of our hands and slips her feet back into her Birkenstocks. 'Come on, Pearl. It's your morning to cook breakfast with Oren and I believe I was promised pancakes.'

Melody turns and immediately trips on a tuft of grass but manages to correct herself as I reach my arm out to stop her. She laughs, wild and bright, then thanks me as Buffy and Willow heave themselves off the grass and follow her as she strides towards the house.

'Do you feel better now you've called your magic back?' Pearl asks as she puts her flip-flops on.

'Am I sensing some cynicism, Miss Newman?' I ask with a smirk.

'Listen. I love Aunty Mel. She can be a bit cringe sometimes, but she has a good heart. It's just hard to take something like this seriously when I know that she found that incantation on TikTok.'

'You not into this kooky New Age stuff, then?'

Pearl sniggers, then apologises. 'Sorry. That's funny because I was the kooky one at school. Everyone called me Pheebs.'

'Pheebs?'

'After Phoebe from *Friends*. I mean, I'm blonde' – she flicks her hair which is the same colour as the sun, I note with a small smile – 'and I'm a vegetarian who buys clothes from charity shops and uses a natural deodorant.'

'That's what that smell is. I thought it was the farm.'

She ignores me. 'So I guess the Phoebe thing makes sense because compared to them, I am a bit kooky. But *this*' – she stops to wave her hand over the grass – 'is a whole other level of kooky for me.'

'*This*' – I copy her and wave my hand over the grass – 'is nothing. Do you know how many of these things I've done with Mum? Last year, we did a retreat in Arizona where everyone sat in a tent and screamed.'

'Screamed?'

'Yeah, *screamed*. It's called primal scream therapy. It's about expressing your emotions and feelings in a safe and supportive environment. I googled it afterwards and it's been widely discredited.'

'I can't imagine your mum doing something like that,' she says as we head back to the house.

'Are you kidding? Of course she didn't. As soon as someone started speaking in tongues, she was out of there.' I thumb over my shoulder. 'We were by the pool at the Four Seasons in Scottsdale within an hour.'

Pearl barks out a laugh.

But I shake my head. 'We're Brazilian. You don't fuck with bruxaria.'

'Fair enough.'

'That wasn't even the worst one, though.'

'What's worse than screaming in a tent?' Pearl asks.

'A sound bath in the New Forest with a dead person.'

'What, like a spirit guide?'

'No, an actual dead person. The person lying next to me died, Pearl. Like, died until they were dead.'

She turns to stare at me. 'What do you mean they died?'

'We thought they were asleep, but they were taking that long sleep.' I raise my eyebrows. 'The last one.'

'You are lying!'

'I was ten. Do you know how traumatised I was?'

When I snigger, Pearl laughs so hard that she needs to stop and rest her hand on the Defender.

'Oh my God, Ren,' she wheezes. 'Thank you. I needed that.'

'Morning, you two,' Aunt Celeste says with a slow smile from the doorway of the house.

She looks down and when Pearl and I realise that we're still holding hands, we let go and jump apart.

As soon as we walk into the kitchen, Jacinta holds up a cafeteira and I almost fall to my knees.

'Graças a Deus e a Nossa Senhora Aparecida,' I say, then make the sign of the cross.

'We have oat milk,' she says, gesturing at a grey carton.

'She likes it black,' Pearl tells her with a smirk. 'Like her heart.'

'And don't you forget it,' I warn, toasting her with my mug.

Aunt Celeste and Jacinta chuckle, but Melody doesn't. 'What were you two laughing about before?'

She's watching us with a frown not unlike the one she gave

us when she found us outside the bathroom earlier. And I get it. Yesterday she had to separate us and this morning, we're laughing like nothing happened, so I don't blame her for being bewildered by how well we're getting on all of a sudden.

I'm equally surprised, to be honest.

But I'm sure Pearl will say something to piss me off in about twelve minutes.

'Renata was telling me about this sound bath she went to,' she says, but then stops as she laughs again.

Aunt Celeste's shoulders shiver. 'The one in the New Forest?'

'Yes!' Pearl shrieks, grabbing Aunt Celeste's hands.

The crease between Melody's dark eyebrows deepens as she watches them crack up. 'What happened?'

But before we can tell her, Oren strolls into the kitchen saying, 'Right! Who's ready for pancakes?'

There's a chorus of *Me*s and raised arms as he starts opening drawers.

'Don't worry, I'll make sure they're vegan,' he says, taking out a wooden spoon and pointing it at me. 'How do you feel about rhubarb, Ren? Iris and Marcus are on their way with some from their garden.'

As if on cue, they wander into the kitchen, the pair of them struggling to step over Buffy, then Willow, who are taking a much-needed nap by the island while they wait for Pearl and Oren to start cooking.

Or, more likely, waiting for Pearl and Oren to drop something.

'Morning,' Marcus says, then holds up a basket full of what looks like watercress with several spears of rhubarb sticking out of it. 'We come bringing the only two things that we've managed to grow this summer.'

'Look at this!' Aunt Celeste tugs out a stick of rhubarb and sniffs it when he dumps the basket on the island. 'I used to have a dress this colour, back when I was young and not covered in dirt all the time.'

I scoff because even when she's covered in dirt, Aunt Celeste out-serves us all.

'I was wearing it the night I met your mother, actually,' she tells me, poking me in the side with the stick of rhubarb, then handing it to Pearl so she can take it – and the others – over to the sink to clean them.

'Yeah?' I say, even though I've heard her tell this story dozens of times.

'It was our first Formal Hall at Sidney and in walks this girl with big hair and a bigger laugh who is just talking, talking, talking.' She waves her hands around. 'She was talking so quickly that no one could understand a word she was saying, only that they had to be near her. So, I made sure that I sat at her table for dinner and that was it.' She slaps the island. 'We've been friends ever since.'

'Hey! Hey! Hey!' Hunter announces as he wanders into the kitchen in dark blue overalls.

Everyone greets him with a cheer that makes the dogs lift their heads, then roll on to their backs when he bends down to rub their bellies. But when he walks around the island to kiss Jacinta, I realise that we're one short.

'Where's Mother Martha?' I ask, sipping my coffee.

Jacinta shakes her head. 'She rarely does breakfast or lunch with us because she's usually at the café.'

'Speaking of Mother Martha,' Oren says, pointing the wooden spoon at me again. 'I've been thinking. Maybe we should make more of an effort to eat vegan, like her, Ren and Aunt Celeste.'

'No chance,' Hunter scoffs, grabbing the cafeteira. 'I need cheese.'

'Me too,' Melody agrees. 'Besides, we've discussed this *so* many times, guys. As long as we consume dairy products in an ethical way, there's no need to be vegan. Just because we have another one in our midst now' – she pretends to glare at me – 'we shouldn't feel guilty. Besides, it's easier for Ren. We weren't raised vegan.'

'Fernanda isn't vegan,' Aunt Celeste says before I can.

Everyone else seems stunned, but I just laugh. 'Are you kidding? Mum's Brazilian.'

'Fernanda could *never* give up red meat.' Aunt Celeste waves her hand and rolls her eyes. 'She tried being vegan while we were at Cambridge, along with some other things that weren't for her, either.'

It's one of my mother's favourite comebacks so when Aunt Celeste delivers it with the playful wink, I know she'd be thrilled.

'Ah. Minha querida mãe,' I sigh again, shaking my head as I take another swig of coffee.

'What time is it?' Jacinta asks, grabbing her travel cup and an apple from the bowl. 'I've got to get to North End Farm. Charlie Boyd's cow is about to go into labour.'

When she dashes out, Oren turns the radio up as a Prince song starts playing.

'Do you guys need any help?' I ask when he hands Pearl a mixing bowl.

'Don't worry,' Melody says. 'They've got it. Besides, you and Mother Martha are doing dinner, right?'

'Yeah,' I say, glancing over at the rota as I feel a pinch of panic about what on earth I'm going to feed everyone once I've exhausted my repertoire of farofa, tapioca and rice and beans.

Not that I'll be able to make any of those things here given the thirty-mile rule, I realise.

I hope they like salad.

'We have, like, ten minutes before breakfast,' Melody says. 'Why don't I give you the tour.'

'Sure,' I say, downing my coffee.

Buffy and Willow come with us, heading out of the front door and turning left again. The door to the mystery room is still closed and if Melody wasn't trying to convince me that it's possible to produce dairy products ethically, I'd ask her what's in there. I was tempted to sneak a look last night on my way back from the bathroom while we were midway through our game of Scrabble, but I thought better of it as I imagined opening the door to be confronted by a roomful of porcelain dolls, or something.

Still, when we pass the windows, curiosity gets the better of me again and I try to snatch a look in.

I'm not as subtle as I think, though, because Melody thumbs at it. 'That's the library, by the way.'

'A *library*?'

She holds her hand up when I gasp. 'That sounds grander than it is. If you're picturing yourself swinging past on a ladder, like Belle in *Beauty and the Beast*, please don't get your hopes up. Although,' she snorts, 'it's you, so it's probably more like the Citadel from *Game of Thrones*, right?'

'The library from *Matilda*, actually,' I tell her, flicking my hair.

'Well, it's nothing like any of them. Just some IKEA shelves and a desk. I love it, though.' She shrugs. 'It's my favourite room in the house. It's where you'll be doing your lessons with Aunt Celeste and Oren.'

'What time do they start, by the way? I need to take a shower,' I realise.

I was only supposed to run down and watch the sunrise, but here I am, an hour later, still wearing what I wore yesterday. My T-shirt is so creased that they probably think I slept in my clothes, which is slightly mortifying. Then I remember that I haven't brushed my teeth, which is definitely mortifying. I cup my hand over my mouth to smell my breath and curse myself for talking so much.

Great, I think, taking a step away from Melody. *The mug of coffee I just downed is really going to help.*

'Don't worry. You've got plenty of time,' Melody tells me, then turns back to the dogs, who are sitting under the tree again and calls out to them. 'Come on, you two. Leave the squirrels alone.'

They bark, sending gravel flying as they gallop over.

They catch up when we reach the back field as Melody and I stop, because there it is again.

That view.

As soon as I look out at the row of trees on the horizon, I feel something in my chest align and I suddenly don't care about my creased T-shirt and my coffee breath and what I'm going to make for dinner tonight.

'OK,' she says with a dreamy sigh. 'I can start my day now that I've said hello to the trees.'

Me too, I think when she steps out into the field.

We walk in step, our arms swinging idly by our sides as Buffy and Willow charge ahead of us until they become two blonde dandelion heads in the distance, bobbing through the grass.

'We each have our favourite time of day here and this is mine,' Melody says as the dogs stop to sniff something in the grass. 'You're pretty much seeing it as I did for the first time three years ago.'

Melody stops to look up as a flurry of swifts swoop overhead.

'Did you know,' I say when they pass, 'that a group of swifts is known as a scream?'

'You would know that, Wednesday Addams.'

I chuckle and nudge her with my hip. 'What was this place like when you bought it?'

'The house was fine, but the rest of the land hadn't been touched for years. I had this grand plan to bring it back to life and become self-sufficient. I thought once I tidied the place up, you know, some weeding here, fix a fence there, mow the grass over there, I could get some chickens, grow some potatoes and start living the good life. But there was a storm a few days after we moved in and when a tree almost fell on the house, I realised that it was going to take more than some weeding and a few potatoes to get this place back on track.'

'That must have been scary,' I say as the dogs run back towards us, panting.

As soon as we catch up with them, they turn around and

charge off again as Melody shakes her head and says, 'I've never experienced storms like the ones here. They're wild. They have nowhere to go but right at you. You should have been here last month. It sounded like the world was ending.'

She whistles and shakes her head again. 'A tree fell across the driveway that leads up to the house. It's so big we can't move it, which is why we had to go through the field yesterday.'

'What are you going to do?' I ask with a frown. 'Are you just going to leave it there?'

'We can't. Driving through the field is fine now because it's summer, but once autumn comes and it starts raining, the field will become a quagmire and we'll be stranded,' Melody says with a shrug as the dogs disappear into a copse of trees. 'At least we'll have enough firewood for the next seventeen years, right?'

'Every cloud,' I tell her as I raise my hand to shelter my eyes from the sun.

She does the same. 'Thank God for Aunt Celeste. I was ready to sell when I realised how much work needs to be done, but she knew it had potential. She was aware of the Sussex Wildlife Trust's Nature Recovery Network, so she knew they were working with local landowners, like me, to create a mosaic of habitats for plants and animals. One day, all the local land will be connected and wildlife will just move between as though it's one.'

'That's a brilliant idea.'

'Right? We're creating a forest garden to improve biodiversity. Come on, let me show you.'

We reach the stand of trees then and I'm relieved because I can't believe how hot it is already. I can feel my T-shirt sticking to my back, which is an unwelcome reminder that I haven't showered yet this morning, but as soon as we walk between the trees and into the shade, I close my eyes and sigh.

When I open them again, the light has dimmed, the scalding sun obscured by the canopy of leaves over our heads, so it twinkles like starlight as Melody leads me over to a cluster of young trees.

'Are these apples?' I ask, stroking them.

'Yes! That's Bramley.' She beams, then points at the others. 'That's Red Falstaff. And those are Orange Pippin. We're also planting Concorde and Black Worcester pears, Avalon plums and Merryweather damsons.'

Buffy and Willow come thundering back to us.

'Easy, you two,' Melody warns.

One of them has a stick, which she drops at our feet.

As soon as she does, Melody picks it up and hurls it away from the delicate dwarf trees. It works because Buffy and Willow immediately chase after it, barking wildly as they disappear in a blur of blonde fur.

'Anyway,' Melody says, 'we're trying to create a woodland corridor for bats and birds. So we're also planting native broadleaf trees like common alder, beech and sweet chestnut. And some berry bushes. Pretty much anything that would be native to a wood like this.'

'Then out here,' we're soaked in sunshine again as she walks back into the field, 'will be a wildflower meadow to support bees and other pollinators. The plan is to eventually make our own honey.'

'What a wonderful way to use this land,' I tell her as we walk back to the house and she points out the compost heap and greenhouse and the decrepit barn the dogs like to sleep in that she wants to convert.

'The one thing being here has taught me' – she stops to show me her hands. 'apart from not wasting money on manicures, is how to protect this land.' She holds her arms out now. 'This is what we're fighting for, right? So, one day, Iris's kid can run around here with Buffy and Willow, picking apples straight from the tree.'

When she starts singing and turning in a circle like Maria von Trapp, the dogs tear over, barking wildly. I let out a sound that's somewhere between a scream and a laugh as they knock her on to her back on the grass and clamber over her as she cackles, arms and legs flying.

Melody sticks her hand up in the air and I grab it and haul her back to her feet as Buffy and Willow roll around on their backs now, barking blissfully as she brushes the fur off her.

She lost a Birkenstock in the scrum and when she slips it back on, she grins.

'Come on,' she says. 'I want to show you something else.'

She's suddenly so excited that she makes us run as she leads me up the field. From this angle, I can see the back of the house for the first time, and as soon as I do, I know *exactly* what she wants to show me.

'Oh my God!' I gasp, then burst out laughing.

She grins as she stands next to it, then cocks her hip, gesturing like it's a prize on a game show. 'Is this not the cutest chicken house that you've ever seen, Ren?'

I laugh again because *this* is what I was expecting.

Not terracotta pots and antique rugs.

It looks like a life-size Barbie Dreamhouse, the wooden slats painted various shades of pink with white trim and white shutters either side of the windows with heart-shaped holes. There's even a turquoise kidney-shaped pool for the chickens to drink out of and a few fake palm trees dotted around the long, enclosed run.

'Look inside!' she shrieks, opening a door.

When I walk over and peer in, I step back and howl with laughter. 'Is that wallpaper?'

'Yes! I had it custom made. Look! It has chickens on it!'

'This is nicer than Riley's flat!'

It smells nicer as well, I realise as she leads me inside.

Buffy and Willow follow us in, sniffing around at our feet as I ask, 'Where on earth did you find this?'

'It's actually a garden shed, but we added this roost bar and shelf, so the girls have somewhere to sit and this ladder. And we put chicken wire over the windows, which kind of looks like leading, right? Oh, and we added these for them to chill in.' She turns to show me the wall of wooden nesting boxes, each with a name painted over them. 'Not that they ever go in the right one, but it makes me happy.'

I snort and shake my head because it's ridiculous.

Absolutely ridiculous.

The whole thing is painted hot pink. Even the vaulted ceiling. And sure enough, the cream wallpaper has a hot-pink William-Morris-style print that has chickens nestled among the strawberries, leaves and flowers.

'I wanted to do this to the big house,' Melody tells me,

patting the roof with her hand with a proud smile when we go back outside, 'but Oren threatened to move out so I did it for the hens instead.'

'I see why you keep it out back.' I laugh.

The locals already think she's a weirdo so Lord knows what they'd think of this.

'Let me introduce you to the girls!' Melody says, holding the door for Buffy and Willow as they pad out.

She walks around to the run where the hens are waddling around, pecking at the straw.

The dogs follow, nudging their noses against the chicken wire, but the hens don't seem to care.

'This is Dolly,' Melody says, pointing at a brown hen with white speckles. 'The black speckled one is Sharon Needles. The red ones in the middle are Beyoncé, Kelly and Michelle, the white one is Marilyn, the gold one is Mariah and the black-and-white one with the red face, strutting around over there, is Moira Rose.'

'You have a very nice house,' I tell them.

'They're our second brood,' Melody whispers as she leads me away.

'Your second?' I ask, pulling a face.

'The first one perished when someone forgot to close the door and a fox got them.'

Someone, I think as Melody blushes, then takes my arm and tugs me back towards the house.

15

My first couple of weeks at the farm are bliss.

I'll be honest, when Melody asked me to spend the summer here, I was concerned. After all, I've never had a 'normal' routine that called on me to get up for school and be home by curfew otherwise I'd be grounded. I've never been grounded at all, in fact. Even when my mother's had to come and retrieve me from a different police cell every other week, she never tried to ground me. Probably because she grew up in a house like that and she was adamant that she didn't want me stuffing dresses and red lipstick into my school bag to change into at my friend's house, like she used to.

It's not like we didn't have any routine at all, though. But given that I barely saw her even when we still lived together, my mother couldn't enforce any real restrictions on how I spent my days beyond demanding that I check in with her assistant, Teresa, and be there when she got back, which might not be until midnight. Most of the time, though, she was in bed by ten-thirty, so she had no idea that I was still up at one in the morning, scrolling through TikTok in my hotel dressing gown. And she'd be gone again by 7 a.m., so wouldn't know that I didn't get up before eleven most mornings and all I'd have for breakfast was a black coffee and a banana.

As long as I followed the few rules she had, she didn't concern herself with what I did or when. And I liked it that way. OK, it wasn't a 'normal' family life, but we aren't a 'normal' family, are we?

So when I saw my name on the rota and realised that I have chores and I have to attend lessons in person, instead of being able to sit in a coffee shop at three in the afternoon watching a pre-recorded one on my laptop, I panicked. Not because I don't want to do those things, but because I don't want to let anyone down. I don't want to oversleep and miss breakfast or forget to close the door to the chicken coop so we lose another brood of hens.

But the moment the sun woke me up that first morning, I stepped on to the charmingly chaotic carousel of life on the farm and I've been riding it ever since. I'm up by six, collecting eggs from the coop or putting the first load of washing on before breakfast. Then I'm actually excited for my lesson with Aunt Celeste and Oren because it turns out that learning about the effect of rising river temperatures on the biodiversity of a local fish community is a lot more interesting when there's two other people to discuss it with.

The only thing I really miss is having lunch in the cemetery with Riley. But I've enjoyed sitting around the table with the family instead, teasing Melody because of something silly she said on her podcast or bickering about what to have for dinner. And I like that we always sit in the same place – me to Melody's left next to Aunt Celeste and opposite Oren – because there's comfort in that consistency.

I mean, it's just a dining chair, but I look at it sometimes and think, *That's mine.*

Plus, I like that we always return to the kitchen. Usually, Pearl, Oren and I will choose a record to listen to then join everyone around the island, each of us tasked with something, even if it isn't our night to cook. Oren will scrub the potatoes because he's the only one who cleans them properly, he insists. And Pearl and I shell peas, which invariably becomes a competition that I win, of course, while the others set the table and slice the bread and light the candles while Melody tells us about an email she got from a listener or an article she read.

Mercifully, Mother Martha takes the lead when it's our turn and I do my best to help, whisking whatever she tells me to and chopping whatever she tells me to and rinsing tayberries and raspberries as she shows me how to tell the difference between the two before we conjure them into a compote for dessert.

Then when Melody heads to bed and the others drift home, Pearl, Oren and I stray outside. It's my favourite part of the day because it's finally quiet. So quiet that I swear you can feel the Earth turning away from the sun while the stars listen as we chat idly on the bench and drink homemade lemonade that tastes like stars as well.

I can't remember the last time it was this hot in England. It's so hot, even at night, that when I sit outside with Pearl and Oren, aching for a breeze to pass and kiss my cheek, I could be on my grandparents' terrace in São Paulo, the smell of lime and sugar in the air, while 'Preciso Me Encontrar' plays and my grandfather sings along.

Time wrinkles then smooths into another day. Then another. Each one tumbling into the next. Each quiet. Ordinary. Normal, I suppose. And it's such a relief not to be constantly firefighting. To not receive an email or comment that sets my day alight and I have to stop what I'm doing to deal with it before it rages out of control.

I should be bored by now, but *this* is living, isn't it? Losing afternoons jumping in lakes with Pearl and Oren, then falling asleep in the sun, not watching my screen flash every few seconds with something else. And something else. And something else. Things that don't matter because when I eventually check my phone, it's already been forgotten and everyone has moved on to the next crisis that can't wait but can.

Plus, not having my phone stops me from checking it every time it buzzes to see if it's Riley. I know I won't hear from Tab, but I figured that he'd have been in touch, at least. But then he was never much of a texter before all of this happened. Even so, the space between replies is getting further and further apart.

That stings, but it doesn't sting as much as I thought it would. Now I only have time to call my mother, respond to the latest flurry of interview requests and event invitations, then go on Live to respond to whatever I missed since I was last on. So I don't have a chance to worry about what people are saying in my comments or to keep track of what Riley and Tab are up to because I only have those two hours a day. Then I put my phone back in my chest of drawers and I don't think about it – or that life – until I take it back out again.

The only time I feel the loss of my phone is when I want to take a photo, but that makes me focus on the moment. Actually *remember* it. So instead of doom scrolling, now I fall asleep running through a maze of memories, some old, some freshly made, turning left to find another, then right to find another. None of them connected, but still intrinsically linked somehow, because all of this is new, like knowing the number of steps it takes to get to my room and returning to a bed that looks the same because no one's touched it since I made it.

It's only been a couple of weeks, but my loud, untidy life is suddenly simple. Ordered. I wake up with the sun, then it's chores. Breakfast. Lessons. Lunch. More lessons. Then, in those precious couple of hours before dinner when the sun is bright and urging us to do something, Pearl, Oren and I head out and just walk. Along paths seamed either side with grass, fields fanning out on either side of us like the pages of an open book as we walk and walk and walk until I learn every turn. Every groove. Past the wildflowers blooming, their throats open and singing yellow as Oren tells us about the magic and mystery of Chanctonbury.

'Melody doesn't just want to live off the land,' he tells me one afternoon as he leads Pearl and I along a narrow path. 'Everything we eat is intentional. Like this.'

He stops and bends down to tug two round leaves from the green cloud sprouting by Pearl's feet. Her white VEJAs are filthy now, I notice, as I look up to find Oren holding the leaves up to us with an eager smile.

She hesitates, waiting for me to take one first.

'Taste it,' he tells us.

Pearl looks horrified, but I've been on enough hikes with my mother to not be afraid to try things, even if the cacao in Costa

Rica tasted nothing like chocolate and the jambú in São Paulo made my tongue and lips numb. But I'm curious to see what the English countryside has to offer, so I bite into it.

'Is it bad?' Pearl murmurs when my eyes widen.

'It tastes kind of like rocket.'

She tries it then and grins at Oren. 'It does.'

'Nasturtium!' He grins back. 'The leaves are full of zinc and vitamin C so they're great to ward off colds. Some people use it as an antibiotic. Plus, the whole plant is edible. The flowers are milder and a bit sweeter.'

He bends down again to pick a hot-red flower and when he hands it to me, I pluck off a petal.

'It's kind of sweet,' I say, handing it to Pearl. 'How do you know all this stuff, Oren?'

'Before I wanted to be a marine biologist, I wanted to be a botanist,' he says as we keep walking. 'That's why I love it here so much. I mean, look at this.' He stops by what looks like a fierce patch of nettles with spears of yellow flowers shooting out. 'This is agrimony. Some people use it for protection.'

He takes a few more steps, then crouches down. 'And these tiny white flowers are eyebright. People use this to treat eye infections. And some people drink eyebright tea because it's said that you'll see the truth.'

My eyebrow quirks up. 'Are these *some people* witches, Oren?'

When he stands up again, he blushes. I'm not surprised, though. Now Oren feels more comfortable around me, he's been sharing some pretty wild conspiracy theories about the climate crisis. But it's the same stuff I've been hearing at protests for years – chemtrails and geoengineering and weather manipulation – and while I do my best to challenge it, he's so convinced that him being into witchcraft isn't out of the question.

He holds his huge hands up and laughs. 'Don't worry. I have no plans for us to become Chanctonbury's answer to the Halliwell sisters. I'm interested in witchcraft in its purest sense because it's about respecting nature and reinforcing people's connection to it. Which, when you think about it, is what we're trying to do on the farm.'

'Yeah, but if we were the Halliwell sisters, I'd be Prue, right?' I check.

He closes his eyes and nods. 'One hundred per cent.'

'I'm surrounded by geeks,' Pearl snorts as we carry on up the path.

When the sun gets too thick for talking – for anything – we stop under a cluster of trees. Oren gets out the tartan blanket that he always keeps in his tote bag and we lie down, the baked grass warming our backs.

It's perfect.

One of those moments I've only ever seen on other people's Instagrams through the Hefe filter.

Except it's actually happening.

The three of us dozing on the blanket as I tell myself that I don't need to take a photo because I'll never forget it. The warm breath of the afternoon against my cheek. The grass swishing beside us. The trees swaying over us, their leaves singing. A little day music that makes me swoon. Everything is so alive I swear I hear it draw in a breath. Hear the bat of butterfly wings and mice burrowing and the hundred little wildflowers surrounding us shivering in the breeze, their petals splayed like hundreds of tiny mouths gulping down the sun.

It's perfect.

But then I feel Pearl move beside me.

I crack an eye open to find her sitting up with a frown. 'Why do you two like science so much?'

'Huh?' Oren grunts, as he sits up as well.

'She's baiting us,' I warn, as I close my eyes again.

'I'm not,' she insists. 'I'm just not fond of science.'

'You can't say, *I'm not fond of science*,' I tell her. 'It's not a pizza topping, Pearl.'

'Ren's right,' I hear Oren say. 'Science isn't something you can have an opinion on. It exists.'

I sit up, throwing my hands up at the trees. 'None of *this* would exist without science.'

She won't budge, though. 'I'd rather discover the mysteries of the universe on my own, thank you.'

'That's a romantic notion,' I tell her, tugging the hairband off my wrist and tying my hair up. 'But the way things are going, there's not going to be a universe to discover for much longer.'

'Exactly.'

When she smirks at me, it confirms that she's trying to wind us up.

Oren falls for it, though. 'So how do we fix it, then?'

'Science is just the *means* of fixing it, but it's pointless if people don't care. You can hit them with as many dire statistics and peer-reviewed papers as you like, but it will never

223

register' – she taps her temple – 'because it doesn't directly affect them. Besides, change is painful. It's painful and difficult and inconvenient so most people won't even try because they either think that we're too far gone to avoid the climate crisis or it's so far in the future that they'll be dead when it happens so why bother.'

'So how do we make them care?' Oren asks, but I already know what she's going to say.

Sure enough, Pearl shrugs and says, 'Empathy.'

'I know we're hopeless hippies, Pearl, but we're not going to love the problem away.'

I try not to laugh, but I'm surprised by Oren's sudden sass.

I shouldn't be, though. He's Melody's brother, after all. It's easy to forget that, given how different they are. Where she's spirited to the point of exhaustion at times, he has an intensity that makes me feel less self-conscious about my own. He's quiet. Sensitive. Attentive. A honey-hearted gentle giant who is clearly very proud of his sister but would rather cheer her on from the sidelines than lead the charge. He seems much happier at the farm, fixing fences and talking with us about changing the world while Melody goes out and shouts it from the rooftops. But every now and then – like now – he'll say something that makes me see a glint of his sister's spirit.

Pearl clocks me trying not to laugh and glares at me before turning back to Oren. 'Yeah, but the definition of empathy is understanding another perspective and letting it guide your actions, right?'

'OK, Kong Qiu.' He chuckles. 'How do we get them to empathise, then?'

'Books. Art. Music.' She reaches into her backpack and takes out her water bottle, which is the same shade of lilac as the T-shirt she's wearing. 'I'll learn more from Emily Dickinson than I ever will from Darwin.'

He barks out a laugh. 'Come on!'

'I will. While Darwin was riding the high seas on HMS *Beagle . . .*'

Despite my best efforts to stay out of it, I can't resist adding, '. . . devising the theory of evolution.'

Pearl ignores me. 'Emily Dickinson was a recluse yet wrote the most captivating poetry I've ever read.'

'Dickinson wouldn't know about the birds she wrote about if it wasn't for Darwin,' I remind her.

She tilts her head. 'And I wouldn't care about those birds if it wasn't for Dickinson.'

Touché, I think.

But I scoff instead. 'Caring or not caring about birds doesn't affect their existence in any way, Pearl.'

'Of course it does! You get that more than anyone, Renata.'

'Do I?'

'I've read the foreword you wrote for the reissue of *The Giving Tree.*'

That catches me off guard. 'How? It's not out until October.'

'They sent me an ARC to review for GreenGirlPearl,' she says, then points her water bottle at me. 'And in it, you said that book is the reason you started Out of Time. Not science, Renata. A book.'

'No, I said it was *one of the reasons* I started Out of Time,' I correct.

225

Oren thumbs at me. 'It's not like her mum is a prominent environmental activist, or anything.'

'Yeah, but that book made Renata understand everything her mother told her, which is . . .'

Pearl holds her arms out as she waits for us to say it, but we just stare at her.

'Empathy!' she sings. 'Would you want to be a marine biologist if it wasn't for that book?'

'*The Giving Tree* is about a tree, not the ocean.'

'You know what I mean,' she says, poking me in the side when I lie back down.

'I'll kick you!' I warn, snatching the water bottle from her and taking a swig before she sees me smile.

'Hey! I need that. I'm *so* hot. I'm burning up.' She grabs my wrist. 'Feel.'

But when she presses my palm to her forehead, I can't feel a thing because I'm burning up as well.

16

'Olá, minha querida filha. Tudo bem?' my mother sings as soon her face appears on the screen of my laptop.

'Good. How's Austin?'

'Hot. How's Chanctonbury?'

'Hot,' I tell her, watching her walk into the kitchen.

It looks like every kitchen in every apartment we've ever stayed in.

Clean.

Neat.

Anonymous.

The opposite of the cheerful chaos at the farm with its constant, easy buzz. The radio always on and the kitchen always cluttered with people, somebody always chopping something or baking something. I wake up to the sound of laughter every morning and fall asleep to the sound of Oren snoring down the hall every night and I suddenly feel very sad for my mother, by herself in that empty apartment.

'You look so well, querida. The farm air clearly agrees with you.'

I study my face on the screen.

I can't remember the last time my skin looked so clear.

'So, you've been doing as I said?' she says, turning to open a cabinet.

'You'd be proud. I actually baked owl bread the other day.'

She grabs a glass, then turns back to her laptop with her eyebrow raised. 'Owl bread?'

'Yeah. Pearl, Oren and I made loaves in the shape of owls for Lammas. Apparently it pleases the spirits.'

I thought she'd freak out but instead she nods. 'Yes, of course. Tuesday was August 1st.'

'How do you know about Lammas?'

'Renata, por favor. I've known Celeste since we were eighteen. I know all about these witchy festivals.'

'She and Oren were *super* excited. We broke one of the owl loaves into four pieces then buried them in the four corners of the barn to protect the fruits of the harvest. Then we shared another one over dinner, to bring us blessings and keep us protected from harm during the upcoming harvest. But, before dinner, we made jam with some of the fruit from Aunt Celeste's garden and took it up to Chanctonbury Ring.'

'What was that like?' my mother asks from inside the fridge as she pulls out a carton of coconut water.

'Spooky,' I tell her, my eyes wide. 'I'm glad we went during the day.'

'What's up there?'

'Just a ring of trees, but I kept thinking about the stories Oren told me about aliens and the devil.'

'O diabo?' she gasps, almost spilling the coconut water as she pours.

'According to local legend you can summon the devil on midsummer's night by running around the ring of trees seven times. Apparently, when he appears he offers you a bowl of soup in exchange for your soul.'

'Renata, you didn't!'

'We tried,' I tell her with a shrug, 'but midsummer was in June . . .'

'Que Nossa Senhora Aparecida nos proteja e nos abençoe sempre!'

'Mum, I'm kidding!' I say with a wicked cackle. 'We just left more bread as an offering to the Earth along with some strawberries and dahlias from Aunt Celeste's garden.'

'Graças a Deus,' she says, her hand on her chest, then takes a long sip of the coconut water.

'Aunt Celeste sends her love by the way.'

'How is she? I miss her.'

'Good. Pearl and I helped her sew some kohlrabi this morning,' I tell her with a proud smile, but as soon as I do, I feel a swift stab as I realise that I probably won't be here to harvest it in the autumn.

'Lovely Pearl. How is she?'

My heart does this weird fidgety thing at the sound of her name.

But I ignore it as I shrug and say, 'Yeah, she's good. Annoying as always.'

'And how's Melody?'

'I haven't seen much of her now school's done. Only at dinner.'

'Before I forget,' my mother says. 'Giles emailed me about your book contract. He was waiting for a response from Penguin, but you can sign it now. I know Melody said there was no rush, but please tell her that I'm sorry it's taken so long.'

When I see myself frown on the screen, I force myself to smile because I'd forgotten about the book.

Melody hasn't mentioned it.

'Melody seems to be everywhere at the moment,' my mother says, as she turns to put the carton back in the fridge. 'Every time I turn on the radio or open the newspaper, there she is.'

'Really?'

I guess that explains why I've barely seen her.

She's always busy, busy, busy.

Always out.

Always on the phone.

Always in the library with the door shut.

She stops to point her glass at me. 'What did you think of her *Teen Vogue* article by the way?'

'I haven't had a chance to read it yet,' I lie.

Melody hasn't mentioned that, either.

'You should, Renata. It's about you.'

'Me?'

'Well, it centres around Out of Time, but the thrust of it is about young climate activists being harassed online. She makes an excellent point about how people your age are scared to publicly engage with these issues for fear of being abused as well. Although, that's the point of the trolls, isn't it? To discourage debate.'

'Yeah,' I say, but I'm not listening as I ask myself why Melody hasn't told me about the article.

After we say goodbye, I look it up.

My mother's right: it's brilliant. But even though it's preceded by the photograph Pearl took of me outside The Dorchester, Tab and Riley are quoted throughout, while I'm only mentioned in passing.

Why would Melody speak to them about Out of Time and not me?

I mean, I'm *right here*.

In her house.

And why would Tab and Riley even speak to Melody?

Weren't they the ones telling me to separate Out of Time from my friendship with her?

I'm tempted to fire off a message to our group chat pointing out the irony, but before I do, I make myself take a breath and read the article again to make sure that I'm not overreacting. When I do, I realise that at the beginning, Melody refers to 'groups like Out of Time', but when she later introduces Tab and Riley, she calls them 'young climate activists'.

That's weird, I think as I check my email.

The most recent unread message was sent twelve minutes ago.

Subject: Time to Say Goodbye

My eyes blur as soon as I see it so I can't see clearly enough to read all of it but I get the gist.

Tab and Riley are quitting Out of Time to start their own group.

I'm consumed by a wave of anger so fierce that it brings fresh tears to my eyes as I reach for my phone. It's been so long since I've called Tab that I can't find her name in my Recents log. I have to search for her in my phone book instead, but when I hit 'Call', it goes to voicemail.

'*Coward*,' I mutter, opening our group chat and sending her a message.

Quitting on email, Tab.

Nice.

She's online and I hold my breath when I see that she's typing. Then she stops.

I wait a beat or two, then type, *Is this really how it ends?*

My message only has one grey check mark, though, and I curse the reception at the farm.

So I try to call Riley and it goes to voicemail as well.

Wait, I think, my stomach turning inside out, *have they blocked me?*

I check Tab's Instagram and the grid is blank with *No Posts Yet.*

I stare at my phone, telling myself that it's just a glitch as I close Instagram and reopen it.

But there it is again.

No Posts Yet.

My hands shake as I do the same with Riley's.

This account is private.

I message him to ask what's going on, but the same thing happens.

And that's how it ends.

With one grey check mark.

17

I'm devastated.

There's no other word for it.

I thought I was doing a good job hiding it, because no one else noticed, but Pearl kept looking at me across the table during dinner while Melody told us about her 5 Live interview. I tried to smile when everyone else did and laugh when everyone else did and congratulate Melody when everyone else did, but Pearl kept looking. And when they all went to bed but I didn't, concluding it was pointless because I knew I wasn't going to sleep, Pearl followed me when I went outside and sat next to me on the bench. But she didn't say a word. She didn't try to fill the stiff silence or make a joke as I sat there, shell-shocked, the horror of it still heavy around my shoulders. She just waited until the anger burned away, but the tears stayed and I told her what happened.

All she said was, *I'm so sorry, Renata.*

Not *I told you so.*

Or even *Fuck Tab and Riley. You don't need them*, like Melody would have.

And I'm glad she didn't because that isn't true.

Even though Pearl saw this coming well before I did, the end point remains the same.

So we sat there, her eyes shining in the dark as mine blurred again.

When they did, it felt like we were sitting on the seabed, somewhere out of reach, the stars shimmering over us like mermaid scales. But then they disappeared, the sky thick as the trees tossed their heads back in the wind and when I felt the first drop of rain on my nose, Pearl said we should go back inside.

She leaned over and kissed me lightly on the cheek as she did. It was only for a second, but it was enough to make me wait before I trusted my legs to stand up and follow her into the house.

That's another reason I can't sleep.

I can't stop thinking about that either.

About her mouth on my cheek, and if I'd just turned my mine . . .

'Nope,' I say into the dark, kicking off the sheet as the storm continues to spit and howl outside.

I can't think about *that* right now.

My head is wrecked enough as it is.

I slip out of my room down to the kitchen, but the light is on and as soon as I walk in, there she is.

'I came to check on Buffy and Willow,' Pearl says, looking up from the sofa. 'They're scared of storms.'

I look down at the dogs, who are fast asleep on the rug at her feet, then up at her and there's a moment where we just stare at each other. I don't know why it's so awkward because nothing happened. It was just a peck on the cheek so why do I suddenly not know what to do with my hands?

Still, it's enough to make me want to lie and say that I only came down for a glass of water then scuttle back to my room, hoping that – much like the storm – this weirdness has passed by morning. But then there's a flash of lightning so bright that it makes the living room windows go from black to white, and when Pearl's hands fist in the blanket around her shoulders, I realise why she's down here and I can't leave her by herself.

'Cocoa?' I ask, walking into the kitchen.

'There isn't any,' she says, then jumps at the urgent crack of thunder that follows.

I almost jump as well so I don't blame Pearl for being scared because the rain sounds like waves slapping the side of a boat that's sinking, the wind singing like sirens saying, *This is it.*

This is it.

I hold up a tin of cocoa to distract her as the windows rattle.

'I brought all the essentials,' I tell her as I root through the cabinets for a pan. 'Coffee. Cocoa. Bourbons.'

'You have Bourbons?' she asks, shrugging off the blanket.

The dogs lift their heads when she stands up, then promptly fall back asleep as she walks over to me.

'Course,' I say on my way to the fridge. 'I know what I'm doing. I also brought a carton of cigarettes to barter with and a spare toothbrush I can turn into a shank if Mother Martha starts with me.'

'Hey, prison jokes are my thing.'

She pulls a face, but I can tell that she's trying not to smile.

Then I'm trying not to as well as I think, *I did that. I made her feel better.*

But just as her shoulders begin to fall, they shoot up as the storm makes its presence felt again.

So I stand back from the open fridge door and point inside. 'Do we have any oat milk? I can't find it.'

She looks away from the window to glare at me. 'Of course there's oat milk. There's, like, two cartons.' She stomps over to the fridge and grabs one. 'See? It was right in front of you, Renata.'

'Thanks,' I say, taking it from her and heading back to the stove.

The windows start rattling again and when she looks over at them, I gesture at the tin of cocoa.

'Can you make a paste while I'm doing this?'

'Sure,' she says, grabbing two mugs from the cabinet. 'I know what you're doing, by the way.'

'What am I doing?'

'Trying to distract me from the storm,' she says as she begins spooning cocoa into each mug.

'I'm just making cocoa.'

She snorts, but she doesn't fight the smile this time as she mixes the paste.

'I can't believe that I used to be scared of you,' she tells me.

'I'm glad to hear that,' I tell her with a slow smile.

That makes her look up. 'You're glad that I used to be scared of you?'

'No, I'm glad that you're not any more.'

We stay like that for a while, the candles burning down and the walls drawing in as we chat about nothing.

And it's nice.

Easy.

If you'd told me back in February, when Pearl and I were bickering in that police cell, that seven months later, we'd be making cocoa while I try not to stare at her mouth, I would have laughed in your face.

'I need to tell you something,' Pearl says as I yank the pan off the stove before the milk boils over.

'Yeah?' I say, glancing back over at her as it bubbles down.

She doesn't look at me, only into the paste she's still stirring. 'You're probably wondering why I'm living here. I told everyone not to tell you because I wanted to tell you myself, but it's never the right time. And I know you've had enough to deal with today, what with all this stuff with Tab and Riley. You don't need my drama as well, do you? But Oren is *stressing out* that he's going to let something slip. He and Melody are a lethal combination of awful liars with big mouths so it's an actual miracle neither of them have told you already so I shouldn't push it any longer.'

She says it all at once and the edge of panic in her voice makes me put the pan down on the stove.

She finally looks up at me.

'I'm just going to say it and I don't want you to be all, like, weird and nice,' she warns with a furious frown. 'Because if you're nice to me, Ren, it will make me cry and I really don't want to cry.'

Don't cry, I think because I don't know what I'll do if she does.

As I watch her eyes fill with tears, I realise that it's not just panic I'm feeling. It's whatever made John Wick take that sledgehammer to his basement floor as I grasp at a series of increasingly hysterical scenarios that range from *She doesn't get on with her parents* to *She's in witness protection*.

But as I'm asking myself if she's here to avoid an unhinged ex, she blurts out, 'My mum died.'

'What the fuck?' I yell.

Like, literally *yell*.

As responses go, that has got to be up there with one of the worst.

But I'm so stunned that it just comes out.

'I'm sorry!' I press my hands to my cheeks, mortified. 'I can't believe I said that.'

Luckily, she laughs.

'Don't apologise,' she says, reaching past me to turn the gas off before the milk boils over. 'I think that's the most honest response I've had so far. Most people cry and I'm the one who ends up comforting them.'

Does she want me to comfort her? I panic.

Should I be hugging her?

Stroking her hair and telling her that it will be OK?

But I'm not the stroke-your-hair-and-tell-you-that-it-will-be-OK kind of friend.

I'm not sure what kind of friend I am, actually, but I suspect it's closer to John Wick.

Pearl doesn't seem to be waiting for me to do any of that, though, as she reaches for the pan and divides the hot milk into the mugs while I just stand there. 'It was in the new year, so . . .' She stops, hearing how that sounds, then laughs again and waves her hand. 'What I mean is that it's not as fresh as it was.'

I nod as she hands me one of the mugs.

The dogs look up again as we walk over to sit on one of the sofas, then Willow comes over to lie across Pearl's feet as I put my mug on the coffee table then turn to face her.

'I'm sorry. I'm so bad with stuff like this,' I say, in case it isn't already obvious.

'What?' She laughs again. 'Feelings?'

'No,' I say, then I think about it. 'Well, yeah, but parent stuff.'

'You talk about your mum all the time.'

'No, *other people's* parent stuff. I never ask about them because of Riley.'

'Riley?'

'Yeah, he grew up in care—'

'Why did I think he was loaded like you and Tab?' she interrupts with a frown.

'No way!' I scoff as I reach for my mug. 'He was in a group home from the age of nine, but that's all I know because he won't talk about it. Like, *ever*. He says that you should never ask anyone something about their life unless they're willing to volunteer it because, chances are, there's a reason why they haven't told you already.'

'I get that.' Pearl nods. 'Mum grew up in care as well.'

'She did?'

'Similar situation to Riley. She never talks about it, either.'

I note that she uses the present tense and it gets me right in the throat.

I wonder if she notices as well because Pearl goes quiet as she looks into her mug while I look at her.

After stirring her cocoa a few times, she says, 'I get what Riley means about not asking people stuff that they haven't told you already. Is that why you never talk about your dad?'

That's breaking Riley's rule, ironically.

But I don't care.

'There's nothing to talk about.' I shrug. 'I've never met him. He peaced out before I was born.'

'Have you ever tried to find him?'

'No,' I snort. 'He has no interest in me so why should I have any interest in him? Mum keeps track of him on Facebook in case I ever do, though. Or if I need a kidney, or something. The one, and only, time I asked about him, she told me that he was living on an ashram in Bali, which is all I need to know, to be honest.'

'I've never met my dad, either,' she tells me with a sniff. 'He died. Heroin.'

'Shit. Sorry.'

I curse myself for another staggeringly inappropriate response.

'It is what it is.' She shrugs, unfazed. 'Until Mum and Melody reconnected, it was always just me and Mum against the world. You get that, right?'

All I can do is nod as I suddenly miss my mother with such urgency that I can't catch my breath.

'But Melody came back into our lives just when we needed her the most.' She stops and turns her cheek away, but I can see the faraway look in her eyes, as though she's standing on the deck of a boat, reeling the memory in as she says, 'It was like she knew, because a month after she got back in touch, Mum found the lump in her breast. It was Melody who made

240

her go to the doctor. And it was Melody who went with her to all the blood tests and the scans and took her for the biopsy, while I carried on going to school and pestering Mum to let me get my ears pierced because I was ten and I didn't have a clue that anything was going on. And it was Melody sitting next to Mum at the kitchen table when she told me that it was cancer.'

Pearl shrugs again. 'The doctors had caught it early so she said that she was going to be fine. And she was. But last Halloween . . .' She dips her head and when she lifts her chin again, there are fresh tears in her eyes. '. . . It had metastasised to her lungs and that was it. By the end of February, she'd gone.'

'Christ,' I choke out, then curl my fingers around my neck. 'That's so fast.'

She nods, then gets that faraway look in her eyes again. 'So when I was arrested at the protest outside The Dorchester, it was towards the end and all I could think was, *What if it happens now and I miss it?*'

My whole face burns as I remember how I acted in the cell.

Shrugging and waving my hand as I told her that it was nothing.

That we were just going to get a slap on the wrist and be sent home.

I feel wretched, but she says, 'How were you to know? I lied. I told you the police had called Mum, when they'd actually called Melody. I don't know what I would have done without her. She promised Mum she'd take care of me, and she has. She's in the process of adopting me, even though she doesn't need to because I'm sixteen.'

'That's amazing.'

'I mean, I miss Mum in a way that I don't think I'll ever get over.' She finally looks me in the eye. 'But I'm glad I'm here because I've never had a family before. It's kind of nice, isn't it?'

'Yeah,' I say with a nod, my chin shivering. 'It kind of is.'

18

Pearl says she isn't tired.

I don't know if that's true or if it's the storm still swirling outside, but she's clearly keen to talk.

'Tell me another story,' she says, in that way you do when you're about to fall sleep.

When you'll say anything.

All the things that you'd never be brave enough to say when you're awake.

That's one of the good things about always moving around: I have plenty of stories, even if they were earned in an effort to make the most of the time I had in places I didn't really want to be. So, if Pearl wants to hear one, I'm happy to oblige. Although, I suspect she doesn't. She's just wants to talk about anything but her mother, so she's doing that thing where she asks me something before I can ask her something and that's OK. So, when the rain eases to a steady shower as the storm tires itself out, I tell her about the polar bears in Svalbard and the elephant sanctuary in Rambukkana and the turtles hatching on the Galápagos Islands.

'I don't even have a passport,' Pearl says, reaching down to scratch Willow's head, which makes her stretch her legs out as Buffy snores on the rug by my feet. 'But then, I've never needed one. Mum had, like, three jobs, so aside from the odd weekend in Newport to see Melody, we couldn't afford to go anywhere. Actually' – she points at me – 'we met Melody in Cornwall for a wedding last summer. Have you ever been?'

'I was in Cornwall last summer!' I laugh, but the sound dies in my throat as I remember sitting on that beach towel with Tab and the heat of her leg next to mine as we looked out at the sea, watching Riley surf.

'No way! What part?'

I clear my throat and say, 'Fistral Beach.'

'We were in St Ives.' She sounds disappointed. 'It would have been funny if we were in the same place.'

'Yeah,' I murmur, looking up at the shadows shivering across the ceiling in the candlelight.

But when I look over at the window, I see that it isn't the candles as the storm gives way to the sun.

'It's over,' Pearl says with a sigh as we sink back into the sofa.

We sit like that for a while, our heads tipped back against the sofa cushion as we gaze at the sun rising through the windows, the honey-thick light suddenly brazen and unavoidable. And I don't know what Pearl's thinking, but I'm thinking about last summer and how I'm kind of glad that she and I weren't in the same place. My cheeks sting as I imagine how Tab and Riley would have reacted if we'd bumped into her, especially if she was with Melody. I probably would have been vile to her as well, joining in with the smirks and eye rolling and the twenty minutes of mocking that would have no doubt ensued as soon as we walked away.

I don't even know who that person is any more.

'Where was your first kiss?' Pearl asks suddenly.

The shock of it makes my heart stutter. When I turn my head to look at her, the golden light slanting through the window strikes the curve of her cheek in such a way that my heart does more than stutter because she looks so beautiful that I have to look away again. When I do, it reminds me of the first time I saw Gustav Klimt's *The Kiss* at the Belvedere in Vienna as a child and I had to turn my back to it because the gold hurt my eyes.

'Come on.' Pearl nudges me with her elbow. 'Tell me.'

'Where was your first kiss?' I say, stalling so I can catch my breath.

She rolls her eyes. 'I'm sure your first kiss was somewhere way more glamorous than mine. But if you must know, it was at the bus stop outside Brighton station.'

'Fine,' I concede with a chuckle. 'Mine was somewhere *slightly* more glamourous.'

'Where?'

'The Túria Fountain in Valencia. I'd just thrown a penny in and wished that she'd kiss me, then she did.'

'And your last kiss?'

This one hurts.

'The toilet of a pub on Earl's Court Road. She said she was drunk, but she wasn't.'

I wonder if Pearl knows it was Tab because she asks, 'When was that?'

'A few weeks before the protest at The Dorchester.'

Pearl thinks about that for a moment, then says, 'Do you want a better last kiss?'

245

I don't know what she means, but I turn my head as she turns hers. Then she licks her lips, and I don't know what happens, just that my hands are reaching for her face and her mouth is finding mine and as soon as our lips touch, it provokes a sound that I've never heard in the back of my throat.

I gasp when we pull apart, her cheeks hot against the pads of my fingers. 'What was that?'

'I don't know,' she gasps back, her eyes black. 'But do it again.'

I lean in as she leans in and it startles me how easy it is. I tilt my head as she tilts hers and we just fit. It's not clumsy like it was with Naomie by that fountain in Valencia, the pair of us giggling and stepping on each other's toes. Or delirious like it was the last time with Tab when she grabbed me by the front of my shirt. Our teeth collided so it felt more like a bite than a kiss, and she tasted of mischief and cider as she licked her way into my mouth, then laughed against my lips before she pushed me away again and said, 'I'm so wasted!'

Looking back on it now, I should have known then that was all we were ever going to be.

But I believed Tab when she said *Soon*.

When she said *Not yet*.

Believed that when we stayed up all night making lists of the things we wanted to do and the places we wanted to go, that our lives would eventually blossom beyond breathlessly kissing when no one was looking.

So, I can't help but ask myself if the same thing is happening as Pearl clings to me the way Tab used to, her tongue slow and warm in my mouth and her hands fisted in my hair. But as she's climbing into my lap, I hear Oren's big, goofy laugh. We spring apart as he thunders down the stairs, then stare at each other, panting.

'You two up already?' he asks as he strides into the kitchen.

'We wanted to watch the sunrise,' Pearl says and, God, she's a good liar.

But Oren just claps his hands and says, 'I was thinking, why don't we have the mushrooms we picked yesterday for breakfast? I think there's enough bread left.'

'Coffee,' Jacinta mutters, charging into the kitchen in filthy denim dungarees. She looks like she hasn't slept, either, as she reaches for the kettle and says, 'The storm made one of Annie Hayes's mares bolt and we've been chasing her through the village since 3 a.m. Christ, I remember when I was your age, kids, and I spent my Saturday nights puking in bushes, not chasing horses. What's happened to my life?'

'Did you catch her?' Oren asks.

'Yeah, but not before she trampled Mrs Flynn's prize peonies.'

With that, the kitchen is full again. I watch from the sofa, my lips still trembling while Oren and Jacinta clean mushrooms and laugh about Mrs Flynn's poor peonies as everyone else drifts in for breakfast.

Everyone but Melody, who is nowhere to be seen as Pearl and I walk over to join them around the island.

'Can we have something a little more upbeat, please?' I ask, gesturing at the radio when Petroc Trelawny announces a track called 'Jesus' Blood Never Failed Me Yet'.

But Oren shakes his head. 'Melody likes Radio 3 on Sunday mornings.'

'She's not even here,' Jacinta points out.

'Mel won't mind, Oren,' Aunt Celeste says, walking over to the radio and switching it to 6Music.

A David Bowie song is playing and we all cheer with relief.

'Can someone slice the bread?' Jacinta asks. 'We'll need two loaves, right? One for us and one for Oren.'

There's a ripple of laughter as he goes to grab another chopping board.

'Ren and I will get the eggs,' Pearl suggests, snatching the wire basket from the island.

'Oh brilliant! Thanks, girls,' Jacinta says, but Pearl is already hurrying out of the kitchen.

I follow, Buffy and Willow at my heels. Pearl's in such a rush that she manages to make it out of the front door before them and I follow to find that everything is deep, deep green after the rain the night before.

I have to trot to catch up to Pearl, but when her blonde hair flashes in the sunshine as she disappears around the side of the house, it's harder to put one foot in front of the other as I think, *Here we go.*

Pearl wants to have The Conversation, doesn't she?

The I Don't Know What Just Happened, Renata. But it Can't Happen Again conversation.

Oh God, what was I thinking?

Why did I kiss her?

Now I'm going to have to spend the rest of summer avoiding her.

When I get to the chicken coop, she's already inside, so I take a deep breath before I go in.

'Listen, Pearl,' I say as soon as I close the door behind me because we don't need to do this.

It was just a kiss.

A kiss so good that it felt like it disrupted the space-time continuum, but whatever.

'Hold on, Ren.' Pearl holds her hand up. 'Can I just say something?'

Before I can respond, she reaches for the front of my T-shirt and kisses me again.

She pulls me to her so suddenly that I stagger forward and she staggers back and when we regain our balance, she lets go of my T-shirt to wrap her arms around me.

No one has ever held me like that before.

Like they want to.

Like they *have* to.

Like they might fall if they don't.

She drops the wire basket and when it lands at our feet, the hens screech.

The sound of it makes us jump apart and stare at each other.

'What were you going to say?' she asks, chest heaving.

'I can't remember.'

I can't even remember my own name.

'Shall we not talk, then?' she says, her green eyes black again.

'I'm good with that,' I tell her, kissing her this time.

Except, it's less of a collision as we melt into it, her hands fisted in the back of my T-shirt.

Mine are cupping her hot cheeks as I hear that sound in the back of my throat again because *Oh God.*

Oh God, oh God, oh God.

Pearl's a good liar, but she's an even better kisser.

When her mouth finally slides away from mine, I immediately miss the heat of her. But before I can catch my breath, her mouth finds mine again. I stagger forward, but there's nowhere else to go in the tiny chicken coop. So we fall against the door and as we do, she knocks the back of her head on the frame.

Pearl laughs into my open mouth and I pull away to ask if she's OK.

'Don't worry, I've got a hard head.' She laughs again.

'We should get back before Oren comes looking for us,' I realise, shaking my head until my eyes refocus.

'I like you, Ren,' Pearl says so suddenly that everything swims back out of focus.

'Huh?' I grunt, once again proving that I shouldn't be allowed to talk to people.

Or Pearl, at least.

'I like you, Ren,' she says again. 'Do you like me?'

'Yeah,' I hear myself say.

And that was easy.

Is this how it's supposed to go? I think as she smiles, and I lean in to kiss her again.

But she stops me. 'What about the others?'

'I'd rather kiss you.'

'No!' She slaps my arm. 'I mean, should we tell them?'

'Do you want to?'

'Well, I don't *not* want to,' she says, which makes my heart fizz. 'But you know what they're like.'

'What do you mean?'

She tilts her head at me as if to say, *Come on*. 'Nothing

happens here. Like, nothing. And I love that. That's one of my favourite things about living here; there's no drama. But how do you think they're going to react when they find out about this?' She stops to gesture at the space between us. 'That horse trampling Mrs Flynn's prize peonies *was* going to be the hot topic of conversation over breakfast.'

'OK,' I say warily, sensing where this is going.

She raises her eyebrows, her head still tilted. 'Imagine: instead of Mrs Flynn's prize peonies, they're talking about us. And instead of breakfast, it's every meal for the rest of the summer.'

'That's an excellent point.'

'I just want to enjoy this because this is the best part.' She sighs dreamily and steps forward to hook her arms around my waist. 'You know? The beginning. When we're getting to know each other all over again and learning things we didn't know before. Fun things.' She waggles her eyebrows, then nudges my nose with hers. 'And I don't want them asking a load of questions that we don't know the answers to yet. Do you?'

'God, no,' I grunt. 'What's the plan, then?'

Pearl shrugs. 'Let's tell them when we know what the answers are.'

'That makes sense.'

'Besides, I don't want this to be weird for Oren. I love hanging out with him. He's like my brother.'

A shiver of dread scuttles across my scalp then as I remember how many times Tab said that about Riley.

'Actually, he will be when Melody adopts me,' Pearl says as my heart throbs ominously.

'I guess so.'

'So I don't want him to feel like he's third-wheeling it with us.'

'Uh-huh.' I nod, taking a step back because here they come. The excuses.

Sure enough, Pearl frowns. 'And what if Aunty Mel's weird? She's no prude, but we're technically living together. Or what if Celeste tells your mum and she doesn't like us sleeping across the hall from each other?'

She's right – after all, my mother only let me stay with Riley because she knew that there was nothing going on between us – but all I can think is, *I'm not doing this again.*

I can't do this again.

I'm about to back out of the chicken coop and tell her not to worry – that it's not worth it – when Pearl closes her eyes and groans. When she opens them again, she shakes her head.

'Sorry, Ren. This was so perfect and I'm ruining it, aren't I?'

'Perfect?' I say with a slow smile.

'Yeah,' she says and she sounds so sure that I let out a silly giggle as she reaches for me again. 'But you should probably know that this won't be the first time I ruin a perfect moment by overthinking.'

'No, it's nice,' I realise when the panic subsides. 'That you've thought about it.'

'You're all I think about,' she whispers, her eyelids heavy.

I lean in to kiss her again, but we jump when one of the chickens shrieks.

Pearl curses under her breath then kisses me quickly on the cheek. 'We should get back.'

We grab as many eggs as we can and as we're stepping back out into the sunshine, Pearl turns to smile at me, and I reach for her hand. But before I can, there's Melody, watching us with her Spice Girls mug.

'Morning,' Pearl and I say at the same time.

'Morning, you two.' She looks between us, her eyebrows rising slightly. 'What are you up to?'

Pearl holds up the wire basket.

She looks at it, then at us. 'It's Oren's day to collect the eggs.'

'I know.' Pearl shrugs. 'But he's helping Jacinta, so we offered to do it.'

'Well, look at you two being so helpful.'

There's a strange beat of silence that Pearl interrupts. 'There's enough for omelettes.'

Melody loves omelettes, but it doesn't seem to register, her eyes on me now.

All I can think is, *She knows* as we follow her back to the house.

As soon as we walk into the kitchen, Melody stops to survey the scene.

'What's going on in here?' she asks crisply. 'Are we having a kitchen party?'

'Yes!' Jacinta says from the stove. 'Come join us!'

But Melody frowns. 'What happened to Radio 3?'

'Sorry, Mel,' Oren mutters, striding over to switch it back.

'That's better,' she sighs, refilling her mug, then heading into the library.

19

'Let's just eat,' Aunt Celeste says with a sigh. 'Mel wouldn't want all of our breakfasts to be ruined.'

'They already are,' Hunter mutters and there's a rumble of agreement.

'We can't eat without Mel,' Oren says with a frown, then pushes his chair back. 'I'll remind her again. She probably got caught up, replying to an email, or something.'

Pearl puts her hand on his. 'You've already reminded her twice, Oren.'

'Oh! You're all here!' Melody sings as she strolls into the kitchen.

'We have been for twenty minutes,' Hunter says under his breath.

But no one else says anything as Melody sits at the head of the table and holds her mug out to Oren.

'This looks delicious,' she says as he refills it.

'Mushroom omelette.' He grins. 'Your favourite, Mel.'

I clock Jacinta's clipped smile as she asks, 'Why are you so busy at eight o'clock on a Sunday, Mel?'

'I've got *so much* on,' she says, eyes wide. 'I can't keep up with the requests since the *Guardian* asked me to comment on that Online Safety Act report. Now I have to go to Salford to discuss it on *Woman's Hour*.'

Iris beams. 'I love *Woman's Hour*.'

'Remember the first time Fernanda was on *Woman's Hour*, Ren?' Aunt Celeste snorts.

I chuckle. 'Yeah. Jenni Murray versus my mother was quite something.'

Melody watches us as we nudge one another, but when Marcus asks what happened, she raises her mug and says, 'Plus, Denmark's climate minister is going to be on my podcast on Tuesday, so I need to prepare for that, as well as my talk at the University of Sussex at the end of the month. There's not enough hours in the day!'

'Have you decided what you're going to focus on?' Oren asks as he butters a slice of toast.

'How environmental activism is evolving. This discussion around the Online Safety Act is perfect timing, actually. I definitely want to talk about how the purpose of online abuse is often to shut down the conversation.'

'That's an excellent follow-up to what you wrote about in *Teen Vogue*,' I tell her with a smile.

'What's that about *Teen Vogue*?' Pearl asks.

There's a stretch of silence as Melody turns to look at me.

When she doesn't say anything, everyone looks at me as well. So I say, 'Melody wrote an amazing piece about how when people my age see young activists being harassed online, it discourages them from speaking out.'

There's a murmur of agreement around the table.

'Why didn't you tell us?' Pearl asks. 'I'd love to read it.'

'I'll print it out for you,' Melody says with a smile that doesn't reach her eyes.

'Do you mention the girls in it?' Aunt Celeste asks and I note that her smile is equally as tight.

But Melody just shrugs. 'Of course.'

There's a tense beat of silence as they stare at one another.

Melody looks away first, turning towards Oren with a warmer smile.

'I used the photograph Pearl took of Ren the day they were arrested.'

That makes Pearl's eyebrows rise slightly as her gaze flits across the table to meet mine for just a second, before she dips her head and stabs at her omelette with her fork.

'That's so cool!' Oren says, hand in his hair so I can see how big his eyes are. 'I can't wait to read it, Mel.'

'Come to my study later and I'll show it to you.' She smiles back, then leans over to press a kiss to his cheek before she pushes her chair back. When she stands up, she casts a glance down the table and says, 'Thanks for breakfast, but I need to prep for my interview with Denmark's climate minister.'

'Of course Mel's not mad at you,' Oren tells me as he, Pearl and I sit in the field after breakfast while Buffy and Willow snore in the sunshine. 'Why would she be mad at you for telling us about the *Teen Vogue* thing?'

'Didn't you notice how her mood changed as soon as I mentioned it? She didn't even eat her breakfast She just got up and left,' I remind him as Pearl and I paint his nails.

Because, let's be real, I was never going to wear lime-green nail polish, but it looks good on him.

'Breakfast was inedible.' Pearl pretends to heave. 'We spent all yesterday afternoon finding those mushrooms and I know they were a bastard to clean, Oren.' She raises her eyebrows at him, but he looks down at his nails. 'And Aunty Mel left us sitting at the dining table for, like, twenty minutes. She could have told us that she wasn't ready so we could have eaten without her or at least tried to keep everything warm, right?'

Oren sidesteps it. 'She didn't mean to leave us sitting there. Her head's all over the place at the moment.'

Pearl nods, then tips her chin up at me. 'Maybe that's why you think she was being weird.'

'Exactly,' Oren says. 'She's not mad at you, Ren. She's just distracted.'

I try to shrug it off, but I can't. 'Melody's not been the same these last few weeks.'

'What do you mean?' Oren asks.

'I don't know. It's like she's avoiding me, or something.'

Pearl laughs. 'Why would she be avoiding you, Ren?'

'Like our book. Every time I mention it, she tells me not to worry about it, that we have the whole summer. I mean, she hasn't even read the outline I sent her.'

Oren shrugs. 'Don't read anything into it,' he tells me, blowing on his nails. 'Mel's just stressed about this interview. This climate minister is the first proper guest that she's had on her podcast and she doesn't want to mess it up.'

'Um.' Pearl feigns offence. 'Are Ren and I not proper guests?'

'You know what I mean.' He chuckles, nudging her. 'Now Mel's signed this deal with the BBC, she's worried about maintaining the balance between her old listeners and the new ones who will be expecting something more substantial than a conversation with her mates.'

'I didn't know that she'd signed a deal with the BBC,' I say when I reach for his hand.

'Me neither,' Pearl says, passing me the bottle of nail polish.

'It only happened last week, but she's super excited.'

'I bet,' I say.

But before I can say anything else, he grins. 'Hey, Mel.'

I look up to see Melody standing over us.

'Look at you three,' she says with a sharp smile. 'I love how close you've become.'

Something about the way she says it makes my shoulders tense and when I cast a glance over at Pearl, I don't know whether it's because she's squinting into the sun, but she looks as uneasy as I feel.

'I hate to break up the party,' Melody says, 'but I need to borrow Ren for a second.'

'Sure,' I say, handing the bottle of nail polish back to Pearl and clambering to my feet.

'Walk me back to the house?' Melody says.

I wait for her to sling her arm around me, but she crosses them as we head up the field.

'About the *Teen Vogue* article,' she starts to say.

I don't mean to interrupt, but I feel awkward. 'You don't need to apologise. I—'

She interrupts me this time. 'I wasn't going to apologise, Renata. I just wanted to let you know that I wasn't hiding anything. I was going to tell everyone tonight over dinner. And

I didn't ask you to contribute because you're supposed to be taking a break, aren't you?'

She gestures back to where Pearl and Oren are sitting. 'This is what you're supposed to be doing on a Sunday afternoon. Hanging out with your friends in the sunshine, painting each other's nails. That's why you're here, isn't it? That's why your mum agreed to let you stay.'

'That and our book—' I start to say.

But she talks over me. 'So, please. Just be in the moment and enjoy the summer. And if you ever need to talk to me about anything, just pull me aside. You don't need to do it in front of everyone, OK?'

When I nod, she nods back, her smile noticeably looser.

'Lunch in twenty, OK? Iris is making roasted cauliflower!' she says, then walks away.

Lunch is quiet.

Or I'm quiet, I should say.

Melody, however, is back to her usual energetic self, holding court at the head of the table as she tells everyone about her new podcast deal with the BBC and the guests she has lined up.

Oren keeps looking between Pearl and me, clearly anxious we're going to tell her that we already know.

But we just smile and congratulate her as she says, 'My show is still going to be weekly, but each episode needs to be under half an hour because my new producer' – she stops to grin and wiggle in her chair – 'I have a producer now, guys. Get me.' There's an excited *Oh* around the table, which makes her toss her head back and cackle. '*My producer* thinks more people will listen because it's less of a commitment than my usual hour.'

'Plus, less work, right?' Hunter says.

But Melody scoffs. 'I wish. Between all the prep I'll need to do, travelling to the BBC Radio Sussex studios in Brighton to do the interviews, then editing everything down, it's going to be *more* work.'

'Won't someone at the BBC edit it?' Pearl asks.

'Oh! And the transcripts!' Melody points her wine glass at her, then at Oren. 'I need your help with that, guys. The BBC are going to publish a transcript of each episode and they've suggested I transcribe all of my old episodes before we launch in September in case any of my new fans want to go back and listen to them.'

'There must be an AI program that can do that,' Oren says.

'There is.' Melody nods. 'But we all know how terrible AI is for the environment.'

Everyone around the table nods back.

'Plus, it's not that accurate and I'm not getting cancelled again,' she snorts. 'Besides, by the time you've proofread everything, discovered the errors then found the right place in the podcast to check what it should be, you may as well have just transcribed it.'

She beams at Pearl and Oren. 'So, you two are on transcription duty as of tomorrow morning. It's going to be tight, though. Today is one month exactly until the new show launches on September 6th.'

'That's my due date!' Iris grins.

Hunter doesn't look as excited, though. 'But Marcus and I need Oren's help shifting that tree out of the road. Surely the storm the other night is a reminder that we won't be able to cut through the field much longer.'

She waves her fork at him. 'We've got plenty of time. Let's not wish the summer away.'

Hunter and Marcus exchange a glance that tells me that they're not convinced.

So, I say, 'Why don't Pearl and I do the transcripts so Oren can help with the tree?'

Melody turns to look at me as though she'd forgotten I was there.

'No, Ren.' She waves her fork at me this time. 'You're supposed to be taking a break, remember? Focus on that. Besides, your mum will kill me if she finds out that I've put you to work. You're a guest.'

I feel the sting of *guest* and say, 'I won't tell her.'

'Don't worry.' She flashes me a bright smile, then turns to wink at Pearl and Oren. 'These two will have it done in no time and you can go back to enjoying your summer together.'

20

'Shh,' I hiss at the elderly hinges of my bedroom door as I ease it open.

I wait a beat for the creak to fade, my heart pounding as I hold my breath, then poke my head out. But I'm greeted by darkness, the hall empty aside from the sound of Oren snoring steadily at the other end.

It's only been twenty-three minutes since Pearl asked me to meet her in the attic, but when I risk a step out into the hall, I've never been more grateful that Buffy and Willow are the worst guard dogs ever. It's so dark that I have to use the torch on my phone to guide me, cursing each traitorous floorboard that tries to betray me until I finally reach the attic staircase.

I have to stop myself taking the stairs two at a time as I head for the door, but when I open it, I can't take another step, because there's Pearl, surrounded by candles.

'Too much?' She winces as I stare at the scene.

It's the most romantic thing anyone has ever done for me, I want to say, but I can't catch my breath.

'Come. Sit,' Pearl says, gesturing at a blanket that I recognise from the sofa.

'Do we need to have *the conversation*?' she asks as we sit cross-legged opposite one another.

'*The conversation*?'

She must feel me tense because she looks me in the eye. 'You know? Where is this going?'

'Ah.' I nod slowly. '*That* conversation.'

'Do you know where this is going?'

'No,' I tell her as I feel a sharp pinch of panic. 'Do you?'

'Of course not.' She laughs lightly, then licks her lips. 'But I like the direction it's going in.'

I let go of a breath.

'Ditto,' I tell her, leaning in to nudge her with my nose.

'Even though you used to hate me.'

'I didn't *hate* you,' I correct. 'I just didn't know you.'

'And you had no desire to know me, did you?'

'That's true,' I concede with a chuckle.

'Because you thought I was annoying,' she reminds me with a playful smirk.

'I still think you're annoying.'

I return her smirk, but when I lean in again, she leans back.

'See?' I say when she won't let me kiss her. 'So annoying.'

But she just laughs. 'Is that why you avoided me for so long?'

'I didn't *avoid* you,' I lie because what am I supposed to say?

If I tell her the truth, she'll blow out the candles and leave me here with the Christmas decorations.

But Pearl just stares at me until I give in.

'*If* I ever avoided you,' I say, 'it was only out of wariness.'

'Of what?'

'I dunno.' I shrug. 'When GreenGirlPearl blew up, I assumed you were jumping on the green bandwagon with everyone else.' I hold my hands up. 'But I was wrong, OK?'

263

Pearl raises her eyebrows. 'Because you're . . .'

'An asshole?'

'*Such* an asshole,' she says through her teeth. 'Rude and smug and *so* intense.'

'Well, this is fun,' I tell her with a theatrical sigh. 'I could be sleeping, but I'd much rather be doing this.'

But she keeps going. 'And belligerent, but in the best possible way.' She smiles to herself. 'I've always envied that, Ren. How you don't give a shit what people think about you. I wish I could be more like that. But you care so much about stuff that I worry that you'll break your own heart.'

When she looks at me again, she groans and covers her face with her hands.

'Sorry. Am I ruining another moment with my overthinking?'

'Of course not. I like it.'

She peeks at me through her fingers. 'You do?'

'Yeah. I like that you think about this stuff.'

When she takes her hands away from her face, she's frowning. 'You don't?'

'I try not to.'

That makes her chin quiver again. 'Oh.'

'What I mean is: I used to be the same. I used to overthink everything. I would stay up at night, replaying conversations, over and over, and cursing myself for something I said on TikTok six months ago.'

'Why did you stop?'

'Because I had to. After my last kiss, she . . .'

'Tab,' Pearl says when I trail off, my cheeks stinging.

I make myself look at her. 'You knew?'

264

'Not for sure. But I figured something was going on between the two of you from the way you reacted when I warned you to be careful of her in the police cell.'

'It's complicated.' I exhale sharply through my nose. 'Actually, it isn't. I knew how I felt and she didn't.'

I shrug because now I'm forced to say it out loud, it really is as simple as that, isn't it?

'Anyway, about an hour after we last kissed, she sent me a WhatsApp with a string of random emojis. It was so bizarre that I'll never forget what they were.' I chuckle sourly. 'A needle, three whales and four bombs.'

'What does that mean?'

'I had no idea, but when I finally summoned the courage to ask, she just replied, *Sorry. Butt text.*'

Pearl snorts then presses her lips together until her shoulders stop shaking.

'I know. It's ridiculous. I spent *thirteen hours* agonising over some random emojis she didn't mean to send. I mean, I was out of my mind trying to decode what she was saying and she wasn't even thinking about me. So I swore I'd never do that again. And, OK, I'm not gonna lie and say that I haven't done it since. I mean, you saw the state I was in last night when she and Riley quit Out of Time.'

When Pearl nods, I feel a strange sense of relief as it suddenly dawns on me why I was so upset. 'But that was more about Riley than Tab. He was my friend, you know? We lived together. He knew me. Like, really *knew* me. I can get over what happened with Tab, but that? I don't know if I can.'

'So you're not over Tab?'

She looks me in the eye when she says it, but I hear the way the words wobble.

'Fuck Tab,' I say and I realise that I finally mean it. 'Yeah, I regret how things played out. But the thing about spending your whole life trying to stop the climate crisis is that you have to live with the constant and very real threat that you're not going to succeed. If that's the case, then I don't know how long we have left before the world ends and I'm not spending it trying to guess how someone feels about me.'

'How do you want to spend it, then?' she asks, her eyelids heavy.

'I just don't want to waste any more time.'

'So, let's not waste any more time,' she breathes as her mouth finds mine in the candlelight.

We kiss until we fall asleep, our legs tangled and our heads on the same cushion.

When we stir again, it's still dark outside, but the candles are waning.

'Tell me a secret,' Pearl whispers, her warm forehead against mine. 'Quick, before the candles burn out.'

'I'm glad the world didn't end before I met you,' I whisper back, still half asleep.

We kiss until the candles die and are replaced by sunlight.

'We'd better get downstairs before Aunty Mel and Oren wake up,' she says when we're drenched in gold.

I groan into her neck, then reluctantly untangle my legs from hers as we force ourselves to stand up.

Pearl reaches down to grab the blanket, and I pick up the

cushions before we walk gingerly to the door. I ease it open as quietly as the stiff hinges will allow and go out first.

There's nothing.

I can't even hear Oren snoring, which isn't good because that means he could be awake. But as I'm about to brave the first step, Pearl tugs on the back of my T-shirt. As I twist around to look at her, she curls her other hand around my throat, her mouth seeking out mine in another deep kiss that almost makes me drop the cushions. But as I'm about to turn and face her, she pulls back and looks at me with a wicked grin.

'One for the road,' she whispers, panting slightly.

I growl because all I can think is, *How am I supposed to walk now?* My knees are weak as I tiptoe down the wooden staircase, my heart thumping as she follows, her hand still fisted in the back of my T-shirt.

We make it to our doors, but as I'm about to slip into my room, Pearl swears under her breath.

'What?' I mouth.

She holds up the blanket, then tips her chin up at the cushions in my arms.

'We have to put these back before anyone notices,' she whispers.

And by *anyone*, she means Oren.

Given that Pearl loves to rearrange the fridge magnets and push every other book back on the shelves in the library to wind him up, he'll definitely notice they're missing.

'Come on,' she hisses, but she's already walking towards the stairs.

I follow, my heart thumping again as she checks if anyone's in the kitchen.

'All clear,' she says, then scuttles in.

The dogs lift their heads – Buffy on the rug by the armchair and Willow in a puddle of sunlight by the table. We lean down to rub their bellies, before hurrying over to the sofa as we hear a door slam upstairs.

She drapes the blanket over the sofa then gives me a look that my heart recognises before I do.

'Don't,' I warn, holding my finger up. 'What if someone comes down?'

'Sorry.' She giggles, grabbing my finger. 'I just waited so long to kiss you and now I can't stop.'

Oh God.

How can I not kiss her when she says stuff like that?

'Come here,' I tell her, but before she can, there's a knock on the front door.

'Who's that at five-thirty in the morning?' Pearl gasps as Buffy and Willow bark.

I have no idea.

It's the first time I've heard anyone knock.

The dogs jump up as I stride over and answer it to find Aunt Celeste looking as breathless as I feel.

'Ren, thank goodness you're awake!' she says. 'Did you get my text? I forgot my key.'

When I see how flushed she is, my heart stops.

Then it starts again, twice as fast, as I ask, 'What's wrong? Is it Mum?'

Pearl's at my side then.

268

'No, no, no.' Aunt Celeste shakes her head. 'It's not Fernanda. It's Dan.'

That doesn't make my heart settle as I ask, 'Is he OK?'

'He broke his leg. It's a compound fracture so it's pretty nasty, but it could have been much worse.'

'Did it happen on his dig?' Pearl asks.

'Of course not! He was excavating a tomb all day, then goes back to the apartment and falls in the bloody shower. You couldn't make it up.' She stops to roll her eyes. 'I'm flying out to Greece to bring him home. I managed to get on the first flight out, but I have to be at Gatwick in an hour. I'm so glad I caught you, Ren.'

She steps forward to pull me into a hug, then kisses my cheek.

She does the same to Pearl, then reaches for my hand. 'I'll be gone a few days, a week at the most, but I had to tell Fernanda, because she only agreed to let you stay because I'm here. She's going to call you later to discuss it, but seeing as you've been here over a month now, she's happy for you to stay until I get back. Although, if you'd rather not, it'll be nice for you to go and see her for a week, right?'

I feel Pearl stiffen beside me.

'Got to go!' Aunt Celeste says with a wave. 'I'll keep you posted.'

'Are you going to stay?' Pearl asks as we watch her ancient red truck carving through the field.

I don't hesitate. 'Of course.'

But as we're turning into each other, Oren comes charging down the stairs.

We step apart and that's how it goes for the rest of the

morning, Pearl and I only able to touch for a moment before we have to stop ourselves. Our hips graze as we follow Oren into the kitchen, then she hooks her little finger through mine as he looks at the sofa with a frown and says, 'Who moved the cushions?'

Then we orbit one another while we help him make breakfast, Pearl's hand catching against mine for a beat longer than necessary every time she passes me something and mine seeking out hers behind the safety of the island. We shouldn't, in case someone sees, but the heat of her next to me makes me want to get closer as we keep looking at each other, then look away, all eyelashes and giggles.

Before I can grab the wire basket and offer to collect the eggs, Melody does.

So Pearl and I have to wait until after breakfast, then offer to take the breakfast scraps out. By that point, we're practically panting as we run outside, and as soon as we're out of sight, Pearl grabs me so tightly, I'm sure that I'll have finger-shaped bruises on my hips later.

We kiss until we hear Melody calling our names, then walk slowly back to the house, hand in hand, the sunlight pouring over us, our shadows flat and black. Pearl snatches one more kiss before we reach the corner that leaves me breathless as I reluctantly let go of her hand in time to find Melody waiting for us on the doorstep.

'There you are!' She beams. 'Are you ready for a day of transcribing, Pearl?'

She slips her arm around Pearl's shoulders, but before she leads her into the house, she looks back at me.

'Have fun today, Renata,' she says, her smile a little sharper.

21

Pearl and Oren spend the next ten days in a row ensconced in Melody's study.

That's what Melody calls it now.

Not the library.

My study.

Not that I mind being on my own. After travelling with my mother, I've mastered the art of wasting days. I'm happy to sit in a café for hours, or to wander around an art gallery, making up stories about the people in the paintings. My favourite thing to do, though, especially when we're in a new city, is to go for a walk. I'll grab a coffee and listen to Mitski while I turn left, then left again and again until I end up back where I started.

I've done it so often that I don't even notice that I'm alone.

Or at least I didn't, before coming here. But since the end of June, my days have been full with chores or lessons or dozing in the sun with Pearl and Oren, doing nothing at all, so I don't know what to do with myself.

The rest of the family is equally unsettled by the tense, slightly erratic energy that now fizzes through the house, disturbing the calm. Melody is always busy, busy, busy. Always out. Always on the phone. The sweet, steady silence suddenly punctuated by the sound of her phone ringing as she sweeps in and out of her study all day. She doesn't acknowledge anyone, just paces into the kitchen while speaking furiously into her phone as she grabs another cup of coffee or checks if a package has been delivered, before pacing back into her study again.

She misses lunch and doesn't finish breakfast. Even during dinner, she sits at the head of the table, passionate and rhapsodic as she commandeers the conversation, telling us about an interview she's done that day or an article one of her listeners has sent her with another wild climate change conspiracy that gets Oren riled up. And we sit and listen, ready to commiserate or congratulate as appropriate before she retreats to her study while we clean up and the rest of the family make excuses about being tired or having an early start.

When they eventually head home, I should get Pearl and Oren back. But every evening this week, while we're trying to decide which of Oren's true crime documentaries to watch, Melody has interrupted us, saying she needs them. Then they disappear into her study, leaving me with nothing to do but stew in my room by myself.

At least Pearl and I have managed to steal some time together. So, as much as I miss her, it almost makes it more exciting. Those desperate, breathless kisses in the chicken coop or when she tells me to meet her in our bathroom and we kiss until we hear Melody at the foot of the stairs, calling her name.

When we reluctantly emerge and rejoin the others I'm sure they know what we've been doing. But no one seems to notice how flushed we are or that my hands are shaking.

So we do it again.

And again.

And again.

'God, I missed you today,' she says with a smile that makes me feel short of breath as we lie in the attic.

I nudge her with my nose. 'Yeah?'

'Yeah. I missed this face.'

She kisses me then rolls on to her back on the blanket with a sleepy sigh.

'What did you do today?' she asks when I do the same. 'Tell me about the world that exists beyond the walls of Melody's study. I vaguely remember daylight. And grass. God, I miss grass.'

'Not much,' I tell her, looking up at the dusty beams. 'After breakfast, I helped Marcus and Hunter.'

'I miss those two as well.'

'They were on top form today. They had a twenty-minute argument about organic fertiliser.'

'Of course they did. They're our Nick and Schmidt. They fight constantly, but they love each other.'

'Yes!' I realise, propping myself up on my elbows. 'That's *exactly* who they are.'

Pearl does the same. 'OK, confession time . . . I got into *New Girl* because of you.'

'No way!'

'Yeah, you used a Nick Miller quote as a caption once and I looked it up.'

'I did?'

'Yeah,' she says, her enthusiasm tapering off as she looks away. 'Something about only getting one wife.'

I realise why she looks away because I remember that photo. It was of me and Tab. I'd never caption a photo of us like that, though, so Pearl really must have been stalking me to have found it on Tab's Instagram.

It makes my heart do that fidgety thing again as I say, 'Well, while we're confessing things . . .'

She turns back to me with a curious frown. 'What?'

'I'm kind of hoping that you have a purse with gems.'

That makes her grin. 'Do you have a saxophone?'

I look at her as if to say, *Of course.* 'All we need now is an alley.'

She laughs, her eyes shining again as she asks, 'So what else did you do today?'

I'm about to shrug and say, *Nothing*, when I remember that my afternoon wasn't completely fruitless.

'I discovered a new spot.'

'Where?' she asks with a gasp.

'You know that path that leads to the village?'

She nods.

'I veered off it and went right instead. I ended up at the other end of the stream by this old tree that has, like, seven trunks so it looks like a massive stick of celery sticking out of the ground.'

Her eyes get even brighter. 'It sounds like something from one of Oren's stories.'

'Exactly! I can't wait to show you because on the other side of the stream, there's this house. This perfect little house with a thatched roof and roses in the garden. It's like something from a fairy tale.'

'Let's go on Friday.' She turns into me and tugs on the front of my T-shirt, her bottom lip wet and the words loose with excitement, like a tap filling up a bath. Filling me as well as she says, 'Aunty Mel's at the University of Sussex all day. We can pack a picnic. It'll be sickeningly romantic. You'll hate it.'

'What about Oren?' I ask.

But I don't know why I'm thinking about Oren.

Not when Pearl's looking at me like that.

'He's going with Melody.' She lets go of my T-shirt and rolls her eyes. 'Someone needs to carry her bags.'

'What do you mean?'

'He's Aunty Mel's assistant now,' she says with a snigger as she lies back down.

I try not to snigger as well, but I can't help it. 'Her *what*?'

'Yeah, he answers her calls and emails and sorts out her diary.'

When did Melody get so busy that she can't do that herself?

Perhaps he offered, I realise, which is something Oren would do.

'In fairness, Aunty Mel's a total scatterbrain and he's pathologically organised so they're the perfect team. But it means I'm stuck with all the transcribing and it's *so boring*. I'm going out of my mind.'

'Are you almost done?' I ask hopefully.

'Please.' She snorts. 'It takes four hours to transcribe each episode.'

'*Four hours?*'

'Yep. And there's, like, one hundred and twelve episodes.' She shakes her head. 'There's only, like, nine days left of August. There's *no way* I'm going to get it all done by September 6th.'

'I can help.'

'I'll suggest it but, please, no more talking, Renata. All I do all day is listen to people talking.'

'So, you don't want to discuss Hurricane Hilary and how

275

extreme weather events are becoming more common because of the climate crisis?'

'Oh my God!' she groans, reaching for the front of my T-shirt again. 'Will you just kiss me already?'

The next afternoon, instead of veering right off the path towards my new spot, I keep going towards the village, smiling as I pass the nasturtiums and the other flowers and herbs Oren pointed out on similarly sunny afternoons.

Bright yellow agrimony for protection.

Delicate white eyebright for attracting awareness.

Hardy green mugwort for expanding insight.

When I reach the village, I realise that I haven't been back since the day I arrived: Melody in that Stevie Nicks T-shirt and those Wayfarers she hasn't worn since. In fact, I haven't seen her in those filthy Hunters, either. Her nails are always polished now and her hair back to being teased to just-rolled-out-of-bed perfection.

I feel a small fizz of excitement at finding myself back here. The tiny high street looks exactly the same: like a page from a Shirley Hughes book. The blue, blue sky. The green, green hills. There's no scruffy black-and-white dog waiting outside the butcher, though, but the Union Jack bunting is still swaying gently in the breeze.

Someone in a neatly pressed pale blue shirt and chinos smiles and nods at me as we pass outside the pub. Given that's usually the prelude to either being hit on or having your phone snatched out of your hand on Earl's Court Road, I'm surprised to find myself smiling back, a slight spring in my step as I continue on.

I wonder what my mother would think if she saw me practically skipping while I smile at strangers. I wouldn't recognise myself either because I'm wearing a dress. It's black, of course, but it has straps, which Pearl took advantage of and pressed a kiss to my shoulder when no one was looking during lunch.

'Ren! Hey!' Keith says from behind the counter as I stroll into Mother Martha's café.

It's not what I expected at all. Given the gentle green exterior, I assumed it would be as twee as the other shops on the high street, but it's a riot of colour. Crayola green and Majorelle Blue and hot pink with plants everywhere and framed prints of Frida Kahlo and Margaret Atwood among the Greenpeace posters.

Plus, it's full – every table taken – which I wasn't expecting, either, especially on a Wednesday afternoon.

'How's it going, Keith?' I smile back. 'Congrats on the Scrabble win last Sunday. Quixotry. Nice.'

'I thought Pearl's head was going to explode.'

'It's the first time anyone's beaten her since I got to the farm.'

He bows, then slings the tea towel he's holding over his shoulder. 'Lovely to see you, Ren, but if you were hoping to catch Mother Martha, she's in Sullington, checking out a potential supplier.'

'That's OK. I'll see her for dinner.'

'I dunno.' He stops to scratch his beard. 'She's not feeling the new vibe at the farm.'

I wince. 'It's a bit intense, isn't it?'

'She says Melody stressing all the time is throwing her chakras out of balance.'

'Sounds painful, Keith,' someone snorts then waves as they leave their empty mug on the counter.

When Keith waves back I ask myself if that's why it's been so quiet at the farm recently.

I've noticed the numbers dwindling around the dining table, but I hadn't thought to question it. After all, Mother Martha is seventy-nine, so I understand why she'd be too tired after being on her feet all day to manage the half-hour walk to the farm. And Iris is certainly too pregnant to. Plus, with Uncle Dan's leg in a cast, I get why Aunt Celeste hasn't made it to dinner since she got back from Greece. But maybe Melody's mood has something to do with it as well. I don't know about throwing my chakras out of balance, but it certainly has me watching what I say because you never know what's going to trigger a twenty-minute rant about how busy she is.

'Don't worry,' I tell Keith. 'Melody will calm down when her podcast relaunches.'

'Hopefully,' he says, but the look he gives me tells me that he isn't so sure. 'I don't blame you for needing a break, though.' He gestures at the table in the corner that's now free. 'What can I get you? Black coffee?'

'Please.'

'We have some of my vegan chocolate cake left.' He leans in and lowers his voice. 'It's better than Mother Martha's, but don't tell her I said that or she'll rip my heart right out.'

He chuckles as he wanders behind the counter, but when I head over to the table, I feel something buzzing against my hip. I ignore it, but when I sit down and dump my tote bag into my lap, I can still feel it.

It takes me a second, then I gasp as I realise it's my phone.

I don't even look at the screen, sure it's my mother, but my throat tightens like a fist when I answer with a breezy 'Hey,' then hear someone chuckle softly and say, 'You didn't block me.'

I open my mouth, but nothing comes out as I hear the note of mischief in Tab's voice. 'How's farm life?'

It's so nonchalant – so fucking *Tab* – like we only spoke yesterday, that it makes my jaw clench.

Not that I should be surprised. This is what she does. How many mornings did we wake up after a night of kissing and making plans only for her to laugh and roll away from me as soon as Riley walked into the room? Her ability to pretend that nothing happened so convincing that I'd ask myself if anything did.

Not today, though.

I know *exactly* what she did.

'What do you want, Tab?' I ask, because we may as well just get straight to it.

There's a tight beat of silence, then she says, 'Ren, we need to talk.'

'Do we?' I ask.

Because what is there to talk about at this point?

'Fine,' she says with a dramatic sigh and I can picture the equally dramatic eye roll. 'I'll talk, then. Riley's been on at me to call you. He says I need to fix this.'

I catch myself smiling with relief because of course he did.

Dear, sweet Riley.

But then the corners of my mouth droop as I realise what Tab's actually saying.

'So you're only trying to fix this because Riley's making you?'

She goes quiet and I don't bother waiting for her to deny it.

'Listen, Tab. Sometimes you break something and it stays broken and you have to live with it.'

She doesn't say anything to that, either, which should make it easier, but I still hear my voice falter when I say, 'If Riley wants to talk, though, tell him I'm open to it.'

'So, that's it? We're done?' she finally says.

I can't help but feel a surge of delight at how stunned she sounds. She probably thought that calling me would be enough. That I'd be so relieved to hear from her that I'd dissolve into tears and plead with her to work this out. But then my satisfaction sharpens to irritation because if she thought that, she doesn't know me at all.

'Jesus, Ren,' she says. 'How did we get here?'

'How did we get here?' I hiss.

Luckily, Keith brings over my coffee and cake so I have a chance to catch my breath.

'Where are you?' she asks as I thank him.

What's it to you? I want to say, but I know Tab.

She's only asking because she wants this to be over already.

'Are you in a café?' she asks. 'Don't tell me. Black coffee, right?'

I wait for my heart to flutter when her voice softens but it doesn't this time because *big whoop*.

She knows how I take my coffee.

Keith knows how I take my coffee.

'If there's something you want to say, Tab, just say it.'

'Ren, I miss you,' she says so suddenly that I drop the teaspoon I'm holding into my mug.

Of all the things I thought she was going to say, it wasn't that.

I figured she'd make a tepid apology, then tell me that we need to move on, like she always does.

280

For Riley's sake, of course.

'Listen, Ren. I'm sorry,' she says and I try not to drop my phone into my mug this time because *holy shit*.

Tab never says sorry.

Like *ever*.

The most you get out of her is an *I'm sorry you feel that way*.

'I am,' she says and I squeeze my eyes shut and press my palm to my forehead. 'I'm sorry, Ren. I'm sorry for everything. Not just for quitting Out of Time, but for how I treated you.' I hear her suck in a breath before she says, 'I was scared, OK? I was scared and confused because I didn't want to fuck everything up. Look what we're trying to do with Out of Time. Look what we're building. The legacy we're creating. I didn't want anything to ruin that.'

I know then that she really is sorry.

Not for losing me, though.

But for losing Out of Time.

'I fucked up, OK?' Tab says as I try not to laugh. 'Is that what you want me to say? *I fucked up*. But we can still fix this. I know we can. So, stop sulking and come home.'

I arch an eyebrow at that, but I refuse to give her the satisfaction of biting back. So, I let her deliver the rest of this clearly rehearsed speech that she's no doubt sure will have me weeping and promising to be on the next train back to London. 'Out of Time is *us*, Ren. Me, you and Riley. There's no Out of Time without the three of us. So let's just get over this petty bullshit and focus on what actually matters: saving the planet.'

* * *

281

Don't tell her, I think that night while Pearl and I are in the attic.

But I have to.

'Pearl, are you scared of this?'

'Of us?' she asks with a frown.

I nod.

'Of course,' she admits, then sweeps her thumb against my bottom lip, her eyelids heavy. 'The good kind of scared, though. Top of the rollercoaster scared. Stepping back after you've lit a firework scared.'

'But are you confused?'

Her smile slips. 'I am now. What's going on, Ren?'

When she sits up, I do the same as I sigh and say, 'Tab called me today.'

'What did she say?'

When I roll my eyes, Pearl chuckles weakly. 'She gave you the big romantic speech.'

'No,' I snort and when I laugh, I mean it because for the first time since I met Tab, there's no doubt.

No need to replay the conversation on a loop until I find something to hold on to.

To keep me going.

Some secret message that Tab couldn't say because she was scared or confused.

No need to ask myself what she meant.

Because I know exactly what she meant.

'She wants back in.'

Pearl's eyebrow jerks up. 'With Out of Time?'

I nod.

'I thought she and Riley were starting their own group?'

'That obviously didn't pan out.'

Pearl smirks, but I see her jaw tighten as she asks, 'Is that all she wants?'

When I nod again, Pearl's brow smooths and the corners of her mouth lift. 'What did you tell her.'

'I told her to get fucked.'

She laughs, her eyes shining in the candlelight as she reaches for my hand, then presses a kiss to it.

'You OK?' she asks softly, kissing my cheek this time.

'Yeah,' I say, because I am, actually. 'I'm not gonna lie, it's sad, but . . . I don't know . . .' My gaze dips down to my hand in hers. 'Spending time with you makes me realise that I didn't know Tab.' When I look up again, Pearl nods. 'Like actually *know* her beyond these big dreams we had about saving the world.

'I don't know.' I shrug, then sigh tenderly. 'It's like we were characters in this play about the audacious underdogs who were going to save the planet.' I ball my other hand into a fist and punch the air. 'Rebel Ren and her trusty sidekick. Except she doesn't want to be the sidekick any more and I never wanted to be the hero.'

'What do you want to be, then?' Pearl asks with a frown.

'I don't know yet,' I say, but then I catch myself smiling as I look at her. 'But I can't wait to find out.'

22

Pearl and I get back to the house as the Defender is pulling in.

When it stops, Oren jumps out.

'Hey, guys!' He waves, then strides around to the driver's side.

'How was the thing at the University of Sussex?' I ask.

'Amazing!' He beams as he opens the door for Melody, and she climbs out. 'Mel was on fire!'

'Stop,' she tells him, waving her hand.

I can't help but smile as she struggles to walk on the gravel in heels. When she catches me watching her, she laughs as she reaches for Oren's arm to steady herself and it reminds me of the evening we met at The Feminist Bookshop. The tense, harassed Melody who is always pacing in and out of her study, phone pressed to her ear, back to being warm and brimming with energy as she cackles and wobbles towards us.

Even if she looks decidedly demure in a neat black shift dress instead of those horrendous boob dungarees. It's the sort of dress my mother would wear, but I still see a glimpse of the old Melody thanks to the smiley face pearl necklace she's paired it with and the obscenely pink lipstick that I haven't seen her wear since I got to the farm. *It's nice to have her back*, I think, as the dogs come tearing around the side of the house.

'How was your talk?' Jacinta asks from the stove as they barge into the kitchen ahead of us.

Everyone is there and I can't remember the last time all of us were together. It surprises me how my chest warms when I see them gathered around the island, helping Jacinta while a John Coltrane record plays.

'Iris,' Pearl hisses when she sees her sitting on one of the dining chairs with her swollen ankles propped on another. 'Aren't you supposed to be on bed rest?'

'Yes,' Marcus says crisply. 'But Melody insisted we come for dinner.'

He glares across the kitchen at her, but Melody isn't paying attention as she scrolls through her phone.

'I'm fine.' Iris waves her hand. 'I'm pregnant, not dying. Besides, I'm going out of my mind at home.'

'Tell me about it,' Aunt Celeste mutters. 'Dan's the worst patient ever. As we were leaving, he announced that he's too exhausted to come. From what, I don't know. I'm the one running around after him all day. He's lucky Melody called to say that she has news otherwise I might have smothered him with a pillow.'

'I do have news!' Melody says. 'News that warrants champagne!'

There's a series of gasps as we look around at each other, our eyebrows raised.

Everyone except Mother Martha, who says, 'We don't have any champagne, sadly. Will red wine do?'

'It will not,' Melody says sternly, then reaches into her leopard print tote bag.

She produces two bottles and holds them up.

'Champagne for us and sparkling apple juice for Iris and the kids!'

There's a cheer as Hunter steps forward to grab them with a rare smile.

'What are we celebrating?' Marcus asks.

'The University of Sussex offered me a job!'

That prompts another round of gasps, then a louder one when Hunter opens the champagne.

'Doing what?' Mother Martha asks.

'They've asked me to be a professor at the School of Media, Arts and Humanities!'

Aunt Celeste looks slightly startled. 'A professor?'

'An adjunct professor, but still!' Melody winks at her, then smiles as she watches Marcus fill a flute with champagne then hand it to her. 'The dean wants me to teach media and cultural studies. She says that with my background in social media, I have a unique perspective.'

'Don't you need a degree to teach?' Pearl asks quietly, frowning at Aunt Celeste.

Melody doesn't hear, though, as Iris claps. 'This is so exciting!'

'Well done, sis!' Jacinta beams.

'I'm so proud of you, Mel,' Oren says, kissing her cheek.

'Oh, Oren,' she sighs. 'It's happening!'

Then she turns to face the rest of us, her eyes wet. 'It's finally happening, guys. People are listening. My platform is growing. It's bigger than Pearl's now.' She laughs, wild and bright. 'Can you believe it? This morning, I hit one hundred and twenty thousand followers! I probably have even more now after my talk.'

'One hundred and twenty thousand, *three hundred and forty-three*,' Oren confirms, checking his phone.

'Congratulations!' Jacinta says, raising her glass.

'Thank you. Thank you. Thank you.' She raises hers back, then curtsies. 'I mean, that's nowhere near the ten million I used to have on YouTube, but I'm getting there, right?'

'You'll be back before you know it,' Oren tells her with a proud smile.

'It's been a long, long road, but it finally feels like I'm getting somewhere, you know? People are recognising me again. *Respecting* me. Subscribers for my podcast have gone through the roof. And now I'm going to be a professor. Can you believe it? Professor Melody Munroe. It has a certain ring to it, don't you think?'

There's another cheer as Aunt Celeste rolls her eyes at me while Melody laps up the applause. I try not to laugh because I can tell she's seething as she raises her glass.

When I do the same, Melody stops and frowns.

'Is something wrong, Renata?' she asks, tilting her head at me.

But I shake mine. 'No. No. Not at all. That's brilliant news, Melody. Congratulations.'

'She's happy for you, Aunty Mel,' Pearl tells her.

But Melody doesn't take her eyes off me. 'You don't look very happy, Renata.'

'Of course I am, Melody.'

'Really?' she pushes, her gaze narrowing.

'She's just surprised, that's all,' Pearl says, coming to stand next to me.

'We all are, Mel,' Aunt Celeste tells her, slipping her arm around my shoulders.

Melody's gaze flicks to her and it's so quiet for a moment that I can hear the fridge hum.

'Surprised about what exactly? That ditzy me can be a professor like you and her mother?'

'No! No!' I say, looking between them, utterly horrified.

But Aunt Celeste's arm tightens around me as she says, 'Of course you can be a professor, Mel. You can be anything you want. I'm just surprised because you've never shown an interest in academia.'

'That's true,' Jacinta snorts, sipping her champagne. 'You barely passed your GCSEs.'

Something flickers across Melody's face.

A moment ago, we were toasting her and now she has tears in her eyes.

I feel awful.

'The students are lucky to have you, Melody,' I say and hold my arm out to her. 'No one understands the power of social media like you do. Look at everything you've accomplished. Your podcast. Your book. All the articles you've written. Plus, a hundred and twenty thousand followers is incredible.'

'It's not *five million*, though, is it, Rebel Ren?' she sneers.

'OK, Mel, I know you're upset, but I need you to take it down a notch,' Aunt Celeste warns.

There's another uncomfortable silence around the kitchen as Melody stares at her.

When Aunt Celeste stares back, Melody turns to me. 'Who cares about followers, Renata? It's not about followers. It's about our commitment to the cause. About our commitment to *each other*. Because women and children, like us' – champagne spills out of her glass as she thrusts her arm out – 'are bearing the brunt of it.'

She turns in a circle to look at everyone. 'More extreme weather events such as droughts and floods, rising sea levels that destroy arable land, and disruption of marine life will result in less food. And less food means that women and children get less as the remaining food supplies will be unevenly distributed. Even more than they are already. So we need to be engaged with and pushing for change, not undermining each other.'

'I wasn't undermining—' I start to say, but she turns her back to me.

'This isn't climate change, it's *everything* change so we need to do everything to stop it!'

'Perfectly put, Mel,' Oren tells her. 'That has to be the opening for your new book!'

I note the *your book*, but I make myself smile as I join in with the applause.

But when Melody wafts around the kitchen as everyone congratulates her, Aunt Celeste leans in.

'Margaret Atwood said that,' she whispers.

But I already knew that.

My mother and I were at the British Library in 2018 when Margaret Atwood made that same speech.

'I don't like the way Aunty Mel spoke to you earlier,' Pearl says a few hours later while we're lying in the attic.

Her jaw is tight as she rolls on to her side to face me and I reach over to graze my knuckles across her cheek as I say, 'She didn't mean it. You know how stressed she is about her new podcast. Plus, I think Aunt Celeste triggered her by questioning the professor thing. She obviously stepped on a raw nerve.'

'Yeah, but Celeste's right.' Pearl sits up. 'Aunty Mel doesn't have any A levels, let alone a postgraduate degree, so I don't blame Celeste for being annoyed at her.'

'You know what Melody's like. She probably thinks professor and lecturer are the same thing.'

'Whatever.' Pearl rolls her eyes. 'The point is, Celeste questioned it, not you, so why single you out?'

'We ruined the moment for her, though, didn't we?'

'Again, *Celeste* did, but she still went off at you.'

'I don't know. She probably thought Aunt Celeste and I were sniggering behind her back.'

'Jacinta was the one sniggering.'

'True, but Jacinta's her sister. She's probably used to that.'

'Well,' Pearl says with a huff. 'I'm just annoyed with myself.'

'Why?'

'I wish I'd said something.'

'Come here.'

She lies down next to me again and when she curls into me, I slip my arm around her.

'I appreciate that,' I say, stopping to press a kiss to her mouth, 'but I'm good.'

'I'm surprised you didn't tell her to fuck off and walk out.'

'The old Ren would have,' I realise. 'But I'm Zen Ren now.'

'Zen Ren?' She scoffs. 'I'll remind you of that next time Melody makes us listen to Ed Sheeran.'

290

I curse under my breath, but as I'm about to kiss her again, she sits up.

'I don't get it,' she says with a frown.

'Get what?'

'Don't you think it's weird that Aunty Mel suddenly wants to teach?'

'Not really. But then Mum's always been in academia so I'm used to it, I guess.'

'If Aunty Mel wants to teach, I'm all for it. But she gave us that barn-burning speech about how this isn't climate change, it's everything change . . .' She balls her hand into a fist and holds it up. 'That we need to do something now! Now! Now! How is teaching media and cultural studies going to help?'

Before I can answer, I'm distracted by a flash in the dark.

When I reach for my phone, she lies back down next to me.

'What?' Pearl lifts her head off my shoulder to frown at me as I groan.

'It's not Tab.' I press a kiss to her forehead. 'It's Mum confirming she's back on September 22nd.'

'Oh,' she says, sounding as deflated as I feel when she lets her head fall back on to my shoulder.

'She has to be back by the 25th because that's when the new term starts at UCL,' I say with a shrug.

'Summer's ending, isn't it?' Pearl says, her breath warm against my neck.

'I know,' I say with a miserable sigh as I feel my phone buzz in my hand again.

I glance at the screen, then sit up.

'Shit,' I mutter as Pearl sits up as well. 'It's Aunt Celeste. She says it's urgent.'

'Quick. Call her now,' Pearl tells me, but I'm already unlocking my phone.

'Oh good. You're still awake,' Aunt Celeste says when she answers.

'What's going on?' I ask, putting it on speaker. 'Is everything OK?'

'It's Dan.'

'Is he OK?' Pearl asks.

I can hear how frantic Aunt Celeste is, her breath quickening in time with my heart. So I'm not surprised that she doesn't ask why Pearl and I are together at two in the morning as she says, 'He was in agony and the painkillers weren't helping so I called 111 and I'm so glad I did because he has acute compartment syndrome.'

'What's that?' Pearl and I ask at the same time.

'It happens when a plaster cast is too tight and restricts the blood flow. We're at Worthing A&E now, but they're moving him to Royal Sussex County because he needs emergency surgery.'

'OK.' Pearl nods. 'Let me wake up Melody and we'll be there in, like, an hour.'

'No, girls. Just stay at the farm for now and I'll keep you posted, OK?'

'No way,' I tell her. 'You can't deal with all of this by yourself.'

'You shouldn't be alone right now,' Pearl says and the way her voice wavers makes me reach for her hand as I ask myself how many times she was alone in hospitals with her mother.

292

'You're so sweet, girls, but I don't even know where I'll be in an hour.'

'It doesn't matter. We'll find you,' I insist and Pearl nods again.

'I'm fine, I promise, girls. But I've got to go. The consultant wants to talk to me.'

'OK,' I say, trying to keep my tone even. 'I love you, Aunt Celeste.'

'I love you too, bug.'

23

'Good, you're up!' Pearl says when we walk into the kitchen to find Oren with his head in the fridge.

He closes his eyes and yawns greedily.

'I couldn't sleep,' he mumbles, grabbing a bowl and kicking the door shut.

'Oren, listen,' I say gently as he lifts the tea towel to admire a ball of dough. 'Uncle Dan's in the hospital.'

He looks horrified. 'What happened?'

As soon as he says it, Buffy and Willow jump to their feet and traipse over, tails swishing.

'The cast on his leg was too tight and it was restricting the blood flow,' Pearl tells him.

'No way!' he says, fisting his hands in his hair.

'Yeah, he's having emergency surgery right now.'

'A fasciotomy?'

'Yes!' I blink at him.

But of course he knew that.

'They had to do it within six hours otherwise he could have lost his leg,' I tell him.

'OK. Let's go.' He nods. 'Where is he?'

'Royal Sussex County,' I say.

'Melody's in the shower, so we'll leave as soon as she's out.'

'Leave for where?' I hear Melody ask, and we turn to find her watching us from the doorway.

'Uncle Dan's in the hospital, Mel,' Oren tells her, his eyes wide. 'He's having emergency surgery.'

But she doesn't flinch. 'How did you know that?'

'Ren and Pearl just told me.'

She looks at us. 'How did *you* know that?'

'Celeste called Ren from A&E last night,' Pearl says.

Melody frowns. 'When?'

'I dunno.' Pearl shrugs, looking at me. 'About two a.m. We were going to wake you up so we could go and be with her, but she told us not to because they were about to transfer him.'

I don't know if Pearl realises what she just said, but, luckily, it doesn't seem to register as Melody watches Oren charge around the kitchen, recovering the bowl and putting it back in the fridge, then turning off the oven.

'Let's go,' he says.

'Hold on.' Melody holds her hands up. 'Everyone just take a breath. When did you last speak to Celeste?'

'I don't know.' I shrug, then look at Pearl. 'Like, an hour ago, before Dan went into surgery.'

'Well, I *just* spoke to her and Dan's fine.'

'Fine?' Pearl repeats.

'Yes,' Melody says with a steady smile. 'He's just been transferred to Recovery.'

'Already?' I say and even Oren looks surprised, his forehead creasing.

'He was in and out in less than an hour. I know it sounds scary, but it's a minor procedure, right, Oren?'

295

His eyebrows rise slightly at *minor procedure*, but then he catches himself and nods.

Melody gestures at him as if to say, *See?* And I don't know if she really believes that being rushed into surgery at six in the morning to have your leg cut open otherwise you'll lose it is no big deal or if all of this is an attempt to keep us calm, but I can't stop thinking about how scared Aunt Celeste sounded.

'All they had to do was make an incision to relieve the pressure and that's it. Right, Oren?' Melody says.

'Sure.' He nods again. 'A fasciotomy isn't that complicated.'

'Exactly. So there's no need to rush to the hospital, is there?'

He shakes his head.

'I want to see Uncle Dan, though,' I say.

'Of course, but let's give Aunt Celeste some space, shall we? Besides, she's not alone. Her sister is there.'

'We can take her lunch,' Oren suggests with a bright smile. 'I can make that broad bean dip she loves.'

'You're so sweet.' Melody kisses him on the cheek, then steps back and claps her hands. 'Right. Until we hear from her, I think it's best we keep busy. Why don't you and Pearl get started on breakfast?'

'Good idea,' he says, switching the oven back on.

But when he takes her Spice Girls mug out of the cabinet, she raises her finger and says, 'Actually, Oren, can you put my coffee in my travel mug? Renata and I are going for a walk.'

Buffy and Willow lead the way as we walk to the back field. It's not even seven o'clock yet, but as Melody and I stand side by side, looking out at the familiar line of trees on the horizon, I know that it's going to be one of those days when it feels like the sun is on a sugar high. It's so bright already that it hurts my eyes.

I wonder if Mum knows about Uncle Dan? I ask myself as I try to work out what time it is in Austin.

'Ren,' Melody says. Snaps, actually, so I'm guessing it isn't the first time she's said it.

'Sorry.' I shake my head then turn to look at her. 'I was just thinking about Aunt Celeste.'

She sighs sharply. 'That's what I wanted to talk to you about.'

'Is something wrong with Uncle Dan?'

I *knew* she was being too calm in the kitchen.

I hold my breath while she sips her coffee, then says, 'Aunt Celeste and I had quite a . . . how do I put this politely?' She stops to snort. 'A *heated* discussion this morning.'

'About Uncle Dan?'

'No, about you, actually.'

'Me?'

'Yes. About what happened last night.'

'Oh, don't worry about it, Melody.' I wave my hand at her. 'I haven't even thought about it.'

'Well, I have,' she says tightly. 'I've thought of little else.'

'Seriously, don't worry about it. I get it, OK? You've got so much going on so please, let's just forget about it. What's going on with Uncle Dan is way more important than what happened last night.'

She stares at me for a moment, then barks out a laugh.

It's so loud – so unexpected – that the sound makes my shoulders jerk up.

'See?' she says. '*This* is why I'm so frustrated.'

'Frustrated?'

'Yes! You think *I'm* the one to blame for what happened last night?'

'Not at all. I was just as—'

But she doesn't let me finish. 'Aunt Celeste certainly does. Her husband is having emergency surgery, yet she still had time to berate me for the way I spoke to the precious Renata Barbosa last night.'

She bows at me, but when I step back, a crease appears between her eyebrows. 'This is just so frustrating. I know I shouldn't compare you to Pearl because her reasons for being here are so different from yours, but as soon as she got here, she fitted right in and now she's a valued member of the family and a trusted confidant.'

That stings more than it should as she adds, 'But it's like you're not even trying, Renata. You spend all day sulking. You just do what's expected of you, then disappear for the afternoon and get home in time for supper.'

What else am I supposed to do? Pearl and Oren are with you all the time, I want to say, but the look she gives me dissolves the impulse to say any more as I see something flash in her eyes.

Something dark, like a curtain falling across a window.

'I have to say, Renata, I'm really disappointed.'

That more than stings. 'Disappointed?'

'For the last two weeks, Pearl, Oren and I have been in my study working fourteen-hour days, fighting the good fight, and

298

what have you been doing? Swanning around, picking flowers and sleeping in the sun.'

She gestures at the field rolling from our feet. 'You don't think that we can't see you through the window? We're in there' – she thumbs over her shoulder at the house – 'busting our arses to save the planet from burning up and you don't even care. I thought you being here would light a fire under us. I thought you'd be a lightning rod. I was sure that you would have given us all jobs by now and you'd be leading the charge on what to do next. But instead you've been pick, pick, picking at me. Criticising everything I do.'

'I haven't—'

She talks over me again. 'Yes, you have. The *Teen Vogue* thing. Sneering at my new job last night.'

'I wasn't sneering. I—'

'And you haven't even mentioned our book.'

'*You* haven't mentioned our book,' I manage to get out.

'Why are you waiting for me? If you really cared about it, you would have been pestering me non-stop.'

That's true, I realise. *Why haven't I?*

But then something kicks at me.

'I have asked you, Melody. Several times, actually, but you keep telling me not to worry about it. *Rest, reset, regroup, Renata.* Remember?'

When she turns her face away and flicks her hair, I try not to raise my voice as I ask, 'Have you even read the rough outline I sent you? Melody, I know you're busy, but—'

'So *that's* what this is about!' She laughs. 'You're jealous because I'm busy? Because you're not the star here?'

My ears – and head – ring with shock as the tears in my eyes make her face blurry.

Unrecognisable.

'The star?'

'Yes. Here you're not Renata Barbosa, one of *Time*'s Twenty-Five Most Influential Teens.'

'I'm not one of *Time*'s Twenty-Five Most Influential Teens,' I tell her.

Which is an odd point to argue given that Melody just called me a stuck-up asshole, but I'm reeling.

'*Time* announced it overnight.' Melody wags her finger at me. 'That's what yesterday was about, wasn't it? Because I dared to stand up to you. When was the last time someone did?'

She arches an eyebrow, but when I don't – can't – respond, she says, 'There are no stars here, Renata. We're all here because we want to be part of something. Not just a family but a movement. A revolution. The world is burning and if we're going to put the fire out, we need to focus. Commit. Put in the work. Be a team.'

That knocks me sideways.

No one has ever accused me of being incapable of those things.

If anything, my mother has always told me that I'm too focused.

'That's what this summer was supposed to be about. Mum wants me to be a normal teenager.'

I don't realise I've said it out loud until Melody shivers with laughter.

'When have you ever listened to your mother?' she asks, and there's a sharpness at the corners of her eyes that I've never seen before. 'That's the trouble. You think that you fight with her so much because you're too alike, but it's actually because you're sick of living in her shadow. You're desperate to know who you are away from her. Well, now you know. This is who you are, Renata.'

Melody looks me up and down with a smirk. 'Lonely. Purposeless. Adrift. You've only been here two months and you've already been forgotten. That's why you're struggling. Not just because you don't know how to be part of a family, but because you know now that it doesn't matter how many millions of followers you have, your mother will always be the star. And that eats you up, doesn't it? Without Tab and Riley and your millions of mindless, sycophantic followers, you have nothing,' she hisses. 'Seeing you here is like the Emperor's New Clothes. You're not radical or revolutionary in the slightest. It's all been for attention, hasn't it? Out of Time, the protests, getting arrested, all of it.'

As soon as she says it, I remember that damp afternoon at the Tate Modern, Melody and I wandering from room to room, gazing at the artwork while I told her everything.

All of my biggest fears about who I am and what people think of me and she stored it away, didn't she?

And now she's throwing it back at me.

Every word.

'Would you even care about fighting climate change if your mother didn't?' Melody presses her hand to her chest. 'I chose this life, but if Fernanda was into football, would you want to be the next Mary Earps? If you really cared then it wouldn't matter what your mother told you to do this summer because you wouldn't be able to stop. But no. You meet a pretty girl and *POOF!* You forget that the planet's on fire. It's such a shame. I believed you, Renata.' She shakes her head. 'I really believed that you were going to change the world.'

24

We all have that door inside of us, don't we? That one deep inside, around that corner we never dare turn. The door we have to keep locked because everything we don't want to think about is behind it. All of those things we've done and haven't done and said and shouldn't have said. Every fear and regret and mistimed, reckless comment that we have to keep behind it because it would devour us whole if we let ourselves remember.

Some people are scared of heights or spiders or clowns.

But I'm scared of what's behind that door and Melody just kicked it in.

What's that line from *The Tempest*?

Hell is empty and all the devils are here.

Well, all of my devils are here as I walk back to the house. Every insecurity I have about myself and my place in the world. All of those unthinkable things that I now can't stop thinking about.

I'm so distracted that I follow her into the kitchen to find it empty aside from Pearl, who is setting the table, and Oren, who is at the stove, folding an omelette. It's Saturday morning so it should be full by now and while I'm grateful not to be immediately confronted by an onslaught of cheery *Hello*s as everyone asks how I slept and what I have planned for the day, with only the four of us, it will be harder to pretend that I'm OK.

But Pearl and Oren are too startled to notice that anything is wrong as Melody strides into the kitchen then shrieks and runs over to the radio to turn it up as a trailer for her new podcast starts playing.

'Where is everyone?' she asks, disappointed that we're the only ones there to hear it.

'Aunt Celeste is at the hospital,' Oren says with a sad sigh. 'Mother Martha is at the café. Marcus and Iris have their NCT group over. And Aunt Jacinta and Uncle Hunter are at Cerys and Nicole's wedding.'

'Oh, yes. That's right,' she says with an easy smile. 'Oh well. Just us, then.'

And just like that, Melody is back to her warm, cheerful self, singing along to the radio as Oren pours her a fresh cup of coffee while she leans against the counter, scrolling through her phone.

'You spoil me.' She grins as he plates her omelette.

While they're giggling at the stove, Pearl paces over to me.

'What did Aunty Mel want to talk to you about?' she asks, her forehead pinched with concern.

'Not now,' I manage to say as Melody spins around to face us.

'Come on, girls,' she sings, wafting over to the table. 'As it's just us, why don't you sit here, Pearl?'

She pats the chair to her left.

My chair.

Then all I can hear is Self Esteem singing about needing to

be braver as Pearl looks at the chair, then at me, as Oren does the same, before we all look at Melody as she sits at the head of the table.

'I'm good here, thanks,' Pearl tells her, sitting in her usual spot.

'If you prefer,' Melody says, her smile slipping for a second.

Pearl watches her suspiciously as she tucks into her omelette and while I appreciate Pearl's reluctance to take my place, it means that I have to sit next to Melody, which I'd rather not do right now.

Melody must know that because she pats the chair again. 'Come. Sit, Renata.'

It sounds like she's talking to a dog, which makes me even more reluctant to sit down, but when Oren looks between us, I do as I'm told before he asks what's wrong and I have to lie and say that I'm fine.

As soon as I do, Melody reaches for her mug and says, 'Why did I implement the screen-time rule, guys?'

Pearl and I look across the table at each other, then at Oren.

He clears his throat and says, 'So we're present and appreciate our time together.'

Melody smiles and reaches over to squeeze his hand.

'But some people don't appreciate our time together, so they don't want to follow the rules,' she says with a pointed sigh, her face hardening again. 'I'm not forcing any of you to be here. So, if you want to go, you can. But if you stay, I expect *everyone* to follow the rules. And while I understand the temptation to use your phone outside of the allotted screen time, if you can't follow the rules, then you can't have one.'

Oren's cheeks flush, obviously assuming that she's talking about him, but we all do it.

We're always looking up recipes or checking words for Scrabble or what song is playing on the radio.

Melody was literally *just* scrolling through her phone while Oren was making her omelette.

'We didn't break the rules, Aunty Mel,' Pearl says tightly, clearly clocking before Oren or I do what prompted this reminder. 'It was an emergency. Dan was in the hospital.'

But Melody shakes her head. 'That's why we have a landline, Pearl.'

'A landline that's in your study that no one heard at two in the morning.'

'Well, I'll get one for my bedroom as well, then. I'm sure they sell them on Amazon, but you all know my feelings about Amazon.' She sips her coffee, then says, 'Perhaps the hardware shop in the village will be able to source one. Renata can make herself useful for once and go in and ask while I'm doing my interview with *Stylist* later.'

Pearl's eyebrows rise at *for once*, but when I glare across the table at her, she looks confused, but takes the hint, exhaling sharply through her nose as she asks, 'What interview with *Stylist*?'

'They're doing a profile on Mel.' Oren beams. 'They're calling it "The New Queen of Green".'

She winks at him, but Pearl is unmoved. 'I thought we were taking Celeste lunch at the hospital?'

'She just messaged me,' Melody says with another shrug. 'Dan's being discharged this afternoon.'

Pearl blinks at her. 'What?'

Even Oren questions it. 'Already? He only got out of surgery an hour ago.'

'Aunt Celeste says they need the bed. Plus, there's less risk of infection if he's at home.'

'I suppose so,' Oren mutters.

Pearl's gaze narrows as she says, 'That's great news, but how were you going to take us to the hospital if you have this interview with *Stylist*?'

'I didn't say that I was taking you to the hospital.'

'She didn't,' Oren chips in. '*I* suggested that we bring Aunt Celeste lunch, didn't I?'

Melody nods, then raises her knife. 'Back to the phone thing. After your allotted time this morning, Oren will collect your phones and they'll be locked in my study until you can have them again this evening.'

Pearl stares at her. 'You can't be serious, Aunty Mel.'

'I'm deadly serious. If you can't follow the rules, then you can't have your phone.'

'But Iris is about to go into labour at any moment.'

'So?'

'So?' Pearl echoes, looking between Oren and I as if to say, *Are you hearing this?*

But Melody is adamant 'We're not unreachable, are we? We have the landline. Besides, this is *your* fault. You did this to yourselves. If you could be trusted to follow the rules—'

'Well, it's a ridiculous rule,' Pearl interrupts, pushing her plate away.

'Do you hear this, Renata?' Melody gestures at Pearl. 'Do you hear the way she's speaking to me? She never used to speak to me like this before you got here.'

'Hold on.' Pearl raises her hands and chuckles bitterly. 'What does this have to do with Ren?'

'It has to do with how much time *you two*' – she wags her finger between us – 'spend online. Look at Oren. He doesn't speak the way you two do. He doesn't swear or raise his voice or challenge me.'

'Because he's scared of you,' she mutters.

Oren turns to look at Pearl with a wounded frown as Melody says, 'Maybe you two should be as well because I'm not going to allow you to speak to me the way you speak to the people in your comments. Not everything is a fight, you know? You're always so angry. So suspicious. On guard. It's because you spend too much time on social media. I know you two think you know it all, but you could learn a thing or two from me.'

Pearl scoffs, her eyes wide as she looks at me across the table.

But Melody ignores her. 'Now eat up. Your breakfast is getting cold.'

25

'Melody's right,' I tell Pearl with a miserable sigh as we wander around the florist, trying to find some locally sourced flowers for Aunt Celeste. 'As soon as I got to the farm, I completely abandoned my purpose, didn't I?'

'No, she isn't!' She looks at me like I've lost it.

'But I have changed, haven't I? I'm nothing like I was in London.'

'Good.' She snorts. 'You were insufferable.'

'You know what I mean, Pearl.'

'Of course I do, Ren, but ignore Aunty Mel. I don't know what's gotten into her,' she says, adding a rose to the bouquet she's building in her hand, then drifts over to a bucket of white chrysanthemums. 'Yes, you've taken a break this summer but it's good that you did because you need to regroup. Now Tab's gone, you can stop with the silly stunts and go back to the digital activism that actually makes a difference.'

That's true, I think as she forgoes the chrysanthemums in favour of a bubblegum-pink carnation. 'You're right. I mean, I guess this is a chance to refocus and finally get rid of the Junior Extinction Rebellion thing.'

'I know I'm right. It's my job to remember who you are when you can't.'

'Because you're my girlfriend?'

I laugh, but the sound dies in my throat as I realise what I've said.

Pearl stops admiring the carnations and when she turns to stare at me, her lips parted, it's all I can do not to bend over and vomit into one of the buckets of flowers at my feet.

But then she smiles, her eyes alight.

'Yes, I am. And, as your girlfriend, I'd like to remind you that all anyone has told you for the last two months is to take it easy. Now Aunty Mel's berating you for taking it easy? I love her, but that makes no sense.'

I don't hear a word beyond, *Yes, I am.*

'Can we take a moment to acknowledge the girlfriend thing?' I whisper as she floats back in my direction.

'Well, I am your girlfriend, aren't I?' she whispers back.

I don't hesitate. 'Yeah.'

'OK then,' she says, her nose wrinkling as she leans in to press a kiss to my mouth. 'Well, that was easy. I've never used the G word before so I'm glad you're not freaking out.'

'I've never used that word, either,' I admit.

That makes her cheeks flush as she says, 'How come I'm the first?'

'I don't know.' I sniff, shuffling awkwardly on the spot. 'I just know, you know?'

She reaches over to tug on the front of my T-shirt. 'How?'

'Because I want to see you in a jumper.'

It's such a weird thing to say, even for me, that I want to throw up again.

'No, what I mean is . . .' I start to say, then cough in an effort to clear my throat.

But Pearl just smiles. 'I know what you mean. I want to see you in a jumper as well.'

I laugh, relieved she gets it.

It's only been one summer, but I want every season.

I want to see her in autumn in a jumper down to her knees and yellow clouds of hawkbit at her feet. And at Christmas, teasing me with mistletoe, her hair smelling of oranges and smoke from the wood burner. And in spring, when everything is green again and the drifts of daffodils salute us as we pass. Then again, next summer.

And the one after that.

And every summer after that.

Which is *ridiculous*.

It's only been three weeks since we first kissed so how can I know that already?

I mean, I don't even know where I'll be in a month.

I don't want to say it, but I have to. 'What happens when the summer's over, though?'

'We'll work it out,' Pearl says with a slow smile.

She's so sure that something in me settles.

We'll work it out.

'So, when should we do the hard launch on Instagram?' Pearl teases, waggling her eyebrows.

I pull a face. 'I don't know if we're *that* serious.'

When she slaps my arm, I snigger, but then I stop as I remember something Melody said earlier.

'Actually, we might not have to,' I realise.

'Why not?' she asks with a frown.

'I think Melody knows about us, which means everyone will by the end of the day.'

Pearl winces. 'Because of what I said this morning?'

'I think so.'

'Oh, so what?' Pearl huffs. 'I don't care if everyone finds out. Do you?'

'Of course not.'

'What about your mum?'

'She loves you, so she'll be thrilled, I'm sure. And if she's weird about us living together here, I can always stay with Aunt Celeste. At least I'll still be nearby and she'll need my help with Uncle Dan, right?'

'Have you heard from Celeste, by the way?'

'I called her earlier but it went to voicemail.'

'Try her again now.'

'I can't. Melody took our phones, didn't she?'

'Now *that*,' she says as she goes over to inspect a bucket of sunflowers, 'is proof that Aunty Mel has lost it. Relaunching this podcast has sent her over the edge.'

'Still, it kind of scares me how easily I took my foot off the gas.'

'Because you needed to. We almost went to prison, Ren,' she reminds me, her eyes wide. 'You acted like you didn't care, but I know you were as terrified as I was. Plus, you had all of that shit with Tab and things were weird with your mum. I mean, you've been raising hell since you started Out of Time so you needed to take a break otherwise you would have burned out. Then what use would you be?'

'That's true.'

'Gladioli!' She points to the sign that says, *Birth flower for August*. 'We have to get these for Iris!'

'Iris is due on September 6th,' I remind her.

'Oh yeah.' She snorts. 'Anyway, ignore Aunty Mel.'

'That's easy for you to say. She isn't questioning your entire life's purpose.'

'Don't let her!' Pearl warns, reaching for a deep-pink hydrangea.

'Aren't hydrangeas a bit granny-ish?' I ask as she adds it to the bouquet.

She turns to glare at me.

'Granny-ish? I think you mean *timeless*. They're my favourite. Especially the pink ones.'

I hold my hands up as she shakes the bouquet at me, then says, 'As for Aunty Mel, again, I love her, but she needs to calm down with this whole . . .' She stops to put on a dramatic voice. '*Pearl, Oren and I are in my study for twenty-seven hours a day, fighting the good fight, while all you do is skip around in the sunshine.*'

'There are twenty-four hours in a day,' I correct.

'It's hyperbole,' she counters, comparing the pink of the hydrangea with that of the roses and carnations then plucking out another one. 'The point is: we're hardly holed up in her study finding a solution to microplastics in the ocean. I'm transcribing her podcast while she and Oren . . .' She trails off as she thinks about it.

'Actually, I don't know what they're doing. All I know is that *Stylist* is only crowning Aunty Mel The Queen of Green because she wrote them a piece about how the government banning face

313

wipes is going to impact your skincare routine that went viral. So, if that's fighting the good fight, then I'd argue that even with your foot off the gas you're having way more of an impact than she is. I mean, she's writing about face wipes while you were on Live yesterday raising money for the green roof project in Rio de Janeiro, so she needs to get off her high horse and leave you alone.'

'Damn,' I say, trying not to smile. 'I had no idea you had it in you, Miss Newman.'

'If she ever speaks to you like that again' – Pearl scowls – 'I'm breaking her Spice Girls mug.'

'Noted.'

'But I won't have to because you're not going to let her speak to you like that again, are you?' She raises her finger. 'I love Zen Ren, but as insufferable as Rebel Ren is, we need her sometimes.'

I nod. 'Don't worry, she's still in here.'

'Good.' She nods back, then gasps. 'Oh, they've got eucalyptus!'

She holds out a sprig for me to smell, then adds it to the bouquet.

'I don't know,' I say, crossing my arms. 'Maybe Melody was trying that whole reverse psychology thing.'

'Reverse psychology?'

'Yeah, like she was being mean to me to reignite a spark, or something.'

'Your spark is just fine, Ren. Aunty Mel is the one who needs to stop and take stock.'

'What do you mean?' I ask as she looks at the bouquet, then adds another sprig of eucalyptus.

'Have you checked her socials recently?'

'No. I barely have enough time to keep up with my own.'

'It's weird.' She stops to blink and shake her head. 'It's like Aunty Mel is two completely different people. The lovely, sweet Melody we know who goes on *Woman's Hour* and writes articles about face wipes, and Online Melody who argues with everyone and retweets the wildest, most unhinged shit you've ever read.'

'Like *what*?'

'All of these nutty conspiracy theories about chemtrails and 5G and something about a harp.'

'H-A-A-R-P,' I correct with a groan.

'What's that?'

'High-frequency Active Auroral Research Program. People are always in my comments warning me that the US government is using it to manipulate the weather to trigger natural disasters.'

Pearl looks up from adjusting the bouquet. 'Why would they do that?'

'Something about mind control and aliens.' I close my eyes and shake my head. 'I don't know.'

'That sounds like something Oren would believe.'

'He does. We had a *forty-minute* discussion about it when I first got to the farm. Don't you remember?'

'No, but I usually zone out when you two start geeking out,' she admits with a chuckle.

'Well, if Melody's tweeting about HAARP, it's *one hundred per cent* because of Oren.'

'Yeah, but isn't it funny how she only tweets about it? She's never said any of this stuff to us.'

'Because she knows Aunt Celeste will annihilate her.'

Pearl arches an eyebrow as if to say, *Exactly*. 'I bet that's why she didn't tell us that she did Eileen Booker's podcast last month.'

'She didn't!' I gasp, horrified. 'Why would she do that? Eileen Booker is . . .'

'A complete wackadoodle?' Pearl says when I can't find a polite way of putting it.

'I was going to say eccentric, but if the tin foil hat fits.'

'I don't know what Aunty Mel was thinking. She claims the BBC have her *booked and busy*,' Pearl says, parroting Melody, 'promoting the new podcast, but I doubt they'd arrange for her to do something with Eileen Booker.'

'No way.' I shake my head. 'They won't be happy about that. Not all publicity is good publicity.'

'That's the thing, though,' Pearl says. 'More people respond to her unhinged tweets than they do to her ones about face wipes, even if it's just to correct her "science" about 5G, or whatever. Most of them are rabid right-wing climate change deniers, though. But the messed-up thing is, the more Aunty Mel does it, the more engagement she gets and the more things she's invited to contribute to. So, in a way, it's working for her.'

'Yeah, until it doesn't.'

'That's what I'm worried about.' Pearl turns to me with a heavy sigh. 'Aunty Mel's worked so hard to get to where she's at so if she takes it too far and loses everything again, I think it will break her this time.'

As we're leaving the florist, Pearl shows me the bouquet with a proud smile.

'It's very pink,' I say, then frown, 'but what's with that one weird eggplant-coloured peony in the middle?'

Her smile loosens, her nose wrinkling as she plucks it out and hands it to me.

I roll my eyes as I take it, then produce the pink hydrangea that I've been hiding behind my back.

Pearl shrieks when she sees it, snatching it and holding it to her chest.

'You remembered!' she says, bouncing up and down.

'You told me they were your favourite, like, twelve seconds ago, Pearl. I'm not a goldfish.'

But she sticks her bottom lip out. 'You remembered.'

'Yeah, whatever,' I say with a sniff and a shrug. 'It's just a flower. Don't make it weird.'

But of course she does, rubbing her hydrangea against my peony as though they're kissing.

'I shoplifted that, by the way,' I lie as she giggles to herself.

Pearl hooks her arm through mine. 'I have the best girlfriend.'

'I think we should see other people,' I growl as she drags me up the high street.

'Tell you what,' she says, her hip knocking against mine as she pulls me closer, 'let's swing by the café to see if Mother Martha's back. You can get a black coffee and resume brooding.'

'I would very much like that.'

'Maybe she'll have some of her hummingbird cake left.'

'I'm not sharing,' I warn because I know what she's thinking. 'That's enough cute coupley shit for today.'

But when she kisses me on the cheek, I have to bite down on a smile.

'Girls!' Mother Martha calls out from behind the counter as we walk into the café.

'Hey!' we say together as she walks out to greet us.

'I'm so glad you came back.' She hugs us both at once. 'Sorry I missed you earlier.'

When she steps back, her eyes light up as she admires the bouquet that Pearl is cradling.

'Pretty! Are those for Celeste?'

We nod.

'She's going to love those hydrangeas. They're her favourite.'

Pearl turns to me with a smug smirk, which I ignore as Mother Martha heads back behind the counter.

'I'm off to see her now,' she says, reaching for a cardboard box.

'Here, let me help you with that,' I offer as Pearl takes my peony.

'Thank you, sweet girl,' Mother Martha says, handing me the box, then rubbing my back with her hand. 'I'm taking her some food. She can't keep eating those awful, plastic vending machine sandwiches.'

Pearl smiles brightly. 'Yeah, but she'll be home tonight, right?'

'No, she's sleeping at the hospital again,' Mother Martha mutters as she looks for her keys.

'Are they not discharging Uncle Dan, then?' I ask with a frown.

She looks equally confused. 'No, he's still waiting for a bed on a ward.'

'I thought he was coming home this afternoon?' Pearl asks as we follow her out of the café.

'Home?' She stops so suddenly that we almost walk into the back of her. 'Who told you that?'

'Melody,' I say.

'She must have gotten confused.' Mother Martha carries on through the door and out into the brilliant sunshine. 'They're discharging him from Recovery, but he's going to be in hospital for a while.'

'Oh no,' Pearl and I say, looking at each other as she stops by her van.

'Dan's very poorly, girls. He almost lost his leg. Poor Celeste is in bits.'

'I feel awful,' Pearl says as I'm thinking it. 'I had no idea. Melody's been so blasé about it.'

'She's probably trying not to worry you guys, but Celeste needs us right now.'

'Of course,' I say, feeling wretched that we didn't go to the hospital earlier.

'We'll come with you,' Pearl says before I can.

'Oh, lovely,' Mother Martha says with a warm smile as she opens the back door of the van.

But as I step off the kerb to put the cardboard box in, I have to wait as she moves stuff around.

'Sorry, Ren,' she murmurs as she tries to make space. 'Just give me a sec.'

'What have *you* been buying from ASOS, Mother Martha?' Pearl chuckles.

'None of this is mine,' she grumbles as she heaves a huge black-and-white bag out of the way. 'It's Melody's. She gets all this stuff delivered to the post office and keeps forgetting to collect it. They don't have the space to store it, so they asked me if I'd take it to the farm, but I haven't had a chance.'

'This is probably PR from brands,' Pearl groans. 'I dread to think how many lists *MelodyLoves* was on. They're obviously bombarding her again. I'll tell Oren to add a No PR notice to her website.'

'I'm sure Mel would appreciate that, darling. She won't want crap from any of these companies, will she? And look at all of this plastic! It's appalling! None of it's recyclable. And Amazon? Come on!' Mother Martha says, sneering at a box, before sliding it out of the way. 'Mel hates Amazon.'

'And SHEIN.' Pearl grimaces. 'Aunty Mel would *never* support them. They approached her about promoting their new sustainable collection, but she refused, even though it would have paid for a new boiler.'

'Because Mel has integrity,' Mother Martha says, closing the van door.

26

It's the perfect evening, the sky the deepest, truest blue as Pearl and I emerge, hand in hand, from the copse with Buffy and Willow at our heels. Before we head back to the house, I stop and turn to look back at the row of trees lining the horizon and I feel the same ache that made me feel so small the first time I saw them, the thought that one day soon, all of this could be gone, making tears gather at the corners of my eyes again.

When something in my chest tightens as I tell myself that I can't let that happen, I know why I'm here. It was never about the book or running away from Tab and Riley; it was so I can see this, wasn't it?

Feel *this*.

Because what's the point of trying to save the planet if you don't appreciate your time on it?

It's time to go, I realise, squeezing Pearl's hand a little tighter. But when she turns her head to smile at me, her hair as bright as the sunshine buttering our cheeks and bare shoulders, it doesn't feel like the end.

It feels like the start of something.

Something that doesn't make me feel small.

It makes me feel like I can do anything.

But then she has to go and ruin the moment by saying, 'I need to tell you something.'

'What?' I ask, my heart hiccupping as I lick my fingers.

They're stained purple from the berries we've been picking and when Pearl winces, I have a feeling that our peaceful afternoon of eating blackberries still warm from the sunshine isn't going to end so peacefully.

'It's about Melody, but I kind of don't want to tell you,' she says, then blushes so furiously that her cheeks are almost the same colour as my fingers, which does nothing to soothe the dread.

'Why not?'

She winces. 'Because I shouldn't know.'

'Know what?'

'We should be sitting for this,' she says, leading me over to the wood pile that Hunter, Marcus and I have been steadily adding to as we try to move the massive tree that fell across the road.

When I do, she plonks down next to me with a heavy sigh. 'OK. Before I tell you, Ren, you have to promise that you're not going to be all weird and judgey about how I found out, OK?'

'Absolutely not,' I say, because let's not start out by lying.

'Yeah, but it's me. You like me, remember?'

'For now,' I say, arching an eyebrow.

She rolls her eyes, then says, 'OK. So I happened to glance at Aunty Mel's inbox earlier and—'

'No.' I hold my hand up before she can finish the sentence. 'No. No. No. *Nope*.'

'What?' she asks with a wounded frown.

'I don't want to know.'

'But I have to tell you!'

'You don't, actually.'

'I do! It's in the Girlfriend Agreement. Kissing, compliments and secrets.'

'I didn't agree to those terms, Pearl.'

'Too late, Barbosa.' She points at me. 'You're in this!'

'Please, Pearl. Things are already weird between Melody and me so whatever it is, please forget that you saw it. Just lock it in a box, bury it in a basement, then set the house on fire.'

'But I can't! I have to get it out!'

'If this is anything to do with nudity, I swear to God!'

'No!' She looks horrified. 'It's nothing like that. But you were right.'

I hate her, because she knows that will get me.

'Right about what?'

'OK.' She holds up her hands. 'Let me just start by saying that it was an accident.'

'What, you just tripped and fell into Melody's inbox?'

She ignores me as she inches closer. 'You know how I use Aunty Mel's laptop when I'm transcribing her podcasts?'

'I didn't but go on.'

'Well, this afternoon, Aunty Mel needed it because she had a Zoom with a producer from Radio 4's *Open Country*. She took the laptop so she could show them around the farm.'

'OK.' I nod, anxious for her to get to the point.

'So, while she was out with Oren, I had to use the desktop and her inbox was open.'

'Which you could have ignored,' I point out.

'I know and ordinarily, I would have, but something caught

my eye.' She cringes, her cheeks flushing again. 'I didn't read anything, though, I swear. I didn't even scroll. The emails were just *right there*.'

'This is the bit I don't want to know, right?'

'It's nothing personal,' she promises. 'It was her old MelodyLoves Hotmail that seems to be mostly junk, but I guess she kept it for this sort of thing.'

'What sort of thing?'

'That's why I have to tell you because it might make you feel better about Aunty Mel blowing up at you.'

'Fine,' I concede, throwing my head back with a groan. 'Just tell me.'

She shimmies closer. 'Remember that stuff we saw in the back of Mother Martha's van the other day?'

'Yeah?'

'Well, that wasn't PR. Aunty Mel bought it.'

'Are you sure?'

'I saw the order confirmations. Not just Amazon but ASOS, Zara, Space NK. Even *SHEIN*.'

'Recently, though?' I check. 'I mean, it's her old MelodyLoves account, right?'

'One hundred per cent.' Pearl closes her eyes and shakes her head. 'I checked.'

'That is weird.'

Pearl's eyes snap open.

'Weird?' She frowns furiously. 'It's *so* hypocritical, Ren. And OK, I get it. We live in the middle of nowhere so she has to shop online, but *come on*! There are *so many* options beyond ASOS and SHEIN.'

Pearl throws her hands up. 'I literally *just* wrote a post last week on GreenGirlPearl about ten sustainable indie clothing brands to support. Yeah, they're moderately more expensive, but surely it's better to buy a few pieces that are going to last than *bags* of stuff that's going to end up in landfill?'

'You know I agree, but we're human. We can't get it right all the time. Mum eats meat.'

'It's not the same thing. Your mum doesn't extol the virtues of veganism then chow down on a rib-eye when she's alone. Whereas Aunty Mel preaches about shopping locally than buys all this crap from brands she knows are damaging the planet!' She arches an eyebrow to stop me when I start to defend Melody again. 'She knows it's wrong; that's why she gets it delivered to the post office instead of the farm.'

That makes me pause. 'Fair point.'

'What pisses me off more, though' – Pearl lets out a frustrated huff – 'is that two days ago she accused you of not doing enough. Yet, here she is, supporting an industry she *knows* I'm trying to change.'

'You need to talk to her, then,' I say, nudging Pearl with my knee.

'Yeah, but how do I do that without letting her know that I was snooping in her inbox?'

'You don't need to tell her that bit. Just have a general conversation.'

Pearl thinks for a moment, then shakes her head. 'Now isn't the time.'

'True,' I concede. 'Maybe wait until the podcast relaunches and she's calmed down.'

'I don't think she's going to calm down any time soon,' she says, pulling a face.

'What do you mean?'

'This is what you were right about, by the way.'

'There's something else?'

Pearl sucks in a breath and tucks her hair behind her ears. 'When Aunty Mel and Oren were done with that Zoom call, they were talking by the front door. The study window was open so I knew they could see me at the desk, but I always have my headphones on while I'm transcribing so they wouldn't have known that I'd turned the recording off while I was *glancing* at Aunty Mel's inbox and could hear what they were saying.'

'Do I want to know?' I ask.

'I didn't hear all of it, but I caught enough.'

'Enough about *what*?' I ask when she raises her eyebrows.

'Well, first of all' – she leans in – 'the dean at the University of Sussex didn't offer Aunty Mel a job as an adjunct professor. They asked her to come in and do a guest lecture for the journalism and media studies students.'

'Where did she get adjunct professor from, then?'

'There's more.' Pearl stops to look around, even though we're alone aside from Buffy and Willow, who are snoring in unison beneath a gnarled oak tree. 'The dean withdrew the invitation this morning.'

'Why?'

'Because they had complaints from students.'

'Oh, that happens all the time,' I tell her, waving my hand. 'I had the same thing when I was asked to speak at the University of Edinburgh last year. The devil works hard but the oil industry works harder.'

'That's the thing.' Pearl casts another glance up at the house. 'It was the Student Sustainability Committee that complained. They said Aunty Mel's an inappropriate guest because of her' – she uses air quotes – '*radical online views and endorsement of people like Eileen Booker.*'

'Shut up!'

She nods. 'There's a petition and everything.'

When I gasp, Pearl gestures as if to say, *See?*

'I told you this would happen if Aunty Mel kept being a disaster on socials.'

'This is not good.' I shake my head. 'This is not going to end well.'

Pearl groans. 'I know. Poor Aunty Mel. It's MelodyLoves all over again.'

As we're walking back towards the house, we see Marcus and Iris's Range Rover driving up the field and by the time we stroll around the side of the house, he's by the passenger door, helping her out.

'How you doing, Iris?' Pearl asks, swinging the basket of blackberries.

'Still pregnant,' she mutters with a heavy sigh.

'We only have ten days to go so Iris is feeling a little uncomfortable,' Marcus says with a tense smile.

'A little uncomfortable?' she scoffs, stopping to pat Buffy and Willow's heads. 'This baby seems to think that my bladder is a trampoline. But God forbid I miss Aunty Mel's podcast listening party.'

She holds her hands up in mock horror and then waddles to the front door as Pearl and I hear footsteps in the gravel behind us and turn to see Jacinta and Hunter approaching.

'Hey!' we say at once.

Jacinta smiles, but Hunter looks as thrilled as Iris, even though he has a bottle of wine in each hand.

'How was the wedding?' I ask.

'Lovely.' Jacinta sighs dreamily. 'Such a beautiful day. I wish we could have stayed longer, though.'

'Yeah, Hay is a long way to go for two days,' Hunter grumbles, then points one of the bottles at me. 'But thanks for jumping on FaceTime with Cerys's niece. She was so excited. She couldn't stop talking about it.'

'Sure. No problem.'

'I'm, like, totally cool now because I know Rebel Ren,' he tells me with a slight swagger.

But Jacinta rolls her eyes. 'You're still not cool, Hunter.'

'She's just mad because Josie didn't call her cool,' he says under his breath as we follow her inside.

'Hey! Hey! Hey!' Jacinta says as we walk into the kitchen.

'You're home!' I gasp when I see Aunt Celeste, rushing over to hug her.

My smile slips when I step back. She looks even more worn out than when I last saw her, the skin under her eyes bruised black and the rest of her skin blotchy from crying or lack of sleep, or both. She's in jeans and a shirt so creased that it looks like she just pulled it off the washing line, which isn't like her at all. Usually, she's so put together that people stop to ask where she got her dress or what perfume she's wearing.

But now she smells of hospitals.

'I couldn't miss the podcast party, could I?' she says, kissing the top of my head.

'Yes, you could have,' Pearl tells her.

'How is Uncle Dan?' I ask, squeezing her arm.

'Much better,' she says and I let go of a breath. 'The consultant says that he doesn't need a skin graft, which is a *huge* relief. I think it's that colloidal silver you gave me, Mother Martha.'

'Blessed be,' she says, bowing her head.

'You're all here!' Oren beams as he strides into the kitchen.

He's clearly fresh from the shower, his hair wet and his eyes bright as he joins us at the counter.

'What can I help with?' I ask Mother Martha.

'Can you make Iris some tea with the mint Celeste brought?' she says, gesturing at the kettle.

'I don't have indigestion!' Iris calls out from the sofa. 'I just need this baby out of me!'

'Ten more days,' Jacinta coos, going over to stroke her hair.

'Yes!' Melody says, appearing in the doorway. 'Ten more days until my podcast premiers!'

Oren cheers when she sweeps in, but the rest of us just look at her, then at each other.

'That's pretty,' Pearl says, gaze narrowing as Melody floats by in a moss-green satin dress.

'Oh, thank you, darling!' She twirls, eyes gleaming. 'I got it from Birdsong.'

'It's from Zara,' Pearl leans in to whisper as Melody flits around, kissing everyone.

'Are you sure?' I whisper back while I fill up the kettle.

'Yes,' she hisses as she glares across the kitchen at Melody. 'I did a post about sustainable alternatives to this summer's high street "it dresses" back in May and *that* was one of them.'

'Not now,' I warn as Melody points at us.

'Did you girls repost the teaser clip I posted earlier?'

'You have our phones,' Pearl reminds her, crossing her arms.

'Oh yeah.' She chuckles.

'Guys,' Oren says, raising his voice over the gentle chatter before gesturing at Melody.

'Thank you for coming,' she sings, then waits.

Oren takes the hint, initiating a round of applause.

The rest of us look at each other again, then join in, albeit with less enthusiasm.

Still, Melody laps it up, laughing and curtsying, then gestures at us to stop.

'Thanks, guys!' She smiles, shivering with glee. 'As you know, I've been working *so hard* relaunching my podcast. We have six episodes in the can.' She stops to wiggle. 'That's a broadcast term, by the way.' She points at us, then winks. 'I'm currently prepping the next six, so I'm thrilled that we're taking a moment to celebrate because I think this will be the last time that we'll be together for a while.'

'Plus, we're about to be one more.' Jacinta beams, stroking Iris's hair again.

It takes Melody a second, then she nods and says, 'Of course! That's why I wanted us to come together tonight, guys. I would have loved for you to come to my party in London next Wednesday

330

when the first episode actually goes out, but with everything going on, I know you can't make it. Still, at least Oren is coming.'

'What about the girls?' Jacinta asks.

Melody makes a show of rolling her eyes. 'Oh, they don't want to come.'

'Yes, we do,' I say, turning to Pearl. 'We're looking forward to it.'

'Oh, don't worry, Ren. You don't need to come. It's just going to be a load of journalists.'

'Yeah, but someone from BBC publicity DMed me, like, a month ago to ask if I'd introduce you.'

She seems slightly startled by that. 'They did?'

When I nod, my stomach turns inside out.

'Shit.' I wince. 'I hope that wasn't a surprise or something.'

'Don't worry, Ren.' Melody smiles smoothly. 'There's no need for you or Pearl to come. I'd rather we celebrated tonight, as a family. You're the first to hear the episode, so I can't wait to find out what you think!'

Oren raises his arm with a cheer and when Melody curtsies again, her eyes shining in the candlelight, I catch Jacinta raising her eyebrow at Aunt Celeste, who tries not to laugh.

'Come on, guys! Mother Martha prepared this beautiful meal in my honour so let's eat and be merry!'

She saunters over to the table and stands at the head as we each grab something from the island.

'It wasn't just me,' Mother Martha says, turning to smile at me. 'Ren and I made everything together.'

'You're being *very* generous,' I tell her as I put the salad bowl down in the middle of the table.

'Don't listen to her, Mel. Ren's an excellent sous chef.'

Melody isn't listening, though, as she gestures at us to sit.

But then she frowns as Oren fills her glass.

'Red wine?' she says, her brow fluttering. 'I thought this was a celebration?'

'This is all we have,' he says sheepishly.

'You should have said that you wanted champagne, Mel,' Hunter mutters as he takes the bottle from Oren. 'We could have stopped in Storrington on our way back from Hay.'

'I shouldn't have to,' I hear Melody say under her breath as she sits down with a sigh.

As soon as she does, Pearl raises her finger and jumps up again.

Melody watches as Pearl rushes over to the sideboard and grabs the white gift bag dotted with brightly coloured hearts that's sitting next to the record player.

She giggles lightly and smiles, but then her face stills as Pearl walks over to hand the gift bag to Iris.

'What's this?' Melody asks as Pearl kisses Iris's cheek, then sits back at the table.

She grins, wriggling in her chair. 'Something Ren and I made for Iris.'

'The bag was Pearl's choice,' I'm careful to point out.

'This is so nice of you, girls,' Iris says as she roots through the lime-green tissue paper, then gasps.

'What is it?' Melody asks, her frown deepening.

'Mother Martha was showing Ren and me how to make candles the other day, so we decided to make one for Iris. We know you guys are having a home birth,' Pearl says as Iris sticks her nose into the glass, then closes her eyes as she sniffs, 'so we figured it might be soothing. It has lavender, sandalwood and clary sage.'

Mother Martha points across the table. 'Clary sage is perfect for reducing cramps.'

'Yeah, so you won't feel a thing,' I promise, which makes Hunter cackle.

'Oh, girls. Come here!' Iris holds her arms out. 'Thank you! You're so sweet.'

'That's lovely, guys,' Oren tells us as we go over to hug her.

'Yes. Lovely. Flowers for Aunt Celeste. A homemade candle for Iris,' Melody says with a smile that doesn't match the sudden sharpness of her tone as she watches us sit down and put our napkins back in our laps.

My stomach tenses, because I recognise that tone and I look over to Pearl to warn her.

She frowns at me as if to say, *What's wrong?*

But then Melody sighs and says, 'Nothing for me, though.'

'Huh?' Pearl mutters, turning to frown at her now.

Melody ignores her, suddenly absorbed in the salad that Oren is piling on to her plate.

When she does, it's as though someone has opened a window as I shiver and look at Pearl again.

She still looks confused, but before she can ask, Aunt Celeste slams the wine bottle down on the table.

'Mel, *what* has gotten into you?'

I don't recognise that tone, though.

Aunt Celeste is always so warm – so steady – but she sounds utterly exhausted.

Not that Melody seems to notice. 'I'm just saying: I have something to celebrate tonight as well.' She holds her fork in the air with another theatrical sigh. 'Not that you'd know it.'

'It's a candle, Mel,' Aunt Celeste says. 'I'm sorry that we stopped talking about you for *two minutes* to acknowledge the fact that your niece is about to give birth to her first child, but not everything is about you.'

Melody is unrepentant, though. 'I just wanted tonight to be about me. Is that too much to ask?'

When she glances around the table, no one responds as we turn to look at Iris, who dips her head as she blushes and stuffs the candle back into the gift bag.

Even Oren looks bewildered.

Melody's clearly expecting him to agree with her, but when he doesn't, she tuts and shakes her head.

'It's always about you, Mel!' Aunt Celeste says. But she doesn't just sound exhausted, she sounds at the end of her tether. When she closes her eyes and pinches the bridge of her nose, Mother Martha rubs her shoulder, then leans in to whisper something that makes her nod.

When Aunt Celeste takes her hand away from her face, her eyes are so red that I rub her other shoulder as she sucks in an unsteady breath then says, 'I'm sorry, guys. I'm really struggling and *this*' – she waves her hand at Melody – 'is too much for me right now. Perhaps I should go home.'

'No!' we all say at once as Mother Martha and I clasp her shoulders when she pushes her chair back.

'Celeste, you've been through hell these last couple of days,' Jacinta reminds her, coming over to hug her tightly from behind. 'So don't you dare apologise. We love you and we're here for you.'

There's a murmur of agreement as Pearl and Iris reach across the table to each hold one of Aunt Celeste's hands as Hunter refills her wine glass, then urges her to eat something.

'As for you,' Jacinta says through her teeth. She stops hugging Aunt Celeste and stands to glare at her sister. 'You've been doing this for weeks and I haven't said anything, but *enough*!'

'*Enough* of *what*?' Melody asks, looking at Oren, but he's looking up at Jacinta.

'*This*!' She jabs her finger in Melody's direction, her whole face red. 'Most of you don't know what Mel was like in the MelodyLoves days, but I do. And *this* is what she was like.'

'Oh, I remember,' Aunt Celeste says with a bitter chuckle as she reaches for her wine glass.

'I know you do. You're the only one here who remembers how *awful* she was.'

Melody looks between them, blinking furiously as they nod at one another.

'Demanding.' Jacinta's face tightens with disgust as she counts off each one on her fingers. 'Dramatic.'

'Egocentric,' Aunt Celeste adds.

Jacinta points at Melody. 'And paranoid. If you didn't agree with her, you were against her, right?'

I'm so stunned that I glance over at Pearl again to find her staring, her mouth open.

Melody, however, is utterly unfazed as she says, 'I have no idea what you're talking about.'

'I'm talking about *this*!' Jacinta gestures wildly at the table.

'Why is *all of this* not enough for you, Mel? We're all here to celebrate this ridiculous podcast that you won't shut up about and it's still not enough. Aunt Celeste's husband had emergency surgery *two days* ago. My daughter is so close to giving birth that I'm scared every time she sneezes. My husband and I drove for *five hours* to came back from Hay a day early *for you*.'

She points at the jam jars of flowers dotted around the table. 'Pearl picked these for you and Mother Martha and Ren have been cooking all day. They made puff pastry from scratch, for heaven's sake. Not even Gordon Ramsay makes puff pastry from scratch, and you're pouting over a candle. *A candle*.'

'I honestly don't know why you're getting so upset,' Melody laughs. 'I was just saying—'

'Enough!' Jacinta balls her hands into fists and holds them up. 'I thought you'd changed, Mel. That you'd learned something, but you're back to being MelodyLoves. Except this time you're being an asshole to Ren and I don't know why. You're always complaining about her, saying that she thinks she's too good to help out.'

Pearl's eyebrows raise at that as Mother Martha says, 'What? She's an absolute delight.'

'Ren's been brilliant,' Iris says then. 'She's been helping us get the nursery ready, hasn't she, Marcus?'

'She has,' he agrees with a nod. 'And she's been helping us shift this tree.'

Hunter winks at me. 'Stronger than she looks, this one.'

'And now you're complaining about Pearl as well?' Jacinta frowns. 'What's going on, Mel? You love Pearl. You're her godmother, but now you're saying that she's talking back to you and being disrespectful, like Ren. Which I don't believe, because I've never seen either of them behave that way.'

'Have you, Oren?' Aunt Celeste asks.

But when he looks at Mel, Jacinta throws her hands up, then leans between Aunt Celeste and me to look at him. 'It's OK to speak up, you know, Oren. Don't be scared of her.'

'I'm not scared of her,' he says in a way that isn't convincing in the slightest.

So Jacinta gives up and turns back to Melody. 'Even if Ren and Pearl were disrespectful, I don't blame them. You've taken their phones away and now you've uninvited them from your party. What did they do?'

But Melody simply shrugs. 'None of you have to live with them, do you?'

'You know what—' Pearl starts to say.

But Aunt Celeste holds her hands up. 'Fine. If you're so unhappy with them, Mel, then they can come and live with me. We have the room and Dan *adores* them. They're the only ones who listen to his stories so he'll be thrilled. Especially as he's going to be housebound for a while.'

'Or they can come live with me,' Mother Martha says. 'I'd love to have them.'

Melody looks on, astonished.

'Everybody just calm down,' she tells them, raising her voice.

'I'm perfectly calm, thank you,' Aunt Celeste says crisply.

But Melody ignores her. 'I love the girls and I love having them here.'

'So why are you treating them like this?' Jacinta asks.

Melody ignores her as well. 'I only took their phones because . . .'

She trails off as she looks up at the ceiling and lets out a small sob.

When she looks back at everyone at the table, there are tears in her eyes.

'Because I'm getting death threats,' she says, weakly.

'Death threats?' Iris gasps, clasping her belly.

'Don't worry, darling,' Aunt Celeste says. 'It's quite common, sadly.'

'*Quite common?*' Melody scoffs, her hand flying to her chest. 'Why are you trying to diminish it?'

'She's not trying to diminish anything,' Pearl tells her. 'She's trying to keep a *very* pregnant woman calm. Besides, Celeste is right. Someone threatens to rape or kill Ren and me at least once a day.'

There's another sharp intake of breath around the table.

'That's *awful*,' Iris says.

But Pearl just shrugs. 'I know, but Ren gets it way worse than I do, right?'

'I mean, yeah.' I shrug as well. 'But that's what happens when you dare to put your head above the parapet. Look at Mum. She's been dealing with threats like that for years. That's why she has Maurice.'

'I thought he was her driver,' Pearl says, eyes wide.

I shake my head. 'I never understood why she needed him until that photo of me at that Extinction Rebellion protest went viral a couple of years ago and I noticed a swift change in tone, let's say.'

Pearl nods. 'The same thing happened to me when I spoke at the *Teen Vogue* summit last year.'

'So, you can see why I'm concerned, right?' Melody interrupts.

'Have you called the police?' Aunt Celeste asks.

'Of course! They're dealing with it,' Melody says with a tender sigh. 'In the meantime, I'm just trying to keep myself, and the rest of us, safe by limiting the girls' use of social media.'

'That makes sense,' Marcus says.

But then Melody exhales sharply and adds, 'I'd rather they didn't go on social media at all because they've told this person too much about me and where I live already. But I can't stop them completely, can I?'

My jaw clenches as I look at Pearl and she looks at Melody.

'So, these death threats are *our* fault?' Pearl asks.

Melody doesn't hesitate. 'Yes! Ren going on Live all the time lets everyone know exactly where we live.'

'Oh, so it's Ren's fault.' Pearl chuckles sourly, throwing her hands up. 'Of course it is!'

I let go of Aunt Celeste's shoulder and turn to Melody.

'First of all, I'm not *on Live all the time*,' I say, sounding much steadier than I feel as something bubbles up in my chest, like a pan of milk boiling over. 'I go on once a day, if that. And, when I do, I'm careful to keep the background indistinct so no one knows where I am because, as I said, I've been dealing with threats for years.'

Melody barks out a laugh. 'You were on Live on the train here!'

'I didn't say where I was going, though.'

'You didn't need to! It was obvious.'

'No, it wasn't,' I say, swallowing back the urge to tell her that she could at least have the decency to look at me. But I can't, because if I lose my temper, she'll use it as evidence of the disrespect she's been complaining about, and I refuse to give her the satisfaction.

So I make sure to keep my tone even as I say, 'My back was to the window, and I did it when there was nothing but fields. No station signs or announcements.'

Melody slams her hand on the table so hard the silverware shivers.

'So why is this person threatening to come to the farm and kidnap me tonight?'

'Tonight?' everyone gasps.

'What do you mean they're coming to get you tonight, Mel?' Oren asks.

Iris looks at Marcus, who says, 'Why wouldn't you tell us something like that?'

'How could you invite us all here knowing that?' Hunter barks, pushing his chair back.

'It's fine,' she says with another shrug. 'The police are dealing with it.'

When she sips her wine, something about it reminds me of the morning she told us about Uncle Dan.

She's being too composed.

Too calm as she turns to me and says, 'This is why I took your phone, Renata. You've put us all at risk.'

'*She* has?' Pearl says.

'How exactly have *I* put us all at risk, Melody?' I ask.

'You have *six million* followers, Renata. Who knows who's been watching your Lives.'

'And *Woman's Hour* has three and a half million listeners, yet you told Nuala McGovern that you live on a farm in Chanctonbury. So, you've hardly been careful about saying where you live, have you?'

That catches her off guard.

I feel a flutter of satisfaction when she flinches as Iris says, 'That's true.'

But Melody recovers quickly.

'Well, all I know is that I've lived here for *three years*, then you get here and look what happens.'

'Yeah, but you did *Woman's Hour after* I got here.'

'She's right, Mel.' Mother Martha points at her. 'I distinctly remember you saying that you live on a farm in Chanctonbury because everyone cheered in the café when you did.'

'There are only a handful of farms here,' Hunter tells her, 'and we're the only residential one so they could have just narrowed it down, then confirmed it through the Land Registry.'

'You can do that?' she asks, her bravado wavering.

'Yeah.' Marcus nods. 'It costs, like, twenty quid online.'

'What? Anyone can just search for a property, even if they don't own it?'

He nods again. 'Plus, didn't you apply for planning permission to convert the barn?'

The skin between her eyebrows creases. 'Yeah.'

'Well, all of your information is on Horsham's Planning Register, then.'

'What?'

'All this person needed to do was to search "Chanctonbury"

341

and the recent planning applications would come up. Then they just needed to click on the application form and they would have your name and address.'

Melody stares at him. 'Are you serious? It's that easy?'

'Yep. It's so you can object to planning proposals that might affect you.'

I cross my arms. 'So it's not my fault that they found out where you live.'

'It's not about that,' Melody hisses, slapping the table again. 'Someone is threatening to come here and snatch me from my bed and all you care about, Renata, is whose fault it is.'

'You're the one—' I start to say, but she won't let me finish.

'Can't you see what you're doing? Stop undermining everything I say.'

'I'm just defending myself. You're blaming me for—'

But she talks over me again. 'All I was trying to do was to create a beautiful, supportive, *intentional* community and within two months of you arriving, you've ruined it and now my life is in danger.'

'You put yourself in danger, Melody!' I manage to get out this time and as annoyed with myself as I am for raising my voice, I'm not going to let her say – or let the others think – that this is my fault.

I didn't do anything wrong.

'What did you think was going to happen when you started regurgitating conspiracy theories on Twitter and riling up right-wing climate change deniers for engagement?' I throw my hands up. 'It might earn you more followers and a few extra bylines, but you can't win with these people. Trust me, I know. What do you think happened to me when I was on Twitter, having it out with Trump and Piers Morgan and everyone else calling me a brainwashed brat for saying, *Hey, can we please stop fucking up our planet?*'

'Is that what you've been doing online, Mel?' Jacinta asks, looking between us.

Melody just shrugs as Pearl says, 'She went on Eileen Booker's podcast.'

'Oh, Melody.' Mother Martha shakes her head. 'You can't associate with someone like her.'

'Why not?' Oren asks with a frown.

'Because most people already think that we're exaggerating about how dire things are. So, when you start spouting about things like HAARP it makes us sound as deluded as the people who say that wind turbines cause cancer.'

'Exactly.' I nod. 'I know you think that you're helping by going toe-to-toe with these people, Melody, but take it from someone who knows: if you kick the hornets' nest, *this* is what happens.'

'I don't understand.' Aunt Celeste shakes her head. 'You've never shared these views with us, Mel.'

'Because she doesn't actually believe any of this shit,' Pearl says when Melody doesn't say anything, just sips her wine. 'She just knows that it gets her engagement, and engagement raises her profile.'

'Well, at least they're talking about me.' Melody shrugs.

'At least they're talking about me,' Jacinta says, nose in the air, mocking Melody's voice. 'Isn't that what you kept saying last time? When I begged you not to tell everyone that your night cream was burning their faces because they were "using

it wrong". But you wouldn't listen because all you cared about was that people were talking about you. Not what they were saying. And look what happened? You lost everything and now you're about to again. Except, this time, you've put us all in danger!'

'Calm down, sis,' she sneers, rolling her eyes. 'You're being hysterical.'

'Melody,' I say in the steadiest way that I can manage given that I'm fighting the urge to grab her by the shoulders and shake her. 'Jacinta's right: you're going to lose everything again. The BBC won't want to be associated with any of this because it will look like they're endorsing it.'

She doesn't listen, though. 'It's just an act, guys. A little theatre to promote the podcast.'

Melody raises her wine glass with a flourish, then points it at me. 'It's like the Rebel Ren thing.'

When she sees the look on my face, she laughs. 'You're nothing like you are online, are you?'

'Melody, that isn't an act. I really am pissed off at what we're doing to the planet.'

'Please.' She snorts, then turns to tip her chin up at Oren. 'You said it yourself that you were terrified of Renata before you met her. Then, when you did, you were surprised by how sweet she is.'

'Yeah, I guess,' he murmurs.

'See.' Melody gestures at him with a smug smirk. 'So don't deny it, Renata. Rebel Ren has worked wonders for you, hasn't it? Look how many followers you have!'

'It's not an act!'

I don't mean to raise my voice again, but what is she talking about?

'We've all seen it.' Melody raises her wine glass at everyone sitting around the table. 'You haven't been remotely rebellious since you got here, have you?'

That should eviscerate me like it did the last time she told me that I'd abandoned my purpose, but once my ears stop ringing, I can hear myself chuckling as I finally realise what this summer has been about.

'Exactly,' I tell her with a shrug.

That makes Melody falter as she stares at me. 'What do you mean?'

'Look how much happier I've been since I stopped arguing with strangers online.'

That's why my mother agreed to me being here, I know then.

She wasn't trying to derail me – and Out of Time – because she thinks I'm damaging the cause.

She wants me to remember *what* the cause is.

It's not how many followers I have or trying to convince the people in my comments that they're wrong. It's about empowering the ones who are willing to listen because that's how you start a revolution, isn't it?

By letting people know that they don't need to wait for someone to tell them to start one.

'Please,' Melody snorts. 'As soon as you leave here, you'll be back to fighting with everyone in your comments before the train pulls out of Chanctonbury station.'

I grit my teeth before saying, 'Me showing my followers that it's not OK for someone to talk to you like you're not a human being is not the same as you arguing with right-wing nuts who are never going to agree with you, Melody. It doesn't matter what you come at them with; they won't change their minds.'

I wait for her to look at me, then say, 'Trust me, I know. It's like a sport to them. Besides, most of them are bots so it's futile to fight with them because they're not even real. And the ones that are will dox you for fun. Plus, Mother Martha is right: countering wild, unfounded conspiracy theories with more wild, unfounded conspiracy theories doesn't help the cause and makes you just as bad as they are.'

'You should *never* have done Eileen Booker's podcast,' Aunt Celeste says.

'I can't believe that you put us all in danger like this for a few extra followers on Twitter,' Jacinta agrees, looking at Iris, who keeps glancing over at the kitchen door. 'Was it worth it, Mel?'

'Look at this, Renata!' Melody jumps to her feet. 'Look what you've done!'

I stare at her. 'What *I've* done?'

'I hope you're happy! You've turned my own family against me!'

'I haven't—' I try to say.

But she won't let me finish. 'You don't have a family, so you want to take mine from me!'

'I do have a family!' I roar, standing up to face her. 'A family that loves me for who I am and who I'm trying to be and I will *not* let you make me doubt that, or myself, ever again!'

'That's right.' Aunt Celeste stands up and slips her arm around my shoulders. 'I can't believe I vouched for you with Fernanda, Mel. I thought Ren was coming here to write a book with you. To have some time in a peaceful place to reconnect with what matters. But I see it now. You've been trying to steal Ren's light

346

from the moment you met her. You've been using her to rebuild your platform and now people are paying attention to you again, you want to extinguish it altogether so you can shine.'

Melody tosses her head back and laughs. 'You're out of your mind if you think *I* need *her*!'

'No, *you're* out of your mind if you think that I'm going to sit here and let you blame Ren because you're so desperate to be famous that you'll destroy a sixteen-year-old girl to get it.'

'Destroy?' Melody recoils. 'And I'm the dramatic one, right? Renata looks just fine to me.'

'You know what? I am fine,' I agree.

Because I don't care any more.

I don't care if Melody thinks that I've abandoned my purpose, because I haven't.

I've never been so sure of myself.

I know *exactly* who I am, I realise as I look at Pearl and she smiles.

I'm Ren Barbosa and I'm going to change the world.

The *New York Times*
Sept. 29, 2025

Transcript of Renata Barbosa's conversation with Connie Carr, nonfiction critic for the *New York Times*, ahead of her review of Barbosa's memoir, *Time and Other Four-Letter Words*. The transcription was requested by Ms M. Munroe and prepared by Felix Montgomery of the *New York Times*.

CONNIE CARR: Hey, Ren. How are you?

RENATA BARBOSA: I'm good, thanks. How are you?

CARR: I'm great. New York is the last stop on your book tour before you head back to the UK to start university next month, right?

BARBOSA: Yeah. When I get back home I have, like, a week to sort my shit out before I move into halls.

CARR: That should be interesting. I doubt many of your classmates will be starting university with a *New York Times* bestseller under their belts already.

[LAUGHTER]

CARR: Congratulations, by the way.

BARBOSA: Thank you. I still can't quite believe it.

CARR: You won't remember this, but we've actually met before.

BARBOSA: I do, actually. It was at the PRH Christmas party last year, right?

CARR: Yes! I can't believe you remember. You must have been introduced to a hundred people that night.

BARBOSA: How could I forget? Your daughter was wearing that black T-shirt with three witches that said *SUPPORT YOUR LOCAL GIRL GANG*.

[LAUGHTER]

CARR: She's going to be thrilled. I'm relieved it's you she's chosen to be obsessed with. Being a mom to a thirteen-year-old is terrifying at the best of times, but when you throw social media into the mix, it keeps me up at night.

BARBOSA: I bet.

CARR: But I've noticed a shift in the last couple of years thanks to people like you and your girlfriend, Pearl. It's so inspiring to see how you guys help channel that fierce, slightly

349

chaotic adolescent energy away from how you look towards who you are as a person and finding your place in the world. I feel a tremendous amount of guilt about bringing a child into this world then bequeathing them a planet that is literally on fire. So, it's reassuring to hear my daughter say, 'You know what, that's not OK, but we're going to do what we can to fix it.'

BARBOSA: She's right: it's not OK. And there isn't a magic button that we can press to perform a factory reset on the planet, but there are still things that we can do to prepare. Or, at least, to not make the climate crisis any worse than it's going to be.

CARR: I must admit that when the press release landed in my inbox announcing your memoir, I was a little surprised. Not that you were writing a book, of course, but I assumed it was going to be a rousing manifesto about how to save the planet, not a memoir. It's unfiltered and unflinching and unsettling, and I'll be honest, I was also surprised by how moved I was by it. You're only eighteen, after all, so I questioned how much you had to say.

BARBOSA: I get that. But I feel like saving the planet is all I've talked about for the last four years. Plus, it's been done. I mean, go and read

Braiding Sweetgrass by Robin Wall Kimmerer. Or *The Sixth Extinction* by Elizabeth Kolbert. Or *Fire Weather* by John Vaillant. And my mum's book, of course.

CARR: *Brick by Brick* was one of our Books of the Year for 2024.

BARBOSA: Exactly. So, what can I possibly add that hasn't already been said?

CARR: Do you really think that you have nothing to add? What about reaching people who aren't already aware of what you've been doing with Out of Time? I thought you were trying to start a revolution?

BARBOSA: I am, but you don't start a revolution by telling people how we're going to mitigate the climate crisis. It actually starts by making them give a shit. That's what the book is about. It's me telling them who I am and why I care and hopefully people will read it and think, 'I want to do something about this is as well.' Once they think that, what happens next is easy. [LAUGHS] OK. Maybe not easy, but it's certainly half the battle. And that's how you start a revolution, one person at a time.

CARR: No magic button.

BARBOSA: No magic button.

CARR: For me, that's what makes this book so special. How beautifully you articulate the anguish of being a teenager and feeling like you're somehow too much and not enough, all at once. You're inheriting a planet that, as you say, has a sell-by date. So teenagers are torn between saying, 'Fuck it!' and sucking the marrow from life while they can and trying to do something about it. And even if you try to do both, you don't feel like you're doing enough of either, do you?

BARBOSA: Exactly. But I want people my age to know that that's OK. There's no 'right' way of doing this. All we can do is try and leave the planet in a better state than how we found it.

CARR: OK. You know what's coming.

[LAUGHTER]

BARBOSA: Hit me.

CARR: Now you've explained why you wanted to write this memoir, what you've chosen to tell us makes more sense because it's all the things you haven't spoken about before. Your childhood. Your relationship with your mother, Fernanda, and your decision not to try and find your father. And then there's all the things that were going on behind the scenes at Out of Time.

BARBOSA: Right.

CARR: But the book stops that evening in the police cell when you meet your girlfriend, Pearl.

BARBOSA: Yes.

CARR: You don't mention what happens after that, which is, perhaps, what people want to know the most.

BARBOSA: I'm sure.

CARR: Is that because all of that is so well documented?

BARBOSA: It's all online. From the police investigation to the court case to Tab and Riley quitting Out of Time and why that prompted my decision to focus on digital activism.

CARR: And Pearl, of course. You talk about the summer you got together and how much you love living in Chanctonbury all the time, but you never talk about Melody Munroe. Which is strange because Melody has spoken about little else but you for the last two years.

BARBOSA: So I hear.

CARR: [LAUGHS] OK. It's clear that you don't want to talk about her.

BARBOSA: It's not that I don't want to talk about her, Connie, it's that I have nothing to say.

CARR: Well, she has plenty to say. Do you not feel the need to rebut any of it?

BARBOSA: No, because I don't care what she has to say about me.

CARR: She certainly seems concerned about what you're going to say about her in this book. She's been discussing it for weeks on her podcast, alluding to something that happened that summer and that there are two sides of the story. In fact, I just received a press release saying her memoir, *How to Lose Friends and Influence People: My Summer with Rebel Ren* will be published next spring.

BARBOSA: [LAUGHS]

CARR: You really don't care, do you?

BARBOSA: I really don't.

CARR: She says that she lost everything because of you. Her platform. Her reputation. Her podcast with the BBC. Even her family.

BARBOSA: And I'm sure she believes that.

CARR: But you don't?

BARBOSA: I think her behaviour speaks for itself. But at least you're talking about her, right?

CARR: What do you want us to say about you, Ren?

BARBOSA: I don't care what you have to say about me.

CARR: Why write a book, then?

BARBOSA: For anyone who needs to know that it doesn't matter what people say about you.

CARR: Is that why the book ends before you meet Melody?

BARBOSA: No, it ends when I meet Pearl because that's when my life started again.

CARR: And what does this new life look like, Ren?

BARBOSA : Not so different from the old one, except I won't be alone when the world ends.

Acknowledgements

This story would not be possible without the courage and tenacity of the people who created the culture of resistance that has inspired young activists like Ren and Pearl. From the Suffragettes and the Civil Rights Movement, to groups like ACT UP, Amnesty International and Greenpeace who channelled our struggles into resistance and fought for social and political change that has made the world safer for those of us who might not otherwise be able to exist as freely – and as softly – as we choose. These rights were hard won, but are easily lost, so we continue to be inspired by you and are grateful for what you have taught us and for what we can pass on to the next generation as they prepare to enter the fray.

Speaking of the next generation, I would also like to dedicate this story to the young people in my life who mean so very much to me. My nephews, Jacob and Nathan, and my adopted nieces, Sienna, Eve and Indie, who are about to inherit a planet that is, as Ren continuously reminds us, on fire. I'm sorry for my part in that. I've only ever wanted to leave the world in a better place than I found it, but I still have hope that it will be, in whatever small way. Even so, it's okay to be angry that so many decisions about your future were decided before you got a chance to live it, but it's important to remember that while the past is prologue, the ending hasn't been written yet.

Forgive me for using a book analogy, but it seemed apt and it's a sweet segue into thanking everyone at Hachette Children's Group for ensuring that this one found you. First, my editor, Lizzie Clifford, for her tireless support and guidance through what was a trying time for me, both physically and mentally. Thank you for your patience, Lizzie, and for your mighty red pen that ensured this isn't two hundred pages longer. I'd also like to extend my gratitude to Laura Pritchard for her insightful feedback which shaped this story into something even more special and for ensuring that each stage – from the copy-edit with Becca Allen, to the proofread with Anna Bowles, to the sensitivity read – ran smoothly, and for transforming a PDF file into a novel.

While we were doing that, the designer, Joana Reis, and the illustrator, Diberkato, were working their magic to produce one of the most beautiful covers I have ever seen. I don't know how, but they managed to conjure Ren and Pearl, these two girls that have been in my head for the last year, and it's nothing short of astonishing. I am so very grateful, and I can't tell you how proud I am to hold it up and say, *I wrote that*.

Write it, I did, but you wouldn't be reading it now if it wasn't for an incredible group of people at Hachette Children's Group that I feel very lucky to have championing it. Em Thomas, Lucy Clayton and Beth Carter in PR, Bec Gillies in marketing, Joelyn Esdelle in production and Katherine Fox in home sales and Jemimah James in export sales. Thank you all for your hard work and creativity and doing what you do so that all of my friends and family can cheer and send me photos of my books every time they see one in the wild. Even my sixteen-year-old cousin who steadfastly refuses to acknowledge my existence on social media now DMs me whenever she sees one of my books on TikTok, and I have experienced no greater compliment.

I don't know if that makes me cool, but it certainly makes me feel loved so I want to take a moment to thank all of my friends and family as well. Not just for the excited photos that they take while they point at one of my books, but also for putting up with me not replying to texts while I'm holed up in my writing cave and for making sure that I eat and see daylight when I'm not.

Someone else who made sure that I ate is Justine Palmer at the Royal Literary Fund, who swooped in to rescue me last year. Without her generous support I honestly don't know what I would have done, and I hope to one day be in a position to do the same for another author.

I'd also like to thank everyone who has had a hand in this story without even realising it. The booksellers and librarians who champion my books and others like it. All of this is for nothing without you. The poets, authors and musicians who inspire me every day and make me want to be a better, more honest writer. The readers who write heart-stoppingly beautiful reviews, make collages and playlists and compare my books to Taylor Swift and Chappell Roan songs. Your joy and enthusiasm reminds me why I have to tell these stories.

Finally, I'd like to thank my agent, Claire Wilson from RCW. Everyone says that they have the best agent, but I actually do so sucks to be you. Claire is my biggest fan and has gone toe-to-toe with my imposter syndrome so many times over the last fourteen years that I wouldn't be writing this now if not for her. I should probably thank Sam Copeland as well, because if he wasn't sick that day, Claire and I may never have met. Although, I truly think that we were destined to be a part of each other's stories.

ALSO BY TANYA BYRNE

Car headlights. The last thing Ash hears is the
snap of breaking glass as the windscreen hits
her and breaks into a million pieces like stars.
But she made it, she's still here. Or is she?

This New Year's Eve, Ash gets an invitation
from the afterlife she can't decline: to join a clan
of fierce girl reapers who take the souls of the
city's dead to await their fate.

But Ash can't forget her first love, Poppy,
and she will do anything to see her again . . .
even if it means they only get a few more
days together. *Dead or alive . . .*

NOT EVEN DEATH CAN TEAR THEM APART.

DON'T MISS

ALSO BYRNE

Mara's ex, Nico, is the girl of her dreams: beautiful, wild and unpredictable. She's Mara's everything, even though Mara's never sure that she's Nico's *anything*. Then Nico goes missing . . .

New Year's Day: A girl is rescued from the sea. She knows she is called Nico, but other than that, she has no memory of why she was in the sea or what came before.

When destiny reunites them, is this Mara and Nico's second chance? Can their relationship make it out of the shallows? And what will happen when they discover the truth behind Nico's accident? Because one day, Nico will remember *everything*.